Inked Caffeine

Monique Duclos

Tellwell Talent
www.tellwell.ca

ISBN
978-0-2288-5417-3 (Hardcover)
978-0-2288-5418-0 (Paperback)
978-0-2288-5416-6 (eBook)

It is only a matter of time. I wasn't expecting to go quite like this, but I guess being tortured makes the most sense. As I slowly spun in circles upside down, I stared down at my blood in the sand. So much was pouring from all my new wounds that the sand had stopped absorbing, and instead, the blood was puddling on the surface. There was nothing I could do but hang here, and no matter how many times I ran the options through my mind, the likelihood of me getting out of this was thin. The options didn't look very good. And even though there were three of them sitting there, watching me twirl and occasionally spit the blood out of my filling mouth, I was alone. I was alone, and nobody knew where I was. Even if they did, they wouldn't know how to get here. Trying to glance at my feet, my cheeks were too swollen and I could only *just* make out the chain wrapped around my ankles. Closing my swollen eyes, I thought back to my apartment and how life was easier back then. But that's always the case, isn't it? You always think back to the beginning when it's the end. And this was most definitely the end. I was just waiting for my body to lose enough blood so that I could pass out. At least if I was unconscious, I wouldn't feel any more pain.

Opening my swollen eyes once more, I whimpered and almost sighed as I watched one of them walk toward me. He had an array of tools all spread out in front of him; he had been using most of them on me all night.

"Ple—please," I croaked, spitting blood off to the si

I wasn't sure why I kept pleading. I knew he wasn't going to stop, but it was worth a try. Maybe it is just human nature to beg for your life in times like these. This time, he had a nail gun in his hand, and I did my best to flail in the chains to get away, but it was no good. There was nowhere I could go. My hands cuffed uncomfortably behind my back, I simply swung back and forth.

"Oh, just fucking stop it, would'ya?" he snapped, grabbing my shoulder and holding me still.

Pressing the gun against my side, he pressed firmly against the trigger and shot into my skin. My screaming echoed throughout the skeleton building but only until I started coughing and choking on my own blood. *This is it.*

Chapter 1

June 2016
Hollywood
Los Angeles, California

The city was quite disgusting in the summertime. The air got thick with heat and the smog made it hard to breathe. Thankfully, I worked indoors fulltime and got to hide away in an air-conditioned building.

"Y'know, I have to ask . . . and I know you probably get this a lot . . ." an older woman said as she rummaged through her purse for her money. "Is that your natural hair colour?" she asked, sliding a ten-dollar bill on the counter.

I forced a laugh, opening the cash register and picking out her change. "Yes," I smiled, handing her the proper amount.

Her eyes widened. "Wow! That's incredible! So . . . vibrant!" she laughed, placing her change back in her purse.

Turning my back to her, I quickly made her coffee, added a smiley face beside her name on the cup, then handed it over across the counter.

"Have a good day," I smiled.

"You as well! Thank you," she smiled back, slowly turning around and leaving.

I stood by until she walked out, then sighed, shoulders sinking. Walking back into the kitchen, Angela, the store manager, was sitting down outside with the fire exit door open, smoking a cigarette.

"Was that Gloria?" she asked, smoke coming out of her nose as she spoke.

I nodded, rubbing my face with my hands.

"What a nutbag," she added, laughing and shaking her head.

Gloria was one of our recurring customers. She was in her late eighties; a short, plump old lady who had short term memory loss. She always ordered a tall decaf with cream and had the same comment on my hair every single day; her polite blue eyes gawking in awe. At first, it was annoying. When I first met her, I thought it was some sort of joke. Then I found out that it was an actual medical illness and it instantly stopped pissing me off. I was used to it now. My hair is a vibrant crimson red and it was not only Gloria who asked me if it was my natural colour or not; I got asked daily.

It was from my mom's gene pool since my dad's hair was blonde. But nobody knew that because nobody knew my parents. I never talked about them. I hadn't seen them since I moved out, but that didn't really phase me since I didn't really get along with them when I *was* living at home. I always preferred to be left alone anyway. Plus, they had my older brother, Aaron, to obsess over. He was a spitting image of my dad, personality and all. He succeeded in school and was on his way to get his law degree.

I never applied for secondary education because of the turn my life took. I never had time, let alone the money. I moved out in the middle of grade twelve and found a cheap little apartment in Hollywood. It was nothing special, but it was home. Working at Starbucks wasn't so bad either. At first, it was just something to keep me busy during the summer, but once I graduated high school, I stayed and I'd been here for six years now. Sad, I know, but it helped pay the bills.

"Hey, so I gotta leave to go pick up Jason from school. You good to shut this place down?" Angela asked, tossing her cigarette and stepping on it.

I nodded. "Yeah, no problem."

"Cool. I'll see you tomorrow then. Thanks, Dallas!" she smiled, grabbing her purse and kicking the door closed behind her.

I sighed and sat down, resting my chin in the palm of my hand. Closing time was just around the corner, so I started cleaning tabletops, tucking in chairs and began to clean all the machines. I removed the remaining food from their displays and packed them away in a take-out box for the group of homeless people I passed every day on my walk home. Nine o'clock came around and the final customer left. After I told them to have a good night, I cleaned their table, tucked their chair in and then started flicking off lights. Yawning, I walked into the kitchen to lock the back door and then grabbed my keys, walked out the front door and locked it behind me.

I worked at the corner of Vine Street and Melrose Avenue. Starbucks was on Vine and my apartment was just up the street, so I didn't have that far of a walk. Five minutes max. I wasn't that far from Santa Monica Boulevard and with the constant volume of tourists, my area was actually pretty safe to be around. Although, looking at the outside of my apartment, you'd think otherwise. It was nothing fancy, and the elevator didn't work, but it got the job done. And I mean, sometimes the building would lose hot water and I would have to hold off showering for a few days, but I guess you get what you pay for, and I didn't have a lot to pay with. It took a while to ignore the constant echoing of sirens from further into the city and the never-ending honking from the depths of traffic on the interstate, but other than that, it was a soothing place to be at night.

"Ey, Dallas!" a man greeted.

Smiling as I approached him, I stopped outside of a pharmacy's parking lot that he called home and sighed, staring at the newest tarp addition to his tent.

"Hey, Rufus. I thought you were going to one of the shelters I told you about?" I asked.

He laughed awkwardly and shook his head, sitting cross-legged on a flattened piece of cardboard.

"Nah. Can't be bothered. I've been livin' here for months. Ain't nothin' wrong with that," he explained.

Rolling my eyes, I continued to smile. There *was* something wrong. He sat in his own urine daily and he smelt awful. I'm not sure when he last bathed.

"It's June and it's only going to get hotter," I mumbled.

"That's fine! I'll sweat off all my fat!" he laughed.

I forced a laugh and rolled my eyes once more. He didn't have any fat to spare.

"Oh well. Where's everyone else?" I asked.

Normally, there were other people here.

He shrugged. "Ditched me for the 7-Eleven on Highland," he explained.

I frowned. "Well, sucks to be them," I said, handing over the take-out box of cookies and muffins. Rufus took it gladly and started laughing.

"Sucks to be them!" he repeated, opening the box and shoving a muffin in his mouth in its entirety. "Thank you very much!" he grinned, crumbs falling out as he spoke.

I laughed. "My pleasure. Have a good night, Rufus," I said, continuing my walk to my apartment.

Rufus was a nice guy. Like he said, he'd been 'living' outside of the same pharmacy for months now. I wasn't sure about his story or his situation, but he was perfectly content with where he was. I had been giving him Starbucks leftovers for as long as I'd known him.

Finally getting to my floor, I unlocked my front door and was greeted by my little grey kitten, Poppy.

"Hi, cuteness," I smiled, tossing my keys on the kitchen counter and bending down to scratch the top of her head.

She was already purring. I had found her one night on my walk home from work. She had been placed in a cardboard box in an alleyway and I was pretty quick to claim her as my own.

"Want some dinner?" I asked, opening the fridge and grabbing a new can of wet cat food. She was meowing and weaving in between my legs as I opened the can. I plopped the meat in her bowl, then poured myself a quick bowl of cereal. It wasn't late, but I was tired and knew I had to open shop in the morning. I quickly ate my Cheerios in front of the TV before heading off to bed.

Every day was kind of the same at Starbucks. We had a lot of the same recurring customers and the odd random that came in, but overall, it was just the same boring, fake smiling shit. I made fresh food every morning for the display up front and brewed almost five fresh pots of coffee, all before opening. I turned on all the machines so they could warm up, and then Angela walked in the back door, yawning.

"Morning!" I called out from up front.

"Yup . . ." she mumbled, dropping her purse and walking out to meet me. "How was your night?" she asked, leaning against the counter and rubbing her tired eyes.

"It was fine. Nothing special," I mumbled.

"Jason had *another* detention yesterday . . ." she said in a very monotone voice. "The principal is talking about enrolling him in summer school," she sighed.

I frowned, walking around her to the front door and flicking on the neon *open* sign.

"What's up with him? What's he doing?" I asked, walking back and sitting down in the kitchen.

She followed. "He's being bullied by a bunch of other kids, so he gets physical. He punched this other kid in the stomach . . ." she explained, opening the fire exit door and lighting a cigarette. "I dunno. I don't know what I'm going to do with him," she added.

Just then, we both got distracted by the bell going off at the front door and we both exchanged looks.

"Wow. Someone's early," I said, laughing a bit, then standing to go greet them.

We'd only been open for a minute or two.

He looked my age, maybe a bit older, and had black messy hair. His shirt was black, his pants were black with holes in them, and he was wearing black and white converse. Both of his arms were *covered* in tattoos, as well as his hands and even one side of his neck. He also had a nose ring on the right side, and his left eyebrow was pierced. I was never one to judge a book by its cover because I've been judged my whole life because of my hair, but I was still intimidated. I arched a brow, staring at his tattooed body up and down, then made eye contact and forced a smile.

"Good morning," I greeted. "What can I get you?"

"Jesus Christ, lookit that hair!" he laughed. "Just a black coffee, please."

Of course, I thought to myself. *A new victim of my hair.* That was the most obnoxious reaction ever, so I smiled and tried my best not to roll my eyes.

"Heh, yeah. I get that a lot. What size did you want?"

"Uh, I dunno. I'll have a large?" he said as a question and I huffed.

I could feel Angela watching us from the kitchen. I pressed the necessary buttons on the register, but just as I was about to tell him the amount he owed, he slapped the exact amount down on the counter. I stared at the money and blinked, a little shocked at how fast he was. This seemed like his first time ordering coffee . . . ever. Taking the money and placing it in the register, I grabbed my marker and smiled back at him.

"Name?" I asked and he frowned, looking around at the empty room. Instantly feeling like a fool, I ducked my head and laughed. "Sorry. Force of habit. I realize there's nobody else here," I quickly added.

He laughed. "It's Jim—" he mumbled, suddenly looking embarrassed and cutting himself off.

"Jim?" I repeated, grabbing his cup and popping the lid off the marker.

"James!" he added, and it made me jump.

Having already written down the letter **J**, I glanced up at him and laughed.

"James . . ." I repeated, hesitant to add the **A** in case he changed his mind.

"Jimmy. My name's Jimmy. Nobody calls me James," he said, suddenly sighing loudly.

I huffed and glanced down at his cup, deciding to write **Jimmy James**. Turning my back to him, I made his boring black coffee, then turned back around to hand it to him over the counter.

"Here'ya go, Jimmy James," I laughed.

He stared at the name and threw his head back laughing.

"No . . . not what I meant. But I'll take it," he laughed.

Leaning back against the counter behind me, I stared at his hand holding his cup and saw that he had a word tattooed across his knuckles. I tried tilting my head to the side to see what it said, but he had already taken a step back to leave.

"Cheers," he said, raising the coffee up, then grabbing a handful of sugar packets.

My eyes widened and I had to hold back my laughter.

"Ha! D'you want some coffee with your sugar?" I asked.

He shoved the packets of sugar in his pockets and shrugged his shoulders, smiling.

"Not sure what I'm in the mood for yet. Have a good day!" he cheered, then left.

I watched him walk down the street past the windows to my left and quickly looked away when he stared back. Heading back into the kitchen, I shoved my thumb over my shoulder and frowned.

"Did you see how many sugars he took?" I asked Angie, and she nodded with a laugh.

The lunch rush came, then ended just as quickly, and suddenly Angie and I were head over heels with dishes.

"I'm surprised that guy actually came in," she said, breaking our silence.

I looked at her as I was drying a group of spoons by hand since the two dishwashers were full.

"Who?" I asked.

"That guy. This morning," she said.

"Oh, we're back to talking about that," I laughed, "why do you say that?"

"Because. I always see him standing at the door or by the windows, staring inside. But then he always walks away. I think he works at the tattoo parlour at the end of the street . . ."

"That would make sense. Did you see his arms? They're both covered! But that's kinda creepy, no? He just stands outside and stares?"

"Yeah, like he's not totally sure if he wants to come in or not."

We both started laughing.

"He's probably like . . . a serial killer or something . . ."

"It's okay. You were polite and made him a coffee. He won't kill you," Angie said, smiling.

I rolled my eyes. "But did you see how many packets of sugar he took? Like, why bother ordering a black coffee?"

"Well, he probably doesn't want to order a quintuple coffee . . . I know *I'd* be embarrassed," she laughed.

I snorted and shook my head. "So strange . . ."

For the past week, the mysterious sugar addict came in at the same time every morning and would always order his large black coffee and then grab a handful of sugar packets before leaving. He also always had exact change. I eventually got used to this routine, as I did with every regular customer, and thought it would be funny if I had the coffee ready and made before he even walked through the door. The cup *always* read 'Jimmy James.' Friday, he walked in three minutes after six, like he did every day, and I had his large black placed on the counter and a little pile of sugar packets placed beside it in a little pyramid. I stayed hidden in the kitchen. He walked in and slowed down, staring at his coffee and arched his brow. Leaning over the counter, he tried to look back into the kitchen and sighed.

"Oi! Firehead!" he called out.

I was originally smiling, but frowned at the nickname and walked out. "Firehead? Really?" I asked, standing across from him behind the counter and crossing my arms.

He smirked and shrugged. "Got your attention."

"*Anything* would have gotten my attention. I work here," I stated, narrowing my eyes at him and smiling.

He did the same in return, then looked down at the sugar pyramid and laughed.

"Har har," he said, placing the change on the counter.

I was grinning and took the money, placing it in the register.

"I know, I'm hilarious. But seriously, dude. Try something new for once! Have you even *looked* at our menu?" I asked.

I heard Angie walk in from the back and could see her face appear in my peripheral but chose to ignore her.

"Not really . . . I mean, I don't want to waste money on something that's going to be too sugary and disgusting," he mumbled, shoving the sugar in his pocket and taking his coffee.

I snorted. "Yeah, because you *hate* sugar!"

He narrowed his eyes, still smirking. "Right. So, you stalking me or something? You know how many sugars I take now?" he asked.

I was still smiling. "Well, you've come in every single day this week at the exact same time and have ordered the exact same thing . . . so yeah, I took note. I mean, I don't know if I got the sugar amount right. Somewhere between four and eight," I smirked and he started laughing. "Aren't you glad, though? Lookit this VIP service!" I grinned, throwing my arms in the air enthusiastically.

He huffed, slowly taking a few steps backwards. "Fine. Tomorrow, I'll order something completely random and throw you off," he said.

I raised my brows and laughed. "Alright then. You do that, and I'll see you tomorrow at 6:03 a.m."

"Dude, seriously?" he laughed, opening the door and walking out.

"YOU CALLED ME FIREHEAD!" I yelled in return.

I watched him laugh and walk off, shaking his head as he passed the windows. Suddenly, I was being shaken. I turned around and grabbed Angie's hands off my shoulders and squeezed her palms.

"What, whaaaat?!" I yelled.

"You made him *laugh*!" she yelled back, laughing herself.

I dropped her hands and walked into the kitchen.

"Heh, yeah. I did. And you know how I did it?" I asked.

She stared at me, genuinely curious. "How?!"

"I was *nice*! You should try it sometime!" Then I started laughing.

Her shoulders sank and she sighed. "Shut up . . ." she mumbled, nudging me then going back to baking muffins.

Angela Bryce was a good friend of mine. She was thirty years old with brown hair that was usually tied up in a ponytail and dark brown eyes. She only came off as intimidating because she was a small, bitter, single mom, and if it wasn't for all the smoking, she'd probably be happier and less stressed. But once you got to know her, like I did, she was actually a lot of fun. Her son Jason definitely kept her on her toes, though. She worked and managed this Starbucks and occasionally worked at a department store in a different part of town. She had helped me out more times than I could count and was there for me the second I decided to run away from home.

We also had a part-time worker named Tiffany, but she was an ignorant seventeen-year-old who thought she was the shit and sat around obnoxiously chewing bubble gum. *Very* stereotypical. She had somewhat of a Valley girl accent when she spoke, usually wore her dirty blonde hair in a huge bun loosely tied on the top of her head, and her acrylic nails were trimmed to an unbelievable length. Her work schedule was all over the place, but we could always use as many helping hands as possible, even if she brought her shitty attitude with her. Either way, she had a relatively good work ethic, and Ang and I couldn't run this place without her. It was just the three of us, and we were a tiny dysfunctional family. I loved it.

Chapter 2

The next morning, I woke up earlier than normal. It was too early for anything good to be on TV and my computer was too ancient to manage anything, so I decided it wouldn't hurt to open shop a little earlier than normal. I showered and got dressed, fed Poppy and then slowly made my way to work. The sun hadn't even thought about rising yet, and Rufus was hidden away in his tent when I passed him. Getting to the shop, I decided to keep things closed until everything was ready for business. Flicking on the lights and turning all the coffee machines on, I walked back into the kitchen to begin baking. Sliding everything into the oven, I walked back out to the front and sat up on the counter with my legs hanging off the edge, sighing. Reaching behind me, I grabbed the remote for the radio from underneath the counter and turned on some music. There was nothing to do now but wait.

Just then, there was a knock on the front windows and it made me jump. I looked up and saw the strange sugar addict, only this time, he was in workout clothes instead of his usual all black attire. Hopping off the counter, I walked over and unlocked the front door.

"Hey . . . you're here . . . early," I mumbled suspiciously, popping my head outside and looking both ways as if this was some sort of prank.

He arched a brow and leaned back out of my way, looking to his left and right as well.

"Yeah . . . what are you looking at?" he asked.

"Nothing," I mumbled, taking a step back. "So, what's up? Why are you here so early? It's not even 6:00 a.m. yet . . ." I stated.

He shrugged. "I don't work today and was going for a run. Saw the lights on, so I figured I'd come get my morning coffee. Plus, I threw you off, didn't I?" he asked, smirking a little bit.

I started laughing. "Yep. Y'did. Especially because *I'm* normally not here this early . . ."

"Can I be here this early? Is that allowed?" he asked.

I shrugged, turning and walking away and going back behind the counter, grabbing the remote to the radio and turning the music down a little bit.

"Sure, I don't care. I don't open for another half hour anyways . . ."

He stayed at the front door, standing awkwardly, and I laughed.

"C'moooon in," I added, gesturing to the empty chairs before disappearing back into the kitchen to check on the muffins.

They still had a few minutes. Walking back out, I stood behind the counter and stared at him as he approached the counter. Today, he was wearing a dark grey sleeveless shirt which really emphasized how covered his arms were in tattoos, and knee-length shorts that showed how his entire left leg was covered in tattoos as well. Stopping at the counter, I frowned when he stuck his hand out and smiled.

"I'm Jimmy," he said.

I shook his hand, laughing a little bit at the thought of 'Jimmy James.'

"Dallas," I said, continuing to shake his hand.

He nodded. "Nice to meet you," he smiled, and we were still shaking hands.

My face dropped and I cleared my throat, releasing my grip and taking a step back.

"So. Venti black?" I asked, turning and grabbing a cup.

"Not today," he said, shaking his head.

I arched a brow, the corner of my lips turning into a smile.

"I'm gonna try something different today . . . lemme try that caramel latte thing . . ." he said, motioning to the menu above my head.

I nodded. "What size?"

"Lar-no! Medium!" he yelled, laughing at himself.

I snorted, grabbing a cup and making him a caramel latte. I handed it to him just as he was rummaging through his pockets for some change, but I held up my hand.

"Don't worry about it. On the house," I said, smiling.

He stared up at me. "But why?" he asked.

I shrugged. "Let's call it a taste test. I'd hate for you to think it was too sugary or disgusting. Then *I'd* be the reason you would never try anything new ever again," I said and he laughed.

"Alright. I won't argue. Thanks!" he said, taking it and taking a sip.

I watched his eyes widen and he instantly took a second sip. I started laughing.

"This is so good!" he yelled, holding it with both hands and walking off to sit down at a table.

I wiped down the counter and wiped down the coffee machine, then quickly made myself a simple two milk and two sugar.

"Told'ya . . ." I smiled, putting a lid on the cup.

Leaving my coffee on the counter, I went back into the kitchen to take the muffins out of the oven before they burned to a crisp, then walked back out, grabbed my coffee and joined Jimmy at the table he was sitting at. He was already halfway done. He licked the whipped cream off his top lip and sighed, sinking into his chair.

"So. Dallas. How long have you been working here?" he asked, taking another sip.

I leaned on my elbows, holding my coffee with both hands.

"Six years," I replied.

He arched a brow. "How *old* are you?" he asked, and I snorted.

"I'm twenty-one. How old are *you*?" I asked in return.

"Jesus. You're just a baby. I'm twenty-five," he said, tilting his head back to chug the rest of his latte.

I laughed, but also frowned. He wasn't that much older than me. How did that make me a baby?

"So, how'd you get so good working here? Like, you make your shit so fast," he asked, licking the final drips of foam from the edge of the cup.

"Six years," I repeated, laughing.

He nodded. "Makes sense . . ."

We talked until the first customer walked in around 8:30 a.m. and I almost laughed. I totally forgot I was even at work. I usually wasn't such a social butterfly, but Jimmy was so easy to talk to and time seemed to be flying. Sighing and standing, I made my way behind the counter to help serve the customer while Jimmy threw out our mound of empty coffee cups in the garbage, stretching and yawning afterwards. He sat back down and distracted himself on his phone until I was done. The customer paid and left with their coffee, so I sat back down with him. He was scrolling and liking things on Instagram, and for a moment, I was distracted, watching him like the odd tattoo picture. I never really got into the whole social media thing. Blinking back to reality once he locked his screen and looked back up at me, I leaned forwards and rubbed my face.

"Why do I feel like today is going to be a slow day?"

"Where's the scary lady?" he asked.

"Who, Ang?" I asked, staring at him between my fingers.

He nodded and I laughed.

"She's not so bad . . . she's just . . . bitter. She doesn't work today. Tiffany is supposed to be in today, but she's usually always running late," I mumbled.

"*Tiffany*," Jimmy repeated, scrunching up his nose and I laughed.

"Exactly. Name says it all. Sometimes, she's great. Other times, not so much. Like, she'll do what she's told but she's not going to be happy about it. So, I guess it's better for me if today is a slow day . . ." I said with a sigh.

Looking out the window, I frowned and smushed my face in the palm of my hand. "God, it looks like a storm's coming in. Can't even see the sun . . ." I mumbled, glaring at the darkening sky.

Jimmy turned to look as well. "Yeah, it called for thunderstorms today . . ."

"In June?" I asked, and just on cue, a huge crash of thunder broke, followed by a flash of lightning.

I jumped, then started laughing. "Eerie . . ."

I stood to go into the kitchen to call Tiffany to ask her where she was. There was no answer. *Shocker.*

"That's annoying . . ." I mumbled, frowning and hanging up.

Just about to walk back out, the phone started to ring behind me. I frowned at it over my shoulder, answering it anyways.

"Starbucks, six fifty-five Vine Street."

"Is Tiff there yet?" It was Angela.

"No. I just tried calling her and there was no answer."

"No surprise. Close shop. There are tornado warnings all over the place," she explained.

My eyes widened and I sighed. I have never been too fond of storms let alone *tornadoes.*

"Okay," I mumbled.

"Okay? I'll talk to you later, but yeah. Just close everything and get home ASAP. Looks like this bitch is gonna hit any minute now. Thanks, Dallas." Then she hung up.

I placed the phone back on the receiver, then stared at Jimmy through the doorway. He was curiously staring back at me.

"What's up?" he called.

I walked back out to him and sat back down.

"That was Angela. She says to close shop because there's apparently a tornado warning," I sighed.

He snorted. "Wow . . . and you served all but one customer . . . well, and me," he grinned.

"Yep. Oh well. That's the last time *I'm* ambitious and open early. Let's go. I just gotta shut shit off."

Jimmy stood by the door, waiting for me to double check everything, and then it started to rain. Started to *pour,* actually. Quickly grabbing a box of pastries, I turned the lights off and joined Jimmy's side at the front door. He gestured to the box in my hands.

"Taking home some unsold goodies?" he asked.

Stepping outside with him and locking the door, we stood under the awning to remain dry from the rain.

"Oh, it's nothing. I just—" I paused because I felt stupid. "—whatever goes to waste, I bring with me and give to the homeless guys by the pharmacy near my place," I explained, shrugging a little bit.

I didn't know why I felt embarrassed explaining this, but I did.

Jimmy smiled. "That's awesome. Well, where do you live? I'll walk you home."

"That's okay. I'll live. I'm only like . . . five minutes up that way," I said, gesturing up Vine Street. "It wouldn't be fair for you to walk home alone afterwards," I smiled.

He shrugged. "At least I offered."

"Haha thanks. What're you up to today?" I asked, trying to direct the conversation away from me.

"Not sure . . . I might go to the parlour and just fuck around. That's what I usually do when I'm bored," he laughed. "Unless the power goes out . . . then I'd be fucked," he thought out loud.

My eyes widened and I arched my brow. "Is that what all your tattoos are? You just . . . being bored!?"

"Basically," he laughed, shoving his hands in his pockets and smiling at me.

"Wow. That's ballsy," I laughed and he continued to smile.

"I'm a ballsy guy."

Another giant crash of thunder went off and I jumped again.

He started laughing. "Okay, well. That's our cue, I guess. Nice to meet you, man. See'ya tomorrow?" he asked, walking backwards and into the rain.

I shook my head but remained smiling, laughing at the fact that within seconds, he was soaked.

"Off tomorrow."

"Oh! Well then, I *won't* see you tomorrow," he laughed. "Alighty then. See'ya around," he said, turning with a bit of a wave.

I waved back awkwardly then sighed, staring up at the dark sky and cursing under my breath. Throwing on my hood, I started to head back home at a fast pace. As I reached Rufus' tent, he was understandably inside. Kneeling in front of it and unzipping the door, I started laughing when I saw that he was playing a card game with a friend.

"Hi!" I called out.

The rain hitting the tarps was uncomfortably loud.

"Dallas!" Rufus cheered. "You're getting soaked!" he pointed out, and I started laughing and knelt down under the tarps.

"Yep! Just heading home now! Wanted to give you these!" I yelled, handing him the overflowing box of treats.

His face lit up. "You didn't have to do that in this weather, boy! Thank you!" he grinned, taking the box and offering his friend something.

He smiled back at me in return.

"It's no problem—have a good one!" I smiled, then zipped the tent back up.

I was absolutely drenched, but I didn't really care. Giving Rufus and his friend those pastries was the best part of the day.

It turned out to not be a full-blown tornado, just a thunderstorm with some intense wind. According to the news, the *real* storm just missed us and was heading south. Poppy and I lounged on the couch all day watching TV. The power went out a few times and I thought about Jimmy tattooing himself and laughed out loud. It eventually went off and *stayed* off, so I decided to call it an early night around 7:00 p.m. What else was there to do anyways? But I was restless. I couldn't get comfortable and my mind was all over the place. I was constantly tossing and turning, and I couldn't turn my brain off. Never having really experienced this kind of insomnia before, I sat up and watched TV until the sun came up; thankful that the power had come back on at some point in the night.

Having the day off felt like a blessing since yesterday had been a waste of time. The sky was blue without a cloud to be seen, so I decided to go for a walk with my iPod and maybe if I felt like it, make my way toward Ralph's and go grocery shopping. Turning down Melrose, I waved at Angela through the Starbucks windows and smiled. Carrying on with my hands in my pockets, I let out an exaggerated sigh. I missed days off, and I loved this weather. Smiling up at the clear sky, I glanced to my right as I walked and continued to smile at the Hollywood sign off in the distance. Suddenly, somebody was calling my name and I almost tripped on my own foot.

"Dallas!" they yelled again, only louder.

I frowned, looking all around. I started laughing when I saw Jimmy running across the street, waving at me. I took out an earbud and smiled.

"Hey!" I yelled back, just as he dodged a taxi and made it across to me.

"Funny seeing *you* here!" he said.

I laughed. "You too!"

"Nah, not really. I work here . . ." he mumbled, shoving a thumb over his shoulder and motioning to the tattoo parlour behind him.

My face dropped as I stared at the giant No Regrets sign. The store front was mainly windows, and inside, customers could be seen sitting and waiting for their appointment. He had told me he worked here too. *Was I subconsciously walking to his work?* I swallowed the lump in my throat and smiled.

"Oh yeah!" I played dumb and he laughed.

"So much for that tornado yesterday . . ."

"Heh, yeah. My power *did* go out though. How about you? Were you tattooing?" I asked with a smirk.

He frowned. "Yeah. And then I couldn't finish. My schedule is crammed too, so I gotta wait to finish it," he mumbled and I bit my lip, trying my best not to laugh out loud. "Oh well. But hey! It's my lunch break! What'cha up to?" he asked.

I shrugged. "Going for a walk, I guess . . ." I said, frowning at the ground.

It suddenly sounded so stupid when it came out of my mouth.

He snorted. "Sounds like a thrill. Wanna go grab a bite or something?" he asked, smiling.

I stopped my music and rolled my iPod up, shoving it in my pocket.

"Sure!"

✎

We ended up going to a cheap pizza joint up on Santa Monica Boulevard. We ordered a large pepperoni pizza and some pop, and then ate in silence out on the patio.

"So. When'd you get that tattoo on your finger?" he asked, pointing to the little black heart on my middle finger.

I stared at it and shrugged. "I dunno. I was like, seventeen or something. The act of a rebellious teen or some shit," I mumbled, forcing an awkward laugh.

"Haha! Been there!"

"What about you? You're basically covered . . . from what I can see anyways," I said and he started laughing and my stomach got tight and did a back flip.

It was a good thing he wasn't paying enough attention to notice my face drop. *Is this what butterflies feel like? What the fuck was that?*

"Yeah . . . I have two sleeves and one full leg. Almost one whole side of my torso is done, my entire back . . . uhhh and then my neck," he grinned. "Oh, and my hand and knuckles . . . obviously," he smiled, flattening out his hands on the table.

His right hand had a black and white rose on it and his knuckles read *patience* across them. I mentally smiled to myself because I had been trying to figure out what his knuckles read. Ignoring the tension in my stomach, I focused back on him and smiled.

"I won't go through them all, but a good chunk of them I did myself . . . my first one I got when I was sixteen? And . . . uhm, and my last . . . ." he sat in silence for a moment, staring out at the streets in thought. I was distracted, staring his arms up and down. ". . . two weeks ago. Other than my failure from last night," he said, looking back at me and laughing. "They're an addiction,

I tell'ya! After my first, I never stopped. And I still want more!" he grinned, sipping his Pepsi.

I laughed. "I get it. I want more eventually, I just don't have the money for it," I mumbled, grabbing another piece of pizza.

He rolled his eyes. "Dude. You're *literally* talking to a tattoo artist. I can give you one," he smiled.

"I'm not gonna get a tattoo from you for free . . ."

"Why not? Supply me with free caramel things and you got yourself a deal!" he grinned, leaning back in his chair and crossing his arms across his chest.

I snorted, then stared down at my pizza slice to distract myself from his forearm muscles.

"Well . . . fine. But I don't know what I'd get!"

"Is the heart on your finger your only one?" he asked, arms still crossed.

I shook my head. "Nah. I also have . . ." I sat back in my chair to bend down and lift a pant leg.

My left leg, from the ankle up to my knee, was covered in extremely realistic flames. I didn't have a reason as to why I had got it done. Looked cool as fuck, that was why. His eyes grew wide and he started clapping. I gave him a strange look.

"Dude, that's awesome! Koodos to that artist!" he yelled, getting some looks from other customers.

I quickly rolled my pant leg back down and sat normally. I didn't like too much attention. He pushed back his chair and stood, and I started glaring at him because the attention from strangers was now full blown. I felt like ducking. He lifted his shirt, practically taking it off, to reveal a huge group of flames starting at his tailbone and climbing their way up to his right shoulder blade. His whole back was covered and I was an emotional wreck because of it. At first, I was angry because now *way* too many people were staring and weren't looking away, and then I felt extremely awkward because he had the greatest body I'd ever seen. He was completely ripped with a six-pack and all, and lean and toned and . . . and I felt embarrassed because was I really getting turned on by this? I had to stop gawking and quickly looked away, feeling my face get hot and red.

"Wow . . ." I mumbled, quickly grabbing my drink and chugging its carbonated goodness while trying to cool down.

This is what I didn't understand. I liked women. I had crushes on girls all through school and even though I never got anywhere with them, I still liked them. I never once thought of a guy like this. But Jimmy . . . Jimmy was different. I instantly felt some kind of connection with him, and I didn't know if I was okay with that.

"So, your parents let you get all those tattoos?" I asked but he shook his head, pulling his shirt back down and sitting once again.

"Nah. They hated them, but that didn't really stop me. Then I moved out when I was like nineteen or twenty or something," he smiled.

"Hey, me too!" I grinned, happy that he was sitting again with all his clothes on. "Well, sorta. I moved out when I was seventeen. I got this older brother who is a complete douchebag—"

"Heh, I sense jealousy," he smirked, leaning back and chewing on the end of his straw.

"No. Not at all. He's a total prick. He made my life a living hell since day one. He's basically the reason I left."

"How much older?"

"Three years. He's going to school to be a lawyer. Mom and dad would gawk over him daily."

"And you?"

I forced a laugh, looking down and staring at my grease covered plate. "Me? What about me? I graduated high school and I've been working at a coffee shop ever since."

"Well, what are your hobbies? Are you interested in going to school?" he asked.

I looked up at him and smirked, peeling a pepperoni off my slice of pizza and chewing off little bites.

"Now you sound like my mom."

"Sorry! Whatever, man. I didn't even *finish* high school and I work at a tattoo parlour! You've already got one up on me!" he grinned, finishing his pop.

I shrugged. The waitress came around and asked us how we were doing, so we asked for the bill. I watched Jimmy check her up and down as she walked away.

"Jeez, she obviously does squats," he whispered, staring at the waitress's ass and I forced a laugh, suddenly feeling very uncomfortable about my previous thoughts.

She returned with our receipt and he was quick to act on pulling out his debit card. I had my wallet in my hand and stared at him with wide eyes.

"No, hey! Not allowed!"

"Too slow!"

"J, seriously. I'm paying for my half."

"Ignore him. I'm paying for both." Then he waved his card around.

She handed him the wireless machine and walked away to help another table. I put my wallet away and leaned on the table, glaring at him.

"You suck."

"My treat! I asked *you* out for lunch, so it's only polite if I pay," he smiled, ripping off his copy and standing.

I sighed, chugging my pop and joining his side as we walked out.

"Thanks, babe!" he called out to our waitress.

I frowned and chewed my bottom lip.

It was a twenty-minute walk back down to Melrose where the parlour was, and the whole walk we talked about tattoos. It was kinda neat hearing all his different stories between his own tattoos and stories of tattoos he had given. Getting outside the parlour, we stood by the main entrance and talked a bit more. Reaching into his back pocket, he pulled out a pack of cigarettes and offered me one.

"You smoke?" he asked, and I politely shook my head.

I wasn't offended; both my parents smoked when I was growing up—both quitting before I left.

He nodded and lit one for himself. "So, you called me J back at the pizza place . . ." he pointed out.

I arched a brow. "Did I?"

"Yeah, I think you did," he smirked and I started laughing.

"Well then. I think you just leveled up to being nickname worthy."

"Leveling up already?! My future looks good. No fair though. Your name doesn't convert into anything shorter."

"That sounds like your problem, not mine . . ." I smiled.

He laughed at me, then tilted his head back and blew smoke out above his head.

Suddenly, a tattooed girl with light blue hair tied back into a messy bun opened the door to the shop and leaned out. She stared at me and smiled,.then looked at Jimmy.

"Hey. Your appointment is here," she said with a thick British accent and he nodded.

"Well, I just lit this. So, they can wait," he smirked, tilting his head back to blow smoke up into the air once more.

"Who's this?" she asked, letting go of the door and joining Jimmy's side.

I saw him stare at her with wide eyes, then look back at me and smile. I frowned because I didn't get it.

"This is Dallas," he said, flicking ash off to the side, and she nodded, still smiling.

"I'm Nils," she said, sticking out a hand for me to shake.

She was equally as tattooed as Jimmy. Her left hand—the one that I was shaking—had a bright colourful monarch butterfly on it, and her knuckles read 'FACE'. I assumed I would have to see her right hand to understand.

"Nice to meet you," I added.

She had a nose ring on the right side, as well as stud under her left eye. Both her arms were covered in tattoos, including her hands and knuckles. It suited her, as odd as that sounded, because I had only just met her. Some people could just pull it off, and it looked like she was *meant* to look this way. Not to mention she was *gorgeous*. Overall, very interesting to stare at. She wore a tank top, showing off all her ink, and black shorts with rips and tears. Her legs also had tattoos on them, but were hard to see since she wore dark nylons, and even though she was wearing Dr. Martens, she was still a bit shorter than Jimmy.

"So, where'd you pick up this piece of junk?" she asked, winking and nudging Jimmy's shoulder with her own.

She had the most beautiful accent and it was almost mesmerizing to listen to. Jimmy rolled his eyes and frowned, turning and smirking at her.

"Thanks, Nilly," he mumbled with his cigarette sticking out between his lips.

I laughed awkwardly. "He found me, I guess you could say," I said, awkwardly shoving my hands in my pockets.

Jimmy turned and stuck his tongue out at her then smiled at me, taking another drag and blowing smoke rings above our heads.

She laughed then leaned on his shoulder and sighed. "Well, we're all going out tonight. You should come with!" she enthused, and my face fell.

I stared back and forth between the two of them and swallowed the lump in my throat. "Uhhhh."

"He doesn't wanna hang out with a bunch of drunks, Nilly. Especially if Jack is coming," Jimmy

mumbled and she frowned at him.

I saw her jaw clench before turning and smiling back at me. "Well, come if you want. We'll be heading out around 8:00 p.m. Just going to a bar up the street," she smiled.

I continued to stare at the two of them like a deer in headlights.

"You have James' number, yeah?" she asked, and I frowned, quickly glancing at him before staring back at her.

"I uh . . . no," I mumbled awkwardly, and she was quick to pull a red sharpie out of her pocket.

"Here. Call him or text him if you're coming," she smiled, taking my hand out of my pocket and writing a phone number across it.

Jimmy ducked his head and sighed, shaking his head a little. Dropping his cigarette on the ground, he stepped on it and squished it flat with his toe.

"I *guess* I'll think about it," I said, smiling down at the marker on my hand.

"Perfect! It'll be a lot of fun, I swear. We're fun," she grinned, wrapping her arm around Jimmy and squeezing him. "But *anyways*. Like I said, your appointment is here," she said, turning and smiling back at him.

He stared at me and laughed, shaking his head in a *she's ridiculous* kind of way. "I gotta go," he said and I nodded, taking a few steps back.

"I figured as much," I smiled.

"I'll talk to you later?" he asked and I nodded.

"James, weren't you listening? He's going to call you later," Nils said and I laughed, ducking my head because I could feel myself starting to blush.

He sighed and looked at her then looked back at me and laughed. "Kay, bye," he said, wrapping an arm around Nils and forcing her to turn around.

"See ya," I laughed, turning away as well.

"Bye, Dallas! It was nice meeting you!" Nils yelled out.

Jimmy quickly turned her around and started mumbling quietly to her as they went back inside. I laughed again and shook my head before walking back home.

INKED CAFFEINE
31

My whole walk home, I was filling myself with anxiety about meeting all of Jimmy's friends. I already felt like a child when I was with him, and I couldn't imagine how I'd feel around a full group of them. Subconsciously walking upstairs to my apartment, I let myself in, closed the door and stared into space. Jumping back to reality, I looked down and saw Poppy rubbing against my leg and meowing.

"Oh. Hey, kitty," I mumbled, tossing my iPod onto my counter and walking over to my couch, slumping into it and sighing.

Nils said they were leaving around eight, and it was only just quarter to four. Slouching deeper into the couch, I covered my face with my hands and whined loudly. That wasn't *nearly* enough time to sit and stress about my potential social get-together.

"What am I gonna do, Pops?" I asked aloud.

Flicking on the TV, I watched the odd show and even a full movie, although I was barely paying attention. I kept staring at my phone to keep an eye on the time, then sighed loudly and got up to pace my apartment for a bit and overanalyze every scenario in my head. I didn't have friends growing up which meant I didn't go out to social gatherings, let alone a bar where people would be obnoxious and drinking. *But at the same time, what do I really have to lose? If I don't enjoy myself, I won't do it again. But then there is humiliating myself somehow . . . I know I'll manage to do it one way or another.* Sighing *once* more, I grabbed my cell from my coffee table and stared at the number on my hand. It took me a minute or two to finally get the nerve to dial, and once I did, I could feel the anxiety raising with every ring.

"James Echo . . ." he answered, and my heart skipped and my stomach dropped.

I swallowed the lump in my throat and exhaled slowly and quietly. "Jimmy? It's Dallas," I said and clenched my eyes shut until his response.

"Heeeyyy! I didn't think you'd call!"

I opened my eyes and sighed, staring at the clock on my stove. It was 7:15 p.m.

"Yeah . . . I was honestly contemplating not coming because I'm socially awkward . . ." I laughed, resorting back to pacing my apartment.

I raked a hand through my hair and started chewing on my bottom lip. He laughed, and I got that weird butterfly feeling in my gut again. I frowned.

"That's even better! You can meet everyone and be less awkward."

I could hear a smile in his voice. Continuing to chew on my lip, I let out the smallest of sighs. *That's what I'm afraid of . . .*

"Yeah, I guess you're right," I said with no enthusiasm.

He laughed again. "Don't let Nils intimidate you. She's just *extra* social, that's all. I mean, she's a *brat* but she's great," he said, and I laughed, feeling myself starting to calm down a little bit.

Only a little bit.

"Nah, she's fine. I liked her."

"Yeah, she's cool," he laughed. "So, shop closes at eight tonight, then we'll be heading out. Wanna just head this way and meet us here?" he asked, and I got anxious all over again.

"Sure," I mumbled, glancing panicked around my apartment as if I'd find something to help me calm down.

"Cool! See you soon!"

Then the line went dead. Staring at his number on my screen, I sighed and added his name as a contact, then tossed my phone on the couch.

"I guess . . . it's time to get ready," I mumbled to myself and went to go shower.

Turning on the water, I heard the familiar echo of pipes clunking and sighed loudly.

"No hot water," I mumbled out loud, holding my hand under the running water and waiting to see if it got any warmer.

It didn't. For some reason, this happened the most in the summertime. My landlord said it had something to do with how many people were doing laundry at once, and that people were showering a lot more, but I called bullshit. He just didn't want to admit that his building was a piece of shit. Sighing once more, I knew I couldn't *not* shower, so I quickly undressed and hopped in. It wouldn't be the first time I had a shower under ice cold water, and probably wouldn't be the last. Unfortunately, there had been many times where I skipped showering for almost up to a week because I couldn't bear the cold, but since I was going out in public and meeting people, I figured it would be best if

I smelled and looked nice. I quickly washed my hair and my body, then got out and could feel myself quivering. I was covered in goosebumps.

Towel drying my hair, I sighed and stared at my reflection. I was overdue for a haircut. I was always in a constant state of messy bed head but wasn't going to obsess over how I looked too much. I quickly brushed my teeth, put on some deodorant, and then stared at my little shelf of cologne. I wasn't a cologne kind of guy, but Angela insisted on buying me a new brand every year for Christmas. I guess trying some out tonight wouldn't hurt. I wanted to be on my best behaviour and hopefully would come out with some new acquaintances. Staring at my final product in the mirror, I sighed, shrugged and turned off the light to the bathroom. Quietly talking to myself to calm myself down, I fed Poppy and then headed out, trying my best not to power walk to the parlour.

It was in sight just down the road and Jimmy was there with a group of about eight other people—male and female, all smoking.

"Dallas!" he chirped, bouncing toward me.

"Hey," I smiled awkwardly. "Thanks for the invite," I said and looked at Nils who was pushing her way through people to come stand with us.

She was quick to pull me into a hug.

We walked up Highland Avenue a few blocks until we got to a bar called No Other Place and I forced a laugh.

"No Other Place? They're sitting high on their high horse," I mumbled.

"No, seriously. They're the best. We only ever go to this place," Jimmy said with a straight face and my face fell.

"Oh," I mumbled, but then he started to laugh.

"Ha, yeah. And get thrown out almost every time!" One of the girls laughed, tossing her cigarette butt behind her.

I stared at the back of her head with wide eyes before quickly staring at Jimmy. "We're gonna get kicked out?" I asked quietly.

He laughed and loosely wrapped his arm over my shoulder. I tensed.

"Don't worry," he replied quietly.

Everyone finished their cigarettes and tossed them outside, then all walked in single file, instantly heading for the bar. It was dark inside since there were no windows and the lights were dimmed. There was a DJ on a small stage playing loud techno music and it was already making my head hurt. The ceiling was decorated with twinkle lights which kind of gave it a magical touch, but the drunk girls stumbling around quickly ruined it.

"We don't need to show ID?" I asked, following close by. Was that not a common thing when entering a bar or club? I had never done this before and only assumed that was the norm.

"Nah. We know the guys here. They're cool. We're here so often anyways," Jimmy explained.

"They don't know me," I added.

"Yeah, but you're with us. We got Caleb's younger brother in once. Plus, we go out for so many smoke breaks anyways, it got annoying having to show our ID every single time."

"Oh . . . cool!" I grinned.

He laughed and brought me up to the bar.

"So. What'cha drinking?" he asked, smiling. "It's on me."

"Oh. I don't know. I'm not much of a drinker. I don't really know any drinks . . ." I mumbled awkwardly.

I was already bad at this.

"Ha, okay. Well, we'll start you off easy and work our way up."

"Are we getting drunk?" I asked, quietly again.

I didn't want his friends to know how lame I actually was, even though they were already all off doing their own thing.

He snorted. "Only if you want to. Jack is gonna be throwing a party later in the fall and *then* we'll be getting drunk. Like shitfaced. And obviously, you're more than welcome to come," he grinned.

I smiled nervously but also kind of liked that I was already being invited to another outing that was in the foreseeable future.

"And who's Jack?" I asked.

If I was going to his house in the fall, I should probably meet the guy, no?

"Oh! Right, right! C'mere . . ." he mumbled, bringing me closer to his group of friends who had all already ordered their drinks.

"Okay, so this is Jeremy—"

He was a taller guy with a thicker build like Jimmy, darker skin than the rest with dirty blonde hair.

"Liam—"

The tallest of the group with super short dark brown hair, cutting it close to a buzzcut.

"Caleb—"

An average looking dude, although his shaggy hair made mine look tame.

"Lilly—"

She was very short, almost pixie-like. She had shoulder length blonde hair, and when everyone was smoking, she appeared to be the only one not partaking.

"Jillian—"

She came from an Asian background, and had long, straight bleached blonde hair, although her natural dark roots were peeking out at the top.

"Megan—"

She had long black hair with hot pink tips and was standing with the other girls, laughing.

"That one is Jack—"

He was standing with Caleb, appearing to be the most anti-social of them all. He had a certain 'surfer dude' aesthetic to him with messy blond hair and a tan.

"And of course, Nils," Jimmy finally finished, pointing to everyone.

No one was really paying attention and were all talking amongst themselves.

"Guys!" Nils yelled, now standing beside me with a drink in hand. They all looked over at her, then looked at me. "This is Dallas," she smiled.

I smiled awkwardly then gave a little wave. A few of them said their hellos and the others acknowledged my existence with a head nod.

Jimmy rolled his eyes and leaned back on the bar. "Bunch of assholes," he mumbled and then tried getting the bartender's attention.

"Don't mind them," Nils said.

I turned around and stared at her, laughing awkwardly.

"They're social assholes and think they're better than everyone else," she said, still smiling.

I forced a smile. "Oh. It doesn't help that I'm a hundred percent awkward," I mumbled.

Jimmy tapped my shoulder and handed me a drink and joined my side. I stared down at the drink and scrunched my nose. It was a dark colour and had ice cubes but smelt sweet.

"Calm down. It's just rum and Coke," he said with a smile, then looked up at Nils and greeted her with a head nod.

"Hey, Nilly," he mumbled, sipping his beer.

She smiled at him. "Jimmy's talked a lot about you at the shop," she stated to me while smirking. Jimmy's jaw tensed then he forced a smile and shrugged his shoulders. "Guilty."

Then he walked off to go join his other friends. I felt a second of panic once he walked away, but instantly calmed myself when I realized I actually really liked Nils.

"So, how long have you two been friends?" she asked, sipping her drink.

I took a baby sip of my drink, anticipating disgusting liquor, but it was mainly Coke, so I gladly took another sip and then cleared my throat.

"Uhm. Not long. Like a week and like . . . two days?" I laughed, then quickly drank the rest of my drink.

It wasn't a large glass by any means, but my nerves were overflowing and I figured drinking was better than talking. I quickly finished it and was kind of disappointed when it was gone. Nils noticed and started laughing at me.

"Want another?" she asked, leaning against the bar.

I shrugged. "Sure."

"Ey! Joey!" she yelled. Then she twirled her finger in the air and looked back at me, smiling.

"What about you? How long have you known Jimmy for?" I asked, stopping her before she made me talk about myself again.

"Oh God, *years*. I moved here with my parents when I was about fifteen. I met Jimmy when I was eighteen. We've been best friends ever since. He's helped me through a lot of shit and vice versa," she smiled. "But there was definitely an awkward spot there for a bit. I fell for him *hard* in the beginning. Felt like a bloody wanker!" she laughed, drinking more of her drink. I huffed at the British slang.

"How so?" I asked.

"We'll just say he wasn't showing the same signs of interest," she laughed again.

There was a moment of silence as she finished her drink, then she sighed a little bit.

"Y'know, he acts all gentle and polite, but he's a tough fucker. He lives up to his appearance, that's for sure. James is the kind of guy you want to keep on your good side."

"Is that a threat?" I asked, forcing an uncomfortable laugh and she snorted.

"No! No, I just mean you'll be safe with him. He's a good guy," she smiled, then made eye contact with the bartender and nodded at him without saying another word.

After making my second drink, he grabbed her a second one as well. She handed me my rum and Coke, then gladly took a sip from her fresh beverage.

"Y'know, you walk around looking like me and James, and it's easy for people to judge . . ." she mumbled, taking another sip.

I nodded, staring off at Jimmy who was laughing with his friends.

"Yeah, when Jimmy first walked into Starbucks, I was kind of intimidated," I admitted and she smiled, nodding.

"Exactly. So, all I mean is . . . he's not. I mean, he can throw a mean punch if he needs to, but other than that, he's just a big golden retriever," she smiled, and I started laughing. "You seem like a cool kid. I'm happy he's finally met someone outside of our group. We all kind of hang out like little hermits," she laughed and then gestured toward her friends. "C'mon. They don't bite," she winked and brought me over to the rest of the gang.

Her face hit a certain spot in the light, and I could swear her eyes were purple, but then again, I never drank alcohol, so who knows.

❧

The night turned out to be really enjoyable. Once I got to know everyone, the atmosphere finally stopped being so awkward and I felt like I could actually talk to a few of them without wanting to be sick. I especially liked Nils. We instantly hit it off which was nice because she and Jimmy were clearly close. Not that it mattered, of course. She told me a few silly stories about him which he probably wouldn't have approved of me knowing, but what the hell. Jack was also really likeable, but kind of obnoxious. He definitely drank the most out of all of us and tried to get on top of the bar to dance which apparently wasn't the first time. Nobody wanted to get kicked out, myself in particular, so we got him down before we got in trouble. Either way, it was absolutely hilarious.

There were a few songs where we'd all stand around in a circle with our heads thrown back, singing at the top of our lungs, and it felt really good. I had never experienced anything like this. I was finally out of my comfort zone and had loosened up a bit, ordering drinks all on my own and even flirting a little. Accidentally, of course. I didn't really realize I was doing it. This one pretty girl came up and was struggling to stand straight, playing with my hair. I awkwardly moved out of her way and laughed a little when she swayed back and forth.

"You good?" I asked, reaching out and grabbing her shoulder to keep her sturdy.

Her eyes were heavy, and she was smiling.

"You have pretty hair . . ." she slurred, pulling some strands and twirling them around her finger.

Glancing down at my hand, she gasped and grabbed my wrist, bringing my hand closer to her heavy eyes and staring.

"Lucky boy! Who's the lucky lady?" she slurred, still examining my hand.

I frowned and looked down, confused about what she was talking about, then huffed when I noticed that Jimmy's phone number had survived my shower. Laughing out loud, I pulled my hand from her grip and shook my head, laughing a little.

"Nah. That's his number—oh! Jimmy!" I smiled, watching as he approached me with a frown. My face fell and I frowned in return, confused.

"Oi!" he snapped, marching over and tapping on her shoulder.

She stumbled to turn around and snorted, bending over and laughing for reasons we did not know. He frowned harder, then looked at me and I shrugged.

"She's drunk," I smiled.

"Fuck yeah, she is. Ey, missy!" he yelled, bending down and picking her up by the shoulders.

She struggled to focus on him and then tried to lean in for a kiss, pursing her lips and leaning toward his face. He turned his head just in time and sighed when her drunken lips pressed against his cheek.

"Good God. Go home. You're drunk," he said, and very gently pushed her in the direction of the exit.

She continued to waddle her way out until she stopped and made a dashing sprint for the bathroom; covering her mouth. We both started laughing. Turning to look at me, he was smiling and gave me a pat on my shoulder.

"Hey, I'm glad you came out tonight," he said and I smiled in return, my cheeks aching.

"I am too," I admitted with a bit of a laugh.

"Yeah, like, lookit you! Facing your fears and everything! Ordering drinks all on your own—" He gestured to my drink sitting on the bar. "Talking to hookers . . ." he trailed off, before turning around and making his way back to the dance floor.

I felt the colour leave my face and my mouth slowly gawked open. "*Hooker!?*" I yelled.

He laughed while he danced with Nils. I remained standing where I was, thinking about the night. She didn't *look* like a hooker. *But mind you . . . what do hookers look like?* Did it really matter? Laughing at myself, I sighed and shook my head. This was the most human interaction I had in a while, *not* including work, and I was actually enjoying myself. A lot, smiling by myself like a moron. I was on an emotional roller coaster and I was the only passenger, sitting front row. I was losing my shit, but I was okay with it. Nils saw me and motioned for me to join them, so I finished my drink and ran over. I wasn't drunk . . . I thought. I had never *been* drunk before, but the alcohol definitely got rid of some of the nerves, and I was never one to dance . . . but here I was . . . facing my fears, just like Jimmy had said.

⌘

Our night ended around 3:00 a.m. when Jack had had enough, and we decided to call it quits. Jimmy and Caleb carried him out while the rest of us walked behind.

"Tonight was a lot of fun. We should a hundred percent do it again," Nils said, drunkenly walking beside me with her arm over my shoulder.

I couldn't stop giggling which only made her laugh harder. My head felt slightly fuzzy, but it was nothing to be concerned about. This was my first time consuming alcohol and I knew I was in good hands.

We got back to the tattoo parlour where everyone went their separate ways except for Jack, Nils, Jimmy and me.

"I'll get a cab with him," Nils mumbled, grabbing a cigarette, lighting it, and then taking a huge drag from it.

"You sure?" Jimmy asked.

"Yeah. There's no way he can find his place alone. That's a lot of alone elevator time," she laughed, taking out her cell phone and calling a cab. "You guys go. I'm good. I'll stay at his place," she smiled and Jimmy nodded.

"Cool. I'll see you later then. Bye, Jacky," he said, patting Jack on the back and then turning to me. "C'mon. I'll walk ya home," he smiled, motioning onward and grabbing a cigarette out for himself.

I turned around and waved at Nils. "It was nice meeting you!" I yelled down the empty street.

She laughed and waved back, grabbing Jack's hand and waving back for him.

Jimmy snorted and shook his head. "Y'know, for a kid that had a fucked up childhood, you've got pretty good manners," he stated and I frowned, placing my hands in my pockets.

"That's *why* I have good manners. I don't want to grow up to be like my family," I explained.

He pursed his lips and nodded. "Makes sense."

There was a moment of silence as we walked up toward Starbucks and then turned left up Vine. The fresh air felt nice on my brain and I could feel myself becoming clearer in the head.

"So, did'ya have fun?" he asked, taking a drag of his cigarette and tilting his head back to blow smoke into the air.

"Yes! Lots! Thank you for inviting me! Well, I guess Nils," I laughed.

"Ha, no problem. We'll have to do it again sometime."

"That's what Nils was saying," I smiled, staring down at my feet as we walked.

"Yeah. Nilly sure likes a good party."

"She said you guys have known each other for a long time?" I asked, staring at him.

He smiled. "Nilly and I? Oh *God* yeah. Yeah, I love her. Like a sister, though. It would never work out between us as anything more than that . . ."

"Why not?" I asked.

I knew Nils had kind of already explained it to me, but I was just curious.

He stared straight ahead and took another drag. "Just wouldn't."

Then there was an awkward silence. I cleared my throat and nodded.

Looking ahead, I saw Rufus' tent and knew he'd be inside sleeping. I didn't want to be the one to disturb and wake him, so I tapped Jimmy's arm and gestured for us to cross the street.

"I'm just up ahead, but that's Rufus right there, and I don't want to bother him," I explained.

He frowned as we crossed. "Rufus?" he asked, and I nodded, looking back at my feet and smiled.

"Homeless dude I give the Starbucks shit to."

"Ohhhh," he mumbled, turning to stare at Rufus' tent as we passed.

Looking back at me, I saw him smiling. Side-glancing, I frowned.

"What?" I asked and he shrugged.

"Nothing. I just think it's really fucking awesome that you do that. Not many people would be so generous," he explained and I shrugged.

"It's nothing. Like . . . I just give him the food that would go to waste anyways. So, why throw it away when it can go in someone's stomach, right?"

"No, I totally get it. It's awesome," he smiled.

Staring back at my feet, I felt my face get hot. "Well, this is me!" I said, motioning to my apartment building once were standing outside it. I turned to face him and smiled. "Thanks for the company. How far do you have to go?" I asked.

He shrugged. "I'm back at the bar. Just up the street from it, actually," he laughed, flicking his cigarette butt away and stepping on it.

I opened my mouth. "That's all the way back! You really didn't have to walk me," I said and he shrugged once more.

"I don't mind. Have a good night, Dallas. I'll see ya later," he smiled, turning on his heel and walking back the way we just came.

I sighed. "Bye, J."

Chapter 4

$\mathcal{A}$ few days went by and Jimmy hadn't come by for his regular coffee visit. I mean, it didn't bother me, but it bothered me. Did I do or say something that upset him? I looked forward to seeing him, and every time I heard that God forsaken bell go off at the front door, my stomach did flips. It never turned out to be him and then my chest would ache. But I think most of all, I was mainly pissed off because of these confusing emotions. My mind wouldn't shut up, and when I thought of him, my heart wouldn't calm down. I felt like a fourteen-year-old girl with a high school crush and it was ridiculous.

A week went by with no Jimmy, so I decided it was time *I'd* go visit him. That's what friends did, right? I asked Angela if I could leave early for reasons she didn't need to know and then made my way down the street to the tattoo parlour. Walking through the front door, I smiled when I saw Nils at the front desk drinking a Red Bull. Gasping and choking on her sip, she turned around to have a coughing fit before turning back and smiling at me with watery eyes.

"Dallas!" she yelled, and I laughed. "Hey, hun! You're not here to get a tattoo, are you?!" she gasped, and I continued to laugh, shaking my head.

"No, no. I'm just here to see Jimmy?" I asked and her face fell.

"Oh sweetie, he's off today. I can let him know you popped by though!" she smiled, and I frowned. "You have his number, yeah? Just give him a call!" she continued to smile.

I was aware of my phone in my back pocket and sighed a little. "You're right. I forgot I had his number," I laughed, faking my enthusiasm.

No way am I calling him. Staring at her for a moment, my face dropped, and I narrowed my eyes.

She arched a brow and laughed. "What's up, love?" she asked.

"Your eyes. They were purple the other day and now they're blue?" I asked and she laughed.

"The purple ones were contacts. Blue is my natural eye colour," she smiled. "But good catch." Then she winked and I smiled.

I opened my mouth to say something else, but then an *actual* customer walked in and I was caught off guard.

"I'll get out of your hair," I said, taking a few steps back before leaving the shop.

Standing on the sidewalk, I stared up Highland and sighed. I knew Jimmy lived up there *somewhere* because that's where that bar was from the other night. I didn't know exactly where he lived, but would it really matter if I did? I had his number and wasn't going to call him, so I *definitely* wasn't going to visit him if I knew what building he lived in. Dropping my shoulders, I turned on my heel and started making my way back home.

⤬

Two full weeks now and I didn't even notice the bell of the front door anymore. It was a quiet Wednesday, barely anyone was coming in for coffee and Angie had left for an appointment for Jason, so I was out front, leaning on the counter and practically falling asleep.

"Well, this can't be good for business," someone mumbled.

My eyes shot open and I looked up to see Jimmy smiling down at me. I quickly stood and almost tripped backwards.

"What? I mean, hey!" I stuttered, rubbing my face and raking my hands through my hair.

Today, he was wearing a black sleeveless shirt and black skinny jeans. It took everything not to bite my bottom lip. I sighed.

"Hey . . ." I said again, only more awkwardly.

"Hey!" he chirped. "Y'miss me?!"

I sighed again. "Yes."

And his face fell.

"Oh. Sorry, man. Work's been ridiculous. Not that I'm complaining, I mean, my paycheques are *awesome*!" he smiled. I said nothing, and he sighed. "So, what's up? What's been going on? Nilly said you came to the shop the other day to see if I was working? Should'a called me! When are you done? Let's go hang out!" he enthused all in one breath.

I laughed, shaking my head. "I'm closing tonight."

"Well fuck, man! That's like . . . that's in like . . . five more hours!" he whined, slapping both hands on the counter and making me jump.

I started laughing again. "Aren't you working today?" I asked.

"Well, yeah but . . ."

"So? I'll come by the shop after I close up," I smiled, taking a wet rag and wiping the counter down, trying to look busy.

I had felt like a neglected puppy these past two weeks, even though I knew I shouldn't have.

Again, his face fell, and he sighed. "Alright . . . I'll be there . . ." he mumbled.

"Kay. See you," I said and faked a smile.

He tapped a little beat on the counter, then took a step back.

"Yep . . ."

After he left, I finally stopped tensing and sighed, falling limp against the counter.

Locking everything up, I stared up at the dark sky and sighed. Standing at the corner of Vine and Melrose, I glanced down toward the parlour and sighed once more. I was comfortable walking around this area at night, but really only to and from work. But I guess I *did* tell him I'd meet him when I was done. Shoving my hands in my pockets and staring at my feet, I started making my way to the parlour. I kept my head down and didn't make eye contact with anybody to assure that I wouldn't get in anyone's way and accidentally bumped shoulders with someone. I glanced up quickly and waved, apologizing. They stopped and started laughing.

"Lil' Dallas?!" they yelled.

I froze and my head shot up as I stared straight ahead and felt a cold shiver run down my spine. I saw the parlour in the distance, but I suddenly couldn't move.

"Aar—Aaron?!" I turned around, the colour leaving my face. "I thought you were living at Yale? What the fuck are you doing here?" I asked.

His eyes were bloodshot, his pupils were dilated and his hands were twitchy; his three friends standing by his side were the same. My shoulders sank, and I knew exactly what was going on.

"Oh . . ." I mumbled, accidentally saying it out loud.

"Phst! What *oh*?! You don't know me!" he screamed loudly.

I put my hands up and took a step back. "I don't mean any—I mean, I didn't mean—"

"Shut the fuck up! *Fuck* Yale and *fuck* lawyers, man!" he yelled.

"Okay, yeah. Fuck 'em . . ." I mumbled, taking another step back.

He smirked down at me and it was almost wicked. "I see you're still just as much of a pussy as the last time I saw you. Pussy back then and a pussy now!" he barked, turning to look back at his friends and laugh in unison.

I let it go.

"Y'know, mom and dad never talk about you . . . they don't even *miss* you! And *no one* was concerned after you left!"

I let that one go too and continued taking my baby steps backwards.

"That doesn't surprise me. You were always the favourite . . ." I mumbled, feeding the beast.

I knew complimenting him was better than him attacking me. No Regrets wasn't far now. If I could just turn and run, I would make it into the parlour where Jimmy would be, and I'd be safe from all this. Growing up, any time Aaron was drunk or high, he usually had some anger controlling issues and I was always the one who got caught in the crossfire. And seeing as he wasn't at Yale and was here . . . said a lot. Not that I knew what he was currently on, but I didn't want to hang around long enough to figure it out.

"Fuckin' *right* I'm the favourite!" he yelled, taking a bigger step forwards and shoving me. *Unnecessary.*

"Aaron, we don't need to—" then he shoved me once more and I tripped on the uneven pavement, falling backwards, but thankfully catching myself with my hands.

Sitting up, I stared at my palms and sighed as I cut them both open pretty severely. It fucking hurt. Aaron and his minions all started laughing, but I kept my cool because I knew where this was headed, and panicking would only make things worse.

"Dallas?!" someone called from behind me.

My shoulders sank. *Thank God!* I looked back and realized I was much closer to the tattoo shop than I originally thought, and Jimmy had come out and was walking my way. It was a good thing he looked intimidating as fuck, like Nils was saying.

"Who the fuck is this?" Aaron snapped, staring Jimmy up and down.

"Who the fuck are you?" Jimmy snapped back, walking around to stand in front of me and crossing his arms.

"I'm his mother fuckin' brother!" Aaron yelled, taking a step forwards and standing an inch from Jimmy's face.

J didn't flinch. He didn't even blink, and Aaron was a tall guy.

"Oh. I've heard stories about you. Dallas doesn't want to see you right now, so I think it would be in your best interest if you just fucked off," he said with a clenched jaw.

Looking at my hands, I sighed at all the blood. But looking up at Jimmy standing in front of me with Aaron and his friends on the other side, made me smile.

"How about you fucking *make* me, y'fucking faggot!"

And Aaron's minions took a step closer as well. I stood and patted myself down, picking pieces of pavement and dirt out of my palms and curling my lip at the blood dripping down my wrists. Looking back at Jimmy, he was tense and his jaw was still clenched.

"J, it's okay. Let's just go," I said quietly, nudging him with my elbow. He didn't budge. "J," I said more sternly.

He narrowed his eyes, then slowly turned away.

"What's wrong? Don't wanna play?!" Aaron yelled.

We both ignored him, calmly walking back to the shop. Their mimicking laughs echoed in the distance until they finally let us be and carried on with their adventurous night.

Getting to the parlour, Jimmy was the only one working, so thankfully he had the authority to close down, even though he was technically supposed to be open for another hour.

"Are you okay?" he asked, locking the shop door behind us and turning off the *open* sign.

I gave a slight nod. Gesturing for me to follow, he led me to the bathroom where he ran cold water from the sink.

"Here . . ." he mumbled, gently grabbing my wrists and forcing my palms under the water.

I tensed and winced at the pain, but eased up when the cold felt soothing. Watching the blood wash away, I sighed.

"Yeah, I'll live . . ."

Turning off the tap, he walked off and I quickly followed. Walking into one of the tattoo rooms—that I could only assume was his—he sat me down on the bed and grabbed my hands, inspecting my palms. I curled my lip when the cuts started bleeding again. Both my hands were numb and suddenly I felt very hot and lightheaded. Being in shock was a bitch.

"Lucky for you, we have supplies for this exact kind of thing!" he smiled, walking into a different room and coming back with a pair of latex gloves, gauze, hydrogen peroxide and some form of bandage material.

I snorted and closed my eyes, trying my best not to pass out. "Do people come in here regularly with ripped up body parts?" I asked, opening my eyes and staring at him.

His face fell. "Dude, we *literally* draw on people with needles and put holes in their body . . . people leave here with wounded bleeding body parts all the time!" And then his smile returned, and he started to set everything up. "But this is also from a basic first aid kit."

"So . . . you know what you're doing?" I asked.

"I have a certificate in first aid," he said, gesturing to a framed piece of paper on the wall.

I smiled. "Well, aren't *you* special," I said sarcastically, smirking.

He returned the smirk, then fell quiet and started focusing on cleaning my hands. Applying the gloves, he grabbed some paper towel and placed them on my lap. Grabbing the hydrogen peroxide, he poured it over my palms, and I winced, understanding that the paper towel was for the mess.

"Fuck . . ." I hissed, closing my eyes and sighing.

"Sorry," he mumbled, quickly grabbing the gauze and dabbing away the blood.

Tossing everything out, he grabbed more gauze, placed it on the wounds, then wrapped both my palms with the bandage. I watched the entire process with interest.

"Thanks," I mumbled, glancing up at him before looking back down at my hands.

He was focused on making sure the bandages were perfect and I felt my face get hot again, this time *not* from shock.

"No problem . . ." he mumbled, peeling off his gloves and tossing them in the garbage, and then leaving the room to put the stuff away.

I swung my legs back and forth, looking around at the framed art hung up on the wall and stared at him when he returned.

"Hey, so . . . sorry for being a dick earlier . . ." I confessed.

He shrugged, sitting in his chair, staring at the floor. "I wouldn't say *dick . . .*" he replied, staring at his feet as he twisted back and forth in the chair. "Buuuuut I *did* sense some tension. Can I ask why?" he asked, now looking up and making eye contact.

It was only now that I noticed his eyes were a deep forest green and my stomach did that backflip thing again. I was quick to look away.

"It's really stupid," I mumbled, focusing harder on the swaying of my legs.

He forced a laugh. "Try me."

I fell backwards and sprawled out across the bed, sighing loudly and staring at the ceiling.

"Well!" I said louder than necessary, followed by another sigh. "Work was slow . . . and y'know."

"You're upset that I didn't come hang out?" he asked and I could hear the smile in his voice.

"I TOLD YOU IT WAS DUMB!" I yelled, closing my eyes and trying my best to push away any blush that appeared in my cheeks. I crossed my arms over my face and sighed once more. "I didn't have many friends throughout school . . . any, to be more specific . . . it's nice to have even just one," I mumbled.

Dropping my arms to my side, I continued to stare up at the ceiling, then felt the side of the bed sink in when he sat beside me.

"I get it. And I'm sorry. The shop has been really busy. My schedule was packed and I've been taking advantage of sleeping in as much as possible," he replied, which I wasn't expecting. "But we're hanging out now, which is cool right?"

I opened my eyes to stare at him and couldn't help but laugh. He had the stupidest grin on his face.

"Yeah," I said, sitting back up and staring at my palms, sighing.

He playfully smacked my shoulder and hopped off the bed. "C'mon," he said, grabbing a set of keys and flicking off a group of lights. "I'll walk you home."

I tilted my head. "Aren't you open for like . . . another hour?" I asked but hopped off the bed anyways.

He shrugged. "It's been a dead Wednesday night. If anybody wanted a piercing or tattoo, they would've come already . . ." he mumbled, walking behind me and locking the door behind us.

For the most part, we walked in silence and it was kind of nice. It wasn't tense or awkward, just neither one of us had anything to say. It was a short walk anyway.

"Dallas! A little late to be finishing work, no?" Rufus called out with a smile.

I smiled in return and rolled my eyes, shoving my bandaged hands in my pockets. "Not coming from work, but good eye, Rufus."

"How does he know the time?" Jimmy whispered and I had to hold back my laugh.

"Rufus, this is my friend Jimmy. He works at the tattoo parlour down on Melrose and Highland," I smiled.

Jimmy leaned forwards and reached out to shake Rufus' hand. "Hiya, Rufus."

"Pleasure," Rufus smiled, shaking Jimmy's hand in return.

"Sorry there's no goodies today," I mumbled, my face falling.

Rufus shrugged and swatted his hand in my direction. "Don't sweat it, boy! You do too much for me already," he smiled. "Now get off these streets. It's late."

"Yes, dad," I mumbled, rolling my eyes and carrying on walking with Jimmy following close behind.

"Close walk to work at least," he said once we got to the outside of my apartment building.

I shrugged. "Still sucks in the rain though."

"*Everything* sucks in the rain. The *rain* sucks."

"That's true . . ." I laughed, then more silence.

"Well! I'll see you tomorrow for my usual round for coffee," he grinned.

I couldn't hide my smile.

"Your palms good?" he asked, staring to walk backwards and pointing to my hands.

I stared down at my bandaged palms and nodded. "Heh, yeah. Thanks again."

"Anytime! I'll see'ya tomorrow, Dal," he said, turning and walking away.

I snorted. "HEY! YOU JUST GAVE ME A NICKNAME!" I yelled after him.

He threw both fists to the sky victoriously. I laughed, shaking my head, then walked inside.

Chapter 5

"*I*'VE GOT A VENTI VANILLA LATTE FOR ANDREA, A GRANDE ICED WHITE CHOCOLATE MOCHA FOR DANIELLE AND A TALL HOT CHOCOLATE WITH WHIPPED CREAM FOR BRIAN!" I yelled, placing the drinks at the end of the pickup counter. Wiping the sweat off my forehead with my arm, I took a deep breath and went back to the backlog of orders Angela was throwing my way. Grabbing a new cup, I started making another hot chocolate, but was distracted by the smoke coming from the kitchen.

"DALLAS, THE MUFFINS!" Angela yelled, gesturing to the door.

"*Fuck!*" I hissed, dropping and spilling the cup all over the floor as I made a dash for the kitchen.

Opening the oven door, I started coughing and swatting the smoke from my face just as Tiffany walked in through the back door. The fire alarm began to scream above me and I groaned in frustration.

"What the fuck?" Tiffany frowned, stepping around me.

"*HELP!*" I snapped, throwing on a pair of oven mitts and reaching in to grab the burnt muffins.

Tiffany walked over and propped the fire exit door open before grabbing the broom and reaching up to stop the fire alarm with the handle. Sighing, she put the broom back where it came from and went out to help Angela. Placing the burnt muffins on top of the stove, I leaned against the counter and did my best to catch my breath, glaring at the black baked goods. The store had air-conditioning, but it did nothing when you were running around like a headless chicken. For some reason, everyone decided they wanted coffee at the same time today, and even though it was all hands on deck, it was hard to keep up with all the orders.

The break between the hours of breakfast and lunch had arrived and we finally had a chance to sit down and catch our breath. Tiffany went outside to talk to somebody on her phone, whereas Angela and I stayed in the kitchen, almost laughing at the shit show we just dealt with.

"Jesus . . ." I panted, resting my head between my knees.

"What a mess . . ." she mumbled, then turned and stared at me. "What's up? You seem distracted today. Something on your mind?" she asked.

My eyes were closed and I was still catching my breath. I tried my best not to smile. *Yes. There's absolutely something on my mind* I thought to myself, staring at my hands.

"No. I just had a bad sleep last night . . ." I mumbled, then stood and stretched.

She watched and arched a brow. "And what the fuck happened to your hands?" she asked, motioning to my bandaged palms.

"Heh?" I stared at them and huffed. "Oh, these. Yeah, I ran into Aaron last night . . ." I trailed off, tucking my hands into my pockets.

She looked concerned. "Oh shit. And he did that?"

"Yeah. It's nothing. Jimmy helped. He stood up to him because . . . well, because I can't. Brought me back to the tattoo parlour and bandaged me up."

"That was nice of him. Kinda funny how things played out between you two," she said, and I looked at her with an arched brow.

"Played out?" I asked and she shrugged.

"Well, yeah. I mean, first he was this weird . . . sugar addict that came in on a daily basis, and now you guys are friends. Kinda neat," she laughed and I snorted.

"Yeah. Neat," I laughed.

"Come to think of it. I haven't seen him in a while . . ."

"Yeah, I know. He's probably busy at work . . ." I trailed off, staring at the wall.

"Well anyway. We better get cleaning if we want to be ready for the lunch chaos," she mumbled, standing and tying her hair up in a ponytail.

The lunch rush came and there was still no sign of Jimmy, but this time, instead of sadness, I felt angry. I had no right to feel this way but that didn't matter. It wasn't like we were the best of friends; we had technically only just met. But he *did* tell me last night that he'd be here, and I got my hopes up. It put me in a sour mood for the rest of the day.

"The restrooms are *clearly* labeled! No, like I said, we're *out* of low-cal milk! Ma'am! The sign on the door says NO dogs!"

"DALLAS!" Angie screamed from the kitchen.

I tensed, turning and glaring at her. "*WHAT!?*" I yelled back, closing my eyes and regretting it instantly.

"KITCHEN. NOW."

I rolled my eyes and sighed loudly, turning on my heel and walking toward the kitchen.

"Tall chai latte," I grumbled to Tiffany, then shoved the cup in her hand before walking through the swinging kitchen doors.

"What the fuck is your *damage*?! You've been on edge all afternoon! What's going on today?! This isn't just lack of sleep!" Angie snapped.

I sat down and linked my hands, twiddling my fingers. I was like an angsty teenager being scolded by their mother. I stayed quiet.

"Dallas, I want answers. Or go home because I can't work with PMSing employees! Especially when they don't even have a uterus! You know you can't talk to customers like that!" she yelled, crossing her arms and tapping her foot impatiently.

Suddenly, Tiffany came back in the room and broke our angry silence with a pop of her bubble gum.

"Uhm, there's a guy here looking for you . . ." she said, staring at me.

I looked up and stood so fast that I got a head rush. I slammed through the swinging doors out to the front and slapped my hands on the counter, winced at the pain, then glared at Jimmy straight in the eyes.

His huge grin quickly faded, and he pouted. "I'm *sorry*!" he whined. "Dallas, honestly. I'm sorry. I was setting up for an appointment and—"

I held up a hand to silence him and sighed, closing my eyes. "It's okay. I don't care. I'm just having a bad day. Do you want a drink?" I asked.

He frowned. "No?" he mumbled.

"Good," I said and walked back to the kitchen and tossed my apron aside. "I'm leaving early. I'll see you tomorrow," I said to Angie, then walked back out to the front. "Let's go," I snapped, walking ahead of Jimmy.

Angela poked her head out of the kitchen and she and Jimmy exchanged concerned looks before he quickly followed me.

"Dal, wait up!" he called, jogging to catch up with me. "Kay, whoa, whoa! Hold up!" he said, grabbing my shoulder and stopping me from walking any further.

I stared at him. "What?"

"What's your deal?" he asked, forcing a laugh. "This can't seriously be because I didn't show up at my normal time?" he asked. I shrugged, and he sighed. "Dallas, I work too y'know. I can't just be hanging around the coffee shop when I have appointments."

"I'm not asking you to."

"Then what's with the twelve-year-old attitude?" he asked.

"No attitude," I replied.

He sighed once more, closing his eyes and rubbing his temple. "Okay well . . . fuck. This is so fucking dumb. You got shit you gotta figure out, okay? Because this is stupid. I like you, man. You're cool to hang out with and now you're just making it a fucking joke," he said, shaking his head. "Look . . . call me when you've . . . sorted out whatever it is you need to sort out . . ."

I ducked my head because I felt defeated and my shoulders sank. Sighing, I looked up to see him already walking down the street with his head ducked and his hands in his pockets.

Like most nights, I decided to have something quick and simple for dinner and sat down in front of the TV with microwavable noodles. I flicked through some channels for a while just to end up watching KTLA. A woman was talking over video footage of Oakland Heights Penitentiary.

> *"—and escaping. Connor Evans, the leader of the group, proceeded to unlock the doors of his fellow inmates. How the six of them escaped the prison has not yet been determined; police are still searching for answers. Residents in and around the Oakland area are advised to stay indoors with their doors locked and blinds closed. If you see any of the six following faces, please call the police immediately. More on this tonight at ten. Now, over to Rhonda for sports—"*

The fork full of noodles never made it to my mouth. I was too busy staring at the TV screen in horror; the six faces of the now escaped convicts staring back at me. I didn't think that kind of shit actually happened. It was rare convicts escaped prison, and now six of them? And in Oakland? Oakland Heights Penitentiary was a maximum security prison made for the worst of the worst and these six were known to group together. Back in 2010, they had caused chaos and havoc. They were all arsonists one way or another and usually traveled with flammables and explosives. They blew up an entire town before getting caught and all thrown into prison with life sentences. It was a good thing Oakland was nowhere near us. At *least* a seven-hour drive north. I turned off the TV and looked down at Poppy who looked back up at me and tilted her head to the side.

"And on that creepy note, I think it's bedtime," I said.

She jumped off the couch and ran into the bedroom before I even got up.

I had Friday off and it was a good time to sit and think about my childish ways. I really was being immature, but I was notorious for wearing my emotions on my sleeve and this was all new to me. I didn't hear from Jimmy all day and he didn't hear from me either. Instead, I spent the day on the couch and watched TV.

Once again, I had a horrible sleep that night. I couldn't get Jimmy out of my head and it resulted in a lot of tossing and turning. I'd overheat and then get too cold, so I got up for a glass of water and sat out on my tiny balcony. There was only enough room for a chair and a little table, but it had a view of the city and it was a good place to sit and relax. I sat staring at Jimmy's name in my contacts for a good five minutes, just reading his name over and over again. I wondered if he'd be awake. It was 4:00 a.m. on a Saturday morning, so he'd probably be asleep, but then again, I wouldn't know unless I tried, right? Staring at his name once more, I cursed under my breath, then clicked it, tapping my leg impatiently as it rang. After the first ring, I gasped and quickly hung up, dropping my phone and staring at it in fear. What was I doing? No one was awake this early *willingly.*

"Idiot . . ." I hissed to myself, closing my eyes and rubbing my face.

But moments later, my phone started ringing, vibrating itself closer to the edge. I stared at it, holding my breath and forgetting how to blink. I quickly leaned forwards and snatched it before it fell, then held it in my hand and stared at the screen, reading his name across the caller ID. I let it ring one more time before finally answering it and bringing it to my ear.

I paused for a moment. "Hello?"

"Dallas?" Jimmy croaked.

His voice was raspy, like he had just woken up. *Obviously* he had just woken up. Some asshole was just calling at him at 4:00 a.m. I closed my eyes once more, ducking my head.

"Morning . . ." I mumbled back.

"Morning . . . it's four in the morning . . . what's up? Everything okay?" he asked.

I slowly slid my hand down my face, hooking my finger on my bottom lip and pulling it down.

I'm such an idiot.

"Fine. Nothing. I . . . dialed the wrong number."

"At 4:00 a.m.?" he asked.

I stared at the sky and fixated on a star.

"Yeah. I meant to call Angela. Needed to know if I was opening the shop or not . . ."

Good one. It was a decent lie and considering how quickly I came up with it, I was kind of proud of myself.

"Oh . . . just as well, I'm awake. I've been meaning to go in early and count inventory," he said and my shoulders sank.

Thank God.

"So, I guess you're going back to bed once you call Ang?" he asked, followed by a yawn.

"Well, I'm pretty sure I'm opening. I'm awake now, so I guess I'll go and get ready as well," I said.

He didn't say anything, but I heard his fridge open in the background.

"Well, I'm gonna go. I'm going to shower and stuff . . ." I mumbled, breaking the silence.

"Alright man. Talk to you later . . ." he said, and then hung up before I could say anything else.

As if I wasn't already behaving like a twelve year old, now we were *arguing* like seventh graders. It was fucking ridiculous. *I* was fucking ridiculous.

I had a quick breakfast, showered and then got dressed. Poppy was still asleep on the bed, so I left her food in her dish for when she woke up. It was 5:00 a.m. when I started walking and I walked past Starbucks and straight down the road toward the tattoo parlour. I knew I had to get this over with and that I'd just procrastinate longer and longer until it was dealt with, so to the tattoo parlour I went. Jimmy wasn't there yet, so I stood outside and waited. Even though the sun hadn't risen yet, it was already unbelievably hot out. Leaning against the wall of the shop, I placed my hands in my pockets and sighed. I could feel the anxiety starting to creep up, so I closed my eyes and tried my best to calm my heart rate. Suddenly looking up, I saw him walking down the street toward me in a sleeveless shirt and a backwards snapback hat. He still wore his ripped up skinny jeans though. Taking out a pair of keys, he looked up and saw me, crossed the street and walked right past me to unlock the door.

"Hey," he mumbled, unlocking the front door of the parlour and walking inside.

His hair was wet under his hat and I immediately felt bad for waking him up so early again. Even though he said he had inventory to do, I knew he was tired, and waking up to shower at 4:00 a.m. probably wasn't how he wanted to start his morning. I followed.

"J, I'm sorry," I said straight up.

"What for?" he asked, tossing his keys on the front desk and flicking on a group of lights.

I sighed, continuing to follow him. "Jimmy," I reached out and grabbed his arm, pulling him back from walking any further.

He stopped and turned around to look at me. "What?" he asked with almost a sigh.

"I like you too, okay? You're the only real friend I've had . . . basically ever. And you can call me socially awkward or whatever you want, but I'm essentially new at this. The only people I talk to are Angela and Tiffany, so you can imagine what it must be like to have a *dude* for a friend. We have things in common. I like spending time with you. My whole life is a routine, so I got used to yours and then you didn't show up for two weeks and yeah, I admit, I reacted like a child, so I'm sorry . . . I don't want to be that weird clingy friend. That's not me. So, can we pretend this fucking preschool shit never happened and just go back to being bros?" I asked, smirking at the fact that I said 'bros'.

He snorted, rolling his eyes and shaking his head. He grabbed me into a head lock and fiddled his hands violently through my hair. "You're such a fucking loser!" he laughed, playfully shoving me away, then walking into his room.

I sighed, fixing the strands of hair that were going the wrong direction and followed him.

"Want that tattoo?" he asked, the conversation suddenly switching.

I ducked my head and started laughing. "So, we're cool? Just like that?" I asked and he shrugged.

"Yeah man, I don't care. I mean, you *were* acting like a child, but you just apologized and explained yourself, so how can I be mad?" he asked, sitting down in his chair and leaning back to stare at me. "So. Want that tattoo?" he asked again.

My eyes grew wide and I stood in the doorway awkwardly. "What? Seriously?" I squeaked.

He started laughing.

"Only if you want. There's no way you're opening an hour early," he said, side-glancing at me and smirking, obviously catching my lie. "It doesn't have to be anything big," he added.

I frowned, biting my bottom lip. "I have no idea what I want, though."

"How about a piercing?" he asked. "Ever wanted one of those?"

"I've always wanted my lip pierced . . ." I thought out loud.

"Done. I'll set everything up," he said and I suddenly felt my adrenaline kick in and I got really giddy and nervous.

"Really?" I squeaked.

He snorted, putting on a pair of latex gloves and taking out a terrifying needle. The giddiness stopped instantly, and my face dropped.

"That's what you use?" I asked.

He nodded. "Yep. Try not to think about it and come sit over here . . ." he mumbled, rolling his chair over to the bed.

I sat down cautiously while he stood and walked closer to me. I didn't have time to take into consideration just how close he'd have to get . . . and come to think of it, he was putting his hands in my mouth. I felt my face getting red and hot again and I had to mentally tell myself to shut up, man up and calm down.

"These. Open," he said, slapping his hands between my knees and gesturing for me to spread my legs.

I stared down at my legs, then up at him and swallowed the lump in my throat. "Uhm . . ."

"I gotta get in closer," he said casually. "C'mon, open." He slapped my knees again.

I quickly opened my legs and he stepped in even closer, frowning and focusing hard on my lips. I felt myself get *extra* hot and I tried to look everywhere but his face but couldn't help myself and ended up staring. His emerald eyes had fragments of gold in them, and I noticed he had a small scar above his eyebrow piercing. I frowned. He had a skinny black marker in his hand. He dabbed a little dot on my lip, then noticed me staring and laughed.

"Got it in a fight," he stated, and I was quick to clear my throat and look away.

"What?" I asked, clearing my throat once more.

He laughed again and turned around to grab a handheld mirror. "The scar above my eyebrow? I got it in a fight," he explained, then held the mirror up in front of my face. "Is that spot okay?" he asked.

I blinked a few times from the mirror being so close, but once I stared at the little black dot, I couldn't help but smile.

"Yeah."

"Cool." Placing the mirror back on the counter behind him, he went back to standing incredibly close between my legs and smiled. "Ready?" he asked.

He smelt like a mixture of cigarettes and a sweet, musky cologne. I nodded ever so slightly.

"Uh huh . . ."

"Okay. This tool here—" he held up what looked like miniature tongs for the barbeque. "—is going to clamp your lip so I can get a grip on it, okay? This doesn't hurt at all," he explained.

I nodded. Grabbing the bottom left corner of my lip with the clamps, he held it out and away from my teeth. With his other hand, he picked up the scary needle and I tensed, closing my eyes.

He laughed. "Dal, I've done these a hundred thousand times, kay? Sometimes, I tattoo all day, sometimes, I pierce all day. Sometimes, I do both. I know what I'm doing."

"Kay," I mumbled back, opening my eyes and staring into his.

I was mesmerized by his eyes once more until he started talking again and I jumped back to reality.

"Now I want you to take a deep breath in . . ."

So I did, but I overexaggerated it ridiculously, making him smile.

"Now exhale slowly."

And then he pushed the needle through my lip, and it stung but didn't hurt nearly as much as anticipated. I clenched my eyes shut and tensed but I had to stay still while he put the piercing inside. Opening my eyes only a little, I was shocked to see that it barely bled. He was almost frowning from being so focused and took the clamps off, but leaned in even closer to focus on twisting the ball on the back of the piercing. Now I was making a conscious effort to look anywhere *but* his eyes, so I drifted down and stared at his neck tattoos. His left side was covered in a splatter of different coloured and different sized stars, whereas the right side simply said the word *cowabunga* in cursive. I did my best to refrain from smiling. Finishing with my piercing, he took a step back and smiled.

"All done! That wasn't so bad, was it?" he grinned, taking a few steps back.

I exhaled loudly, and he laughed, walking away and coming back with a sucker. I stared at him. "Blood sugar," he confirmed.

"Ah."

And I took it gladly; ripping off the wrapper and shoving it in my mouth.

"Okay, so you can eat and drink whatever you want but it's just going to feel weird for a bit. But I want you to brush your teeth after every meal for the next three days. I don't want any infection starting. It sounds like a lot of maintenance, but trust me. Just brush your teeth more than normal and use mouth wash. Oh! And saltwater rinse. We had this girl get her tongue pierced and she didn't listen to basically *any* of the aftercare I told her about and she came back in two days later and her tongue had gone numb and the piercing was rejected," he said all in one breath.

My eyes went wide, and I gave him a terrified look.

He laughed. "So, clean mouth, okay?" he grinned and I nodded.

He stood in front of me and smiled, then stared down at my hands. "How are your palms?" he asked, gesturing to them.

I shrugged. "Healing, I guess . . ." I mumbled, every word feeling different with the newfound metal in my lip.

He pursed his lips and nodded. "Good . . ."

Then that awkward silence came back.

"Well, man. As fun as that was, I really gotta start doing inventory. You open up soon anyways, right?" he asked. "I know you only came down here to talk, so . . ." he smirked.

I ducked my head since my face was bright red.

"Yeah, I should go," I mumbled, completely ignoring his observation.

Hopping off the bed, I stopped in the doorway and stared at him.

"Doesn't this place not open until noon? How long does inventory take?" I asked.

He was sitting in his chair and now every one of his drawers were opened.

Huffing, he looked back at me and smiled. "You'd be surprised. Plus, I told Nils I would do her inventory for her too. Then I gotta clean—there's always stuff to do before opening," he explained.

"I should probably give the place a good clean too," I thought out loud.

"Probably not a bad idea."

"I'll see you later?" I asked and his face fell.

"Now . . . don't get mad, but—" he started, and I started laughing.

"J, it's fine."

"I just have lots of appointments and I'm swamped!" he whined, and I laughed again.

"It's *fine*. I *guess* I'll live," I winked. "My routine OCD will have to survive another day of disappointment," I said dramatically.

He snorted and started laughing. "Shut up."

"But thanks for the freebie," I smiled, poking the ring out a bit further with my tongue pressing against the back.

He leaned back into his chair and smiled at me. "Anytime, but now you owe me!"

"I'd gladly give you shit for free, but you have to show up for that to happen!" I yelled, then left laughing.

I slowly walked back to Starbucks, every so often rolling the back of the piercing on the tip of my tongue. My lip felt ten times its original size even though I couldn't really feel it at all. It was definitely a weird sensation, but I couldn't help but play with it, which really only made it hurt more. Eventually, the pain became a soothing numb feeling and I forgot all about it.

I didn't end up giving the shop a clean since I didn't have time. I wasn't planning on an impromptu lip piercing and now I had to open up in twenty minutes. I preheated the oven while I made a fresh batch of pastries, then walked out to the front to turn on the coffee machines. Taking out my phone to glance at the time, I gave myself a nod of approval and turned on our *open* sign. Going back to the kitchen, I placed the pastries inside the oven, then sighed.

I looked down at my bandaged hands and made the decision all on my own that it was time they came off. It would probably be good for them to get some oxygen. Grabbing the corner of the bandage on my left hand, I slowly started to peel it back and unwind it from my palm. There was a sudden shock that shot through my whole arm and it made me clench my eyes shut and flinch. The wound had started to heal around the gauze. Sighing with frustration, I stood and walked over to the sink and held my hands under cold water, soaking the gauze and instantly making it easier to remove. It still hurt like a bitch, but it was manageable. A few of the smaller cuts started to bleed again, but I ignored them since the major part of the injury was already starting to heal and that's all I cared about. Once both hands were free from their bandages, I turned the water off and gently dabbed them dry with paper towel. They were so swollen—swollen and bruised and actually looked disgusting.

How was I supposed to deal with hot beverages all day? Or customer service? I already got dirty looks with the bandages *on*, I could only imagine the looks I was going to get with them *off*. I sighed, sitting in one of the chairs and twirling in circles. Maybe taking the bandages off wasn't the best idea. Staring at my palms a bit more, I sighed loudly and sunk deeper into the chair.

If Jimmy hadn't come at that exact moment that night, Aaron probably would've continued to beat the shit out of me like he always did, and God would only know the outcome. These gashes on my hands were nothing compared to what he used to do when we were younger. Jimmy took me in and helped me when he really didn't have to and there wasn't anything I could do to repay him. Especially when I was acting like a child. Our entire relationship thus far had only been him giving and me taking and giving nothing back in return.

It was then that it really hit me. I really liked this guy. And the more I told myself not to like him, the more I wanted him. It didn't make any sense. What made him so special to spark such an interest in my mind? I lived in Los Angeles. I saw 'weird' guys like him all over the place and I'd never once thought of them as anything more than a stranger on the street. So why now? He made me happy, but he didn't have to make me *this* happy. These were new feelings but were starting to feel a little too comfortable and I wanted them to stop and stay away forever. Was this honestly the beginning of something I had no control of?

Or was I just confused because he was my first *real* friend? My shoulders sank and I sighed once more.

It was then that I decided that I was going to spend as much time *away* from him as possible and grab control of these new emotions. Maybe if I saw less of him, I'd lose this confusing state of mind. But did I really want that? I'd also be losing a friend and I honestly and truly did enjoy his company. It was harsh and *very* immature, I know, but I didn't know what else to do. What other option did I have? Tell him I was falling in love with him and that I had to stop seeing him so I could return to being heterosexual? No. I didn't think so. This was logical in my mind and that's all I needed to comfort me.

Chapter 6

Half an hour after opening, I had a small lineup of people, but it was nothing I couldn't handle alone. It wasn't anything chaotic by any means. I've been doing this long enough that I could efficiently get the job done in a timely manner, even with my injured hands. Thankfully, I only had to do a half-day, and both Angela and Tiffany showed up at noon.

"Hey," I mumbled, untying my apron and folding it up.

Walking past Tiffany as she exited the kitchen and I entered, she stared at my lip and her eyes went wide.

"Hey," Ang mumbled, shortly following Tiffany.

Also staring at me, she gasped and quickly turned around. I gave a quiet chuckle and quickly tossed my apron on the kitchen counter.

"Hey! Wait! What's that on your lip?!" she called just as I opened the fire exit door.

"Nothing!" I laughed in return, allowing the door to slam shut behind me.

Walking around to the front of the store and stopping at the corner intersection, I looked down Melrose to my left. Staring at the sky for a moment, I contemplated going to visit him because deep down that's all I wanted to do. I even started walking, but was quick to twirl on my heel and walk back toward Vine. This happened a few times.

"No!" I finally yelled to myself and made someone walking past me jump. "Sorry," I mumbled, then set a stern path up Vine toward my apartment.

I power walked the entire way, ran up the stairs, then plopped down on the couch once I got inside. I was out of breath like I had just come back from a marathon. Eventually removing my shoes, I turned on the TV before standing and stretching. Feeling the back of my lip piercing with my tongue, I slightly winced when I got a pinch of pain.

"Teeth. I need to brush my teeth," I mumbled to myself, making my way to the bathroom.

Looking at my reflection in the mirror, I froze for a moment and just stared at myself. The lip ring wasn't anything drastic, but it was enough to give me *some* confidence boost. Tilting my head to the side, I smiled a little before sighing. Feeling my brain wander to Jimmy standing inches from my face and the gold speckles in his eyes, I smacked my hands atop the counter and yelled.

"*Stop* it!" I snapped, smacking my head and sighing.

Staring back at myself in the mirror, now frowning, I grabbed my toothbrush and ran it under some cold water. Applying a small amount of toothpaste, I started brushing my teeth, still frowning at myself. Closing my eyes, I ducked my head and carefully brushed around my lip. Opening my eyes once more, I stared at my sink and froze when I saw how water stained it was. The water in this building had always been pretty harsh, and if I didn't keep on top of cleaning, everything would get covered in rusty water stains. *Note to self: buy Lysol.* Spitting and rinsing my mouth, I turned off the water, and gave myself one more look before leaving the bathroom and making my way back to the couch.

I watched Netflix for a solid four hours until I finally felt myself doze in and out, my eyes slowly staying shut for longer periods of time. Thankfully, I finally fell asleep. I had been up since 4:00 a.m. after all. Hours went by when I was abruptly woken by my phone buzzing in my pocket. Opening one eye at a time, I placed my phone to my ear and closed my eyes once more, sighing.

"Hello?"

"Hey ya! I went by SB and you weren't there!" Jimmy whined.

I wanted to smile but I also wanted to sigh. I was excited to hear from him and that's what upset me.

"Yeah, sorry. I forgot I only worked until the afternoon."

"I *guess* that's okay. Just don't let it happen again," he started laughing and I couldn't help but smile. "So what'cha doing right now?" he asked.

"I fell asleep on the couch . . . just woke up."

"Hard work giving people coffee?" he asked with a mimicking tone.

I opened my eyes and sat up, gasping loud enough for him to hear. "Now hold on just one minute—"

Suddenly, there was a loud, aggressive knock on my door, and it made me jump. I spun around to stare at it and frowned. "No wait, actually J, hold on just a minute. Someone's at my door."

"It's me," he said, and I could hear that he was outside and smoking.

I started laughing, slowly getting off the couch and making my way over to the door as I rubbed my tired eyes. "Really? Because that'd be fucking creepy since you don't know what floor I'm on *or* my room number," I laughed, walking up and peeking through the peep hole. I felt my stomach drop and could feel the colour leaving my face. "Uh . . . can I call you back? It's Aaron . . ." I mumbled, and Jimmy's side of the conversation suddenly got very quiet.

I opened my mouth to say something again but was interrupted by Aaron banging on my door again. I jumped and took a step back. How did he know where I lived? Other than the other night, we hadn't seen each other in five years. *How in God's name is he at my front door right now?*

"I'm on my way," Jimmy said, his tone doing a complete one-eighty.

"No, no! It's okay," I said, cautiously stepping forwards again and looking through the peep hole. "He looks beat up, believe it or not. I'm fine. I'll call you shortly."

"Call me the second he leaves. Or the second he *doesn't* leave, and you want him to . . ."

"Will do. Thanks," I said and then I hung up before Aaron kicked the door down. Shoving my phone in my back pocket, I closed my eyes and exhaled slowly. "Okay . . ." I mumbled quietly, placing my hand on the handle, cautiously opening the door, and staring at my brother's beaten face. "Aaron," I said in a nervous tone.

His left eye was squinting and was a nasty blend of black, blue and purple. His nose was bleeding, his cheekbone had a gash straight across it and his shirt was soaked in blood that I could only assume was his own.

"What the fuck did you do now? And how the hell did you find out where I live?" I asked.

He forced himself in but lost his footing and fell, quickly grabbing ahold of my kitchen counter to hold himself up right. Unfortunately, his hand was covered in blood from trying to stop his bleeding nose, so now my counter looked like a crime scene. I closed the door behind him and watched him struggle. I could hear him choking on his own breath until he started crying. Normally, it would make me happy to see him in such a state. Normally, the role would be reversed . . . but this was unusual, and it was starting to freak me out.

"They're here," he spat and I arched my brow.

"Who's here?" I asked.

"Don't you watch the news?! The convicts! The escaped convicts!" he yelled, losing his grip on the counter and falling to the floor, crying harder.

My eyes widened, and I subconsciously reached out and locked the door behind me. "Here? As in, LA?!" I squeaked.

"Who the fuck do you think did this to me?!" he yelled, glaring at me over his shoulder.

I sighed. "Okay. Just calm down for a second. How—"

But I was cut off by another bang on the door. Tensing, I looked through the peep hole again, but frowned when I saw a police officer standing on the other side. Unlocking the door, I opened it and took a step back.

"Officer? How can I help you?" I asked.

The policeman placed both hands on his accessory belt and leaned forwards, peeking around my apartment just as Aaron ran into the bathroom. I took a step back, more confused than ever.

"What's going on?" I asked.

His stern look slowly turned into a huge grin and he motioned down the hall. "LOOKS GOOD GUYS! C'MON!" he yelled, pushing past me and walking toward my couch.

Taking another step back, I almost fell over when forty—no, *fifty* people came pouring into my apartment. Aaron returned from the bathroom a few moments later and had washed off every single injury. He was wearing a clean shirt and was now crawling on the floor laughing hysterically, and giving the police officer a high five from the ground. The gash he had on his cheek was a latex Halloween prop and he threw it at me, still bent over laughing.

"Aaron?!" I screamed.

There were five other police officers, but these were women and they were standing on my coffee table and undressing. I slammed the door shut and squeezed my way through the bodies, trying to find my asshole of a brother who had already disappeared in the crowd. My place was *not* big enough for this many people. Someone had already found my aux cord attached to my stereo and was now blasting music so loud, I couldn't hear my own thoughts and my heartbeat was in unison with the bass. Getting to my balcony, Aaron was outside rolling a joint with some of his friends.

"Dude, that was *perfect*!" one of them cheered.

"Excuse me!" I yelled, forcing myself between the two and standing an inch from Aaron's face.

He instantly stopped laughing and shoved me, clenching his jaw. I stumbled back, quickly grabbing onto the railing before I fell on my already wounded hands from this exact same incident.

"Don't even fucking *try* it," he growled.

"Aaron, you can't just invite all these strangers into my house and throw a fucking party!" I snapped.

I winced when I heard something smash back inside, followed by cheers and screaming.

"Looks like I just fucking did," Aaron snapped in return.

Closing my eyes, I took in a deep breath before exhaling slowly. "How did you find me?" I asked, staring back at him.

He took a drag from his joint and turned to blow the smoke out in my face. I closed my eyes again, sighing once more.

"Nick saw you one night. Told me about it. So, I had you followed," he explained, now staring out at my view with a sick smile on his face. Glancing down at my hands, he smirked and snatched my right hand, flipping it over to stare at my slow-healing injury. "Nice hands. They still hurt?" he asked, pressing his thumb into the wound.

"Fuck off!" I snapped, quickly pulling back and wincing at the pain.

He laughed, the joint resting on his bottom lip. "Where the booze at?" he yelled, shoving past me and walking back inside.

I rolled my eyes. *You're not going to find any booze, but whatever.* Watching him run inside and join his friends, I felt my whole body tense with rage.

"Aaron, I'm going to call the police!" I yelled back inside, frowning.

He threw his head back laughing. "The police are already here!" he yelled in return, staring up at the half-naked women on my coffee table.

I sighed, leaning against the railing and looked out at the view of the city, rubbing my throbbing palm. It was almost 8:00 p.m. and the sun was just starting to set. I looked in the distance and saw the Starbucks intersection. Sighing again, I closed my eyes and tried to calm myself down.

"Fuck it," I mumbled to myself, then dug for my phone.

I originally wasn't going to call him back and that would've hopefully been my first sign that I didn't want to hang out anymore; only he would have panicked and rushed over anyways. Either way, I needed help and he was the only person who would help me right now. I didn't see how Angela could've helped with this one. Realistically, I *should've* called the police, but I quickly hit redial on Jimmy's number and anxiously placed my phone to my ear, tapping nervously on the railing.

"Hi," he answered quickly.

"I'm coming over," I mumbled.

"Done. What's up? What's happening? Want me to meet you halfway? I can come to you if you'd like."

"No, it's fine . . . I'll tell you all about it later. I just need to grab my cat and get out."

"Cat . . ."

"Yeah. Is that okay? Can we crash at your place tonight?" I asked, and closed my eyes and bit down on my bottom lip. *Hard*. I couldn't believe the words were coming out of my mouth.

"Oh yeah, yeah! I'm done shortly. Meet me at the parlour?"

"Already on my way."

"Cool. See you."

"And J?"

"Yo."

"Thanks."

"Ha! Any time, dude! Just hurry yer ass up!" And then he hung up.

Shoving my phone back in my pocket, I ran inside to start gathering my things while the party continued to go on. Squishing my way through the crowd, I ran to my bedroom where I saw a small circle of people smoking a joint and blowing the smoke in Poppy's face, all laughing hysterically.

"HEY!"

She was cornered in the far end of my room with all her fur on her back raised, and she was hissing.

"LEAVE HER THE FUCK ALONE!" I screamed, shoving them out of the way which was easier than I expected because they were all high.

Picking her up, I grabbed a bag, opened my closet and started throwing random items of clothes inside. I placed Poppy inside the bag as well and closed it just enough that she could poke her head in and out whenever she pleased. Pushing past more people, I made my way to my bed and grabbed my phone cord from the wall, then forced my way to the kitchen where I opened a cupboard and grabbed a handful of Poppy's canned wet cat food. Getting to the bathroom, I could feel my heartbeat in my face and was starting to panic. Grabbing my toothbrush and toothpaste, I made my way to the front door. Thankfully, I kept my phone and wallet in my pocket, so really, I had everything that was important to me. The apartment was a lost cause at this point. I would deal with it tomorrow.

Opening my front door, I glanced back and gently played with my lip piercing with my tongue. Aaron was standing on my couch and in his hand was my 3D puzzle of the globe. It took me *forever* to complete. Holding it above his head, he made direct eye contact with me before smashing it into the ground. Wincing at the impact, the puzzle burst into a million pieces and I sighed, turning on my heel and closing the door behind me. The party could be heard down the hall.

I quickly ran down the flights of stairs, got to the street and power walked back toward Starbucks.

"Hey, Dallas!" Rufus cheered.

"Hey, Rufus," I mumbled, not bothering to stop, and walking past him.

I knew it was rude, but at the moment, I didn't really care. Reaching Melrose, I continued to power walk until I reached the tattoo parlour where Jimmy was already waiting for me, smoking a cigarette. He smiled once I reached him. Unfortunately, I felt relieved to see him.

"So, your brother is throwing a party at your place? That's what I gathered with the small information you gave me. That, and the noise in the background on the phone," he smiled, tossing his butt and stepping on it.

I sighed. "Yes, only stupider and more complicated. You sure you don't mind me staying at your place?" I asked and he shrugged, pressing the button for the crosswalk.

"I don't give two fucks, dude," he laughed.

"Cool. And you're cool with cats? Like, you're not allergic or anything?" I asked, turning my back to him and showing him Poppy curled up in my bag.

He poked his nose inside and started laughing some more. "Wow. Classy. Yeah, cats are cool. It's little," he smiled, reaching in and letting her sniff his hand.

"Her name is Poppy. I found her abandoned in an alleyway!" I smiled.

He started laughing. "Adopting stray cats . . . feeding the homeless . . . what *don't* you do?" he teased, shoving his hands in his pockets.

I continued to smile. Crossing once the light changed, we made our way up Highland and Jimmy huffed once more.

"She's cute. Does she pee everywhere? What about barf—"

"J, it's a cat, not a human baby. She's litter trained—ohhh . . . I forgot her litter back at my place." I saw him tense, but we continued to walk. "It's fine! I'll make something . . . how far is your place anyways?"

"Up Highland. Past No Other Place. Like, closer to Sunset Boulevard," he mumbled.

I stopped walking and stared at him, eyes wide.

"Seriously?!" I whined.

"Hey, you invited yourself over. Quit yer bitchin'," he laughed, and I sighed, jogging to catch up with him.

"I know, I know. I'm sorry. Seriously, Jimmy. Thanks. I owe you *big* time!"

"Heh, yeah. You owe me for a bunch of shit now!" he laughed, gently shoving me.

Walking a bit in silence, I stared down at my feet and played with my lip ring, wondering what Aaron's party was doing to the inside of my apartment. I could feel the anxiety raising, then suddenly Jimmy's voice snapped me out of it and I jumped.

"Hmm?" I asked, looking at him.

He huffed. "So, what are your plans like tomorrow?" he asked.

I shrugged. "Nothing. I have tomorrow off. I'm hoping Aaron and friends will be gone so I can assess the chaos he leaves me," I sighed.

Jimmy frowned. "That guy's a total asshat, isn't he?" he asked and I snorted, nodding.

"That he is."

When we finally got to his place, his apartment building was shockingly nice. It was called The Highland and almost looked brand new.

"New build?" I asked, looking up at the tall building.

Taking out his keys, he pressed a little grey key fob to a box which beeped and unlocked the front door. Holding the door for me, he shrugged.

"I think it's a few years old?" he mumbled, walking to the elevator and pressing the button to go up.

The front lobby smelled like eucalyptus and had quiet classical music playing in the background.

"It's really nice here," I said aloud, looking all around.

Makes my place look like a piece of shit. My front lobby smelled of damp concrete and had *no* music playing. It was extremely cold, no matter what the temperature was outside, and other than providing the front door, its sole purpose was where tenants picked up their mail in tiny mailboxes inserted into the wall.

Stepping into the elevator, he held the key fob to another little box, then pressed on the appropriate floor number.

"And I like the security," I laughed. "If I lived here, no *way* Aaron could throw surprise parties."

"Move in, then," he said, and I chocked on my spit and started coughing. He waited for me to finish and held back a laugh. "I mean, there's still apartments available. We were full for a while, but then a few moved out," he added and I started laughing, clearing my throat.

"Oh. Yeah, I don't think I could afford to live here . . . I mean, by the looks of it. I can *just* afford my shithole," I mumbled.

Once the elevator doors opened, I followed Jimmy down a hallway with apartment doors on either side. Turning a corner, I stopped and almost gasped. There was an opening with a beautiful view of the Hollywood Hills. It was nighttime, so all you could see were the lights from the houses of the rich and the light pollution in the sky, but there was something very calming about it. Down below was an open patio with a few barbeques and tables with chairs and even a few fire pits. It appeared open to tenants but looked untouched.

"Wow," I mumbled out loud and Jimmy laughed.

"The idea is nice, but I don't think I've ever gone down there once . . . and I've been living here for two years," he mumbled, continuing to walk and lead the way.

Turning another corner, we finally got to his room and the inside was a very similar setup as my own, only . . . nicer. It was a studio. As soon as you opened the door, the kitchen was on the left. The fridge was instantly beside you, followed by the stove and an L-shaped counter in front of you. Around the corner on your right was the bathroom and he also had the luxury of having his own washer and drier. My building had the laundry room in the basement, and I had to share with the rest of the residents. It was awful for an introvert like me.

"Dude, this is so nice," I mumbled, still gawking.

He closed the door behind me and smiled, placing his keys in a little bowl that was on the L-shaped counter.

"Welcome," he mumbled, stretching his arms above and behind his back.

Sitting on the floor, I opened my bag and allowed for Poppy to come out and explore her new surroundings. Other than the alleyway I found her in, she had only ever been in my apartment, so this was going to be strange for her. Looking past the counter, I saw Jimmy's bed. It was just a box spring and mattress on the ground pressed up against the wall, but had the fluffiest black duvet I had ever seen. It was also king sized. On the wall in the centre of the room was a huge flat screen TV with a black couch in front of it. Beside the TV to the left was a glass door that led out to a balcony much bigger than my own. The walls, although plain grey, were decorated exactly like his room at the shop with his drawings and doodles framed and hung all over the place.

"Mi casa es su casa!" he smiled, taking off his shirt and walking off to the bathroom.

I couldn't help but gawk at that too, finally getting a glimpse of his entire back tattoos.

Sitting on the floor with Poppy, I watched as she sniffed every surface with her ears pinned straight back. I ended up laying down where I was and tossed my bag, sprawling out on the floor and sighing loudly. Jimmy came back from the bathroom and was now wearing a black hoodie that said **Los Angeles, California** on it in white. Tourist shit. They sold them everywhere in every size and every colour on The Blvd. He glanced down at me and laughed, stepping over my body and opening the fridge.

"Comfy?" he asked.

I closed my eyes and nodded. "Absolutely."

"Beer?"

"Nah."

"What do you mean, *nah*?" he asked, turning around and staring at me.

"Don't drink."

"What do you mean you *don't drink*?! You drank with us at the bar!" he yelled.

I opened my eyes and glared at him, my lips turning into a grin.

"I mean, I don't drink *casually*. Never got into it."

"Dude, you are *literally* the legal age. That's usually when kids your age take advantage of alcohol!"

"*Kids my age*," I mimicked. "You just made me sound so young . . . and yourself so old," I laughed.

"I am *not* old! I'm only four years older than you!"

"Yeah, well . . . you just made it sound like you were twenty years older!" I laughed, sitting up and stretching. "But *fine*. If it means so much to you, I'll have a goddamn beer."

"Great! It tastes like piss!" he enthused, opening the fridge again, grabbing me a bottle, smacking the lid off the countertop and popping it off.

"That's reassuring," I laughed, taking it from him and examining it. "Smells like piss."

Sighing loudly, I pressed the bottle to my lips and took a swing. Closing my eyes and forcing it down, I gagged. Opening one eye, I stared at Jimmy with the bottle in hand and shrugged.

"Could be worse, I suppose . . ." I mumbled, then took another sip.

"That's the spirit!" he grinned, taking another sip from his own and walking over to the couch.

I sighed and slowly got up to join him. Poppy was currently sniffing out the bathroom. Sitting on the couch beside Jimmy, I groaned loudly and leaned my head back, closing my eyes. Stretching my neck, I sat back up and saw him staring at me. I frowned.

"What?" I asked, and he shrugged.

"Nothing. How's your lip?" he asked, taking another sip from his beer.

I shrugged in return. "S'good. The pain is gone. I'm kinda used to it now. I like it," I smiled, pressing my tongue against the piercing and staring down at it.

I mentally reminded myself to make sure I brushed my teeth after my beer. I didn't want any infections or rejections to happen, like Jimmy explained. He smiled at me.

"Good."

We ended up staying up for most of the night, drinking beers and talking. Thankfully, we didn't drink enough to get drunk because that could have been dangerous on my end, but we *did* do a lot of talking, which I guess was kind of nice. I've never really just . . . *talked* with anyone before.

"So, did you hear about those escaped convicts up in Oakland?" I asked and he nodded while sipping his fourth beer.

"I heard something along those lines . . ."

"Apparently, they're a gang . . . they all escaped together, and they blow shit up and it's intense."

"How does this have to do with anything, man?" he laughed, finishing his beer and opening a fifth.

I stopped drinking since his tolerance was obviously higher than mine and I didn't want to say anything or *do* anything I'd regret . . .

"Well! Aaron showed up at my door and his face was beat in and he was bleeding everywhere—"

"Good."

"So, he walked in and started crying, going on about how they were here, and they beat him up."

Jimmy choked on his sip and started laughing. "They like blowing shit up, but instead they decided to beat up some random white kid?"

"Let me finish!" I laughed.

"Sorry!"

"Then there was a knock on my door and it was a police officer . . . and he walked in along with like, fifty other people and Aaron came out of the bathroom all cleaned up and . . . well, *not* beat up . . . like all his cuts were fake. Like, special effects makeup fake. It was fucked up," I explained, zoning out at the floor and shaking my head. "And to think that he has nothing better to do with his life but to come up with ideas like that . . . clearly a lot of thought was put into it. He said he had me followed and that's how he knew where I lived," I added, forcing a laugh.

"Wooooow. I didn't know shit like that actually happened. Sorry to hear that, dude," he said, and I stopped staring at the floor to stare at him.

I shrugged. "Yeah . . ." Then I leaned back and stared at the ceiling, sighing. "So, I tried sticking up for myself very briefly and well . . . he just shoved me and I knew where that was going. He saw my hands and pressed his thumb into my palm and it actually really fucking hurt . . ." I mumbled, looking down at my hands.

It seemed the gashes were all in different stages of healing: some sore and red, others were scabby and gross.

"What a fucking prick," Jimmy mumbled quietly, shaking his head. Staring down at my hands, he gestured toward them with a slight head nod. "Why'd you take your bandages off anyways?" he asked, and I shrugged.

"Thought they were healed enough that I could. Thought some air could do them some good," I mumbled.

He huffed, placing his beer on the coffee table and reaching out to take my hands into his. I swallowed the lump in my throat.

"Yeah, but then we should've rebandaged them. They still look tender . . ." he mumbled.

"Yeah so . . . that's when I called you . . . sorry." I added, trying to get back to my story and awkwardly taking my hands back before he noticed how much I was starting to overheat.

I placed my hands in my lap and stared at him.

"Don't apologize! Shit happens . . . apparently. We'll go back in the morning and hopefully they'll be gone," he said, grabbing his beer and taking another sip.

"And if they're not?"

"Then we'll figure it out when the time comes . . . why didn't you call the cops?" he asked and I shrugged with a sigh.

"I'm not entirely sure. I thought about it . . . briefly. Then I called you . . ." I mumbled.

He smiled ever so slightly, then there was a long silence.

"So, like . . . what happened to you guys? Why is he such an asshole?" he asked, playing with his beer bottle cap and bending it in half.

I started laughing. "How much time do you have?" I asked and he shrugged.

"We both don't work tomorrow," he smiled, tossing the bent cap on the table and sipping his beer.

Chapter 7

2004
North Hollywood
Los Angeles, California

$\mathcal{D}$allas was nine years old. Growing up at school was always a struggle for him as it had always been hard for him to make friends. Not that he wasn't likeable; he was very polite and well mannered, but kids always thought his hair colour was odd and he was very shy because of it. He was never ambitious enough to step out of his shell and for this, he always hung out on his own. Unfortunately, this forced him to grow up a lot faster than most kids his age, and he matured very quickly. He learned how to take care of himself and how to deal with situations most nine year olds would cry about. Not to mention, his parents were never easy on him either. His older brother, Aaron, was very obviously the favourite out of the two which was also another contributing factor to his shyness.

On this particular spring afternoon, it was raining, and the kids were still forced to go outside for recess. Dallas had forgotten his raincoat at home and had nothing but a sweater and was getting drenched. So, he decided to seek shelter under the slide on the playground until the bell rang to go back inside. The rest of the kids were having the time of their lives: jumping in puddles, throwing mud at one another, not to mention intentionally jumping up and down above Dallas' head to get him covered in gross dirty playground water. He tucked his knees up to his chest and sighed, frowning out at the dark sky.

Walking by with her group of friends was Dallas' crush, Becky Richards. Unfortunately, the feelings weren't mutual and when she saw Dallas, she started giggling with her friends. He ducked his head and sighed, resting his chin on his knee. Aaron walked by with his friends and even though he was well aware that his younger brother was being bullied, he chose to ignore him.

"Aaron!" Dallas yelled, crawling out from under the playground and up to his brother's side. Aaron sighed and looked down at him. "What?" he mumbled, rolling his eyes.

"Can I borrow your jacket? I forgot mine at home," Dallas said, crossing his arms against his chest and shivering.

"Fuck no. That's your own fault," Aaron snapped.

He was thirteen and was graduating this year to go into high school and swearing was already part of his everyday vocabulary—in the schoolyard at least—he wouldn't be caught dead saying those words in front of their parents.

"But I'm cold. And wet," Dallas said, pouting.

Aaron shrugged. "Also not my problem," he said and went to walk away.

Dallas reached out to tug on his sleeve but regretted it instantly.

"I SAID *NO*, DALLAS!" Aaron screamed and forcefully pushed him back, making him fall in the wet muddy grass.

Every kid on the playground—including Becky and her friends—stopped what they were doing to point and laugh. Trying his best to hold back tears, Dallas slowly climbed out of the puddle and stared down at his now dirty soaked clothes. Aaron and his group of friends stood by and laughed at him before walking off. Watching his brother walk further and further away, Dallas glanced over his shoulder at his classmates laughing at him and felt his bottom lip start to quiver.

"Oh my goodness, Dallas!" someone yelled, running over to him with an umbrella.

He looked behind to see one of the teachers running toward him with a look of concern.

"Are you alright?!" she asked, bending down in front of him.

He ducked his head and his hair hung heavy in front of his face, his eyes now filling up with tears, but there was no way he would allow them to fall. He shook his head, bottom lip quivering again and she sighed.

"Do you have a change of clothes in your locker?" she asked and he shook his head again. She sighed once more and stood, helping him to his feet and gently placing an arm around him. "I'll call your mother to come pick you up," she said and he stared up at her with wide eyes.

"No!" he yelled, pulling against her arm and starting to walk backwards. She stared at him and arched her brow.

"Why not? Don't you want to go home?"

"No . . . yes. But no. She'll be mad," he explained.

The teacher sighed and smiled. "Don't be silly. I'll talk to her. She has no reason to be mad. C'mon. You're going to catch a cold," she said, placing her arm around him again and leading him inside.

Sitting outside the principal's office, he was given a blanket to wrap himself in and a cup of hot chocolate. Regardless of his newfound warmth, he still shivered. The teacher walked out with a smile on her face and kneeled down in front of him.

"Your mother said that she's on her way, so just wait right here, okay? Change into warm dry clothes as soon as possible or you're going to get sick," she smiled.

He forced a smile himself and nodded. "Okay. Thank you, Miss," he said.

She gently placed a hand on his shoulder and stood. "Have a good rest of your day, Dallas," she said and went back outside for the rest of recess.

A few minutes later, Victoria showed up and power walked inside.

"What happened?" she asked, quickly kneeling in front of him.

He stood and gently folded the blanket on the chair.

"Aaron pushed me," he explained.

She raised a brow and tucked her crimson hair behind her ear.

"What *really* happened?" she asked, standing and placing her hands on her hips. "Did you get bullied at recess again?" she asked.

Dallas sighed and started heading toward the front door. "Yes. But it was Aaron that pushed me, mom," he said, staring at her with his big blue eyes.

She followed him outside and opened her umbrella as they walked to the car.

"Okay. If that's the story you want to go with, that's fine. But you're going to have to tell your father the truth. You know how he feels about lying," she said.

Dallas sighed again and said nothing for the rest of the car ride.

Once they got home, he quickly ran inside and went straight upstairs to his bedroom. Slamming his door shut, he dropped all his clothes so he was only in his boxers and jumped into bed, curling into a ball under the covers and bursting into tears. His bed was the only place he felt safe to let his emotions get the best of him and this was where he would stay for the rest of the day until 4:00 p.m. when Aaron would get home. Coming inside and kicking the front door closed behind him, he dropped his bag and ran upstairs, skipping a few steps at a time, then banging on Dallas' bedroom door.

"Hey, faggot. What'd you tell mom?" he asked, letting himself in before Dallas had a chance to gather himself. "You better not be chirping," he snapped, sitting on the end of his bed.

Dallas didn't say anything, so Aaron grabbed the blankets and threw them off, then burst into hysterics when he saw him curled in a ball in his boxers.

"You're so gay!" he laughed, throwing the blankets on the ground, then leaving, going to his own room and kicking the door closed.

Dallas sat up, eyes bloodshot from crying, and crawled to the edge of the bed where he grabbed his blankets and curled back into a ball.

2008
North Hollywood
Los Angeles, California

"Aaron, stop it!" Dallas screamed, bending over to protect himself as best as possible while his older brother kicked him repeatedly in the stomach.

He was pressed up against the lockers and had nowhere to go. It was lunchtime and the hallways were empty as all the students were out and about, getting their fresh air of the day, whereas Aaron was inside, hunting down his brother with his friends for shits and giggles. Dallas knew better than to go inside where he'd get trapped, but he had to stay in for biology help. Being in his first year of high school and Aaron in his last, it was clear who was the alpha.

"Oi!" a teacher yelled down the hall, poking their head out of their classroom.

Aaron instantly stopped and he and his little minions ran off laughing. The teacher had done their job and casually went back inside their classroom, leaving Dallas on the ground, where he proceeded to cough until he saw blood. Leaning on his hands and knees, he struggled to catch his breath. His eyes were watering, and he decided it was time to go to the bathroom. Going into the first stall he could, he fell to his knees and instantly threw up blood and his lunch.

This wasn't the first time this had happened. It was practically a monthly thing for Aaron to hit him so much and so hard in the stomach that he'd cough or throw up blood. But no matter what he told his parents, they didn't believe him. Plus, Aaron would just punish him the next day for being a tattletale. So eventually, Dallas just stopped speaking all together. This didn't help with the friend-making factor. The guys didn't talk to him and the girls wanted nothing to do with him.

He stood in front of the mirror of the boys' bathroom for a solid five minutes, regaining himself. He rinsed his mouth and splashed his face, breaking out in a cold sweat and starting to shiver. Suddenly, the bell announcing that lunch was over echoed through the halls and he sighed. Heading back out to his locker and gathering his things that were scattered across the floor, he walked against the crowd and went outside where he proceeded to walk home. It wasn't a far walk—ten minutes give or take.

Thankfully, his parents weren't home because they weren't too keen on how much he'd been skipping lately. At least this way, he'd be home to catch the phone call from the school. He went inside and locked the door behind him and even wore his shoes upstairs to make sure he left no trace that he was home early. Closing his bedroom door behind him, he sat at the end of his bed and let out a long and exaggerated sigh, wincing when his stomach ached.

Looking over at his desk, he stared at his current project which was a 1500 piece puzzle. He was halfway done. Taking off his shoes, he sat down and instantly started looking for the next piece. This was his happy place. Puzzles calmed his mind. He liked to build things, and this kept his brain busy so he didn't have to think about his current bodily wound.

2011
North Hollywood
Los Angeles, California

Dallas was seventeen years old. It was a Saturday night in late December and even though California didn't get that cold in the wintertime, it still definitely wasn't eighty degrees anymore. Nights could still get pretty chilly. He was minding his own business with a new puzzle while Aaron, who was home from Yale for Christmas break, was downstairs talking loudly on the phone and loudly playing video games. Their parents were out for the night. The TV was turned up loud and regardless that he was *sort* of having a conversation with a friend, occasionally Aaron would scream at his game, then start laughing, and Dallas was finding it hard to concentrate on his thoughts. Sighing loudly, he decided to call it quits and resulted in reading a book in bed, since that at least didn't involve much thinking. The TV and Aarons' voice suddenly got quiet and Dallas frowned, staring at his doorway, anticipating the worst.

"DALLAS!" Aaron screamed from the bottom of the stairs, making Dallas jump, then sigh.

"What?!" he yelled back.

"C'MERE!"

Rolling his eyes, he closed his book and slowly got out of bed, walking to the top of the stairs and staring down at his brother.

"What?" he asked again.

"I'm going out," Aaron said.

"Okay. I don't care."

Aaron smirked, zipping up his jacket. "Just letting you know. Didn't want'cha getting all freaked out being alone or anything," he said and Dallas rolled his eyes and sighed.

"I think I'll be fine, Aaron," he mumbled, rolling on his heel and heading back to his bedroom.

Aaron laughed and turned to throw on his shoes, then ran up the stairs, skipping a few steps at a time and heading to his room where he grabbed a zip lock bag of weed and his bong.

"Peace out!" he yelled while running down the stairs, then slammed the front door shut behind him.

Dallas sighed once more, only this time it was a sigh of relief.

A few hours went by and Dallas jumped when the front door burst open with Aaron and a few of his friends stumbling in and laughing obnoxiously. Taking a chance at being the only *real* adult in the house, he paused his music and went downstairs to see Aaron and his friends lighting a bong in the living room, and a girl kneeling on the coffee table starting to undress.

"Aar, really?" he sighed, leaning against the door frame. "Mom and dad will be home any minute. Can't you at least take this outside?"

"Have you *seen* it outside? It's fucking cold, man. Just shut the fuck up and mind your own fucking business!" Aaron snapped, swatting his hand in Dallas' direction.

"Dude, I totally forgot you had a brother!" one of his friends snorted, falling back in the couch and laughing hysterically.

"Hahaha! I know, man! Sometimes I do too!" Aaron snorted back.

Dallas rolled his eyes and exhaled slowly to calm himself down. "Mom and dad will be home and you know they're gonna flip shit when they smell that stuff," he said calmly, gesturing toward the pot. "And what's she doing? Is she one of your friends or did you find her at the corner or something?" he snapped, staring at the now half-naked girl in the living room.

"Dude, just shut up! She's with me! Guys, let's move this to the kitchen. I know where my dad keeps the good stuff," Aaron enthused, running to the kitchen with his little posse not too far behind.

The girl picked up her pile of clothes and slowly walked past Dallas, sliding her hand across his chest and down to his crotch. He shrugged her off and made a disgusted face, walking away.

"Aaron! No!" he yelled, following them into the kitchen.

Aaron quickly turned around and shoved Dallas into the nearest wall, denting the drywall and bringing a threatening first up to his face.

"You need to fuck right off," he growled, clenching his teeth together.

Dallas was used to this and turned his head, looking the other way and frowning. Aaron pushed him one more time, then walked off to join his friends in the kitchen. Dusting himself off, Dallas turned to head back upstairs, deciding that he didn't care amore and he *hoped* Aaron would get caught. But as soon as the thought crossed his mind, something that sounded expensive smashed in the kitchen. He clenched his fists and sighed, turning on his heel and marching back into the kitchen.

"Aaron, *enough*!" he snapped, and pushed through the small group of people, picking up the bottles of alcohol and snatching the bong out of Aaron's hands.

He took a step back and kept his stance, frowning at the group of them. Aaron's blood was boiling, clenching his fists and glaring at his brother.

"Yo, dude. Your brother's fuckin' whack, bro," a friend said. "Let's dip," he said to the rest and they all made their way to the front door.

The girl quickly threw on her clothes and stared at Aaron as she left. "See ya, Aar," she mumbled before closing the door behind her.

Dallas turned to watch them leave and turned back to have Aaron punch him square in the jaw. He fell back and dropped everything, the bottles of alcohol smashing as well as the bong, glass going everywhere. The shards of glass cut Dallas all over his arms but nothing too serious, although his now bleeding nose didn't help.

"Aaron, what the fuck!?" he yelled, crawling backwards and bringing a hand up to his face to stop the bleeding.

"I was trying to get with her tonight, man!" he yelled, walking forwards while Dallas crawled backwards.

Struggling to stand up, he continued to block his nose with his arm and swallowed the disgusting mound of blood in his mouth.

"She wasn't even sober! Did she even want to have sex with you?"

"It wouldn't have mattered!"

"So, you were going to have sex with her without her consent, is what you're telling me," Dallas said, narrowing his eyes and dropping his arm.

The blood was still coming from his nose and it was all he could taste. He dusted off the small shards of glass from his skin and his clothes, then sighed.

"No! Fuck, bro! Just shut the fuck up! You don't know what you're talking about! You're just always in the fucking way!" Aaron yelled, shoving Dallas back again. "And now my bong is broken, my pot's all over the floor, and dad's good shit is everywhere! How are you going to explain that when they come home?!"

"I'm not. *You* are. None of this is my fault," Dallas said calmly, bumping into the wall behind him.

Cornered again, he thought to himself. Aaron was angry and Dallas had nowhere to go. Inhaling sharply and holding his breath, he could see his own reflection in his brother's burning eyes.

"You need to just fucking disappear, you fucking faggot. You've been on my case since the day you were fucking born," Aaron hissed, now bringing his voice down to an unnerving whisper.

"Aar, I—"

But this time, he wasn't given a chance to have a comeback. Instead, Aaron brought his arm up and slammed his forearm into Dallas' face, instantly knocking him unconscious.

Midnight came around and Aaron had left the scene almost as soon as Dallas fell to the ground. Mr. and Mrs. Penske walked in and Dallas' unconscious and bleeding body was the first thing they saw. Victoria dropped to her knees beside her son's body and hugged him.

"Oh my God!" she screamed, lifting his head onto her lap and staring up at her husband.

He stood above them with his arms crossed, shaking his head. He walked past and into the kitchen, slowing down when he started stepping on all the glass.

"For fuck's sake!" he yelled. "My good stuff!"

"Scott! That seriously cannot be your main concern! Look at his face!" she screamed, eyes filling up with tears. "Who would do this?!"

"Nobody did this, Victoria. He's done this to himself. He's finally fallen off the edge and now he's into drinking and drugs. It's always the quiet ones, y'know. They never tell you anything until it's too late," Scott growled, walking around the house, looking for more damage. "Where's Aaron?" he snapped, standing back at the front door with his hands on his hips.

Victoria took out her cell phone with shaking hands and started to dial. "I'll call him," she whimpered.

Just then, as if on cue, Aaron calmly came through the front door with bags of snacks he bought at the convenience store, whistling. First, he saw his dad and frowned.

"Oh. Hey, dad, mo—oh my God!" he dropped the bags and ran to Dallas' side, also dropping to his knees. "What happened?" he gasped.

Victoria dropped her phone and burst into tears, grabbing Aaron and pulling him into a hug. "Your brother is an alcoholic drug addict!" she screamed, crying hysterically into his shoulder.

With his father standing behind him and out of sight from his face, Aaron felt a small smile play at his lips, knowing perfectly well that his plan had worked and now he would get zero of the blame.

Quickly wiping the smile off his face, he gasped. "Oh my God . . . I never would have guessed. He was always so quiet."

"That's what I said," Scott growled.

Gently removing his mother, Aaron stood and walked into the kitchen.

"Oh no. Dad! Is this your good whiskey?" he gasped, turning around and staring at his father with wide eyes.

Scott closed his eyes and clenched his jaw, nodding. "It is."

"What are you going to do with him?" Aaron asked, looking down at Dallas' unconscious body.

"Therapy. First thing in the morning," Scott said before Victoria could open her mouth.

She closed her eyes and cried harder. Aaron helped his dad carry Dallas' body up to his room while Victoria cleaned up the mess, all the while still crying. They placed him in his bed and placed his blankets on top.

"We'll have a family talk with him in the morning," Scott said, turning and leaving the room.

Aaron watched his dad leave, then turned back to Dallas and smirked. "I have great pleasure in saying . . . I told you so," he hissed, punched him once more in the face, then left his room and closed the door.

That morning, Dallas woke up with a screaming migraine and his entire face felt swollen and bruised. Probably because it *was* swollen and bruised. He sat up slowly and looked over at his alarm clock that read 4:30 a.m. in bright red numbers which only made his head hurt more. Closing his eyes and sighing, he sat up straight and carefully stretched. Getting out of bed, he walked over to his mirror and flicked on his table light, wincing at its brightness. Trying his best to examine his face with the light that was given to him, he almost didn't recognize himself. His entire nose was swollen black and blue, and the blood was now dry, having dripped from his nose to his top lip. *Nice of my family to clean me up a little bit.* He had a giant green and yellow bruise on his forehead, making it hard for his right eye to stay open, and his right cheekbone was twice its size. He sat at the end of his bed, staring at his reflection, and was quick to push back tears once his bottom lip started to quiver.

Suddenly taking a stand, he grabbed his school bag and shoved in as many of his belongings as he could, as well as keeping his schoolwork inside. He grabbed a second bag and made it overflow with clothes, grabbed his laptop and grabbed his cell phone, then forced open his bedroom window. It was the second story, so it wasn't really *that* far of a drop, but it was still going to suck nonetheless.

The school bag went first, followed by the bag of clothes, then he paused as he sat on his windowsill with his legs hanging out. Looking back at his room, he didn't even have to think twice before turning back around and taking a leap. He made sure to jump further than his pile of bags and forced himself into a summersault afterwards. It was a soft landing considering how hard the ground was. Quickly grabbing his bags and throwing them over his shoulder, he made a run for it down the empty streets to get as far away from his house as he could. He ran and ran until he physically could run no more and stopped to bend down, resting his hands on his knees to catch his breath. His throat burned and his lungs were aching from the harsh cold air he was inhaling, but he knew he had to keep going, so he picked up the pace to a quick walk. Digging his phone out of his pockets, the time read 5:20 a.m. and he knew there was only one person he could call.

"Hello?" the voice croaked from the other end.

"Ang? It's Dallas."

"Dallas, hey . . . what're you doing up so early? Is everything okay?"

"No. I need you to come pick me up. Can I meet you at the movie theatre on Victory Boulevard near my house?"

"Uh, yeah . . . let me just get dressed. What's up? Where are you now?"

"I'm about twenty minutes from the theatre. I'll tell you everything in the car."

"O . . . kay. I'll see you shortly," she mumbled and then hung up.

Angela Bryce was Dallas' boss at Starbucks. He worked there part-time while also attending school; anything to keep him out of the house as much as possible. It was also handy getting an income so when the day came for him to move out, he'd have some money saved up. Obviously, the time came sooner than he expected, but he at least had enough for a few nights in a hotel room.

Finally getting to the movie theatre, Angela was already parked outside waiting for him. He ran across the road and got in the passenger seat. He threw his bags in the back, then sighed, sinking down in the seat and covering his face, finally allowing himself to burst into tears. Angela drove back to her house in silence, the only sound in the car being Dallas' soft sobbing.

Chapter 8

**Present Time
Hollywood
Los Angeles, California**

"*J*esus Christ, Dal. That's intense . . ." Jimmy said, eyes wide.

I shrugged. "Yeah. It is what it is . . . I'm over it now."

"So, what did you do after that?"

"Well, I told Angie everything and made her promise that she wouldn't call the cops or my parents. I didn't want to have to face them ever again, and I assured her that I could take care of myself. She brought me back to her place to help clean me up and insisted I stay there for a while until I got myself back on my feet. I only stayed about a week until I left there in the middle of the night to go find a hotel room."

"Holy shit, dude . . ."

"Heh, yeah. She wasn't very happy with me when I showed up for work after that, but she'd done enough already, and it didn't feel right living there. She has a son and he didn't need to see me squatting. So, I got a shitty motel and spent all my savings and lived there for about a month. I transitioned from part-time to full-time and did the rest of my schoolwork online, saved every dollar I made and started renting my shitty ass apartment."

"Fuck."

"Yeah . . . fun, right?" I laughed awkwardly, then sighed. "So now that piece of shit is in my apartment, destroying everything I've worked for. He's right . . . my parents didn't care that I left. They didn't even *try* looking for me . . . not that I would have wanted them to . . ." I mumbled, zoning out at the floor. "He's so much bigger than me. I don't know why I bother trying to stick up for myself."

"Well, we can go get it back," Jimmy mumbled, and I quickly looked at him.

"Jimmy, no."

"He doesn't scare me," he smiled. "I like the challenge."

"He's like . . . six feet tall or some shit," I mumbled, trying not to smile.

I mean, Jimmy was a few inches taller than I was, but Aaron made me look tiny. I stood at an average height of five feet and eight inches, but whenever Aaron towered over me, I quivered.

"It's not always height that matters. I got the muscle," he grinned, flexing both arms.

I started laughing, shaking my head. "No. Next time we run into him, which I'm hoping isn't any time soon, you can beat the shit out of him then, okay? Just not while he's in my apartment . . ."

He was still grinning. "Deal!"

"So, what about you? You said you moved out early on too?" I asked, suddenly becoming very embarrassed by my situation.

He shrugged. "Yeah. Not as dramatic as your story though . . ."

"Ha, good! It shouldn't have to be dramatic. What happened?"

"Walked in on my dad sleeping with this girl I knew . . . so I left . . . ha!" he said, grabbing his beer from the table and finishing it.

I stared at him and blinked a few times because I wasn't sure what to say.

He shrugged. "Yeah. I just kinda left. His bad karma, really. I was at the parlour with Nils, got home around the same time as my mom and we both heard something upstairs. I went to check it out and caught my dad in the act. I left and he came after me, and from what my mom told me, she filed for a divorce like . . . that day. The divorce didn't actually go through until like . . . a month later. But yeah. That's my story," he mumbled with a shrug.

"J. That's pretty dramatic . . ." I said with a forced laugh.

"Oh . . . haha, yeah, I guess."

"Where did you go?"

"At the time, I went to the shop to see Nils. But I ended up living with my mom for a bit. But then she started fooling around with the wrong kind of guys. They were kind of abusive in more ways than not . . ." he said, pausing for a moment. "So, I moved in with Nils!" he grinned, then stared down at his hands, fiddling with the empty beer bottle; his face was slowly falling. "Yeah . . . her and I have been friends for a long time . . ." he mumbled, smiling to himself.

He seemed to have zoned out for a moment or two and I felt myself staring at the tattoos on his arms; he had since taken off his hoodie and was wearing a t-shirt. Biting my bottom lip, I was hesitant, but asked anyways.

"Is that what this one is all about?" I asked, pointing to a tattoo on his forearm.

It appeared to be your classic 'mom' tattoo, written in a banner wrapped around a heart, only his . . . was covered in scars, all of which looked almost intentional. His smile faded and he stared down at his arm; it was obviously a sore subject.

"Oh. Yeah. Not my finest moment," he huffed, gently sliding his fingers over the raised scars. Continuing to stare at his arm, he sighed, then stared back at me and smiled. "Well, that was fun! So, what do you want for dinner?" he grinned, getting up and heading back into the kitchen.

Poppy had made herself comfortably at home and was asleep on Jimmy's bed. Thankfully, Jimmy had an empty shoebox and we used it for her temporary kitty litter. And thankfully, she was smart enough to understand and use it.

"It's almost midnight," I laughed.

"So what! Time doesn't matter when food is involved! What do you want, pancakes? I feel like pancakes . . ."

I woke up the next morning with my legs tucked up to my chest and my neck aching from being bent all night. I was sweating and it didn't help that I was curled up in a sweater with the hood over my head. The sun was beaming through the wall of windows and I suddenly became very aware of how hot I was. Slowly stretching my neck side to side, I looked in front of me and laughed when I saw Jimmy in the exact same position. His neck was kinked to the side from using the back of the couch as a pillow, his arms were crossed and his legs were hanging off the couch by my side. I had no recollection of falling asleep, but we were both obviously tired as we had fallen asleep where we were. Glancing to my right, I smiled at our dirty plates from eating pancakes. Jimmy had made a huge stack and we ate them all, just half past midnight.

Slowly getting up, I had to take a minute to stretch since my entire body was cramped up, then made my way to the kitchen to figure out his coffee machine. I wondered why he bought Starbucks when he had a perfectly functioning coffee machine right here, but I didn't think about it for too long. I heard him groan and saw him stretch his legs out across the couch and his arms above his head. Stretching his neck back off the side of the couch, he whined loudly and then started laughing.

"What the fuuuuucckkkkk," he said. "Why did we fall asleep like thaaaattttt?"

"Hahaha I know. My neck kills. How do you take your cof—wait . . ." I laughed at myself. "Eight million sugars. Right . . ."

I heard him huff. "You got it," he mumbled, his head still hung back and his eyes closed.

He was silent while I got everything ready, pouring us both mugs of fresh hot coffee. I started scooping spoonfuls of sugar into his and looked over my shoulder, laughing when I saw that he had fallen back asleep.

"J!" I yelled.

He jolted awake, then whined again when he got whiplash. "What time is it?" he asked, rubbing his eyes.

I looked at the clock on the stove. "8:15 on the dot," I said.

He groaned louder, turning over and shoving his face into the back of the couch. "It's my day off! Why am I awake so early?"

"You said you'd help me get my apartment back," I stated, walking over and sitting on the arm rest of the couch, making sure I didn't sit on his feet.

I nudged his leg with my foot and reached out to hand him his coffee. He awkwardly bent his arm behind his back and took it, keeping it elevated since his face was still pressed into the couch.

"Thank you . . ." he muffled.

Reaching for the remote, I turned on the TV and flicked through some channels until I got to the cartoon network. He slowly turned over and sat up, sipping his coffee with his eyes still closed and his hair all over the place.

"Not a morning person?" I asked, smiling.

"I am when I need to be . . ." he mumbled.

"Well, today you need to be! We need to get ready and head back to my apartment and take it back!"

He started laughing, taking another sip of his coffee and slowly opening his eyes to look at me. "Dal, it's an apartment, not a pirate ship . . ."

"Basically the same thing. C'mon, let's get ready!" I enthused, sipping more coffee, then standing and nudging his foot.

He groaned loudly, holding the coffee above his head and laying back down.

Half an hour later, I finally got him to get dressed so we could start heading toward my apartment. Turning onto Melrose, I side-glanced at him and smiled. He was quick to notice this and frowned.

"What?" he asked.

"Nothing. Just weird seeing this side of you, is all . . ." I mumbled, staring down at my feet as we walked.

I sensed he was still frowning.

"What side?" he asked, and I shrugged.

"Sleepy, bed heady, and in sweatpants," I laughed, noting that he was wearing black and white Vans, and they weren't tied.

He stared up at the sky and laughed, shoving his hands in his pockets. "I can't be perfect *all* the time!" he grinned. "Plus, you talk in your sleep," he said, smirking at me and nudging me with his shoulder.

My face fell and I stared straight ahead. "I do? What did I say?" I asked.

Oh fuck.

He laughed again and shrugged. "Nothing really. I couldn't make it out. I'm pretty sure it wasn't even English," he explained and I felt myself cool down.

"Ha!"

"And everyone has bed head," he added, and I snorted.

"Good defense," I said, sticking my tongue out.

He frowned again. Shoving my hands in my pockets and looking down at my feet once more, I couldn't stop smiling.

Suddenly distracted by a parade of fire trucks screaming by with their sirens on, we both stopped walking to watch them speed by. Drivers were panicking to get out of their way and pulling off to the side. The trucks slammed on their brakes and made a hard left, turning up Vine Street. Jimmy turned and stared at me with wide eyes.

"Y'think—" he started, but I didn't give him time to finish before I broke out into a run.

"Y'chasing fire there, Dallas?" Rufus yelled, laughing with his homeless friends.

I ran right past him and didn't even acknowledge what he said. Jimmy was quick to catch up to me once I stopped outside my apartment building. Well, what was left of it anyways.

"Holy shit . . ." he whispered, staring at the giant flames before us.

We both had to jump back when a few windows exploded, sending glass everywhere.

"Excuse me! You two! We need you to stand back until we can contain these flames!" a fireman yelled, pointing at us to step further away from the building.

Jimmy was standing behind me and grabbed onto my shoulders with both hands, pulling me back and forcing me to stand with him and the rest of the crowd that was watching in awe.

"Dallas, I . . ." he started, but never finished.

My shoulders dropped and I stared at my feet, shaking my head. "Whatever," I mumbled, sighing.

I looked up once more and jumped as the roof collapsed and people screamed. Jimmy quickly placed a hand on my back to hold me up right, then gave me a comforting squeeze on my shoulder. Jumping at the sound of somebody screaming my name, I looked to my left and saw Mrs. Sparks—another tenant—marching up toward me, eyes swollen with tears, and cheeks flushed red.

"No . . ." I whispered, shaking my head and feeling my bottom lip begin to quiver.

"This is all your *fault*!" she cried, reaching me and grabbing my shoulders.

Jimmy frowned and took a step back, clearly confused. "Hey, lady—"

"J, it's okay," I mumbled, clearing my throat.

Mrs. Sparks kept her grip on my shoulders and shook me, although didn't quite have the energy or the strength to do so aggressively.

"All your fault," she repeated, clearly in hysterics.

Releasing my shoulders, she began punching my chest, but barely hitting me at all. She was an elderly woman, so her shaking fists didn't affect me as much.

"I'm—I'm sorry," I stuttered, tears now falling down my cheeks.

"Ma'am? Ma'am!" a police officer yelled, quickly running up to us and pulling Mrs. Sparks off of me.

Wiping my tears away with my arm, I tried calming my breathing. "It . . . it wasn't me. I promise you," I explained, sniffling back my runny nose.

Mrs. Sparks curled into the police officer and bawled her eyes out, while the officer gave me a funny look.

"Why would you assume it was your fault at all?" he asked, wrapping an arm around Mrs. Sparks, and I sighed.

"I also lived here," I explained.

"Oh. I'm sorry for your loss," he mumbled, glancing at the burning building to our side.

Another floor of windows exploded, and people screamed and jumped back. I was distraught. Blinking away my tears, I suddenly felt Jimmy's hand on my shoulder and it warmed me up.

"Wanna go back?" he asked quietly.

I glanced at him over my shoulder and sighed as Mrs. Sparks and the police officer walked away.

"Sure. There's nothing left here . . . I hope the bastard is still inside . . ." I mumbled, turning on my heel to head back in the direction we just came.

"Uhhhh don't get your hopes up," Jimmy said, nudging me and pointing straight ahead.

I looked up and saw Aaron stumbling around on the sidewalk further down from where the fire was. Shoving Jimmy's hand off my shoulder, I sprinted down toward

Aaron and shoved him with as much strength as I could physically manage.

"*MOTHER FUCKER*!" I screamed, shoving him once more before he could retaliate.

"Dallas! Hey!" he greeted, a huge fake grin on his face and eyes bloodshot. He stumbled backwards.

"What the fuck did you do?!" I screamed, shoving him again. "You burned down the entire building?! That wasn't only *my* home, Aaron! Other people lived there too!" I continued to scream.

It's a good thing he was still a little out of it, otherwise I wouldn't stand a chance.

He forced a laugh. "Party got a little wild..." he mumbled.

"A *little*?" Jimmy asked, now standing behind me with his arms folded across his chest.

Aaron glared at him. "Who the fuck *are* you, buddy?"

"Yeah, I figured you wouldn't remember. Last time we met, you were a little coked out," Jimmy smiled.

Aaron narrowed his eyes when Jimmy stepped up and stood beside me. "Who's the friend, Dallas? New bodyguard? You're hiring people to pick your fights for you?" he snapped, but stared down at the ground and swallowed awkwardly, looking like he was about to throw up.

"Nah. This fight I'm handling all on my own," I snapped, taking another step forwards and smirking when he jumped. "Aaron, that was my home. Everything I owned was in there. Just be thankful I got Poppy out of there or you'd seriously be sorry."

He started laughing and it only made me angrier. "Dallas—" he started, but I was *beyond* done listening.

Gritting my teeth together, I stepped forwards and clenched my fist, punching him straight in the face. His nose instantly started bleeding and his right eye squinted shut.

"Dal—" he mumbled, falling back onto his ass.

I stood above him, staring down at him for the first time in my entire life. My fist was screaming in pain since that had to be the first time I ever punched anyone, but it felt good.

"You were out of my life for *years*. Let's keep it that way, okay?" I snapped, narrowing my eyes.

Jimmy still stood behind me, smirking and nodding. I turned on my heel and started walking back toward Melrose and he was quick to follow.

"That was kickass!" he yelled, grinning.

I forced a laugh. "What a fucking asshole . . ." I mumbled, shaking my head. "I've never wanted somebody dead so bad in my entire life," I sighed, then looked down at my red knuckles and pouted.

"Punching people hurts . . ." I mumbled, rubbing them.

Jimmy snorted and started laughing at me. "Yeah, but I think he got it a bit worse . . ."

Jimmy unlocked the door and we both walked in; Poppy jumping off the bed and running toward us to greet us. I picked her up and cuddled her in the crease of my neck, kissing her face repeatedly.

"Hi little loaf . . ." I mumbled into her fur.

Jimmy opened the fridge and grabbed himself a beer, offering me one.

I shook my head. "It's not even noon—it's not even 10 a.m.!" I laughed and he shrugged, popping off the cap, closing the fridge with his hip and walking off with the bottle attached to his lips.

"It's 10 a.m. somewhere," he mumbled, taking a huge gulp.

I rolled my eyes. "You could've died today!" I said to Poppy, now holding her up above my head like something out of *The Lion King* and she squirmed and meowed a few times.

Placing her back on the floor, I went to go join Jimmy on the couch. Letting out a big sigh, I placed my feet up on the coffee table and he rested his legs on top of mine.

"Now what?" he asked, taking another sip of his beer.

I shrugged and threw my head back, closing my eyes. "I gotta start looking for a new place, I guess . . ." I mumbled, opening my eyes and staring at my reflection in the TV screen in front of me.

He took another sip, then placed the bottle between his knees. "Well, y'know . . ."

"J, no," I mumbled, turning to look at him.

"You don't even know what I'm going to say!" he yelled, laughing a little.

"You're going to invite me to stay here and I can't!" I yelled in return.

"You said so yourself that you wanted to live here but you couldn't afford it! This way you can!"

"No."

"Why not?!"

"Because! You've already done *so* much for me! I can't just . . . I can't stay. That wouldn't be fair."

He forced a laugh. "Dallas. How wouldn't it be fair? I'm *inviting* you to stay."

I let out a long and exaggerated sigh and didn't say anything, staring at his legs resting up on mine.

"Dallas," he said more sternly. "C'mon, think about it. Shit happens for a reason," he explained and I forced a sarcastic laugh.

"Oh yeah? And what reason would that be? What did I do to get such bad karma?" I asked, arching a brow at him.

"This isn't bad karma! Everything happens for a reason. Just think . . . if Aaron didn't beat the shit out of you growing up, you probably would have never moved out . . ."

"Uh huh . . ." I smirked.

"And if you didn't move out, you wouldn't have met me!" he grinned and I snorted, closing my eyes and shaking my head.

"Where is this going?" I asked, opening my eyes once more and staring at him.

"If Aaron didn't set your apartment on fire, then you wouldn't be sitting here on my couch with me sitting beside you, inviting you to move in with me!" he continued to grin, only this time, he threw his arms up in the air.

I started laughing and sighed. Staring at him and narrowing my eyes, I tried weighing out the pros and cons, but couldn't come up with anything. Sighing loudly, I gave in.

"Fine," I said, leaning my head back on the couch and closing my eyes.

He perked up and smiled wider. "Woohoo! It'll be fun!" he yelled.

I quickly held up a hand to calm him down and opened one eye to stare at him. "*Only* until I find a new place."

"Yeah, yeah. You'll like it here too much, you won't want to leave!" he grinned, grabbing his beer and chugging it, standing to go grab another.

I started laughing, shaking my head.

"Did I tell you there's a rooftop gym and pool?" he asked, kicking the fridge closed with his foot and walking back toward me with a new beer attached to his lips.

I turned to stare at him with wide eyes and mouth open. "What!?" I squeaked and he nodded with a smirk.

"I'll show you later," he mumbled, walking back toward me and sitting back down on the couch.

"Okay, well . . . I gotta go buy a whole new wardrobe because I only have what I packed . . . and where am I going to sleep? You only have one bed," I laughed.

He looked around his small apartment and huffed. "Oh yeah . . . I guess . . . we'll take turns between bed and couch until we buy you your own bed," he grinned.

Chapter 9

$\mathcal{A}$ few days later, I was standing behind the counter at work, cleaning one of the machines, when two police officers walked in. I didn't think anything of it; we've served many officers before. Cleaning my hands, I turned to them and smiled.

"What could I get—"

"Dallas Penske?" one of them asked, and my face dropped.

"Yes?" I asked.

"We're going to need you to come with us," the other explained, and I frowned, grabbing a towel and drying my hands.

"Uhm . . . pardon? What's this about?" I asked.

I was embarrassed. I didn't even know what I did, and yet everybody who was sitting and enjoying their coffee was staring right at me like I was some sort of criminal.

"We just need you to come in for some questioning."

"Questioning about what?" I asked.

Wasn't this the part where I said I wouldn't talk unless I had my lawyer? Only problem was, I didn't *have* a lawyer. Nor could I afford one. And I didn't even know what I was being questioned about! Nervously biting my bottom lip, I stared back and forth between the two officers, awaiting one of them to speak.

"Regarding your apartment. And the fire," one of them said, and I felt the colour leave my face.

"What?! But I had nothing to do with—I can't just *leave*. I'm the only one here. I'll have to call my manager to come in and take my place," I explained, reaching into my back pocket to grab my phone. "Give me two seconds . . ." I mumbled, quickly dialing Angela's number.

I was very aware of how hard my hands were shaking. She was quick to answer, and I was quick to explain the situation and she hung up and got here as fast as she could. While we were waiting for Angela to show, I made them both coffees and they sat at one of the tables and talked.

"Well, like . . . should I call Tiffany and I can come with you?" Angela asked almost instantly upon arriving.

I shook my head and forced a smile, even though I was scared shitless. "No, no. It's okay. They're just going to ask me a few questions," I mumbled, glancing at the two police officers over my shoulder.

Angela stared at me with worried eyes and I grabbed her shoulders and gave them a reassuring squeeze.

"I've texted Jimmy, so he doesn't freak out when I don't come home . . . I'll keep you both updated," I smiled, and her shoulders sank.

"Okay," she breathed.

As if I wasn't awkward before with people just staring at me, now I had to get into the back of a cruiser. There was no scene to be made, and yet everyone standing at the intersection of Vine and Melrose, gawked. Putting on my seatbelt, I took a deep breath in and closed my eyes as the car revved to life. Suddenly, the door beside me opened and Jimmy got in. I jumped and both officers freaked out.

"It's fine, it's fine!" Jimmy yelled, also putting on his seatbelt and throwing up his hands in defence. "I'm his roommate! Whatever you have to ask him, you'll have to ask me too," he explained.

I stared at him, eyes still wide, but knew I had to go along with whatever story he was telling. The officer in the driver's seat stared at me in the rear view and I shrugged.

"I texted him," I mumbled.

"Your landlord didn't say anything about you having a roommate . . ." the officer in the passenger seat mumbled.

Jimmy shrugged, sinking lower in his seat and staring out the window. "I just moved in like . . . two weeks ago," he mumbled.

I stared out my window as well and smiled. He was a good liar. Quick, too. Both officers stared at each other and sighed.

"Okay," one of them mumbled, placing the car into drive and pulling back onto the road.

Jimmy nudged my leg and smiled at me. I did my best not to laugh out loud.

I had never been to the police station before. I had never actually dealt with police *ever*. And there was a reason: they intimidated the *fuck* out of me. Jimmy and I were led to an interrogation room and from what I knew from every crime show, that mirror definitely had people on the other side, watching our every move.

"Morning. I'm Detective Marsh," a woman mumbled, walking in and shaking both of our hands.

Jimmy sat beside me with his arms crossed, looking unimpressed. I mean, I only *told* him where I was going; I didn't expect him to show up, let alone come for the ride.

"Which one of you is Dallas?" she asked, sitting down across from us.

I swallowed the lump in my dry throat. "I'm Dallas," I squeaked, raising a finger.

She nodded and leaned both elbows on the table, staring at me. "So. Why'd you set your apartment building on fire?" she asked.

My mouth dropped open and I was instantly appalled and taken back.

"*What?!*" Jimmy snapped, sitting forwards.

Detective Marsh sat back and frowned at him.

"You think *Dallas* caused the fire!?" he continued to snap.

She arched a brow and stared back and forth between the two of us. "Well, investigation proved that the fire *did* start in your residence. And witnesses said you were throwing a party the night of . . ." she explained, and I rolled my eyes so hard, I felt my eyelids twitch.

"Oh, for fuck's sake . . ." I mumbled, crossing my arms and sinking lower in my chair.

She glared at me.

"Pardon my attitude, but I wasn't *home* that night."

"Then where were you?" she asked, and suddenly Jimmy's lie of being my roommate didn't cut it anymore.

He was my alibi. He was my proof that the fire wasn't my fault. Turning and staring at him, he didn't seem to be bothered by our situation at all, and casually shrugged his shoulders.

"At my place," he stated, and the detective frowned harder.

"I'm sorry? Are you two not roommates?" she asked.

I sighed.

"I lied when I said that we were roommates. I just said that so I could tag along. I'm here for moral support," Jimmy explained.

I covered my face with both of my hands and sighed once more. We were going to jail for sure.

The detective sighed and leaned back in her chair. "Okay. I need this to start making sense *right* now!" she snapped, and it made me jump.

Sighing, I leaned forwards and rested my elbows on the table. "The fire was caused by my older brother, Aaron Penske. He came to my apartment three nights ago and threw a huge party. Easily fifty people were there. I didn't want to take part, so I packed a bag and I left," I explained.

Her body language loosened, and she sighed. "Aaron Penske," she repeated, and I nodded. "I didn't want to make the assumption that you were related . . ." she mumbled, closing her file and linking her hands on the table.

I glanced at Jimmy and we both frowned at her.

"I don't follow . . ." I admitted.

She sighed once more. "This actually makes things extremely easy for us. We have a nice big fat file on your brother, Dallas. This won't be his first rodeo with the police," she explained.

I huffed and crossed my arms, sitting back and smiling. "Why does that not surprise me?" I mumbled.

"But I want to hear the rest of your story anyways. So, please continue. Aaron showed up to throw a party, and then what?" she asked.

"I went to Jimmy's place," I said.

"I'm Jimmy," he smiled with a little wave.

She grabbed the file that had been sitting in front of her and began to take notes.

"I spent the night. We went back to my place the following morning to see the state of things, since . . . y'know . . . the party 'n' all, but when we got there, it was already burning to the ground."

"And where is your brother now?" she asked, still writing.

I shrugged. "No fucking clue. We saw him stumbling around and I punched him in the face . . ." I mumbled, showing her my bruised knuckles for proof.

She glanced up and smiled. "Okay, well . . . luckily for us, we know of a few places we can look to find Aaron," she explained. "He bounces around from place to place. Last time we had a run in with him, he was at his drug dealer's house. So that will most likely be our first stop."

"Good. Catch the fucker and put him behind bars already. Can we go now?" Jimmy asked, sliding back in his chair and standing.

Detective Marsh sighed but did the same. "You can leave," she said. "Thanks for your help and sorry for any confusion." Then she reached to shake our hands once more.

Standing outside, waiting for the bus, Jimmy stretched his arms above his head and yawned. I was still sort of in shock from the whole thing.

"Well *that* was fun!" he moaned, now stretching his neck.

I stared at him and smiled. "You didn't have to come *with* me," I explained. "I only texted you so you'd know where I was. I wasn't sure how long that was going to take."

"Nah, it didn't feel right leaving you to do that on your own. I don't trust cops. They can be snaky sometimes," he mumbled.

The bus stopped in front of us and we got on, sitting at the back.

"Well, thanks."

"No problem."

"No, J. Seriously. Thanks. I was honestly losing my shit. I thought I was going to go to jail for something I didn't do," I huffed.

"I would've bailed you out," he smiled, staring out the window.

I laughed. "Oh yeah?" I asked, and he nodded.

"Yeah. You can't get out of being my roommate *that* easily," he said, looking at me and sticking his tongue out.

I laughed harder.

∞

A month in and I was really happy I decided to move in with Jimmy. It was *way* more fun than living on my own (no offense to Poppy), but I wasn't about to tell him that. We had created a schedule that worked for both of us when it came to buying groceries, making dinner, laundry, etc. He said he loved to cook and offered to do it every night but honestly, how could that be fair? I didn't *love* to cook, but I could do it. Plus, there were far too many times when he'd practically crawl into bed after a long day of work, and I wasn't going to expect him to cook then.

Obviously, my plan of avoiding him went down the drain the same day I had the idea, and I wasn't really one to like change because I lived such a routine, but this change I liked. This change I could deal with. He did, in fact, have a rooftop gym and pool and it was so rarely used that every time we went up, it was empty. The view was spectacular with the Hollywood sign in sight to our left and the city skyline further away to our right. We watched a *lot* of sunsets up there.

❧

August 17th was my twenty-second birthday. Normally, Ang gave me the day off and I'd lounge around my apartment doing nothing, but I didn't want Jimmy to know and make a big deal out of it, so I casually went to work like every other day. I told him I was only doing a half day, from noon until closing, because realistically I didn't want to *really* work a full day on my birthday.

"Yo, it cool if I come with you? I'm gonna grab my coffee and head to the shop early. That kid is coming in with that huge back piece so I wanna get set up."

Today he wore a dark grey beanie which I had never seen before, but staring at him made my stomach do that thing again. That was happening a lot lately.

"Yeah. I'm heading out shortly though, soooo—"

"Yeah, I'm ready!" he grinned, quickly putting his shoes on.

It had become a ritual that he'd come with me to get his coffee on the days our schedules matched up. Sometimes, he'd even get coffees for everyone else at the shop.

"I think I'm just going to be selfish and get myself a drink today. Don't feel like being nice," he grinned.

I snorted. "Selective selfishness. I like that."

We walked inside and Angie was already staring at me, looking unimpressed.

"What are you doing here?!" she yelled.

My face dropped and I widened my eyes, tilting my head a little and staring at her. I ever so slightly shook my head, not wanting her to blow my cover.

"What do you mean?" I asked, eyes getting wider.

Jimmy frowned, looking back and forth between the two of us.

"Not once have I made you work on your birthday, Dallas. I'm not about to start now! Tiffany is on her way, and you have nothing to worry about!" she huffed, tossing her hair out of her face and going to wash her hands.

Jimmy gasped and turned to face me, grabbing my shoulders and shaking me. "IT'S YOUR *BIRTHDAY* TODAY?!" he screamed.

He had been trying to figure out when my birthday was all month, and up to this exact moment, I had been successful at keeping him guessing.

I closed my eyes, head hanging limp and bobbing as he continued to shake me. "Yes," I sighed.

"WHY DIDN'T YOU TELL ME!? THIS CHANGES EVERYTHING!"

I quickly looked up at him and pouted. "Noooo. Whyyyy. You're being selfish today, remember? Keep being selfish," I whined.

Angie finished washing her hands and marched up to me, pushing me around so I was facing the door. "Jimmy. You take him home and make sure he does nothing all day!" she ordered.

"He can't. He has to work," I grinned, looking at her over my shoulder.

"I'll call in sick!" Jimmy yelled.

I spun around and stared at him. "What?! No! You can't! The kid with the back piece is coming in today!" I yelled back.

He shrugged. "So? I could be sick. He doesn't know."

"J, no. That'd be super shitty of you," I laughed.

"You'd almost say it was . . . *selfish* of me," he grinned.

I sighed and rolled my eyes, continuing to laugh. "Shut the fuck up," I snorted. Sighing once more, I started back and forth between him and Angela, then felt my shoulders drop. "Fine. I'll go home and do nothing. *You* keep working and *you* go to the parlour and do your job."

"Damn straight," Angie said, hands on her hips and smirking.

I stuck my tongue out at the both of them and turned on my heel, leaving the store. Jimmy gave Angie a high five, then ran to catch up to me.

"So what'cha wanna do today?" he grinned, shoving his hands in his pants pockets.

I started laughing. "*I'm* going back to the apartment. *You're* going to work and doing another session on that kids' back," I said.

He threw his head back and whined loudly to the sky. "But I don't *wanna*! I wanna come back home and hang out with yooouuuu!" he yelled childishly.

I was still laughing and started giggling. "How about I come hang out with you until he gets there?" I asked, smiling at him.

He started bouncing up and down like a rabbit, still following beside me as we headed toward the tattoo parlour. "Yeah, yeah, yeah!"

I snorted and rolled my eyes. "Y'know, for a twenty-five year old, you sure don't act your age. And to think, you haven't even had your coffee yet," I laughed and he frowned at me, the bunny hopping stopping instantly.

"Hey, yeah! Wait! We didn't even get our coffee! Fuck!" he whined, glancing back the way we came.

I snorted and continued to walk toward the parlour.

"Whatever. I'm young at heart. You're just a wise old fart," he smirked, nudging me with his shoulder.

I laughed harder.

Entering the shop, I briefly waved at everyone as I walked into Jimmy's room with him.

"Hey kiddo! What's cookin'?" Nils asked, popping her head into Jimmy's room, Red Bull in hand.

I sat on the bed and smiled at her, dangling my legs. "Hey Nils. I'm good, how about—"

"IT'S HIS BIRTHDAY TODAY!" Jimmy yelled, taking out his tiny containers of ink as well as his tattoo gun.

I sighed, shoulders slouching. "You're obnoxious, you know?" I mumbled, frowning at him.

Nils started laughing, walking in and sitting beside me. She wrapped an arm around me and gave me a little squeeze. "Well, happy birthday. We'll have to celebrate tonight, no?" she asked, now looking at Jimmy.

"No!" I yelled.

Jimmy was grinning at her, then smirked at me.

Patting me on the back, Nils got up to leave. "Right. It's settled then. I'll call you later," she said, then threw Jimmy a finger gun before leaving, her head tilted back as she cleaned off her energy drink.

My mouth dropped. "You guys didn't even talk! What's settled?! Nobody said anything!?" I yelled, crossing my arms and frowning.

Jimmy continued to set things up, that smirk still playing on his lips. "Nilly and I don't need to use our words. We're just *that* good. Tonight's gonna be fun," he smiled.

I sighed, laying back on the bed and frowning at the ceiling. The room was silent for a moment as he finished gathering everything he needed for the next tattoo session, then suddenly I felt his eyes on me.

"Wanna give each other tattoos while we wait?" he asked, grinning.

I turned to look at him and frowned. "You're fucked. You have a problem. You're an addict," I said, starting to laugh again.

He shrugged. "So, do you wanna?" he asked, ignoring my comments.

I sat up and sighed. "James, no! That shit's permanent!"

"So!? I'm covered, so it doesn't matter if mine looks bad. I'm awesome, so yours will look good either way!" he said.

I rolled my eyes but was still smiling. "Thanks."

"C'mon! It'll be fun! Time killer! Then you can go home and do nothing or whatever . . ."

I sighed once more, louder this time, leaning all my weight on my palms on the edge of the bed. Staring at him, I bit my bottom lip and played with my piercing, then rolled my eyes.

"Fine."

"Yes! Me first!"

"Okay . . . what do I do?" I asked nervously.

He grabbed another chair and pulled it up beside him, tapping on the seat to make me sit. "Take this . . ." he mumbled and handed me the tattoo gun. "And come over here . . ." he said, this time grabbing my chair and rolling us both around to switch positions. "Now go!" he grinned, throwing his arms up in the air.

I started laughing and stared at him. "Well, what am I doing?"

"I dunno. That's half the fun!" he enthused, spinning around to grab me a pair of gloves as well as a pair for himself.

I closed my eyes and sighed, shaking my head. "Well, are we doing matching tattoos like a bunch of losers or just randomly giving each other tattoos?" I asked, staring at the tattoo gun in my hand.

Gently putting it down, I struggled to put the gloves on and frowned when my pinky finger got stuck.

"Dal, you're over thinking the whole point of this game—"

"I didn't know it was a game . . ." I mumbled quietly, fixing my pinky and picking the gun up again.

"Just whatever comes to mind, do it! You'll get a feel for how hard to press on the pedal and how hard to press with the gun . . . either way, I can take the pain," he grinned, turning around and grabbing a little plastic lid.

He filled it with black ink, then turned to look at me, and I was staring at him with wide eyes; mouth opening and closing—speechless. He started laughing.

"Okay. Never mind. We'll try something else . . ." he mumbled, looking around the room.

I had no idea what he was looking for.

Staring back at me, he smiled. "Where is the tattoo going?" he asked and I frowned.

"I have no idea. Uhm . . . your . . . hand?" I asked, staring down at his already tattoo-covered hands.

He laughed and spread both hands out on the bed in front of us. "Which hand?" he asked and I frowned once more.

"Uhm . . . left!" I smiled.

I had no idea what I was doing and this was terrifying that I was on the spot for something so permanent. Keeping his left hand on the bed, he rolled closer to me and I felt my whole body tense up.

"Okay. Hold this like you would hold a pen . . ." he instructed, adjusting my fingers around the gun.

I swallowed the lump in my throat. "Like this?" I asked, looking down at the gun in my hand and he smiled and nodded.

"Exactly. Now . . ."

Placing his hand on top of mine, he awkwardly leaned into me and brought both our hands toward his left hand on the bed. Reaching out with his foot, he slid the pedal closer to him and pressed down a few times.

"Okay . . ." he mumbled, now focusing.

Dipping into the ink, he brought the gun back to his hand and pressed a little dot on the side of his thumb. I could feel myself overheating, but at the same time, I was trying my best to focus on the task at hand.

"Feel that?" he asked, looking at me.

God, his face was close to mine; I could smell his cologne again and it made my stomach do *that thing*.

"Yep," I squeaked.

I wasn't sure what I was supposed to feel, but I rolled with it. Rolling away—thank God—he kept his left hand spread out on the bed and smiled at me.

"The canvas is all yours," he said, and I sighed loudly.

"Okay, okay, okay," I panicked, dabbing the gun in the black ink and pressing down on the pedal.

Taking a slow exaggerated exhale, I brought my face close to his hand and stuck my tongue out to focus. He didn't even flinch. I think he was more focused on watching *me* focus. I tried my best to make the font as pretty as possible and to my surprise, it was kind of easy. It was like writing in slow motion. I had to continue to wipe away the ink and he only bled a little, but after about twenty minutes, I was done and I was proud. I rolled back and grinned.

"Ta da!" I said, now throwing my arms in the air.

He looked down at it and stared laughing. "Mistake?" he read out loud, looking at the slightly cursive writing on the outside of his left index finger.

I nodded. "Yeah. Because this game was a *mistake!*" I laughed. "Now whenever you look at your finger, you'll be reminded how *dumb* you are!" I said and he threw his head back laughing.

"Thanks, Dal," he said, shaking his head and continuing to laugh. "Okay smartass . . . I know exactly what to give you," he said while cleaning up his finger and wrapping it with a clear saran wrap looking bandage.

"Your right hand, please," he smiled, taking the gun from me, putting on his gloves and quickly changing the needle.

Dabbing it in the black ink, he gave me one last little smirk before beginning to draw on the outside of my right index finger. I don't know how he could withstand the pain I was experiencing. There is barely any skin on your fingers, but a lot of nerves. It hurt. It felt like he was drilling into my bone more than my skin and I didn't want to watch because it only made the pain that much worse, so I looked away and bit my bottom lip, continuing to play with my piercing. It hadn't even been five minutes and he was done and I started laughing when I heard him stop the gun.

"Ta da!" he said, mimicking me.

I looked at my finger and threw my head back laughing harder than before, bringing my hand close to my face and examining it from every angle.

"Let's make?" I said out loud, glancing at him.

"MISTAKES!" he yelled, holding his hand in the air and I covered my face laughing. "I just gotta add an s to mine . . ." he added, bringing his hand down and staring at his finger.

"Oh my fucking God."

"You thought you could out smartass me! But I am the master smartass! Now I just made your rude tattoo into something so fucking childish!" he yelled, laughing so hard that he could barely speak.

"We have friendship tattoos now, you know that, right?" I asked.

My cheeks hurt from all the smiling I was doing.

He nodded, still giggling. "I know. We have basic white girl best friend tattoos," he laughed.

"Let's make mistakes," I said, now shaking my head. "So stupid," I snorted.

"Right?!" he yelled, throwing a hand up for a high five.

Laughing and shaking my head once more, I slapped my hand against his and smiled back at my finger.

"That was actually kinda fun . . ." I mumbled.

"*Right?!*"

Then, as if on cue, his appointment showed up for his back session. I watched Jimmy's face fall as he wrapped my finger and he sighed.

"Hey, buddy! I'll be ready in a few seconds!" he called out, then looked at me and pouted, finishing the wrap. "Sorry."

"Hey, no no! This was fun!" I said, smiling down at my bandaged finger.

"Don't think I'm kicking you out . . ."

"J, I don't think you're kicking me out. It's fine. I'll see you later," I laughed, getting up and stretching.

He nodded. "And if John is out there, you . . . pre-paid for this one," he explained, quickly cleaning up his space.

I turned to look at him and arched my brow, staring down at my new tattoo once more.

"John?" I asked.

He nodded, now getting his things set up for his appointment. "Owner. He's not to keen on freebies," he winked.

My face fell and he laughed.

"He's rarely here, but I'm just saying, if he is . . . it's nothing to worry about," he added.

I swallowed the lump in my throat and nodded. "Kay."

"Now get outta here. And make sure you don't do anything today! Angela's rules, not mine!" he yelled as I started walking out of the room.

I forced a laugh and left waving.

"Well. C'mon. Lemme see," Nils said, leaning on the front desk.

I showed her my now red and swollen index finger and laughed again. "His says 'mistakes'," I grinned.

She snorted. "Perfect. Happy birthday, kiddo. We'll see you tonight," she winked.

I scrunched up my nose, stuck my tongue out at her and then left.

I successfully did nothing all day. I lounged around the apartment watching TV with Poppy and ate junk food in nothing but sweatpants. It felt nice to have a full-out lazy day. I made the bed and did some dishes, but other than that, I just watched TV and napped. I didn't live an exciting life. Jimmy finally came home around 10:30 p.m. and was yawning; his hat was missing, his hair was a mess and there was ink all over his hands. I knew he would be home around this time, and I made sure to put a shirt back on before he walked in.

"Hey-yo," he yawned, tossing his keys and kicking the door closed.

He walked over to the couch and flopped over the back rest, sighing loudly. I quickly sat up to get out of his way and started laughing.

"Long day?" I asked.

He nodded slowly. Sluggishly lifting his head, he looked at me and pouted. "Would it be okay with you if we didn't go out tonight?" he asked quietly.

I was still smiling. "J, I didn't want a big thing anyways. I don't like all the attention being about me. I'd be much happier if we stayed in tonight. We can order Chinese food or something."

He closed his eyes and fell limp against the couch, groaning loudly. "Oh my God, that sounds perfect," he whined, now sprawling his arms out straight across the couch.

I got up and headed toward the kitchen, reaching on top of the fridge and grabbing the menu for the Chinese restaurant I got him hooked on.

"Just the usual?" I asked, picking up my cell phone.

He gave me the thumbs up, so I dialed the number and gave them our order, requesting for delivery.

Watching *American Dad* and waiting for the food to come, Jimmy had changed into a clean shirt and sweatpants, then fell asleep on the couch. Moaning in his sleep, I glanced over to see him uncomfortably trying to change positions. My arms crossed, I quickly moved them out of the way when he decided to lay on his back and stretch his legs out on top of me. Laughing, I rested my arms on his shins and went back to watching TV. Moments later, there was a knock on the door and he jolted awake. Nudging his legs off me, I got up to go get the food. Walking back with my arms full, I pushed the coffee table out of the way with my foot and sat down on the floor with all the food. Whenever we ordered Chinese food, we ordered enough for a family of six, so we *had* to sit on the floor to make room for everything. Turning on the PS4, I searched for the controller so I could click on Netflix. Lately, we were binge watching *The Big Bang Theory*. Jimmy finally got off the couch and walked to the kitchen to grab us napkins and plates, then came back with a lit numbered birthday candle. Turning around and staring at it, I started laughing and sat back, watching as he shoved it into one of my chicken balls.

"What the fuck?" I laughed. "Why the number nine?" I asked, staring at the lit candle.

He sat down across from me and shrugged. "They didn't have any twos. But they did have a nine, so . . . I figured it was better than nothing," he smiled.

Laughing even harder, I suddenly felt a choke in my throat and felt a pout coming on.

"Happy birthday!" he yelled, yawning afterwards.

Still laughing, I smiled at the candle with sad eyes. Not once had I ever had *anyone* celebrate my birthday, let alone like this. I usually sat alone in my apartment with Poppy and watched movies until I fell asleep. The birthdays with my family were selectively picked from my memory. Regardless that we didn't go out with everyone, I was happy just to spend it here with Jimmy. He saw the sadness in my eyes and his face dropped.

"What's wrong?!"

I was quick to shake my head. "Nothing. I love it. I've just never had . . . *this* before," I said, sniffling, quickly blinking away any tears. "It's always just been me, myself and I," I added.

He started laughing and threw another chicken ball at my head. "Well, cut it out, man! And blow that candle out before you get wax all over everything! But make sure you make a wish."

I went back to laughing and shook my head. "You're a fucking freak," I said, leaning over and blowing out the candle.

Chapter 10

We still hadn't bought a bed, but we had been keeping our word about taking turns between the couch and the bed. I didn't mind, to be completely honest. The bed was nice, and the couch wasn't awful; I was just grateful to not be homeless. This week, I had the bed, but I couldn't sleep. We decided to keep the air off to save some money, so we slept with all the windows open to get some air flow; regardless that the air flow was hot and filled with pollution.

I kicked all the blankets off and was sprawled out across the entire bed in only my boxers. Jimmy had one leg hanging off the couch and the other hooked over the back, both arms doing the same. He was snoring. I couldn't get comfortable and was making the sheets damp from all the sweat. Even Poppy was sleeping in the kitchen on the cool tile floor. Rolling onto my back, I stared at the ceiling and sighed. The room was glowing from the city lights outside. Abruptly getting to my feet, I pushed open the balcony door and stood outside, leaning against the railings and looking at the busy street below.

Highland was packed with cars, even at this ungodly hour in the morning. In LA, everybody always had somewhere to be. Hearing sirens further down the road, I looked to my right and saw a firetruck trying to make its way through the crowded street. They ended up going on the other side of the road and drove against the traffic since that side seemed to be less busy. They got to Hollywood Boulevard which I could *just* see in the distance, then turned left. Shortly after, a police cruiser and an ambulance came screaming after. I almost laughed out loud. The city was never quiet. There was a small breeze, but it was hot and smelled like city smog. Then again, it was better than nothing.

I turned around so I could see Jimmy inside, awkwardly sprawled on the couch, also in nothing but his boxers. I sighed. We were roommates now which I never saw coming, but I also didn't really plan for my brother to burn my apartment building down to the ground. *How did this all happen so quickly?* Jimmy and I only met back in June and yet here I was . . . standing on his balcony in my boxers, sleeping in his bed. I tensed when he yawned, stretching his arms, then turning over; his back now facing me. I felt my eyes staring at his tattoos, then I felt my stomach get tight, so I quickly turned back around to stare out at the city skyline.

It was then I noticed that I could see Starbucks from here. We were high enough that we cascaded over the shorter buildings, and because of that, I could see all the way down to Melrose Avenue. The far corner was Vine Street and right there was the Starbucks I worked at. Kind of cool. Sighing and smiling, I had to be more thankful for where I was. Things were shitty in the beginning, but I made a new beginning for myself and it really did turn out better than I first anticipated. And after meeting Jimmy, I felt like things were only going to get better. I felt a wider smile play at my lips and this time, my sigh was a positive one—a sigh of relief. I could feel myself letting things go instead of holding onto them for the first time in my life and it felt good. I turned on my heel and walked back inside, leaving the door open and walking to the kitchen to grab myself a cold glass of water. I chugged it back and then got back into bed, forcing myself to fall asleep.

That same morning, I woke up to the smell of eggs, bacon and coffee. I smiled, opening my eyes.

"Morning!" Jimmy greeted, throwing the bacon up in the air, then catching it again with the pan.

"Morning . . ." I yawned, sitting up and scratching my messy bed head.

"Did you have an equally shitty sleep?" he asked, turning around and flicking off the coffee machine.

I nodded, yawning once more before getting out of bed. "I'm gonna shower quick. I was sweating all night."

"Nice! Good thing the bed's all yours this week," he laughed, winking at me.

I stuck my tongue out at him, then went to the bathroom and closed the door, starting the shower.

When I got out, I saw that he had neatly organized a designated eating area on the couch in front of the TV with coffee, a glass of orange juice, and bacon and eggs and toast for each of us. I came out with a towel wrapped around my waist and laughed.

"What's the occasion?" I asked, walking over and taking a piece of toast.

I shoved its entirety in my mouth at once and smiled at him.

"No occasion!" he smiled.

I walked over and grabbed my clothes for work, then went to get changed in the bathroom. When I came out, I caught Jimmy tossing tiny pieces of bacon to Poppy.

"Oi!" I yelled, running over and picking up the remaining pieces from the ground and throwing them out.

They both frowned at me.

"No, no. No human food," I said, shaking my finger in front of his face.

He snorted. "Human food? It's meat! Cats eat meat!" he said.

"Still! It's fatty and greasy. She's still little. I am not secured financially to be paying for any vet bills."

"You're no fun," he huffed, stabbing his eggs with his toast.

I finally sat down on the couch and started eating my breakfast.

"But seriously. What's the occasion?" I asked, sipping my orange juice.

He frowned again. "No occasion. I can't make a nice breakfast for my roomie?" he asked, nudging me and starting to smile.

I started laughing. "When are you gonna drop the whole 'roomie' thing?" I asked, since he had been throwing the word around since I officially moved in.

He shrugged. "Novelty hasn't worn off yet," he grinned.

I rolled my eyes, then stuffed my face with bacon. Casually glancing at my phone, I started choking.

"That's already the time?! I gotta go!" I yelled, quickly standing and chugging my coffee, followed by my orange juice.

Jimmy looked up at me pouting. I smiled and shoved the last piece of toast in my mouth while hopping on one foot and putting a shoe on.

"Sorry, J!" I spat. "I didn't realize that was the time. I gotta open the shop today!"

He shrugged. "Yeah, so do I," he mumbled with a mouth full of food.

I forced a laugh. "Yeah, only the difference for you is you open at noon. I should be opening *now!*" I said, now bouncing on my other foot to put on my other shoe.

He stared at me and sipped his coffee with his pinky in the air. I wiped my mouth of any crumbs and started laughing.

"Okay well, I'm doing a long shift today. I gotta cover for Angie tonight, so I won't be home until later."

"Aight," he mumbled, stuffing his face with more toast than his mouth could handle.

"Keys!" I called, keeping mine in my hand and throwing his keys toward him.

He casually reached up and caught them without even having to turn around while I made a sprint down the hallway toward the elevators. This was usually how our mornings went. He was the cool, calm and collected one; he never had a care in the world if he was late or on time. Whereas I, even when I thought I was on time, was always hurrying as if I was running late. We had grown a coordinated routine where I would scramble around him and he would just sit there, hence me throwing the apartment keys at him and he blindly catching them like some sort of circus act.

"BYE, J!" I yelled just before the door slammed shut.

Work was completely uneventful. Serving coffee to people every day all day was starting to get really tiresome, and now that I was living with Jimmy and had to buy my life back, I found myself thinking of different job opportunities. Not to mention the rent I was going to be paying Jimmy in the meantime.

After Angie left, I slowly cleaned for the rest of the night until it was time to close shop. Nine o'clock came, I locked the front door to the building and slowly made my way to my new home. My walking commute had gone from five minutes to over half an hour, but I couldn't complain. I don't know where I'd be without Jimmy. Key fobbing my way in, I opened the door and saw him passed out on the bed with Poppy. His hands were covered in ink again and his hair was messier than normal. I turned all the lights off except for the kitchen and opened the fridge to make myself dinner but was surprised to see a plate with pizza on it. A little post-it note sat on top that read: *look, pizza!* with a smiley face and a pizza slice doodle. I looked back at Jimmy's motionless body and smiled. I ate in front of the TV, the volume barely noticeable, then stripped everything so I was just in my boxers. Even this late at night, it was almost ninety degrees out. Opening the balcony door for that smoggy wind flow, I walked back to the couch and puffed the pillows a few times before passing out.

The next morning, I woke up and frowned, looking around the room to find Jimmy asleep on the couch with myself in the bed. I sighed, quickly standing up and shoving his shoulders.

"J," I mumbled.

He groaned, turning over and shoving his face into the back cushions.

"J!" I said once more, shaking him harder.

"Whaaaaaat," he whined.

"Did you move me over to the bed?" I asked, still frowning.

He shrugged. "You're still on Bed Week," he mumbled.

"Yeah, but you were passed out on the bed last night. I was fine on the couch . . ."

He shrugged again.

I sighed, biting my bottom lip and playing with my piercing. "How'd you do it?" I asked.

After all, I *was* only wearing boxers last night. He turned over and stared at me with one eye half open, his hair sticking to his face. I tried to hide my smile.

"Do what?" he asked.

"Move me. How'd you move me over to the bed?" I felt my face get hot.

"I dragged you, then kinda . . . tossed you and folded you," he said with a smile, stretching and yawning, then turned back over, hands ruffling through his hair.

"Haha, oh. Is that all?" I instantly felt myself cool down, but I still had to walk away. "Do you work today?" I asked, walking toward the kitchen and turning on the coffee machine.

"Nah. I'm giving myself the day off because last night was a shit show."

"Yeah, I noticed. You're still covered in ink," I pointed out.

He looked at his arms and sighed. "I'm gonna shower . . ." he mumbled, sitting up and shuffling off to the bathroom.

"Well, I'm only a half day today!" I called once I heard the shower start running.

Making myself a coffee, I leaned against the counter and took baby sips because it was still piping hot. Jimmy suddenly opened the bathroom door and stood out completely naked and I choked on my coffee, turning away laughing.

"JAMES!" I yelled.

He frowned. "What? We're all bros here," he said, slowly walking toward me. "Poppy on the other hand . . . I'm a little concerned about her. She should look away. Not to mention, she's underage," he said, grinning with his hands on his hips.

My back to him, I sighed, turning around and making sure my eyes remained in contact with his. I refused to look anywhere else.

"You're a half day, huh? We should go buy you your bed today then," he said.

I stood my ground, trying my best not to look as nervous as I actually was. He stood in front of me smirking, got unnecessarily close, then reached behind me and grabbed his mug of coffee over my shoulder.

"Thanks for the coffee," he grinned, then walked back to the bathroom and kicked the door closed.

I let out a huge sigh of relief and felt my shoulders drop. I could feel my heartbeat in my face. Looking at the time, I groaned because it wasn't time to leave yet but I had to get out of this building. Fast. I felt awkward even though I had no reason to be. Guys were naked in front of each other all the time, like in change rooms 'n' shit—that was half the fun of being a guy . . . right? *Right?!*

"Well I gotta get going!" I called out, closing my eyes, half expecting him to call my bluff. I held my breath waiting for him to respond.

"Okay! I'll see you later!" he called back.

Slowly exhaling, I opened my eyes and grabbed my keys to the shop. "Okay . . ." I mumbled to myself, opening the door and leaving.

Reaching the street, I untangled my earbuds and sighed loudly as I did so. I could still feel my heartbeat in my face and thinking back to what just happened, I started laughing. Shaking my head and sighing once more, I got my earbuds untangled and placed them both in my ears.

"Oh, James . . ." I mumbled to myself, grabbing my iPod and searching for a certain song.

Lately, I had been binging Twenty One Pilots, and their album *Blurryface* was currently living on repeat. Staring up at the sunrise, I smiled at its beauty and began my walk to work. I was going to be *way* too early, so I decided to take my time. I had to admit, I kind of missed Rufus. It had been a while since I last saw him. I wondered what he'd been up to. He was probably wondering about me as well. I hadn't brought him Starbucks freebies in almost a month and the longer I thought about it, the more I reassured myself that I'd bring him some today after work. Even if it was now out of my way, it was the nice thing to do.

Not even getting two blocks away from the apartment, I could already feel myself working up a sweat. It wasn't even 6:00 a.m. yet and was already seventy-eight degrees out. Gotta love that Californian heat. The walk was just over half an hour from Jimmy's apartment, but I didn't mind. The change in scenery was nice. Plus, it was nice that I could walk to work every day. I didn't know where I'd be if I had to buy a car and had that as another expense. Or public transit. Gross. Public transit around here was disgusting.

But as pleasant as walking was, sometimes the city had its downsides. For example, the hooded person who had been following me since I left the apartment. Highland wasn't a sketchy area, but this person in particular gave me a bad gut feeling. I glanced at them over my shoulder to see if I knew who it was, but their head was ducked and I couldn't make out a face. I quickened my pace only a little, just to test the stranger, and sure enough, they did the same. Squeezing my phone in my pocket, I kept my fingers wrapped around it in case I had to make any quick decisions, but was so preoccupied by the person behind me, I didn't pay attention to what was in front of me and bumped into someone else.

"Oh!" I looked up and stepped back, now bumping into the stranger behind me. Looking back and forth between the two, I frowned. "Okaaay . . . can I help you?" I asked, still looking back and forth.

I mentally pinched myself for always being so polite. I shouldn't be standing around making friends; I should be *running*. Taking out both ear buds, I shoved my iPod in my pocket just as the guy behind me took out a baseball bat from behind his back and hit me in the back of my legs. I fell to the ground and my first reaction was to grab my legs and tuck them up.

"*Dude*, what the *fuck*?!" I screamed.

The same guy smacked my knuckles with the bat, then swung at my right knee cap. I screamed in immense pain, feeling it shatter as I tried to crawl away.

"Fuck off! What the fuck did I ever do to you?!" I screamed, knuckles bleeding and blood now seeping through my pants.

The guy I bumped into the first time walked around me and grabbed me under my armpits, picking me up and walking backwards, dragging me out in front of him. I flailed my one leg as best as I could, screaming and fighting against him.

"No! Stop!" I yelled.

He dragged me into the closest alleyway, the guy with the baseball bat walking in front of me. Once dropped, I quickly crawled backwards until my back hit the wall. I was sweating and shaking, tears pouring down my face.

"Who . . . who are you? What do you *want* from me?" I stuttered.

Suddenly, another man turned the corner and walked into the alleyway, also wearing a hoodie. He pulled the hood off and glared at me, nose crooked. My eyes widened and I gasped, feeling sick to my stomach.

"Aaron . . . I . . ."

"Yeah, who's the fucking squealer now, huh? Suddenly not so tough. Where's your gay ass bodyguard, Dallas?" he spat, walking closer toward me.

I tried backing up further, although it was impossible with the wall behind me.

"Aaron, you burned down my fucking house! You tricked me into throwing a party in my own apartment and then you burned it down!" I screamed. My voice was cracking.

My good hand was holding my bad knee, blood soaking through my pants and covering my palm and fingers. He walked until he stood directly above me and he glared down at me. Taking the bat from his friend, he smacked it repeatedly in his palm.

"The police came looking for me. They kicked down my dealer's front door. *He's* in jail. I got out," he explained.

I was happy to hear that the police had found him . . . although, somewhat disappointed it didn't pull through.

"Mom and dad *really* aren't gonna miss you . . ." he added quietly. "They already think you're dead anyways."

I curled into a smaller ball, waiting what was to come next.

"Actually, no one will miss you. No one will even notice that you're gone. Goodbye, baby brother . . ." he said, then swung the bat as hard as he could into my rib cage.

I took a few beats until I finally blacked out, choking on my own blood.

⌘

I had to blink a few times before I could fully open my eyes; the lights above me were so bright.

"Oh, thank God," a voice said and I quickly felt two hands on my arm.

I slowly turned my head to my left and had to blink a few times before Jimmy's face finally came into focus.

"J . . ." I croaked and then clenched my eyes shut.

Everything inside me was screaming in pain.

"Hey, shh. You don't need to talk. I'm right here, okay?" he said quietly.

My eyes still shut, my skin ached when my tears fell down my cheeks. Jimmy's thumb gently rubbed back and forth on my wrist.

"What . . . happened?" I whispered, now barely opening my eyes to stare at him.

His bloodshot eyes said he had been crying. "Aaron. He had some punk ass friends with him again . . ."

"I know . . . but what happened?" I asked more sternly. "How did I get here?"

"I found you," he said.

I opened my eyes fully and stared at him. "What? How?"

I wanted to speak louder but my lungs wouldn't allow it. I saw his face go pink and he ducked his head, sighing and laughing a little bit, almost embarrassed.

"J?" I squeaked.

"Dal . . . you know how you can see Starbucks from our balcony?" he asked, looking back at me.

"Yeah . . ."

"Well . . . whenever we *don't* walk together in the mornings, I stand out on the balcony and watch. I watch until I see you get to work."

"You do?" I asked, looking at him with sad eyes.

Making direct eye contact, his eyes started to water. Their colour appeared darker than normal.

"Yes. It's not that I think you need *protecting* or whatever . . ." he quoted with bunny ears. "But I feel like I need to protect you regardless . . ." he sighed and looked back down.

I smiled. "Jimmy . . ." I mumbled.

This guy . . .

He shrugged. "So, when you left this morning . . . I finished my shower and stood out on the balcony to have a smoke and watched until I saw you get to work. Only . . . I never saw you get there. It freaked me out. After you told me the story of you and your brother's history . . ." he trailed off and sighed. "That day you punched him was kick-ass, but I knew he'd want to get his revenge. His ego sounds too big to let you get away with that," he said, staring back into my eyes. "And who knew if the cops were going to find him . . ."

I was anxiously chewing the inside of my cheek. "So, what did you do?" I asked, my eyes filling with tears again.

He stared at his thumb that was still stroking my skin. "I got dressed and called you. And when there was no answer, I ran. I ran until I found you, which to my surprise didn't take very long. I thought he'd kidnap you for sure and bring you somewhere where no one would be able to find you . . . but I saw three hooded guys walk out of an alleyway, one with a bloody baseball bat and I knew exactly what happened."

"Did you kick their asses?" I asked, letting a small smile play at the corner of my lips.

He shook his head, his face remaining serious. "I wanted to, trust me. I wanted to beat them to *death*. But I didn't. You were my priority," he said.

I let out a little sigh, then finally stared straight ahead to see my right leg in a cast.

"Your kneecap is broken, and you have six broken ribs. You're lucky you don't have a punctured lung. And your knuckles are fine, in a sense. I mean, none of them are broken. Just bruised and bloody," he explained.

I looked down at my torso and saw my entire chest wrapped up and bandaged. I felt my face tense and my lips instantly turned into a pout. Biting my bottom lip, I clenched my teeth and closed my eyes; wincing when the tears fell onto my sensitive skin. I couldn't sob since harsh breathing hurt too much, so instead, I took quick little inhales and long and exaggerated exhales. Jimmy sat in silence, his thumb still slowly stroking my wrist.

Chapter 11

The healing process was a slow and painful one. I had never broken anything before, and here I was in a full leg cast, and torso cast—which I didn't even know was a thing. I was given a wheelchair since crutches involved too much movement of my core and I wasn't supposed to exert myself. Thankfully, Jimmy's elevator worked, although I didn't do too much coming and going from the apartment. I spent most of my days on the couch heavily drugged with pain medication until the two week mark came and Jimmy brought me back to the hospital to get some X-rays done. I felt guilty, to be honest. He was working extra shifts at the shop while also taking care of me. We ended up arguing whether I got the bed or the couch and I *insisted* on taking the couch.

"J, I spend my whole day here anyways, usually asleep. If anything, the bed is harder for me because I'd have to move," I said.

Since I was taking up the whole couch, he sat on the coffee table facing me, his arms resting on his knees while he frowned.

"Then stay in the bed and I'll turn the TV to face you," he mumbled and I frowned.

"No. You're working hard like . . . full days, seven days a week. You deserve the bed."

"You're broken!" he fought back, sitting up and clenching his fists.

"I don't care! I don't want the bed! I'm honestly more comfortable on the couch!" I yelled, then closed my eyes and winced.

Talking was exhausting, let alone yelling. He noticed this and sat closer to me, his body language instantly changing.

"I'm sorry, I'm sorry! The couch is what you want, then the couch is what you get!" he said all too quickly, and I forced a laugh, placing a hand on my ribs.

"It's fine," I whispered.

Staring at him, I sunk deeper into the couch and exhaled slowly.

"Just . . . please. You're working so hard for the both of us on top of taking care of me and taking me to all my appointments. You come home every night exhausted. Just take the bed," I said, staring directly into his eyes.

He sighed. "Okay."

The following afternoon, I was mind-numbingly scrolling through Netflix, uncommitted to starting anything new, but also not in the mood for anything I had already seen. I had eventually settled for *Lord of the Rings: The Fellowship of the Ring*, but ended up falling asleep not even fifteen minutes in. Waking up hours later, I winced at the kink in my neck and sighed loudly, tilting my head to the side and rubbing the sore spot. Staring at the TV, I frowned at the fact that the PS4 had turned itself off, and I was staring at my reflection in the black screen.

"So much for that . . ." I mumbled to myself, grabbing the television remote and turning it off.

Sighing loudly, I leaned back in the couch and stared up at the ceiling. Glancing to my side, I saw that the sun had already set and I had successfully done nothing all day. I was beyond bored and still had a long healing process ahead of me. Whining and uncomfortably trying to get comfortable, it was then I noticed on the ceiling, in the far corner of the room, was a big, fat, black spider. I *hated* spiders. Hate was putting it lightly. I was borderline terrified of them.

"How long have you been there?" I asked, staring at it.

I suddenly didn't want to look anywhere else, just in case it decided to make a run for it. Sighing loudly, I painfully sat up on the couch and leaned against the back pillows, tensing when the spider moved an inch.

"No! No. You just stay where you are," I mumbled, refusing to blink as I continued to adjust myself into a sitting position.

It moved again and started following the length of the room along the ceiling.

"No, no, no, no, nooooooo. Pleeeeease stay still," I whined, my eyes going wide.

Quickly glancing at the coffee table, I saw my phone. Looking back up at the spider, I slowly and painfully reached out and grabbed it with the very tip of my fingers.

"Gotcha!" I smiled, staring at the time on my lock screen.

Jimmy would be home any minute now and I would make the spider his problem. Unless he was also scared of spiders, then we would be in trouble, but something about him told me he wasn't. I didn't know any one else who had such an irrational fear like me, except Angela. Once there was a spider in the kitchen at work and it was the end of the world as we knew it. Complete chaos; neither one of us being able to catch it or kill it. We ended up propping open the fire exit door and herding it outside. Pathetic, but terrifying. Unfortunately for me, I couldn't even move from the couch.

Staring back up at the eight-legged demon, I whimpered when I saw that it had left where the ceiling and wall met and was now crawling toward me upside down on the ceiling. My shoulders sank and I felt my heartbeat quicken.

"Come ooonnn!" I whined, tensing where I sat on the couch.

It wasn't crawling in a straight line, but it was still coming toward me nonetheless. Quickly staring around the room, I searched for an escape, but there wasn't any. My wheelchair was too far out of reach, and there was no way I could get to the bed on my own. Sighing and whining at the same time, I forced a laugh at how pathetic I was. Of *course* this had to happen.

Sitting up almost perfectly straight, I winced at my ribs but continued to stare up at the spider as it now approached directly above me. I held my breath and draped my arm over the back of the couch, holding myself in an upright position. For a moment, it didn't move and neither did I.

"You can smell my fear, can't you . . ." I mumbled, glaring at it.

Taking a few more steps, it stopped once more before dropping an inch on a web. I jumped and everything screamed in pain.

"Don't you—*fuck! Ow!*" I snapped, closing my eyes and placing my hand on my core.

Glaring back up at the spider, it dangled an inch from the ceiling and didn't move.

"Fuck you!" I yelled, grabbing onto the couch once more to sit up.

I tensed when it dropped another inch, but this time, I forced myself up to sit on the arm rest of the couch.

"Don't you fucking dare!" I yelled, but it obviously didn't speak English and suddenly dropped down onto my lap.

I started screaming and without hesitation, threw myself over the back of the couch and crashed on the hardwood floor. Flailing my arms and my one leg, I threw my blanket off and crawled backwards.

"*FUCK!*" I screamed, wrapping my arms around my core and biting my lip.

Hearing the front door unlock, I laid flat on the floor and whined in pain. Everything in my body was screaming and even though Jimmy walked in with Nils, both laughing at something, it took him only a point of a second to notice me.

"*Dallas?!*" he yelled, dropping his keys and running to my side.

"I'm fine, I'm fine! Just—*erugh!* There's a spider!" I whined, keeping one arm wrapped around my ribs while I pointed to the pile of blankets with my other hand.

He looked like he was about to pick me up, but froze and frowned at me.

"What?"

"Spider! There's a spider in the blankets!" I continued to yell.

Nils closed the door behind her and walked up to the pile of blankets, grabbing one end and lifting it to give it a good shake. Still in pain, I tensed. Sure enough, the little fucker came running out from underneath the blanket and made a run toward the kitchen.

"Ew," Nils mumbled, stepping out and stepping on it with her boot.

Jimmy, still on the floor with me, turned to stare at me and arched a brow.

"So . . . super scared of spiders, are'ya?" he asked, smiling a little.

I sighed loudly and laid out flat on the floor, closing my eyes and frowning.

"Terrified," I mumbled, resting my hand on my chest.

"How did you end up on the floor from the couch?" Nils asked, picking up the dead spider with a Kleenex.

I opened my eyes to stare at the two of them and pouted.

"It was on the ceiling and it crawled above me, then dropped," I explained, still pouting.

They both laughed and Jimmy sighed.

"Ya'big dummy. That fall probably hurt."

"Fucking killed," I said and he laughed again.

Staring at me, he sighed. "Well, how are we gonna get you back up?" he asked and I shrugged.

"I didn't think about it as I was throwing myself over the couch," I admitted.

He sighed. "Come on, then . . ." he mumbled, placing one arm behind my back for support while his other hand grabbed mine.

He was strong, and even though it hurt for me to curl myself, he pulled me up onto my feet. My leg cast made it awkward, but we made it work. Throwing my arm over his shoulder, I hopped over to the couch and he cautiously sat me down. Nils took her boots off at the door and started laughing, coming over and joining me on the couch.

"Dramatic evening?" she asked, bringing her legs up and sitting cross-legged.

I leaned my head back, closed my eyes and sighed. "You have no idea."

Week four, I could feel cabin fever kicking in. Thankfully, my knee was healing a lot faster than anyone had anticipated, and I had downgraded to a smaller and thinner cast. As for my ribs, I had three more weeks in my cast before there was even *talk* of it being removed, but at least now I could use crutches and I had gotten rid of the wheelchair. I think Jimmy was relieved that I was semi-mobile, but every move I made when he was around, he treated me like a child.

Personal hygiene was also a difficult issue since my casts couldn't get wet. Sitting on the toilet, I sat in my boxers while Jimmy wrapped my leg cast with plastic bags and taped them down so no water could get in. Painfully holding my arms above my head, I winced in pain as he did the same to the cast on my torso.

"Good?" he asked, standing and taking a step back.

I looked down at my body and sighed, looking up at him and forcing a smile. "Yeah. Thanks, J," I mumbled, beyond sick of the process.

Pulling back the shower curtain, he leaned in and turned the water on, then stared at me and bit his lip, shoving his hands in his pockets.

"Only a little while longer," he said and I nodded.

Standing in front of me, he reached out and I was quick to grab his hand and force myself into a standing position. It was a fifty-fifty group effort of both him helping me up, and me trying to help myself. I was pathetic, really.

Getting to my feet, I sighed loudly and rested all my weight on my good foot.

"Yeah . . ." I mumbled, smiling at him.

He took a step back and continued to stare at me with sad eyes, then sighed. "Okay. Call if you need help with anything," he said and I nodded.

"Will do. Thanks."

Then he left, closing the door behind him. Removing my boxers was the hardest part of the whole process, but there was no way in hell I was going to let him help me with that too. The shower itself took twice as long since I had to always hold onto something as I washed my hair and body, but I was determined and always got the job done. Getting out, I slowly lowered myself back down on the toilet and threw on my clean boxers, leaning back and sighing loudly.

"Jaaammmeesss," I whined, closing my eyes and leaning my head against the wall, my wet hair dripping on my face.

He walked in with scissors in hand, used to the routine. I slowly towel dried my hair as he cut the tape off my leg, then raised my arms when he did the same to my torso.

The second week of October, I finally got the leg cast off *and* the cast for my ribs. It felt good to finally be out of my plaster shell, but I felt very vulnerable. I wasn't back to work yet, which I hated. It wasn't like I was making money while I was off, and I knew it meant Angela had to work twice as hard. I'm the one that got hurt and yet the only two people in my life that really mattered to me were also affected and forced to work overtime. I was in a constant state of gratitude and guilt.

I started going to the shop with Jimmy almost every day since I was encouraged to walk and get my strength back up. Plus, in the long run, it was also good for my lungs to regain my cardio strength. The first few days *sucked*. It wasn't *that* far of a walk, but my body wasn't used to it mentally or physically and I'd always end up having to stop and lean against a building to catch my breath.

"This is so fucking stupid. How can walking make me run out of breath?" I panted, bending over and resting my hands on my knees.

Jimmy stood in front of me and stared down at me with a concerning look, a cigarette sticking out of his mouth.

"I can give you a piggyback ride," he smiled and I huffed, standing back up and slowly stretching my back.

"That would defeat the purpose, J," I mumbled. "Whatever. It's fine. Let's keep going," I said.

Nils was always so enthusiastic whenever I walked in. Jimmy had to constantly remind her to keep her energy on a down low around me since I was 'fragile', which always resulted in gentle hugs.

"I think I could get used to this. Stop healing. Or better yet, just get a job here! We can always use an extra set of hands!" she grinned and I laughed, following Jimmy into his room where I instantly laid down on the tattoo bed to catch my breath.

"He doesn't wanna be Shop Bitch, Nilly," he laughed, sitting on his chair and starting to set up.

I closed my eyes and smiled. "That would be fun. But sorry. I'm at least *good* at my job at Starbucks," I said, resting my hands on my chest and Nils scuffed.

"You're good at your job here too," she said, opening a can of Red Bull and taking a sip.

I opened my eyes at the sound and stared at her, starting to laugh.

"What *is* it with you and that energy drink?" I asked.

She took another sip and shrugged.

"Oh yeah. Nilly is hella addicted to that shit. It's best not to ask," Jimmy mumbled, continuing to set up.

Turning my head, I watched him gather his little containers of inks and sighed, lifting my leg up and rubbing my knee; I could see Nils staring at me from the doorway.

"Have you heard anything from the police yet?" she asked and I shook my head.

"No. There's nothing they can really do. We have no proof that Aaron did it other than Jimmy as a *sort of* eyewitness," I explained.

"Yeah, and saying I saw three guys leave an alleyway holding a baseball bat isn't really a lot to move forward with," Jimmy added.

Leaning against the door frame, Nils sighed.

"So like, where's this guy live? When do we get to go kick the shit outta him?" she asked, mainly staring at Jimmy.

I stared around the room at Jimmy's art and laughed.

"Trust me. If I had that information, the shit would already have been kicked out," he mumbled darkly, cleaning his tattoo gun but keeping his back to us.

My face fell and I turned to stare at him, side-glancing at Nils. She scrunched up her nose and gave me a little wave, quietly leaving the room. It was quiet for a moment as I stared up at the ceiling and went back to stretching my leg.

"Soooo the doctor said I could go back to work starting Monday . . ." I mumbled.

"I can walk you in the morning," he said and I frowned, looking back at him.

"Oh. Okay, cool. Thanks," I smiled, lifting my other leg and stretching it the same way.

"It's nothing . . ." he responded in a monotone voice.

I frowned again. "J, it's not nothing. You've gone beyond expectations of helping me out for more than two months straight. I don't think you really understand how grateful I am. If it wasn't for you—"

"Okay, Dallas. I know. You're welcome. I don't really wanna talk about it anymore, okay?" he snapped, turning and staring at me.

I jumped a bit because I wasn't really expecting the comeback, then sighed. "Okay . . . sorry . . ." I mumbled.

He ducked his head and sighed, turning around to face me. "Look, I'm sorry. But it was a *much* different experience for me."

I arched a brow and forced a laugh. "For you? I was the one—"

"I don't mean it like that! I just mean . . ." he stopped what he was doing and leaned back in his chair. "I would watch you go to work for a reason. And Aaron just amplified that reason. You were passed out in a puddle of your own blood. It was just dripping out of your mouth like nothing . . . I see blood almost every day and it's never once bothered me . . ." he sighed. "So just . . . yeah, it's over with now and you're healing and let's just forget about it, okay? And if we ever, God forbid, run into your brother again, I'll fucking kill him on the spot. Got it?" he asked while staring at me.

I didn't say anything and simply nodded.

We walked back to the apartment that night in silence.

"So, I'm off tomorrow and I was thinking we could finally go buy your bed?" he asked and I nodded.

"Yeah, but J . . . a bed means I'm staying. I still wanna look for my own place," I added and he arched his brow, almost laughing.

"And have you been? Looking, I mean," he asked.

Unlocking the door, he walked in before me and I closed it behind us, staring at the ground and frowning.

"Well . . . no . . ."

"So, why bother? It's so much fun living with me!" he smirked, kicking off his shoes and opening the fridge in search for a beer.

I kicked off my own shoes and stared at him, snorting. "But I can't just—you've done *so* much for me already. Like more than the *last* time I said this . . ." I laughed, walking over to the couch and sprawling out.

I did this almost every night once we got home because I was *exhausted*.

"Yeah, and I'm going to *keep* doing stuff for you even if you don't live here. So, why don't you just make it easier for me and stay?" he asked smiling, bringing a beer to his lips.

I sighed. Staring up at the ceiling, I stayed quiet as I thought about the pros and cons. And unfortunately, there were mainly pros and barely any cons.

"Fine. Then this whole . . . lack of rent thing has to stop. Let me pay you for the months I've missed."

"Hell no! You can start paying as of right now, but no catching up . . ."

"Why not?!" I whined, sitting up and staring at him.

"Because I said so," he smiled, sipping his beer once more.

I overexaggerated my sigh. "Fine."

"So, you're going to stay?" he grinned, practically bouncing over to stand above me.

I was lying on my back and stared up at him, frowning.

"I'll stay," I mumbled.

He held his beer with his mouth and started clapping like a child. "Woohoo!" he cheered into the bottle, then bent down and ruffled both hands through my hair.

I started yelling and curled into a ball until he walked back into the kitchen laughing.

"So, what do you want for dinner, *roomie*?" he asked, putting down the beer and searching through the fridge again.

I groaned loudly since we had *just* gotten rid of the whole 'roomie' thing.

"Food," I mumbled back, smiling up at the ceiling.

He threw a cherry tomato at my head and I started laughing.

The following day, we *did* end up going bed shopping and it was way more fun than necessary. What started out as casually walking through Ikea, turned into playfully pushing each other over onto mattresses. But eventually, I lost my breath and bent over on one of the beds, hugging myself.

"Sorry . . . I forget about the broken rib thing sometimes . . ." Jimmy said, staring at me with concern.

I waved my hand at him, trying to catch my breath. "It's okay. I do too," I panted.

"Okay. We'll get serious now. No more pushing around. What kind of bed do you want?" he asked, placing his hands on his hips and looking around.

I sat up straight and stretched back, feeling my spine crack; the stretch feeling both awful and amazing on my core.

"I don't know . . ." I paused. "J, where's this thing going to go?" I asked, looking up at him.

He bit his bottom lip and continued to look around at all the mattress setups, then shrugged.

"I dunno. Beside mine?" he smiled.

I started laughing. "There's no room . . . there's a reason bachelor apartments are called so . . ."

"I'm not a bachelor!" he yelled in defense and I snorted.

"I mean . . . *technically,* you are," I smiled and he turned to look at me, appalled.

I ducked my head and started laughing. "Either way. I don't think your place is made for two beds . . ." I added, standing and stretching once more.

He sighed. "Well . . . what are we going to do then? You need a bed . . ."

Both of us were silent, looking around the store.

"We could look for a newer, bigger apartment?" he asked and I frowned.

"I'm not making you pack up and move just because of me. If that's the case, then I can just look for my own place," I said.

"I mean, you *could*, but do you really *want* to?" he asked with a smirk.

I smirked in return and rolled my eyes. "No."

"Exactly. So—"

"We could just keep sharing the bed and couch?" I asked, cutting him off and forcing a smile. "I honestly don't mind," I added.

He thought for a moment, then sighed loudly. "I mean, fine. But only until we figure this out. There *has* to be a way to fit two beds in there . . . we'll figure something out . . ." he mumbled. "And you're still getting the bed for at *least* another week!" he added.

I laughed. "That's totally fine with me," I smiled, and we made our way toward the exit.

Getting off the metro at Hollywood and Highland, Jimmy was telling me a story about a huge tattoo he had coming up, but I could barely pay attention. Every now and then, our hands would brush or our arms would bump. I didn't think he was doing it on purpose, but it also didn't bother me. I was staring at my feet as we walked and was smiling to myself every time we accidentally touched.

"Hey, so I forgot to tell you. Remember that party I told you about back when you came to No Other Place with us?"

"Jack's party?" I asked and he nodded.

"Yeah, yeah! That's tonight aaaaand I told Jacky we'd be there?" he said, more so as a question than a statement.

I laughed and shrugged. "Sure. I need more friends anyways. I only have you . . ."

"And Angela. And Nils!"

"Yeah, but I would never hang out with Angie outside of work really . . . it'd be too weird. Next thing you know, she'd be asking me to babysit her kid. And Nils, I only ever small talk with her at the shop."

"Well, she likes you, so that's all you need to know. So, is that a definite yes?" he grinned and I nodded.

"Sure!"

"Cool. I think you really hit it off with Nils. She's a babe, eh? Maybe a step further tonight? Further than shop small talk? Alcohol always helps," he grinned, this time purposely nudging me.

I continued to stare at my feet and frowned. "Doubt it . . ." I mumbled, kicking a pebble.

He started laughing and patted my back. "Jeez, have a *little* faith! Not *all* girls bite," he joked.

Chapter 12

We took turns showering and getting ready. We planned on making a pit stop at the beer store before making our way to Jack's place.

"Now, before we get there, you need to know that Jack's parents are *loaded* and he's an only child, so he's super hella spoiled. Like, spoiled is putting it lightly."

"And he decided to become a tattoo artist?" I laughed.

Jimmy shrugged. "Yeah, well, he's an amazing artist. And why get a job where you have to work hard to make good money when your parents just pay for everything," he laughed.

I frowned. "How old is he?"

"He's my age. I mean none of this as an insult! You know Jack, he's a cool guy. I'm just warning you . . . he's got a nice place and he's definitely arrogant about it. So just . . . compliment it and move on. Don't feed the beast."

I nodded. "Got'cha."

We got to the beer store and bought a little bit of everything and then caught the next bus uptown where Jack lived. Looking out the window, I slowly watched the apartments like ours turn into houses which eventually turned into nice houses and finished at oversized condos. After passing West Hollywood and Beverly Hills, the bus came to a stop just outside Century City which was more of a commercial district filled with condos and skyscrapers. A *very* pricey area. When the bus stopped and Jimmy stood up to leave, I started laughing and shook my head.

"Of *course* this is our stop . . ." I mumbled.

He glanced at me over his shoulder and grinned. "Told ya!" he laughed.

We got off the bus and walked toward some tall black gates.

"There's a code to get in?" I asked and Jimmy nodded, pressing the necessary numbers into the keypad and smiling at me over his shoulder when a little light turned green.

Seconds later, the gates started to slowly open. Walking inside, we buzzed Jack's room and got the green light almost instantly.

"Can you tell I've been here before?" he laughed, holding the door for me to go first. "Personally, I prefer our key fob system," he explained as we stepped into the elevator. "Like . . . here, someone just has to learn the code to the gate, right? Granted, there's security, but still . . ."

"And our place?" I asked, not quite understanding his point.

"Our place, *we* have the key to open the doors and make the elevator do its thing. Like . . . you'll have to *kill* me to get inside the building. Here, you can just cheat. Y'know what I mean?" he asked, seriously having obviously thought about this before.

I stared at him and started laughing. "Sure," I snorted.

Turning my attention to the floor numbers, I stared at our illuminated thirty-two and saw that it was two floors from the top. As soon as the doors opened, I followed closely behind Jimmy like a child following his mother. I was nervous. I knew I'd be the only baby in the room, and I wasn't much of a drinker anyways. Like I said before, I didn't have friends, so it's not like I got out very much to go to parties and such. Plus, Jimmy's friends were all tattoo covered, cigarette smoking 'cool' looking people. I felt extremely out of place when I was with them. Even though I hung out with a few of them already, this felt different for some reason. This was one of their houses, which everyone had been to already. Yet again, I was the odd one out. Maybe if I got super drunk, I'd be extra likeable and sociable, and all of these worries would disappear. Alcohol made this all come naturally, right? Walking down the hall toward Jack's door, you could already hear the music.

"Don't his neighbours get pissed off?" I asked and Jimmy laughed.

"Nah. His neighbours are probably already in there."

We got to the door and it was wide open, so we just walked right in. Instantly, Jimmy saw a group of his friends and walked up to them with arms open, yelling with excitement. I awkwardly followed with an equally as awkward smile on my face. I recognized these guys from the shop but had never been formally introduced. He exchanged bro hugs with a few of them, then reached back and grabbed my arm, pulling me forwards into the group and wrapping an arm over my shoulders.

"*This* is Dallas!" he grinned, saying it like I was some big deal.

I looked around at everyone and smiled. "Hi," I said awkwardly.

"So *you're* Dallas! I'm Evan," he smiled, reaching out and shaking my hand. "Jimmy's told us so much about you!" he enthused.

I arched my brow and glanced over at Jimmy who was grinning.

"You're all he fucking talks about at the shop. Even when you're already there!" the girl to my right laughed.

I turned to Jimmy and laughed. "Oh really?" I asked.

He shrugged. "Just trying to get you some street cred, man. C'mon over here, let's go see Nilly!" he urged, grabbing my arm and walking off.

I tried my best to wave goodbye to the others. "Nice finally meeting you!" I quickly yelled, tripping along behind Jimmy.

"That's Evan and Maria. Evan is kind of an in-and-out friend. Sometimes he hangs out with the gang, sometimes he doesn't. As for Maria, she used to be a piercer at No Regrets forever ago, but then she quit to go to a different parlour. No hard feelings, though! She still hangs out at NR a lot," he explained, and I nodded.

Walking up to Nils, she had already been drinking and smiled when she saw us.

"Hiya boys!" she greeted, pulling the two of us into a hug.

I winced only a little bit since my ribs were still tender.

"YO! JACKY!" Jimmy screamed, going on his tippy toes to wave at Jack over the crowd, and then running off.

"D'you want a drink?" Nils asked and I shrugged.

"Sure. He just ran off with our stuff anyways . . ." I mumbled, following her to the kitchen.

"Soooo? How are Dallas' injuries?" she asked, helping herself to the fridge. Suddenly, she turned around and stared at me with wide eyes. "Oh shit! And I just hugged you! I'm sorry!"

I laughed. "It's all good. Injuries are doing . . . alright," I said, side-glancing at Jimmy over my shoulder.

He was still with Jack, playing around with the iPod and changing song after song. Nils saw this and laughed, popping the lid off a beer for me.

"You've really seemed to kick it off with him, eh? Friendship tattoos 'n' everything," she said, handing me the beer.

Leaning in, I started laughing and asked her to repeat herself since as soon as she started talking, Jimmy and Jack figured out the surround sound and started *blasting* techno music.

"I just mean, he really likes you. You're all he talks about at work. Kind of annoying, actually. It's a good thing you're cute or I'd be *really* annoyed," she smirked, winking at me.

I forced a laugh. "Yeah . . . well, y'know. We're roommates and he said he's never had one since you two lived together, so I know he's excited."

"Yeah, but even before you moved in . . . y'know he never used to drink coffee?"

"I believe it."

"Seriously, dude. You make this kid really happy," she said, suddenly getting really serious.

She must've been a bit older than Jimmy to refer to him as a kid, but I didn't think too much of it; I was too preoccupied on my head spinning with all this new information of Jimmy talking about me. Apparently all the time, too. I smiled.

"Well, he makes me pretty happy too . . ." I said, staring at Jimmy across the room who was laughing with Jack, and not really realizing I was talking aloud.

"Oh! So, does that mean you're . . ." she trailed off and never finished the question but stared at me for a response just the same.

I tilted my head to the side.

"I mean, I totally get it if you're not comfortable saying . . ."

"I don't follow," I frowned.

"I assumed you weren't because he also wouldn't shut up about how he was going to hook you and I up," she snorted.

I laughed awkwardly. "Yeah, he told me that too." I felt my face get hot.

She smirked. "But seriously. Are you?"

"Am I what?! I don't know what you're getting at . . ." That awkward laugh happened again.

"Nilly bo billy! Fananana fo filly!" Jimmy yelled, running over and wrapping his arm around her shoulders. He grinned at me. "Oh! Looky you! You'll drink beer now but never when I offer you one at home?!" he yelled and I laughed.

He wasn't drunk, but he was obviously already having a good time.

"Yeah, that's because you always offer me one before fucking lunchtime!" I yelled back, smirking.

He shrugged, clinking our bottles together and chugging the rest of his, then looked at Nils and smiled. "What'cha guys talking about?"

She laughed. "Nothing. Saw him empty-handed. Got him a beer," she said, staring back at him.

I grinned, holding my beer up.

Jimmy stared back and forth between us, then shrugged. "Coolio. Well, Jack got out the double funnel, so c'mon!" he yelled, placing his beer in his mouth, grabbing both me and Nils by our hands, and pulling us through the crowd to the living room.

Nils laughed and rolled her eyes, and I was petrified.

"'Double funnel'? What does that mean?" I squeaked and Nils continued to laugh.

"You'll see."

The double funnel was exactly how it sounded, with a funnel at the top and two tubes going down in opposite directions. The end of each tube had a valve attached, so once the tubes were filled with alcohol, it was a three-two-one countdown before each player would open their valve and race to empty their tube the fastest. I'd never done a funnel in my life, let alone a double one. Lilly and Caleb were already in the middle of a chugging battle and Lilly was kicking Caleb's ass. Finishing her side first, she stood and flipped everyone the finger, sticking her tongue out. Caleb was still on his knees, bent over laughing.

"Yeah, she's good at sucking *and* swallowing!" he yelled.

People started laughing and cheering.

"Whatever. Still beat your ass," she smirked, walking over and grabbing herself another drink, then sitting on one of the couches.

"Lil and Cal are dating. They're always making inappropriate jokes with each other," Nils explained, standing beside me and drinking her beer.

I stood back, simply watching and enjoying the entertainment until Jimmy made eye contact with me and grabbed me by the front of my shirt.

My face fell and I instantly resisted. "J, no," I said.

"Nonsense. Let's go. You 'n' me," he said, forcing me into the middle of the circle.

The music was still playing loudly and everyone that was attending the party was watching. I hadn't had nearly enough alcohol for this.

"C'mon, Jacky. Let's do this!" Jimmy yelled, getting on his knees and grabbing his end of the funnel.

I slowly and slightly painfully did the same and stared at him with wide eyes. I had no idea what I was doing. People started clapping and cheering even louder, making my ears ring.

"J, I—"

"Take this," he said, placing my end of the funnel in my hands. "Now, he's gonna pour that in at the top and our tubes are going to fill. This valve opens your tube and you just have to drink as fast as you can . . . you'll get a feel for it pretty quickly and you'll basically just open up your throat and swallow it whole," he explained, this time leaning into my ear so I could hear him properly.

I nodded and he grinned, leaning away.

"Don't be scared, but I'm pretty fucking awesome at this," he said.

I looked at Nils who was sitting on the couch across from us, arms crossed with a beer in hand and she smiled and nodded.

"He is," she said.

I bit my bottom lip and played with my lip ring for a bit before sitting up straight with my tube in hand.

"Ready?" Jack asked and I nodded.

"Fuck yeah, bro!" Jimmy yelled.

Jack held the funnel and opened a beer, pouring the entire thing in at once, foam included. It was very nerve wracking, having no choice but to swallow something that was coming at you at fast speed. It felt like you were going to choke and drown if you didn't swallow, but Jimmy was right; the first few gulps were hard, but I got a feel for it quickly and started chugging as fast as I could. I glanced over at him and he was giving Jack the peace sign with his free hand, but then I felt my face lose colour when I realized it wasn't a peace sign at all and Jack opened a second bottle of beer, pouring it in right away. People were going nuts. I closed my eyes, but at this point, the beer was going down like butter and I didn't even feel it. Feeling my tube empty out, I bent over coughing and everyone started screaming even louder. I looked up, my face all red, and started laughing.

"DUDE! THAT WAS FUCKING AMAZING!" Jimmy laughed, patting me on the back. "NO ONE'S EVER BEAT ME BEFORE!" he yelled.

I continued to cough and wiped my mouth with my shirt, letting out a big sigh.

"That . . . fucking sucked," I mumbled.

He continued to laugh and stood, ruffling my hair. "Yeah it did! Good job, though! Again in an hour?" he grinned, fluffing my hair once more, then walking off with Jack.

Nils walked over and gave me her hand to stand up. "Wow. I don't think I've ever seen anyone beat him at his own game," she said.

I stumbled a bit and felt the room spin. Looking at her in a daze, I started laughing. "His game?"

"Yeah, man. He was the one that came up with the double funnel. For our group of friends anyways. Pretty sure it's been invented elsewhere, but I don't have the heart to tell him," she said, smiling.

I blinked slowly and shook my head. "It's effective," I said.

She started laughing and nodded. "Wait until the second round . . . so about what we were talking about before . . ." she mumbled.

I swayed back and forth and stared at her with blurred vision. "Right. Yeah, I didn't understand what you were getting at . . ." I mumbled, finding the couch and leaning on it for support.

This time, she leaned in, but leaned in so close that her breath touched my neck and gave me shivers. "Gay," she said, then leaned back.

The wideness of my eyes was impossible to hide, and I stumbled backwards, falling onto the couch.

She smiled and took a step back. "Thought so. Well hey, no judging here. Definitely no judging from him either," she said, shoving a thumb in Jimmy's direction.

I stared at him and watched him laugh so hard with Jack that he had to grab onto his shoulder to hold himself upright.

Sighing, I stared at my feet. "He doesn't know . . ." I mumbled quietly, staring up at her from the couch.

"Then tell him," she said, shrugging while taking a sip of her beer.

She leaned over and grabbed a carrot and ranch dip from the coffee table, placed the carrot between her lips and shrugged once more before walking away.

Originally, my plan was to drink so much I wouldn't have to socialize, or at least be in a state where socializing came easy, but at this point in the night—and we're talking very early on—it was time to drink for other reasons. The two beers from the funneling hit me hard but wasn't enough to get me where I wanted to get. I wanted to approach Jimmy and ask him for round two, but I suddenly felt very nervous. I had no *reason* to feel nervous. *He* wasn't there for the conversation I just had with Nils. He had no idea. Staring at him from across the room, he was standing at the balcony door with Jack, laughing at something. Holding my breath for a second or two, I exhaled loudly before walking up to him and poking his arm.

He turned and smiled when he saw me. "What's up?" he asked, grinning.

"Wanna go for round two?" I asked.

He started laughing. "Already?"

"Sure! It was fun!" I smiled.

He patted my back laughing and led me back to where the double funneling was still going on. We watched as two people competed against each other, then it was our turn.

"Jacky! Hook us up!" he yelled, waving Jack down.

This time, Jack was a bit more intoxicated, and came stumbling over laughing, spilling the beer in his hand all over the floor.

Jimmy's face fell and he sighed. "Second thought . . . you go have fun. We got this," he laughed, patting Jack on the back.

"Nah, I can do it!" Jack yelled, lifting another bottle of beer up to his face to focus on taking the cap off.

"Jack . . . it's not a twist off. Just . . . gimme this!" Jimmy laughed, snatching the booze from Jack's hands and shoving him off.

"How are you going to pour it at the same time?" I asked, grabbing the funnel and handing it to him. I was back to being unable to make eye contact.

"O ye of little faith," he smirked, smacking the lid off the coffee table and then holding the funnel above our heads. "Ready?" he asked.

I frowned and grabbed my tube. "Do I kneel again?" I asked and he started laughing.

"Yes," he said, and so I carefully knelt down and only winced a little bit once on my knees.

He did the same and held the funnel up even higher, making sure neither one of our tubes got kinks in them. Filling the funnel with the beer, he held his tube with his teeth before placing the empty beer bottle on the floor and side-glancing at me.

"Annnndddd go!" he yelled, opening his valve at the same time as me and beginning to chug while still holding funnel above our heads.

Nils noticed us from across the room and ran over with another beer, popping it open and pouring it in. The second time around wasn't nearly as scary as the first and I already felt like a pro. Jimmy handed the funnel to Nils and looked over at me smiling, but I was too focused on not choking. Suddenly, two more people ran over with drinks and poured them in as well. The cheering was catching everyone's attention and bringing them all back to watch me and Jimmy race. I couldn't feel my face. It was numb and tingly, and the room was already spinning. I'm pretty sure someone added vodka in there and it took everything not to instantly throw it back up. I finally glanced over at Jimmy who was trying his best not to laugh until he reached out and pushed me over. I grabbed onto my tube with both hands and carried on drinking while also trying my best to not burst into hysterics. Jack came running from the kitchen with a bottle of whiskey and that's when I had to call it quits. Finishing the liquid that was still in the tube, I quickly pulled back before Jack had a chance to start pouring and everyone started cheering when the foam from the beer poured all over me. Jimmy quickly did the same but closed his valve so no foam came out.

"Jack, no!" he choked, holding up a hand and bending over laughing. Dropping the funnel, he crawled over to me still laughing. "You're fucking soaked!" he laughed.

I laid on my back and closed my eyes, laughing so hard I wasn't even making a sound. The room continued to spin, and it wasn't until right this second that I realized I also couldn't feel my legs or feet.

"You good?" he asked.

Eyes still closed, I took a deep inhale and nodded slowly. "Mmhmm . . ." I mumbled before letting out a huge burp.

We both broke into hysterics all over again.

"Fuuuuuuck," I laughed, covering my face with both my hands.

"I'm gonna go for a smoke . . . y'wanna come?" he asked.

"Nah . . . gonna lay here . . ." I mumbled, sliding my hands off my face, and slowly opening my eyes and smiling up at him.

He patted me on my forehead and stood up to head out onto the balcony with Nils to go smoke. Even though I just drank enough alcohol to last me a lifetime, I was suddenly extremely thirsty and needed a drink. Slowly getting to my feet, I stood still for a moment or two to make everything stop spinning, then made my way to the kitchen. Jimmy had placed our bag of booze in the fridge, so I helped myself to rum and Coke. I knew there was a written rule somewhere about liquor before beer or vice versa but I had no idea. I wasn't a drinker, so everything else was foreign to me, whereas rum and Coke was the universal party drink . . . I thought. Either way, that last funnel had beer *and* liquor, so whatever the rule was, I had already broken it. Grabbing the bottle of rum, I found myself a cup and grabbed a can of Coke. Mixing the two, I took a sip and made a disgusted face. I was obviously no alcohol scientist and the ratio of pop to booze was completely wrong, but whether the drink was tasty or not wasn't my intention, so I closed my eyes and drank the whole thing. I shook my head and stuck out my tongue.

"Bleh!" I said, but grabbed another can of Coke and made another.

Chapter 13

Four beers—three of which were funneled at high speeds and included one science experiment of booze, and two rum and Cokes later, I was wasted. The things I thought were funny before got even funnier and once I started laughing, it was almost impossible to stop. I didn't stand out though, which was good, because everyone else around me was already plastered.

Drink in hand, I stumbled toward Jimmy who was talking to a new group of friends.

"Hi!" I greeted, bumping into him and laughing.

He looked at me and laughed. "Hi! How's it going?" he asked.

He seemed much less drunk than me. I leaned into him laughing and snorted a bit, grabbing onto his shoulder to support myself from falling. I felt more hyper than anything. Hyper with the addition of numb body parts.

"Good!" I giggled.

Frowning a little, he took my cup and brought it to his face, smelling it. His face fell and he frowned harder, forcing the cup back in my hand.

"Dal, is this straight rum?" he asked.

His friends had walked away at this point, but I kept giggling, now resting my forehead on his shoulder for support.

I closed my eyes and continued to giggle. "Probably isssss by now! Ran out o' Coke!" I slurred, laughing afterwards.

"Ooookayyyyy," he mumbled, grabbing my wrist and bringing me back to the kitchen.

Taking my cup again, he poured it down the drain, then opened the fridge and grabbed a beer. Smacking the cap off the counter and tossing it in the garbage, he placed the bottle in my hand and pointed his finger directly in my face.

"No more rum!" he ordered, poking my nose, then walking away.

I was still focused on my nose after he poked it, then I stared up to see that he had already left.

"Kay!" I grinned, staring at the beer in hand.

I drank the beer and it *did* taste better. Better than the shitty ones we drank at home, but that was the rum talking. I went back to socializing with strangers and even made a few friends. I thought. I mean, I instantly forgot their names but that wasn't the point. Things were blurry and thinking was hard and if I stood still for too long, I'd sway. Plus, walking now involved holding onto people or furniture. The beer wasn't helping my drunken situation either and it sort of confused me why Jimmy gave it to me in the first place since it was still four percent alcohol. But I guess that was my original plan. There was dancing on tables at one point in the night until Jack dug out the karaoke and a bunch of us did that for the next three hours.

Once the energy started to die down, we all sat around in Jack's living room—whether it be on furniture or the floor—talking to one another. I wasn't in the talking mood and so I sat on the couch beside Jimmy, sunken back into the cushions and focusing on how dizzy I was. Leaning my head to the left, I rested on a pillow and did my best to focus on Jimmy and Nils talking. They were both laughing and Nils punched him in the shoulder.

"We don't need to talk about that ever again, understand?" she laughed, covering her face with both hands and shaking her head.

I frowned. There was always something so odd between those two. I had never seen a relationship as strong as theirs, and yet there seemed to be some skeletons in the closet.

"You doing okay down there?" Nils asked, and I blinked my attention back to her.

"Hmm?" I mumbled, staring at her and smiling.

Jimmy sipped his beer and turned to look at me over his shoulder, also smiling.

"I'm doing A-OK," I smiled, making an O with my finger and thumb.

They both laughed and Jimmy turned back around, sipping his beer once more. Feeling my smile fade, I slowly closed my eyes and allowed myself to fall asleep. I suddenly felt exhausted. I wasn't sure how much time had passed or how long I was asleep for, but I suddenly sat up wide awake when Jimmy smacked his empty beer bottle on the table. Everyone started cheering and I rubbed both eyes.

"Y'okay, love?" Nils asked, sitting beside me and giving me a slight nudge.

I stared at her and blinked slowly, not understanding how Jimmy got from one place to another, or what time it was. Starting to smile, I sighed and stretched my arms above my head.

"Mmhmmm," I mumbled.

She laughed and pat my leg. "Okay, good. We're about to play a game, if you're interested," she explained.

Turning to stare at the table in front of me, I blinked slowly at the green beer bottle quickly spinning in circles. It took me a minute to comprehend what I was staring at, and once I did, I felt my face fall. Staring at the spinning bottle, I slowly averted my gaze upwards at the person sitting directly across from me, and felt myself get cold. That couch had way more people squished on it than the one I was currently sitting on. Left to right sat Jeremy, Lilly, Evan, Megan and then Jimmy. My couch only sat myself, Nils, Jillian and Caleb. Beside me on my left, Matt had a sofa chair to himself, and beside him sat Jack on the floor. Maria was on the floor behind Jack, curled up with a pillow and a blanket and was fast asleep.

The screaming and cheering from everyone in the room turned into a quiet, muffled moan and I felt myself finding it difficult to swallow. Looking at Nils, she was staring back at me, but also contributing to the cheering and screaming. Staring back at the bottle, I held my breath as it came to a stop and felt the weight of the world fall off my shoulders as it pointed to Lilly and Caleb.

"Oh my God, what are the chances?!" she giggled, standing from the couch and running over to kiss Caleb on the lips.

It was more than a kiss; it was a mini make out session. Everyone was laughing. Sitting on Caleb's lap and wrapping her arms around him, she looked at Nils and smiled.

"You spin. We're done playing," she stated and Nils huffed.

I hyper focused on the bottle again as Nils reached out to spin it.

The bottle ended up facing across Megan and Nils and everybody screamed in an uproar; the two girls killing themselves laughing as they leaned across the table and gently kissed one another.

"I mean, it's not like that's the first time we've kissed," Nils laughed, sitting back down beside me.

I snorted when I looked over and saw Jack's face fall.

"What?!" he yelled and everybody laughed again. "I HATE THIS GAME!" he added and Megan leaned over to look at him.

"Should've paid attention instead of rolling your joints. You could've sat somewhere other than the *floor!*" she teased, before reaching out and spinning the bottle.

I got the familiar feeling of my stomach dropping. It seemed to be a reoccurring thing. Watching as it slowed down, I sighed once more as it faced Jillian. Everyone cheered again.

"Jiiiiilllll," Megan smirked, leaning across the table and kissing her.

Laughing, Nils looked at me smiling.

"You still good?" she asked, and I smiled and nodded.

"All good," I slurred slowly.

"Good," she said.

Staring back at the bottle once Jillian spun it, I felt sick all over again. It stopping facing Jimmy and while I felt a relief once more, I almost instantly panicked because I realized *he* would be the one to spin it next. But I was being silly. The likelihood of it landing on me was one in a million, right? The screaming almost numbed my ears and both Jillian and Jimmy laughed.

"Lucky you!" Nils teased, nudging Jillian's arm. "No one *ever* gets to kiss James!" she added.

I swallowed the lump in my throat and felt my eyes look away once the two exchanged a quick peck. Now that it was Jimmy's turn to spin, I felt my body tense and I did my best to keep my face as neutral as possible. Forgetting how to blink, I felt my stomach drop and licked my dry lips. The screaming in the room was enough to make me go deaf and it took me a minute to really understand what I was staring at. Blinking slowly, I stared up at Jimmy who looked horrified sitting across from me.

"Uhm . . ." he mumbled and Nils started clapping.

"Yes! I *love* this game! C'mon, James! It's not like this is your first rodeo!" she cheered and he shot her a look.

Remaining petrified, I stayed where I was and became obnoxiously aware of how dry my mouth was.

"Dallas, love, you have to get off the couch for this," Nils said, placing her hand on my shoulder.

"C'mon, dude, let's get this over with," Jimmy mumbled, laughing as he stood and sighing.

Shaking his shoulders around, he cracked his neck side to side and I frowned. *Do I seriously have to go through with this? Is there no way out of this?! Is this what I was missing at parties all these years?! I hate this!* Sighing, I got off the couch and leaned in closer to the table. I was cold but was also very aware of how much I was sweating. This was awful. Could everyone see me sweating? Was I visibly shaking or was that just in my head? Leaning closer and closer, I unfortunately locked eyes with him and felt sick to my stomach.

"Wait! I think I'm going to be sick! And I wanna see this!" Nils suddenly yelled, and I jumped, leaning away.

•

Jack and almost everybody whined loudly as Nils took off for the bathroom and Jimmy started laughing, side-glancing at me before sitting back down on the couch. Nils was gone for longer than any of us had expected and eventually people went about doing their own thing. And just like that, the game was over. Thank *God.*

Sitting on the couch and eating a carrot, I saw Nils finally emerge from the bathroom and make her way out to the balcony. Eating the rest of my carrot, I slowly got off the couch and stumbled my way toward the balcony door. Walking out, I saw her sitting on the floor, smoking a cigarette.

She glanced up at me and smiled. "Hiya," she said.

I sighed and smiled in return, slowly dropping to my knees and resting my head on her lap. She laughed, switching her hands with her cigarette and wrapping her other hand around me.

"Sorry about that," she said and I closed my eyes.

"About what?" I asked quietly.

"The game. I didn't think it was going to land between you two," she explained and I smiled.

"It's fine. At least it didn't happen," I said and she forced a laugh, taking another drag and gently exhaling the smoke.

"Nope. Bluffing," she said.

Opening my eyes, I leaned my head back and stared up at her. "What?"

"I bluffed. I didn't feel sick in the slightest. I'm not as drunk as the rest of you," she laughed, taking another drag.

I continued to stare at her feeling confused. "I don't get it," I mumbled and she smiled, placing a hand on my head and twirling her finger around in my hair.

"I saw how terrified you were and I felt bad," she explained. "You looked like *you* were going to be sick," she added.

I turned my head and closed my eyes once more, nodding slightly. "I *felt* like I was gonna be sick," I slurred.

My entire body felt like it had gained fifty pounds and I felt super dehydrated, but alcohol couldn't fix that. I wanted nothing more than a giant bottle of cold water.

"Alright, Dally! Time to go home!" Jimmy announced, standing in the doorway.

I groaned, rolling over so my face was pressed into Nils' thigh. She laughed, patting my back and stood, lifting my head and gently placing it on the cold mosaic flooring.

"I stopped drinking a while back. I'll give you guys a ride," she whispered to Jimmy as she walked inside.

"Hey . . . how ya doing?" he asked, kneeling down to my level and poking my back.

I groaned again. "Sleep," I slurred, feeling drool slip between my lips.

"Yeah. I figured. C'mon. Nils is going to give us a ride home. It's four in the morning," he said, grabbing me under my armpits and forcing me to my feet. My bad knee gave out and I fell forwards, but he was quick to catch me and throw my arm over his shoulder, walking me to the front door. "Thanks, Jacky. Always a pleasure," he said, patting Jack's unconscious figure on the couch.

The whole elevator ride down, I was leaning all my weight on Jimmy, face pressed into the kink in his neck and my eyes closed. *I could fall asleep right here, standing like this, even though I can't feel my feet,* I thought. His familiar scent of cigarettes and cologne filled my nose and I wanted to smile but still couldn't feel my face. For all I knew, I was probably already smiling.

"Kid can drink a lot . . ." Nils mumbled quietly.

"I'm pretty sure this is his first party . . . he's not a drinker. His body probably doesn't realize what's hit him," Jimmy mumbled back.

"How old is he anyway?" Nils asked and Jimmy huffed.

"Turned twenty-two back in August."

"Really? He's mature for his age, that's for sure . . . poor guy. He'll feel it when he wakes up. I pity him already," she laughed a little.

"He'll be fine. Lesson learned, I guess," he said.

"I think he drank the most out of all of us. Well, except for Jack, of course," Nils laughed.

I felt the elevator stop, and this time, both Jimmy and Nils helped walk me to where her car was parked.

"I know. I'm not sure *why* he drank so much if he didn't know what he was doing . . . at one point, I caught him drinking straight rum," Jimmy explained and Nils giggled.

I was half asleep at this point. They helped me get into the back seat where I laid on my side, then Jimmy got in the passenger seat while Nils drove. They quietly talked amongst each other and I was conscious enough to hear the entire conversation. The first few minutes they talked about different clients they had recently and the tattoos they had to do but then it went quiet and nobody said anything.

"So . . ." Nils started. "How's it been with a new roommate?" she asked.

"It's been a lot of fun, actually. He's a cool kid."

"That's good. I know you were getting pretty lonely there for a while . . ."

"Yeah . . . he doesn't have his own bed yet though. We don't really have the space."

"Oh God, James. I hope you two don't share . . ."

"No! No. We take turns between the couch and the bed. Just until we figure something out, I guess . . ."

"Good. Because I don't think he knows. I mean, I know for a fact that he doesn't know."

"Don't think he knows wha—oh. That. Yeah, I know. I don't think he knows either . . ."

"But on the plus side . . . well, after the funnel, he and I got talking and—"

And suddenly, I became very aware of where this conversation was going, and I didn't like it. Neither did my stomach. I abruptly sat straight up and hit my head on the ceiling of the car, closing my eyes the second the headache started.

"I FEEL SICK!" I yelled, my voice overpowering Nils' completely.

Jimmy turned around and stared at me, already undoing his seat belt. "Okay! Nils, could you just—"

"Already on it," she said, quickly slowing down and pulling over.

Jimmy was already out of the car before it came to a complete stop and was opening the door for me. I crawled out and crawled into the bushes on the side of the road where I proceeded to empty out my entire stomach. I winced in pain as my sore ribs screamed at me. Picking off a large leaf and praying it wasn't poisonous, I wiped my mouth with it and sighed, sitting up and groaning. Jimmy bent over and placed a hand on my back.

"Y'okay?" he asked and I nodded slowly.

"I just want to go to bed . . ." I said, my head feeling much clearer and my stomach feeling emptier.

And with that thought, I realized that I hadn't eaten anything almost all day. That was alcohol poisoning waiting to happen.

"I know. Not much further," he said, helping me to my feet.

I slowly walked to the car and crawled back in, this time laying on my back. Jimmy got back in the passenger seat and sighed, turning back around to stare at me.

"Let's pick up the pace a little ..." he mumbled, clicking his seat belt back on.

"Do you need help?" Nils asked as we stood at the front door of our building. Jimmy shook his head.

"No, no. I got him. Thanks for everything though. See you at work."

They waved goodbye to each other, then Jimmy and I headed inside, my arm around his shoulders again.

"Sleepy . . ." I mumbled for the millionth time as we made our way to the elevator.

"I know. The bed is waiting for you upstairs," he said.

I shook my head slowly. "No. You're bed. I'm couch."

"Dallas, no. You're wasted. You can have the bed. We discussed this earlier. You're still sleeping in the bed for at least another week."

"I'm sick of the bed. I want the couch."

This was false. I wanted nothing more than to sprawl out in the big comfy bed.

"Nope," he mumbled.

"Share the bed with me," I said.

My mouth just kept moving and I had no control over what came out.

He laughed then sighed. "No. It's okay. I want the couch," he said.

The elevator stopped at the appropriate floor and we slowly made our way to our door. Getting inside, I kicked off my shoes, then made a dash for the couch. Jimmy was faster to react than I had anticipated—and I probably didn't move as fast as I thought I did—and was quick to grab the back of my shirt and pull me back.

"Ah, ah! Bed," he ordered, grabbing my shoulders and leading me away from the couch.

"Jaaaammes, nooooo," I whined, leaning back into his hands and pathetically trying to fight back.

It was useless. Laughing, he got me to the bed and spun me around so I was facing him.

I frowned. "It's not fair," I mumbled.

"Oh, I know. Life isn't fair, is it?" he mimicked, resting his hands on my shoulders, then giving me a little push.

The back of my legs hit the bed and I fell backwards. Panicked, I reached out and grabbed the front of his shirt at the last second, forcing him to fall with me and land on top of me. Gasping, he quickly sat up and stared down at me with wide eyes.

"Dude! Your ribs!"

"*Dude, your ribs*!" I mimicked and he frowned.

"Y'little shit," he laughed, poking my sides.

I curled into a ball and started giggling which only encouraged the poking until it went into a full-blown tickle fight. I was laughing so hard, I wasn't breathing. Eventually, it actually became an issue and I pushed him off to the side, although this time he grabbed onto me and flipped me so I was laying on top of him. Both calming down almost instantly, I found myself staring directly into his eyes which were staring right back. For once, I wasn't uncomfortable or awkward and I wasn't squirming to get away or hide my face. We were both just . . . staring. Taking me completely by surprise—although I did nothing to stop him—he gently placed a hand on the back of my neck and sat up ever so slightly, gently pressing our lips together. It was nothing extreme, but my stomach was on the Olympic gymnastics team and had won the gold medal, doing one flip after another. I closed my eyes and felt my whole body warm up, almost leaning into it. He suddenly pulled away and I slowly rolled off, laying beside him and staring at the ceiling in silence.

Chapter 14

That morning, I woke up and my throat felt like it was on fire. Not to mention the little construction workers with jackhammers in my head, drilling into my skull. I closed my eyes and groaned. Opening my eyes and turning my head, I jumped a little and froze when I saw Jimmy fast asleep beside me. We had fallen asleep exactly where we left off, on top of the blankets and sprawled out awkwardly, but now his hand was resting on my stomach and our legs were entwined. I closed my eyes and sighed, rubbing my face with both my hands and slowly getting up, removing his hand and walking to the kitchen.

Keeping my eyes closed, I grabbed the biggest cup we owned and filled it with cold water and ice cubes, chugging it instantly and then refilling it. I repeated this about four times before I finally decided it was time to pee for what felt like the first time in a week. Looking down at my clothes, I sighed when I remembered a shit ton of booze being poured all over me. I reeked and felt sticky. Flushing the toilet, I opened the bathroom door and jumped when I felt my phone vibrate in my back pocket and make a noise I had never heard before. Frowning, I took it out and stared at it.

"Instagram?" I mumbled to myself, clicking on the notification. Apparently, in my drunken stupor, I must've downloaded the app and uploaded pictures? All of which were partially blurry and completely embarrassing. Everyone from the party had already started following me and my few drunk pictures were flooded with likes and comments. Glancing at the time, I sighed, closing my eyes and locking my phone before putting it back in my pocket. It was 10 a.m.

"That's great," I mumbled, mentally thinking to myself that I'd try to delete Instagram later.

Looking back up at Jimmy, I froze when I saw that he was slowly waking up. I panicked, suddenly remembering what had happened earlier this morning. Was the kiss on purpose? Did he think I'd be too drunk to remember? *Was* I too drunk to remember and the memory was just a figment of my imagination? There was no way . . . we were *basically* just cuddling. I decided to play it cool and walked out rubbing my temple.

"Morning . . ." he mumbled, sitting up and shaking his hair around with his hands. "How are you feeling?" he asked.

"I hurt," I claimed, walking over and sitting on the couch, and petting Poppy who was asleep on the armrest.

"There's Advil in the bathroom," he yawned.

"I'm fine," I said in a tone a little too bitter than I meant it to be.

He arched a brow and stood. "Okay . . . want a coffee?" he asked, stretching his arms above his head and tilting his neck side to side.

"Sure."

There was silence in the room while he prepared the coffee machine.

"Going to the parlour today?" I asked.

"Yeah, later in the afternoon 'til closing. What about you? Wanna come with?" he asked, crossing his arms and leaning against the counter.

"Nah. I think I'll stay in and nurse this hangover."

Thank God. I can hyperventilate alone.

"Probably not a bad idea," he smiled. "What'cha gonna do today?" he asked, pouring the coffees and adding the necessary cream and sugar.

He walked over and sat on the other arm of the couch, reaching out to hand me my coffee. I instantly got up and awkwardly stood in the kitchen with my arms crossed.

He ducked his head and sighed, laughing a little. "Dal. If this is because of earlier . . ." he started, looking up and staring at me.

I felt tense. At least he had just confirmed that the kiss wasn't just a dream, but I didn't know if that made me feel better or worse.

"Of *course* this is because of that!" I suddenly snapped, surprising myself.

His face fell.

"What the fuck *was* that?!" I yelled.

He placed his coffee down on the table in front of him and stood, facing me but keeping his distance.

"I didn't do it to freak you out . . ."

"*Really?!* Cause you fucking freaked me out!" I yelled.
God, I was such a child.

"Dallas . . ." he took a step forwards, but I interrupted and took a step back.

"We've been friends for *how long now* and you couldn't have just *told* me you were gay?!" I continued to yell.

"It's not really something I go around announcing to people! And I didn't do it for shits 'n' giggles either! It's not like you tried to stop me!" he yelled back.

He had me there. I was practically pouting, looking away in defeat. I didn't say anything, and he sighed, walking back to his coffee and taking a huge chug, regardless of the temperature.

"You know what, fuck this. I'm not going to argue with you about something you *clearly* wanted and I'm not going to apologize either. I'm going to work early. I'll see you later," he mumbled, tossing his mug in the sink and walking out, slamming the door shut behind him.

I winced when it closed, then sighed. *I'm not really sure why I'm even upset. I've been beating myself up since day one about just possibly having feelings for this guy and now that he has them too, I am mad? No. I am scared. I am fucking scared! This is fucking crazy. I can't be gay. I cannot be gay.* I never thought in a million years that my life would come to this, but then again, who really sits around thinking of these types of things? I felt guilty more than anything. I had lost my cool and now he had walked out. We lived together for fuck's sake! Where the hell was he going to go when his shift was over? But more importantly, what the hell was I supposed to do by myself all day? I didn't start work again until Monday, and it was only Saturday morning. Normally, I'd be going to the shop with him and Nils, but I think we all knew that wasn't going to happen. He was probably freaking out to her right now about the whole situation. God, my head hurt. Frowning at my coffee on the table by the couch, I sighed loudly and stared at Poppy who was still asleep.

"Well, Pops . . . looks like it's just the two of us again . . ." I mumbled.

She wasn't listening. This cat could sleep through anything. Walking over and grabbing my coffee, I joined her on the couch and turned on the TV, deciding this was where I was going to waste my day. I kept it quiet since my head was pounding harder than it was before, although it didn't take long to smell my clothes and it instantly made me feel sick. Chugging the rest of my coffee, I took a shower and threw my clothes in the dirty hamper before making my way back to the TV.

I sat and watched TV all day, but I wasn't really watching TV at all. I wasn't paying an ounce of attention. My brain was rambling, and I didn't notice until I realized I had been biting my nails all afternoon. At one point, I ditched the couch and decided to lay on the floor instead. Laying flat on my back with my arms and legs sprawled out like a starfish, I stared up at the ceiling and pouted. Smiling slightly at the gentle *ba-dump* from Poppy's paws hitting the floor, she cautiously walked up to me and sniffed my forehead.

I stared up at her and smiled. "Hi, kitten . . ." I mumbled, reaching up and scratching her on her head.

She sat where she was and bent down to rub her head against mine, instantly purring. I closed my eyes and sighed, continuing to smile at my personal healer. Ditching my head, she walked along my side, rubbing her head against me the entire time, then stopped and stared at me until I pet her. I eventually sat up and crossed my legs, continuing to smile at her and pet her as she walked circles around me.

"Pops, you're so lucky . . ." I mumbled, leaning on my knee and watching as she walked off to clean her tail.

Moving from her tail, she began licking her paws and wiping behind her ears.

"You don't have any of this relationship shit to think about . . ." I added.

Finally sitting up, she turned to stare at me, meowed at me, then jumped up to the top of the couch. Sighing, I stood and walked over to turn off the TV. Placing my iPod in Jimmy's docking station, I clicked on *shuffle* and began cleaning.

Tidying helped keep me distracted, but it wasn't until I went to make the bed that I got anxious all over again. Staring where both Jimmy and I were asleep only hours ago, I started chewing on my bottom lip and remembered the kiss. Feeling sick with butterflies, I whined loudly before beginning to pace around the apartment. After changing my clothes and feeding Poppy, I grabbed my phone and wallet, locked the front door and left. I decided I would go to Starbucks since that was the only place I could really go.

I was uncomfortable. I hadn't left the apartment by myself since the incident with Aaron and I was out of my comfort zone. Getting to the street, I looked up and down Highland and took a deep breath.

"You got this . . ." I mumbled to myself.

Making my way down Highland, I was on high alert the entire time. Stopping at the corner and staring at the tattoo parlour, I stared inside the windows and sighed when I saw Nils working at the front desk. Suddenly, Jimmy came out of his room and I tensed, turning and quickly continuing down Melrose. Walking past the alleyway where it all happened, I slowed down and glanced down its dark creepiness.

"Don't be ridiculous. It wouldn't happen again," I said aloud, then quickened my pace.

Finally getting to Starbucks, I walked through the back door and Angela jumped and whipped a dish towel at me.

"Dallas!" she snapped. Sighing loudly, she calmed down and frowned at me. "What are you doing here?" she asked.

I stayed silent for a bit, awkwardly swaying back and forth.

"What's up?" she asked, turning around and cleaning down the kitchen space.

"Nothing. I'm just gonna . . . I'm gonna stay here tonight, I think."

She turned back around to face me and arched her brow. "Aaaaaand why would you do that?"

"Because . . ."

"Aw, Dal. Not this again. What happened?"

"No! Not the same thing! Nothing happened!" I yelled quickly in defense.

She frowned. "What's going on?" She stopped cleaning and put her hands on her hips.

Angela and I were close, and honestly, I knew I could tell her anything and trust that she wouldn't judge . . . but it was such a weird topic and made me really uncomfortable, so naturally I was even *more* uncomfortable than necessary. I sighed loudly and she tapped her foot impatiently.

"Dallas. Speak up," she ordered.

I whined, then hunched down in one of the chairs, ever so slightly twirling in a circle with my toe. "It's so awkward and makes me really uncomfortable and I really don't like talking about it, let alone *thinking* about it, so I'm just going to tell you and that'll be that, okay?" I spoke quickly.

She narrowed both eyes. "Okay?"

I took a deep breath like I was about to tell her the longest story known to man, but "Jimmy and I kissed" was all I said.

Her eyes bugged out and she ran up to me, both hands covering her mouth. She squealed a little bit, but I was quick to hold up a hand and tell her to shut up. There were still customers in the front anyways.

"You *what*?!" she squeaked.

I sighed, covering my face with both my hands. I could feel myself overheating.

"I told you I'd tell you and then we'd drop it!"

"Yeah, yeah but whatever! Tell me what happened! Oh my God! Who kissed who? And did you like it? Is this why you moved in with him? Oh my God, Dallas. I had *no idea*!" She was getting louder.

I frowned up at her and grabbed a handful of hair, tugging on it. "Enough. We were drunk . . . well, *I* was drunk. He didn't drink as much as I did. It was earlier this morning, like 4:00 a.m. kind of early . . . and I dunno. *I don't know!*" I whined, my shoulders sinking, and I ducked my head to look at my toes.

She calmed herself down and bent down so she could look up at me. "Hey . . ." she said softly, poking at my chin so I'd look at her. "I don't judge, okay? Your life, not mine. I think it's kind of sweet anyways," she smiled.

I rolled my eyes and she laughed.

"I'm serious! This guy has had a serious thing for you since day one . . ."

"You think so?" I asked, sitting up straight.

She laughed, closing her eyes and shaking her head, followed by a long sigh. "Ohhh boy. And Dallas? Seeing you now . . . I think you have, too . . ." she said, ruffling my hair, then standing back up.

I felt my face go red.

"You're coming home with me tonight. I'm not letting you sleep on the cold hard tiled floor of a Starbucks. You can stay in Jason's room. He's with his dad this week. Think your doctor will let you start work a few days early?" she asked, smiling and winking.

I grinned up at her. "Absolutely. Thanks, Ang."

"What about him? Does he know you're here?"

I went back to pouting and staring at my feet. "No. I kinda freaked out this morning. It's complicated. He's at work right now, expected to be home in two hours, give or take . . ."

"That's why you came here?"

"Exactly. Always been my home away from home," I said, forcing a smile.

She sighed. "Okay, well at least help me clean up before closing."

"Of course!" I smiled.

"But you're going home in the morning and sorting this out."

"You just finished saying we'd come to work together tomorrow!"

"Not anymore. I just changed my mind. I'll call Tiffany."

"Angela . . ."

"Nope. I don't care. You're a big boy now. You have to handle this like an adult and not just run away from it."

"No, seriously, Ang. I can't. Facing him about this gives me serious anxiety. He's probably freaking out too . . ." I begged, standing and following her around the kitchen. "I bit all my nails down!" I added, shoving my hands in her face.

She sighed. "All the more reason to sort things out!"

"No. Please. One week. Just give me one week."

She sighed again and covered her face with her hands, then frowned at me. "Fine. But if he comes to the store during your working hours, you're on your own."

"I can guarantee you that he won't."

I cleaned the entire kitchen and made it spotless while Angie worked the front. Closing time came sooner than anticipated, and suddenly, we were driving back to her place. It wasn't a far drive to her small suburban house, so I was thankful there wasn't too long of an awkward silence for her to start asking questions. Setting me up in Jason's bedroom, she sat at the end of the bed and handed me a glass of wine. I scrunched up my nose and she laughed, rolling her eyes.

"Drink it! Good for the nerves!" she said, forcing the glass into my hands and taking a sip from her own. "So, I know you don't want to talk about it, but . . ."

"Ang . . ."

"I know, I know! But I just have to ask. It's the mother from within wanting to come out again."

I sighed. "What?"

"Is this for real? Like, I don't mean for that to sound as harsh as it is, I just mean . . . are you sure this isn't a crush?" she asked.

I played with my lip piercing. This subject made me so uneasy, but I sat in silence as I thought about what she had just asked.

Sighing, I looked up at her and pouted. "No. It's not. I really like this guy. I don't know what it is about him . . . I can't say I've felt this way since the first day I met him, but it's pretty damn close. I mean like . . . he's sparked an interest since day one," I explained.

She was nodding. "Okay, well as long as you know. And as long as you're happy. You deserve to be happy, Dallas."

"Thanks, Ang," I smiled.

"And the story you told me about him watching you get to work on time?" She placed a hand on her heart. "Adorable."

I started laughing and ducked my head, blushing. "Yeah . . ."

We sat up most of the night talking, not only just about me and Jimmy, but that did end up being the main topic. Once she got all of her 'mom' out, she couldn't stop squealing about how 'adorable' we were, and it only made me blush more. She had finished her glass of wine and had moved onto finishing mine.

Lying down on the bed, she yawned. "It's almost midnight and I'm sleepy. I think it's bedtime."

"Heh. I think so too. We have to work in the morning, anyway."

"Goodnight, Dallas," she mumbled, then slowly made her way to her own bedroom, flicking the lights off on her way.

It was dark and I was comfortable enough, but I just wasn't tired. My body was drained, but no matter how much I bundled myself in the blankets, my mind wouldn't shut off. I found myself staying up all night just thinking about Jimmy *again*.

One week is what I *attempted* to do and it was awful. Especially because I left Poppy there with him, like the asshole I was, which forced him to take care of her. But that was the least of my concern. I worked every day like normal and would end up at Angie's house later. My mind was slowly clearing itself until Wednesday night, when I offered to go grocery shopping so Angela could kick back and relax. Ralph's was a decently priced place over on La Brea Avenue, which was pretty close to where Jimmy and I lived, but the likelihood of him *also* grocery shopping was low. Angela gave me a list, so all I had to do was go in, get the stuff, and get out. Should be easy enough. It was nighttime and a weekday at that, so the store was basically empty.

I walked around with a shopping cart and was listening to my iPod with only one ear bud in. Almost at the home stretch, I had a few more items to look for that were on Angie's list when I looked up and saw *him*. We saw each other at the exact same time, and I felt like I was going to throw up. Realizing the awkward situation, I quickly turned down a random aisle and stayed there. Leaving my cart, I walked to the end of the aisle and cautiously peeked around the corner, frowning when I didn't see him.

"Dallas," he spoke from behind me.

I jumped and spun around, tugging my earbud out and taking a step back.

"Jesus!" I squeaked.

He leaned against the shelves and crossed his arms, arching a brow at me.

"So, you're avoiding me," he stated.

"I'm not . . ." I mumbled, falling into the shelf and sending boxes of tampons crashing to the ground.

He continued to keep his brow arched at me and watched me fail at picking all the boxes up, clumsily shoving them back on the shelf.

"Just getting your monthly tampons?" he asked.

Shoving the last box on the shelf, it fell again and I sighed loudly. "I gotta go," I mumbled, turning on my heel and going to leave, completely abandoning my cart full of food.

He sighed. "Dal . . ."

But I was already gone. I quickly left the store and got in Angie's car, burning rubber out of the parking lot and racing back to her place.

"Stupid, stupid, stupid!" I yelled to myself, breathing heavy and watching the road with wide eyes.

I burst through the door and tossed Angela's keys on the kitchen counter. She was sitting watching TV with a glass of wine.

"Dallas?!"

"Going to bed!" I called, running upstairs.

"Where are the groceries?! Dallas?!"

I ran into Jason's room and slammed the door shut behind me, jumping into the bed and closing my eyes, trying to force myself to sleep.

The next day, I had a full shift and Angie had a half day. Walking up to the front door, we unlocked it and walked inside, flicking on all the lights. Turning on the necessary coffee machines, she went to the back door and pushed it open to get some air flow throughout the building; she did this almost every morning. Jumping at the resistance behind the door, she sighed loudly and called out to me.

"Why do I have a feeling this has something to do with you?" she asked, her hands on her hips as she looked down at the little pile of groceries carefully leaning against the wall.

Everything was there, neatly bagged and paid for. The receipt was in one of the bags as well as the list, and even the remaining items I never grabbed were there as well. Sighing loudly, I leaned against the wall and whined.

"What's going on?" she asked, staring at me.

"I saw him at the grocery store last night. I panicked and made a run for it," I said, ducking my head.

Sighing once more, she grabbed a handful of bags and brought them inside. Looking at the receipt, she shook her head. "Dallas, he paid for all of this," she said.

I grabbed the remaining bags from outside and jumped up on the counter, resting my face in my palms.

"Yeah . . ." was all I could say.

"This has gone too far. You're acting childish," she said, now frowning.

I stared up at her with sad eyes then stared down at my feet. "Yeah . . ." I said again.

Leaving at noon, Angela packed the car with the groceries and gave me a handful of cash.

"I know he's gonna come by today. How can he not? And when he does, *please* give him this money. I can't have him buying me a week's worth of groceries because of a little fight you two are having, got it?" she snapped.

I took the cash and nodded.

"Good. I'll see you back at home," she said, then drove off.

I was anxious for the rest of the day, scared he was going to show up at random because Angie was right; if he came during store hours, I had nothing to do but face the music. Thankfully, that didn't happen, and it was already almost 9:00 p.m. Locking the back door, I walked through the dark building toward the front door when I saw Jimmy walking past the windows of the store to my left. At first,

I felt my body react with excitement; that soon switched to anxiety and I was quick to run and lock the door the second he got there. I saw his shoulders sink and he sighed, resting his forehead on the glass and staring at me.

"Dallas. C'mon. Stop making this weird."

"I'm not making it weird! *You're* making it weird!" I yelled, taking a step back from the door.

"Please. Let me in. Can we please talk about this?"

"There's nothing to talk about," I mumbled.

Oh, how I was wrong.

"I fucked up, I know. I'm *sorry*. Can we *please* just pretend it never happened and go back to the way things were? Your cat is still at my place . . ."

"I'll get her tomorrow."

"Yeah? And where are y'gonna live?" he asked, now standing and frowning at me.

"I'll figure something out."

"Dallas, stop being so fucking ridiculous! It was one kiss!" he yelled, smacking the glass with his hand.

It made me jump and I pouted. "Could you just go? Please? I'd like to leave . . ." I mumbled sadly, disconnecting eye contact and staring at the floor.

Staring at the ground, he sighed. Keeping his hand on the window, he stared at me one last time.

"I'm sorry," he mumbled, and then turned and walked back down the way he came.

I watched him through the windows until he was out of sight, then quickly unlocked the front door, locked it behind myself and then power walked to the bus stop.

Chapter 15

I had Friday off and spent the whole day lounging around Angela's place watching TV. I mean, I wasn't *really* watching TV. I was just kind of staring at it, not really taking in what I was looking at. I felt bad for how I was treating Jimmy and was starting to hate myself. He was just trying to help and I was back to being childish. I couldn't really explain what was going through my head. I was mad and confused, but more than anything, I missed him. Not that I didn't like Angela's company, but I preferred his. And I think that alone was saying something. I missed him and I liked him. I *liked* him. *Is it maybe time I just come to accept what I've been feeling all along? I've been trying to push back these feelings for months, and for what? What is the issue anyways?*

That moment when he kissed me, I was happy. I had never felt that kind of happiness before, and I know that wasn't just the booze talking. I was almost relieved that he was the one to make the move, because I knew I wasn't going to do anything, even in my drunken stupor. From day one of knowing Jimmy and being with him, he had been nothing but helpful and kind and I'd . . . well, I'd been a pain in the ass. He said 'everything happens for a reason' and I think maybe he was right. If it wasn't for him . . . the list could go on, but if it wasn't for him, I'd probably be dead. He took me under his wing and legitimately took care of me because he *cared* about me. And I was throwing it all away, all because of a little kiss that inevitably I *wanted?* Fuck that. It was time I finally took matters into my own hands. Between calling me, paying for Angela's groceries and coming to the shop to talk to me—I blew him off every single time when all he was trying to do was explain himself and set things right. I had no excuse other than being chickenshit.

Turning off the TV, I paced around the living room for a minute or two. I could feel my heart rate rising as I thought about what I was going to do. And all that was, was going back to Jimmy's place and confronting him. Was that so bad? No. Did it have to be scary? Of course not, but I was playing it out to be terrifying in my head.

"Clean. I need to clean . . ." I mumbled to myself, going to the kitchen and taking out all of Angela's cleaning supplies.

It was something I usually did in my own apartment when I had too much on my mind. I felt like I could clear my head while I cleared the clutter—regardless that Angela was already a pretty neat person. So, I took it to the next level and vacuumed every room, as well as mopping the bathroom and kitchen. I cleaned the windows and dusted every surface that needed dusting. It took me a good portion of the day, so that when I finally sat back on the couch, exhausted, it was nighttime.

Looking out the window, I glared up at the sky and frowned when I couldn't see a single star. Walking out to the front door and stepping outside, I sighed when I saw that it was *pouring*. It had been a hot summer with barely any rain, so honestly, we could use it, but . . . now was not the time. Walking back inside, I sat back down on the couch and sunk into the cushions.

"Fuck," I mumbled, staring at my reflection in the TV and overthinking everything all over again.

Making popping noise with my lips and tapping on my legs, I looked around the clean house and sighed. Closing my eyes and leaning my head back against the couch, I whined loudly before sighing again.

"Okay," I said to myself, quickly standing and grabbing my phone and wallet.

Earlier in the week, I had snuck back into Jimmy's apartment to grab myself a change of clothes. That alone almost gave me an anxiety attack, but I walked past the parlour and saw that he was working, so that was my green light to rush to the apartment. But that being said, I didn't have much to pack up from Angela's, and even though she was still at work and would probably be mad at me for ditching her place for the second time in our friendship, at least she was coming home to a clean house. I knew if I texted her ahead of time, she'd Mom Talk me and I'd psych myself out.

"Now or never. It's now or never," I prepped myself, adjusting my bag on my back and leaving the house.

I locked the door and hid her spare key under the welcome mat, then threw up my hood and made my way to the closest bus stop. Getting on at the Fountain Avenue stop, I knew it would take me down far enough that I would only have a short walk to the apartment. Only now, there was thunder and lightning and I only had a hoodie. The universe was fed up with me as well. Thanking the bus driver and stepping off, I sighed and put my hood back up; although within a few feet, I was already soaked. Thankfully, the walk to Jimmy's apartment was only three minutes, but regardless, that three minutes in torrential downpour felt like forever. Key fobbing my way in, I shivered at the air-conditioning in the front foyer and rushed my way to the elevator. I could feel myself start shivering and even after removing my hood, my hair was dripping wet underneath.

"Maybe I should wait . . ." I mumbled out loud, pacing back and forth. "No, no, no. Now is the right time. You're already here. But what if he's mad . . . I mean, *obviously* he's mad. What are you going to say? And how are you going to say it?"

I was having a full blown, one-sided conversation with myself, and I didn't have any answers. Suddenly, there was a ding and the elevator stopped to let me get on. There was someone already inside and they smiled politely at me, having come up from the underground parking.

"Heh. Got stuck in the rain, did ya?" he asked, and I jumped.

"Pardon?" I asked. I wasn't listening.

"You're soaked," he pointed out.

I looked down at my outfit and sighed. "Oh. Yeah. Ha, it's really coming down out there," I mumbled, then started nervously fidgeting with my own hands.

I watched the numbers above the doors and sighed once the elevator came to a stop and the doors opened for me. Clenching my jaw, I exhaled slowly and stepped out. Walking down the hall, I stopped to look out at the view. I had never seen it rain so hard.

"I don't know. I don't *know!*" I panicked, going back to pacing.

I was playing with my lip ring so aggressively, it had started to feel irritated, and it wasn't until there was a giant crash of thunder and lightning that I stopped and continued my walk toward the apartment.

"Okay, okay!" I sighed.

Stopping outside the door, I stared at it and reached for the handle, but froze. My phone went off and I jumped.

"Fuck," I hissed, struggling to take it out of my pocket since my hands were starting to shake.

"*I'm trying not to freak that you're not here. Please tell me you're with Jimmy. Also, thank you for cleaning. The house looks and smells wonderful! Xoxo.*" It was Angela.

"Not . . . now," I mumbled and put my phone back in my pocket.

Staring back at the door, I took one deep breath before making a fist and knocking. I held my breath, feeling like I was going to be sick. There was a second or two of clicking as Jimmy unlocked the door on his side before opening, and once he did, his eyes were wide with surprise. I was pleasantly surprised to see that he was topless.

Opening his mouth to speak, I cut him off by stepping in, dropping my bag, kicking the door shut behind me and pressing my lips against his. I walked forwards, making him walk back until he hit the wall and I grabbed his face with both hands. Pulling back for a second, he stared confused at me, but I had a momentum going and wasn't about to stop and think about it now. Leaning forwards again, I brought our lips back together; smiling when he spun us around to press me against the wall instead. Sliding my hands down his neck, I pressed each fingertip into his back and did my best to press him in closer. I could feel every muscle and it only encouraged me to kiss him harder. Forcing his tongue into my mouth, he tasted like cigarettes and it was an oddly comfortable flavour. Feeling myself overheating, I remembered that I was soaking wet, thus making *him* wet with my hoodie. Pulling back, I quickly grabbed the bottom of my sweater and pulled it up and over my head, tossing it to the side before pressing our lips together again. His arms wrapped around me, I could feel that he was smiling, and when I jumped at another crash of thunder, he started laughing into the kiss.

He started walking backwards, all the while our lips still attached, so I was quick to follow. Stopping when his legs hit the bed, he pulled back to stare at me and catch his breath.

"Are you okay?" he asked.

My throat was dry, as I too was catching my breath, but I laughed and nodded. "Yeah," I panted.

"Good," he said, leaning in, kissing me again, and sliding his hands down my side and stopping at my hips.

Finding his way to the front of my pants, he undid the button and zipper, but honestly was taking too long and I was sexually frustrated and impatient at this point, so I pulled my pants down for him. They were wet and uncomfortable anyways. Kicking off my shoes and socks, I pulled back to catch my breath and Jimmy started laughing. His face was flushed red and we were both already sweating. Grabbing my shoulder and spinning me around, he pushed me so I'd fall back on the bed. This seemed familiar. Crawling back, I peeled off my wet shirt and saw that he was starting to undress in front of me. I had seen him naked briefly before but was too shy to look. Now that I was allowed, I didn't want to look away. I had never seen anybody with such a perfect body before. His boxers were tight and my stomach clenched with butterflies, and before I could crawl back any further, he slowly lowered himself on top of me. I reached up to grab behind his neck and pulled him down to kiss him harder than before. He was still smiling. Straddling his legs on either side of my waist, he sat up and stared down at me, still catching his breath.

"What . . . *what?*" he panted.

I could feel my heart beating throughout my entire body and all the nerves I had before had vanished. All that was left was desire, and the longer I stared at him, the harder I craved him. Licking my lips and brushing my hair out of my face, I cleared my throat and smiled at him.

"You wanted us to make mistakes . . ." I panted.

He sat down on my pelvis and arched a brow, although smirking.

"Well . . . I don't think this is a mistake at all," I smiled, leaning up and pressing my lips against his again.

The morning came and we both woke up around the same time with the sun beaming in through the windows. The floor was covered in our clothing. Yawning and stretching, I turned my head to see Jimmy beside me and smiled.

"Morning."

"Good morning. Have a good sleep?" he asked and I smiled and stretched once more.

"*Very* good sleep. And you?" I asked.

He shrugged. "Can't complain," he smiled, but then there wasn't much else to say and I instantly felt awkward.

"Angela's. Sorry I didn't—"

"It's okay. I kinda figured you'd be with her," he said, holding up a hand before I threw words up everywhere.

"Heh, yeah. Where else do I have to go?" I mumbled, glancing down at my hands and awkwardly fiddling with my fingers. Sighing, I turned to look at him but was quick to stare back at the ceiling and blushed. "Did you have a shitty week too?" I asked.

He yawned and stretched his arms above his head, sinking deeper under the covers and turning on his side to stare at me. He must've sensed my sudden fear of eye contact.

"I can guarantee mine was shittier, actually," he said with a smirk.

Still staring at the ceiling, I frowned and sighed. "Sorry," I mumbled, and then there was that awkward silence again.

"So . . . about that kiss . . ." he started.

Unable to hide my smile, I finally turned on my side and forced myself to stare at him. "Which one?" I asked, still smiling.

He snorted, but then his face fell and he remained staring at me.

I frowned. "What?" I asked and he sighed.

"I'm sorry. I didn't mean for any of this to happen. I didn't mean to freak you out . . ." he explained, and I started shaking my head.

"You don't have to apologize for anything. I overreacted and I'm sorry for that . . . I'm fine with it. With this . . ." I mumbled and he frowned.

"This?" he asked.

I hesitated for a moment, then smiled. "Us," I said, feeling my stomach get tight.

Ducking his head and blushing, he let out a little laugh. "Oh. I didn't know that was a thing," he said.

My face dropped and I felt myself instantly get hot; I rolled back on my back and stared at the ceiling again. He started laughing.

"Well . . . I had a lot of time to think . . ." I mumbled, starting to fiddle with my fingers again. "And I think I just freaked out because this is all so new to me . . . and I obviously didn't know I was . . . y'know . . ."

"Of course," he said, tucking his arm under his head and resting on his forearm.

"And . . . I'm fine with it. I think if we just take baby steps. Because I really like you, Jimmy. I have for a while now," I said, slowly shifting my eyes to stare at him.

My mind was screaming and I felt sick. This was the hardest, and the weirdest, thing for me to say. But it wasn't a lie. I knew I had been feeling a certain way for a long time and pushing it away obviously did nothing . . . so, here I was.

He was nodding. "Yeah, I got that," he laughed.

I felt everything tense and I quickly turned on my side to stare at him with wide eyes. My face remained hot at this point. "What?! How?! For how long?!" I squeaked and he kept laughing.

"Dal, I've been playing this game a bit longer than you . . . my gay-dar is a little more advanced than yours . . ." he laughed and then winked. "Why do you think I kissed you, y'butthead!? I knew you liked me. I thought it was what you wanted."

"It was! It is! It just . . . I dunno . . ."

"I know. I didn't mean for it to be so alarming . . . it just felt like the right timing. I've been wanting to kiss you for fucking ever, but never had the chance. And . . . it's not something you just take lightly and start throwing around, y'know? I just didn't know how to approach it. Not that you being drunk was the right opportunity—"

"No, I get it. I'm just a coward."

"Dallas, you're not a coward. Honestly. I can remember very clearly the first time I kissed a guy. I was a mess. Coming to terms with being gay was probably one of the most stressful times of my life."

"Really?" I asked, almost feeling hopeful.

Obviously, I wasn't the only one in the world going through this.

"Yeah . . . I was nineteen, so just a kid really . . . met this guy at a party and we got to know each other after a while . . ." he mumbled, rolling onto his back and smiling up at the ceiling as he spoke.

"Lemme guess, you turned him gay too?" I asked, sticking out my tongue.

He threw his head back laughing, then threw his hands up. "Hey! You both made the decision! I was just the motivator! It's not my fault that I'm charming as fuck!"

"Phst. Yeah, alright," I laughed, rolling my eyes sarcastically.

He snorted. "Nah. We both kinda 'turned' at the same time, I guess . . ." he added with bunny quotations.

We both laid in silence, although finally and for once, it wasn't awkward.

"So . . . what does this mean?" he asked.

The dreaded question.

I twiddled my thumbs and shrugged. "Are we like . . ."

"I dunno . . ."

"Cause like . . . I'm totally fine with . . ."

"Yeah, me too . . ."

"Okay cool."

"Cool," he ended.

More silence.

"Well . . . I'm off today. I think I'm gonna go back to bed," he added.

I huffed. "I think I'm going to stay up for a bit . . . my brain is a little too . . . awake," I laughed.

He smiled. "I get it. Okay, well . . . see you . . . when I . . . wake up," he laughed, pulling the blankets up to his chin.

I sat up and stretched, smiling at him, then grabbed my boxers. "Thanks, J, for being so understanding . . ." I mumbled and he shrugged, his back to me.

"S'not a big deal . . ." he said. "Night!"

Then he curled up and closed his eyes. I'm not kidding when I say he fell asleep almost immediately. He was a master when it came to passing out, whereas I on the other hand, was a nervous wreck and wasn't sure my mind would allow me to sleep ever again.

If I wasn't overwhelmed with emotions before, I *definitely* was now. I let out a long-exaggerated sigh and finally got off the bed, standing and raking my fingers through my hair. This was crazy. This was *fucking* crazy. Pacing the room for a minute, I finally sat down on the couch and quietly turned on the TV; quickly turning the volume down. I'm not sure how long I was there for, but I watched until my eyes could watch no more. I looked over and saw Jimmy's motionless body and started chewing on the inside of my cheek, ever so gently playing with my lip ring. Everything was screaming to go join him, but I was awkward as hell and scared shitless. I closed my eyes and let out a slow exhale, trying to calm myself down before grabbing the remote and turning off the TV. Looking around at our clothes on the floor, I had to laugh. Last night was fun and scary all at the same time and that was putting it lightly. Standing, I went over to the bed and stopped dead in front of it, staring down at Jimmy's resting body.

My brain was screaming at me to get it over with, but I remained frozen. Clenching my fists, I gently moved back the covers and slowly got under them, pulling them up to my chin. Everything was so much easier last night when my adrenaline had taken over. This morning, not so much. I glanced over to see if he noticed me get in bed, but he was passed out cold. As soon as I let my body calm down, I realized how comfortable I was and I felt my eyes get heavier, blinking slower and slower until my eyes soon stayed shut and I passed out.

I woke up some time after six that night to the smell of garlic and the sound of sizzling. Slowly opening my eyes and yawning, Jimmy's side of the bed was empty. I looked over my shoulder and saw him cooking in only his boxers. Taking this moment to appreciate that he wasn't aware that I was awake yet, I stared at his tattoos. His entire back, from the waistband of his boxers all the way up to the top of his shoulder blade, was covered in flames. I already knew this, but I never got a chance to *stare* at it like I did now. It was so realistic; it was hard to believe it was a tattoo. And then I wondered who did it. I never saw Nils or Jack's work, so maybe it was one of them? His arms were covered as well, but I saw those regularly. Then there was his leg, but it was such a collection of random things, I couldn't really make any of them out. Rolling onto my back, I stretched my arms and yawned once more. Sprawling out across the bed like a starfish, I looked to my left and saw the sun going down outside; Netflix playing *The Walking Dead* in the background.

"Good morning . . ." I laughed, sitting up and rubbing my face.

He jumped at my sudden acknowledgement, then turned around and smiled at me. "Morning! Hungry?" he asked, glancing at me over his shoulder.

As if on cue, my stomach let out a huge grumble and I laughed, placing a hand on my gut. "Always," I smiled.

Getting out of bed, I sat on the edge and stared back at his flames once more. Biting my lip piercing, I stood and cautiously walked up behind him, resting my chin on his shoulder and watching him cook. My entire body was tense, but I was trying my best.

He glanced at me and laughed. "Hi."

I smiled back. "Hi."

Feeling the anxiety pick up again, I quickly gave his shoulder a little peck, then turned on my heel and made a dash for the bathroom, slamming the door shut behind me.

I could hear him laughing. "Wow! A shoulder kiss! Lookit you being all brave 'n' adventurous!" he called out.

Quickly going pee, I flushed the toilet, then wandered over to the sink, staring at myself as I washed my hands. I was smiling, but partially zoning out, just daydreaming at nothing. Looking down at my feet, I couldn't stop smiling and I could feel my pulse in my face. I felt like I had the most energy in the world and could do anything, but I knew that was just the adrenaline talking again. Turning off the water and drying my hands, I stared at myself once more and sighed.

"Well, now I can do everything I've been wanting to do for so long," I said as I walked out of the bathroom.

"You wanted to do things before? How long?" he asked, smirking.

I stuck my tongue out at him and grabbed new clothes. Regardless that I was just butt naked in front of him, I walked into the bathroom to change. I sighed when I came back out.

"So. Now that it's nighttime and we're both wide awake . . . we've become nocturnal completely by accident," I mumbled, staring at the dark sky.

Turning off the air, I opened the door to the balcony and smiled when I saw Poppy lounging on the couch.

"Heh. That'll change quickly when you have to wake up for work tomorrow morning," Jimmy said.

"That's true," I sighed. "Fuck work. I'm so done with it," I mumbled, sitting on the couch and slouching as I gently pet Poppy.

"And you're still so young! Good luck in the future," he laughed. "But fuck the future. In the present, we have pasta!" he grinned, handing me a plate over my head.

"Ooooh! Thank you!" I smiled.

He threw on his shorts from earlier and we sat on the couch, watching Netflix while we ate. Even though the craziest of crazy things had just happened, we carried on with our lives like nothing happened and I liked that. I didn't want things to change or feel awkward.

"So, what things did you want to do earlier?" he asked, grinning.

I threw a noodle at his head. "Just forget about that!" I laughed.

Focusing back on the TV, Jimmy sighed and picked up the remote for the PS4. "I'm sick of *The Walking Dead*. Wanna watch something else?" he asked, going to the menu.

I laughed and shrugged. "You were the one that put it on in the first place."

"I know, I know. I like to think it gives good survival tips, y'know?" he mumbled, turning the PS4 off entirely.

I laughed. Changing back to cable, he flicked through some channels until he got to the cartoon network and *American Dad* was playing.

"Perfect. I fucking love this show," he smiled, sinking lower into the couch and continuing to eat his pasta.

Suddenly, after a few minutes into the show, it changed itself to the news and it made me jump.

"Breaking news! This just in, escaped convicts have been seen in Santa Barbara! Residents are being told to stay inside their homes on a lockdown until further instructions are given. Do not leave your home at any time! These men are armed—"

Jimmy quickly picked up the remote and turned the TV off as the screen showed all six of their faces, but only for a brief moment. Neither one of us said anything and the room got very quiet.

"Jesus . . ." he whispered.

I swallowed the lump in my throat. "I thought they would've caught them by now . . ."

"Yeah, but if they caught them, that'd be all over the news too . . ."

"True . . . you don't think they'll make it down to us, do you?" I asked, staring at him with wide eyes.

"I don't know . . . we're a pretty major city . . . we could be their main target. They're all originally from here, anyway . . . except for Benji Manalis. I think he's from Arizona . . ." he said and my eyes got even wider. He started laughing and playfully shoved my shoulder. "I'm just teasing, Dal!" he snorted. "Finish your food. They'll catch 'em."

"And if they don't?" I asked, and he shrugged.

"Then we will," he laughed, grabbing the remote and turning the TV back on.

The news was still talking about the escaped convicts, so he quickly flicked through a few channels. Unfortunately, every channel was featuring the same thing. Sighing loudly, he grabbed the PS4 remote again and went back to Netflix.

"Fine," he mumbled, scrolling through his list of saved TV shows. "News can't catch us here," he smirked.

I zoned out at our city view through the glass door and nervously bit my bottom lip. I was a big baby when it came to stuff like this. I considered myself pretty independent, but I never wanted to step on anyone's toes or get in anyone's way, especially if it was a situation where I'd lose. That's why I could never really stand up to my brother. I didn't like conflict; I was neurotic and paranoid. I *hated* horror movies and all around anything that would scare me, and I've always been a baby like that. So, the fact that there was this gang of mass murderers roaming the streets of California did *not* sit right with me. Not that it really sat right with anyone, but this was definitely something I'd lose sleep over until they were caught.

My focus was brought back to Jimmy when he started talking again as he continued scrolling through shows.

"So, I think we should try and go back to bed at a decent time, like maybe like nine or ten? That way we won't *completely* fuck up our body clocks and are functional tomorrow . . ."

"How are we going to go back to bed when we only just woke up?"

"I have sleeping pills if you want? It doesn't take much for me to fall asleep, even if I'm not tired. Once I get comfortable enough, I'll be out," he grinned.

I started laughing. "No, I know," I snorted. "Yeah, let's do that. No sleeping pills for me though. That sounds . . . unnatural," I frowned.

After we finished our dinner, we sat out on the balcony for a few hours, talking and enjoying the night.

"So, does this mean we're dating?" he asked with a huge smile, lighting his cigarette and instantly taking a drag.

The question took me off guard and I started blushing; thankful that he couldn't see. "Uhm . . ."

"No pressure by any means. I know we talked about taking it slow, but just like . . . if we had to give it a title . . ." he added, blowing smoke out as he spoke.

I stared out at the downtown skyline and smiled. *Fuck yeah, it means we're dating . . .*

"I mean . . . I'd say so, yeah . . ." I mumbled awkwardly.

I side-glanced at him and saw that he was still smiling, also staring out at the skyline while he smoked his cigarette.

"Cool," he mumbled.

Yeah, it *was* cool, but I had no idea what I was doing. I had never dated anyone before and he seemed liked a veteran pro.

Turning and looking at me, he huffed. "Y'okay?" he asked.

I was staring at my hands, nervously fiddling with my fingers. "Hmm?"

"Are you okay?" he repeated.

I shrugged but nodded. "Yeah. I just . . . this is all very new to me," I forced a laugh.

Leaning back in his chair, he nodded and took another drag from his cigarette. "I don't bite," he said, and I laughed, glancing back out at the city.

My brain was scattered. I wasn't sure how to collect my thoughts and I jumped when Jimmy started talking again.

"Nils will be *thrilled*," he added.

I laughed but frowned, not understanding the statement. "Oh?"

"Yeah, she's wanted this since day one. Almost as badly as me," he confessed and I continued to frown, saying nothing.

Suddenly, against my will, my jaw stretched out into one of the biggest yawns and made my eyes water. He noticed this and started laughing.

"See? You're not *completely* nocturnal," he said, squishing the end of his cigarette and flicking it off the edge. "C'mon. Let's go to bed," he added, standing and patting my leg.

I tensed at the touch.

Heading back inside and leaving the screen door open, I quickly went pee and came back to see Jimmy confidently undressing and getting into bed. I closed my eyes and started laughing. This was going to take some getting used to . . .

"Y'know . . . it's great things turned out the way they did. It's been really hard for me not walking around my own apartment naked," he stated, pulling the covers up to his chin.

I continued to laugh and walked around turning all the lights off. Standing at the other side of the bed, I bit my lip and pushed back any fear I felt creeping up, then started taking off my clothes.

"I mean . . . I'm not saying I would've *hated* you walking around naked . . . but I definitely would have been . . ." I paused, "alarmed, to say the least," I laughed, getting into bed beside him.

"Yeah right! I tested those waters and your whole face went bright red!" he cackled.

I brought the blanket up over my body and frowned. "When?"

"You, coffee. Me, naked. And then you said you had to go to work *early*," he explained with air quotes. "Which was a *lie!*"

I stared at the ceiling, remembering the day, then frowned at the thought.

"Yeah, that was also the same day that Aaron attacked me . . ." I mumbled, and he sighed.

"Well . . . I mean, yeah . . ." he mumbled, also staring up at the ceiling and frowning. "Well, shit. Thanks for taking *that* turn," he said and I forced a laugh.

"Sorry." I turned to look at him and saw that he was still staring at the ceiling, but his eyes were heavy. I smiled. "Comfortable?" I asked and he nodded and yawned, turning on his side and pulling the covers up over his head.

"Night!"

Then he was silent. I glanced at him to stare at the back of his head, shocked that he had turned to fall asleep that quickly. I mean, sure I was tired, but . . . I wasn't about to fall asleep anytime soon. Staring at the ceiling once more and sighing, I dropped my arm off the side of the bed and jumped but smiled when Poppy rubbed up against me. Shortly after, she jumped up on the bed and curled up beside me, closing her eyes and purring. I continued to pet her and smiled at her. Glancing back at Jimmy, I frowned when I saw that he was breathing deep and slow. Fucker was already asleep. I wish I had that talent, but instead, here I was alone in the dark, again, with nothing but my thoughts . . . again.

Chapter 16

I woke up to my alarm screaming the next morning and my body was not prepared for it. One eye opened after the other and I glared at my phone, reaching over and slowly turning off the irritating sound. I looked over my shoulder with only one eye open and saw that Jimmy was still asleep; no reaction to the sound whatsoever. He was like a sleeping guru. I sighed and stretched both arms above my head, yawning. Slowly getting dressed, I fed Poppy, then opened the door to leave. I'd just eat at Starbucks. It made sense. I made fresh food every morning along with fresh coffee, so what was the point of using our food?

"Want me to walk you?" a little voice asked from the bed.

I stopped in the doorway and looked over at Jimmy's motionless body; his bed head sprawled all over his pillow and his eyes poking out above the blankets.

I smiled. "No, that's okay, J. Thanks though. Sleep in," I said and he gave a little nod.

"Okay. Be safe and have a good day . . . text me when you get to work," he added.

I continued to smile. "Thanks, J. You too. And I will," I said, then quietly closed the door and left.

Even though I had just spent a week without Jimmy, I still power walked to work. Regardless that it had already been two months, I was still on edge when I was alone on the streets; especially because I had to pass that *stupid* alleyway to get to work. I never walked with my iPod anymore. Instead, I walked with my head up, aware of all my surroundings. It was kind of nice, even though I felt like I was scanning everything around me. It almost helped me to enjoy the little things, like the weather and the sound of birds singing. I mean, when they weren't being drowned out by traffic and sirens, which was rare. I got to work and walked inside, yawning so wide it made my eyes water.

"Hah, good morning!" Angie grinned from behind the counter, already filling the front display with baked goods.

"Morning," I mumbled, walking back to the kitchen and grabbing a muffin.

Taking a bite, I grabbed my phone from my back pocket and started a conversation with Jimmy. We had never texted each other before, and it honestly felt kind of weird.

"*At work*" was all I said. I figured it was all I *had* to say, and knowing him, he probably fell back asleep.

"Rough night?" Angie asked, winking at me.

I couldn't hide my smile and walked past her to grab my apron from underneath the countertop.

"Maybe."

"Well, did you talk it out? I figured you went back to his place when you weren't home Friday night . . ."

"Yeah, sorry. I got your text and meant to reply but I was . . . distracted. I guess you could say we talked . . ." I smirked, fiddling with some dishes to try and look busy.

I could feel her eyes on me and when I turned around to look at her, I smiled. She had her mouth covered with both hands and her eyes were wide.

"Oh my God! You banged!" she yelled, and I gasped so hard, I choked on my own spit. "Tell me *everything*!" she gasped, running over and forcing me to sit down.

I started laughing and felt my face go red, instantly overheating. "Nooo, I don't wanna talk about it. It's too weird!" I whined.

"Dallas. You can't do that. Don't leave me hanging! I *need* to know!"

"I'll give you minor details," I said, my cheeks aching from all the smiling I was doing.

Angie ran and grabbed another chair, pulling it up in front of me and grinning. Taking a deep breath in, I forced myself to relax, then sighed.

"When I didn't work Friday, I basically sat around the house doing nothing all day, my thoughts picking away at me and it was driving me crazy. I ended up cleaning the entire house—"

"I saw that. Thanks, by the way."

"Ha, no problem. So, I basically just made the choice. I made the decision that this is real and that I'm okay with it and I went back to his place, knowing perfectly well that he'd be home, and knocked on the door," I explained.

Angie had her legs tucked up to her chest and she was hiding her smile behind her knees. Hard to believe that she was a thirty-year-old woman and even though I loved her, it *was* my personal life and she didn't need to know *every* detail of that night.

"He answered . . . and yeah," I added, and she threw her arms up in frustration.

"*And yeah?!* What yeah?! What happened?! Did you kiss?" she screamed.

I was laughing and nodded.

"Oh my God. Like . . . like *kiss* kiss?" she asked and I nodded again. She covered her face squealing.

"Ang, c'mon. This is the kind of reaction I'd expect from Tiffany," I laughed, then frowned at the thought of talking to Tiffany about . . . *anything,* really.

"I'm sorry, I just . . ." she calmed down and dropped her legs. "I'm just so happy for you, Dallas. Honest to God. You two are fucking adorable."

I ducked my head, blushing. "Thanks."

"So, then what?" she asked, resting her arms on her knees and getting closer to my face.

I rolled my eyes and sighed, but couldn't stop smiling. "Why do you need to know?"

"Oh, I already know. I just wanna hear you say it," she grinned.

I stood up and walked off laughing, pacing the room. "What?! No! If you already know then I'm done talking!" I yelled and she was cackling.

"Did it hurt?" she asked.

I stopped pacing and stared at her in disbelief, eyes wide and mouth dropped open. "*Angela*!" I yelled.

"What? I'm just curious," she giggled.

Thankfully, saved by the bell, our first customer walked in. I glared at Angela and stuck my tongue out, then walked out to serve the customer.

"Good morning," I greeted.

"Lookit that hair!" Gloria enthused.

⚭

The day was just like every other day. Busy in the morning, busy at lunch, then barely anyone after that. It felt nice that Jimmy and I had sorted things out because for the first time since the beginning of the summer, I could finally relax all my emotions and not feel stressed about . . . well, anything. He knew I liked him, and I knew he liked me and there were no complications. I hadn't seen Aaron since the dreadful incident back in August and even though he beat the living shit out of me, I was healed, and I was thankful to be alive and I was thankful for people like Jimmy and Angela. I looked over my shoulder to see her working hard in the kitchen and I smiled to myself.

I decided that at the end of my shift, I'd head over to the parlour to visit Jimmy before he finished *his* shift.

"Goodnight, lover boy! I'll see you tomorrow!" Angie called, flicking the lights off behind me as I walked out of the store.

I laughed, waving at her through the windows as I walked down the street toward the parlour. Walking inside, the only light on was from Jimmy's room. Cautiously walking toward it, I peeked my head in, making sure not to startle anyone that was getting something put on them permanently, only he had no client and he was cleaning up.

"Hey!" he grinned, looking up at me from his chair.

"Oh! I thought you had an appointment?" I asked, walking in and sitting on his bed.

"Nah. Fucker cancelled . . ."

"Oh . . . so what have you been doing all night?" I asked.

He shrugged, then lifted up his pants to reveal a bandage on his right calf. It was a slice of pizza as a little

T. rex. I also saw his pink ice cream cone and I laughed, shaking my head.

"You're going to run out of space soon . . ."

"Eventually . . . then I'll just use you. You're an empty canvas," he grinned, wiping down the surfaces of his countertops and kicking drawers closed.

I laughed and rolled my eyes.

"Ready to go?" he asked, standing.

I dangled my legs back and forth and played with my lip piercing. He turned and looked at me, hand above the light switch, about to leave.

"What's up?" he asked.

"Well . . . y'know. It doesn't have to be tonight. I mean, I don't *want* it to be tonight. But I was just thinking . . . I mean, I was just wondering . . ."

"Dal, spit it out," he said, sitting back down and facing me.

"I just wanted . . . like, I mean . . . you *could* use me as a canvas, if you wanted . . . only if you wanted . . ." I said awkwardly.

He started laughing. "Oh yeah? What did you have in mind?" he asked.

I shrugged. "I dunno. I want something on my chest. Chest pieces look cool. I just don't know what of yet . . ."

"Well. That's kind of the important part, no?" he joked, sticking out his tongue.

"I haven't thought that far . . ."

"How about a heart?" he asked, sitting back in his chair and twirling around to grab his portfolio. I arched a brow. "A heart . . . on my chest? Where my heart is?" I asked.

"Yeah. We can even put it slightly to the left, so it's more accurate . . ."

"J . . . a tattoo of a heart above my heart?" I said, snorting.

"Well, when you say it like that . . . I've actually been doodling something I think you'd like. I'll show you what I mean . . ."

He flipped through pages of his portfolio where he had pictures of tattoos he'd done on himself and others, along with paintings he'd done and plain pencil doodles.

"Ah ha!"

He handed me the book and I looked down at a sketch of the most detailed heart I'd ever seen. None of that fake cartoon stuff. It was a legit, anatomically correct heart with veins and arteries and everything. It looked like it could have been out of a medical book.

"J . . ." I whispered. I couldn't take my eyes off it. "You drew this?" I asked, looking at him.

"Yeah . . . just kind of whipped it up one night waiting for the shop to close . . ."

I mentally rolled my eyes. *If only*, I thought to myself. Such a unique talent, and he just used it to doodle when he was bored.

"I love it."

"Ha, thanks. So, don't you think that'd look rad like . . . right here?" he asked, rolling closer to me and poking me in the chest.

I nodded. "Yeah! But in—"

"Colour, of course. Obviously," he winked, then took the book back. "Cool, well I'll have to look at my schedule later tomorrow. I'm not sure when I'll be able to fit you in . . ." he mumbled, placing the book back in its rightful place, then standing and stretching.

I was grinning from ear to ear.

He looked at me and laughed. "Let's go home," he mumbled with a yawn. "Halloween is coming up. *So* many people get tattoos on Halloween," he sighed, locking the door behind us. "It's one of our biggest days for walk-ins . . . which, now that I think of it, I should update my social . . ." he yawned, taking out his phone and opening his Instagram.

It was then I remembered that I also had an account.

"Oh yeah. I have one of those. I should probably delete it . . ." I mumbled, pressing the button at the crosswalk, then taking my phone out as well.

Jimmy giggled. "Yeah. I came across your page. I don't think you should delete it. Use it! But change your username, if anything," he laughed, and I frowned.

"In my defense, I was wasted when this happened. I don't even remember getting it," I explained.

The crosswalk light changed, and we crossed; Jimmy's face deep in his phone as he created a Halloween post.

"Good enough," he mumbled, posting his picture, and shoving his phone back in his pocket.

Yawning again, he stretched his arms above his head. "Yeah, apparently Meg bullied you into getting it. And then you thought it was a great idea to post *only* drunk pictures. I'd take those down," he laughed, and I frowned.

"Everyone's seen them already anyways. What's the big deal?" I asked.

He shrugged. "Nobody likes drunk party pictures," he laughed again and I continued to frown.

"Just . . . delete the drunk ones and post new ones. Post like . . . a picture of our apartment and talk about how I'm an *awesome* roomie," he grinned, throwing an arm over my shoulder.

I burst out laughing. "Yeah. *That's* what I'm gonna post," I mumbled, rolling my eyes.

Life was good. It was great, actually. Jimmy and I were a real couple—which was still totally weird—and slowly but surely, I wasn't afraid to show it. My wounds were a hundred percent healed and I could move and twist my ribs normally without anything hurting. The odd time, I'd feel a pinch here and there, but nothing I couldn't live with. I'd rather a random pinch than being dead in an alleyway. As for my knee, it actually healed way better than my ribs did.

Jimmy's work was getting noticed more and he was snatching more and more clients as the weeks went by. He even got to hire his own apprentice who took all his consultations and bookings and essentially made his appointments for him. His name was Aiden, he was twenty years old and had but one lonesome tattoo. He was an aspiring tattoo artist and had no experience behind the gun, but whenever Jimmy had the time, he'd show him the ropes. Regardless, he was super outgoing, paid close attention to detail, and was great for the job. Plus, it was one less thing for Jimmy to do, since lately, he was swamped.

One day I had off, I spent the entire day at the shop and hung out with Nils when she wasn't busy; Jimmy being busy all day. I was cashing someone out who had just gotten their nose pierced and when Jimmy finally had his first break, he came up behind me and gently squeezed my side.

"Hey," he smiled, kissing the side of my neck.

It sent shivers down my spine.

"Working hard?" he asked, reaching under the desk and grabbing a water bottle from the mini fridge.

I smiled at him and closed the register. "Yep!"

"He's a natural Shop Bitch," Nils laughed, leaning on my shoulder.

I smiled back and forth between the two of them, then Jimmy laughed and sighed, rolling his eyes before heading back to his room.

"We've been through this. Don't get any ideas," he said, closing the door behind him to start working on a new sketch for a new appointment.

Nils giggled. "He doesn't know what he's talking about. Ignore him and work here," she smiled, winking and heading back to her room.

Joining me behind the counter, Aiden sighed and stretched his neck side to side. "Shit, he's gonna be buusssyyy," he mumbled, grabbing the schedule from under the desk and flipping through the months coming.

I grabbed myself a water and glanced down at the schedule as well. Spying everyone's names, Jimmy had full days almost every single day. As proud as I was, I knew he was going to be exhausted.

We stayed late that night after the shop had closed so he could tattoo the heart on my chest and I won't lie, it fucking hurt. It hurt so much, but I didn't want to come off as the biggest baby in the history of babies, so I sucked it up. The realistic heart went on the left side of my chest, directly on my peck and he was currently doing the finishing touches around my nipple. I was grabbing the edge of the tattoo bed so tight that my knuckles were white.

"I'm impressed," he said, wiping away some of the ink and dipping his needle back in the black.

"Hmm?" I mumbled, turning my head and looking at him.

He was focusing on tattooing but smiled a little.

"Usually the nipple can be pretty spicy. You're actually taking this really well."

I turned my head back and stared at the ceiling, tensing my body and closing my eyes when he went back to colouring.

"Oh good, so it's not just me."

"Ha! Why do you say that?"

"This fucking hurts," I said, laughing a little bit.

I couldn't move too much since he was working on my chest, after all. The whole session took us almost to one in the morning, but it was all worth the wait and all worth the pain. It looked amazing and I was obsessed with it. He finished the final touch and rolled back in his chair to examine it, while I crunched up awkwardly and tried looking down at it.

"How's it look?" I asked.

He couldn't stop smiling and rolled back up to dab it with the cloth a few more times.

"Fucking amazing. If I do say so myself," he smiled.

"Heh. Well, it's your artwork," I smiled, laying back down.

He laughed and pulled his gloves off, rolling in closer and resting his chin on my shoulder. "Thanks babe," he mumbled, leaning in closer and gently kissing me on the lips.

I was still smiling. Sighing, he rolled back and stood, starting to clean everything up.

"Well. It's late. Pop's is probably piiiiiissed," he said, tossing the necessary things in the garbage.

I slowly sat up and closed my eyes from feeling a head rush, but then gasped when I saw the final tattoo in the mirror.

"Holy shit, J. It's amazing," I whispered.

He smiled, then gasped. "Oh! Bandage! Almost forgot! You distracted me!" he laughed, grabbing the giant saran wrap bandage and sticking it on.

Watching Jimmy's success was an eye opener. It really got me thinking more about my future and what I wanted to do, because I obviously wouldn't be working at Starbucks forever. But seeing how I never went to college or university or had the money to go even if I wanted to . . . it made things a little harder. I didn't really have any hobbies either; nothing to spark the interest of a possible career. Jimmy had been drawing since he was a kid and he was good at it and found a way to make money doing what he loved. I . . . was good at making coffee. And I hated— not that he made more than me, because he deserved ever penny—that he was paying for almost everything and I was just a small sprinkle of money on top to help with groceries here and there. I obviously helped with rent too, but I usually lived paycheque to paycheque and never really had any savings left over.

Eventually manning up, I asked Angela for budget help and stayed late one night after closing.

"I'm staying late tonight" I had texted Jimmy just to give him a heads up.

"That works. I'm just finishing up then I'm heading to the gym. It's been too long."

"The gym?" I asked out loud.

He was already working long shifts; I couldn't wrap my head around where he got the energy to go to the gym, but to each their own.

Angela and I sat down and went over my expenses and what I could do to actually *save* money instead of just spending it all. It was a positive experience, that was for sure, and I even ended up leaving with a raise.

"God, all it took was for me to complain about money issues to get a raise?" I laughed.

She rolled her eyes and sat back in her chair, folding her arms across her chest. "Well, I mean . . . not that I *want* you to leave, but you *have* been working here for a long time. I'm happy you're discovering all of this on your own . . ."

"Yeah . . ." I mumbled with a slight smile.

"But . . . I don't know if I'm even allowed to give you anymore raises. I'm not even sure I'm allowed to give you *that* raise, but fuck 'em. You deserve it," she laughed and I smiled at her.

"Thanks, Ang."

"It's just that . . . you can only pay a barista so much, y'know?" she asked, and I nodded.

"No, I get it. I truly do appreciate it."

"You know how you could make some more cash?"

"How?" I asked, genuinely interested.

She sat up and stretched, smirking at me. "Babysitting?" she asked quietly, and I started laughing, tucking my chair in and taking a few steps back.

"Nope! Can't rope me into that one again!" I called out, opening the front door.

"C'mon! One night!" she yelled back.

"Night, Ang!"

Chapter 17

November 21 was Jimmy's twenty-sixth birthday and what originally started out as a huge party at No Other Place turned into a tiny quiet dinner with just him, Nils and me. Jack had planned a huge surprise party at the bar for friends only, but got side-tracked by a family emergency in New York. We all piled into Nils' car and dropped him off at the airport, and he assured us that he wanted the party to go on. So, we opted for the beach.

Nils, Jimmy and I were dressed to our best and made our way to the Santa Monica Pier.

"Okay. I've seen these things all over the place. Have you ever tried one?" Jimmy asked, gesturing to a pile of scooters and looking back and forth between me and Nils.

She shook her head and laughed, whereas I frowned and stared at him, confused.

"You've never been on a scooter before?" I asked and he frowned back at me.

"I've obviously been on a scooter. But these are different! They're electric! You just like . . . stand there and press down this little button!" he enthused, walking up to one and holding it up right.

Most of them were lying on their side and not parked right at all. The electric side of them sparked my interest, and suddenly I wanted to try one out.

"Well, how do they work?" Nils asked and I giggled.

"You wanna ride the scooter in your dress and heels?" I asked and she looked insulted.

"Oh course! Even *more* so because I'm in a dress and heels! It's like you don't know me at all," she smirked, winking.

I started laughing. "Okay, okay. Let's get some then."

"We can take them to Uno Dos Taco," she grinned.

Jimmy was still figuring out how to activate the scooter he had in his hand. "Okay. So, we have to download this app . . . and then they take our Visa information. They're fifteen cents a minute."

"Nice!" I smiled, grabbing my wallet from my back pocket and grabbing my Visa.

Eventually getting three scooters figured out, we made our way to Uno Dos Taco up the street and I couldn't stop laughing. I mean I was honestly in hysterics. Jimmy and I were both in extremely expensive suits and Nils was in a dress with heels . . . and we were scooting down Ocean Boulevard, making our way toward a taco joint.

They were simple things, really. There was a button to go, and a button to brake. There was a little bell on the side to notify pedestrians when you were near, and even a little headlight on the front. They also went surprisingly fast; reaching a shocking speed of fifteen miles an hour. I loved it. I wanted to ride these things everywhere.

We got to Uno Dos Taco and bought three family packs of practically everything, then scooted our way back to Pacific Park.

"Well, now what do we do with the scooters?" Nils asked, stepping off hers and sipping from her drink.

"Uhm . . . lemme see . . ." Jimmy mumbled, also stepping off his scooter and looking at the app on his phone.

The sun was in the beginning stages of going down and the parking lot at the pier was starting to pack up. It was obviously a popular place for watching sunsets.

"We just tell the app that we're done with the ride," Jimmy explained, frowning at his phone while he tried to figure everything out.

"Rate your ride," I spoke out loud, also staring at my app. "Excellent!" I grinned, pressing the necessary button.

Nils started laughing. "Yeah, I'm going to rate it the same thing. That was so much fun!"

"Fuck walking. Let's take these bad boys everywhere we go. They probably have them back at home too, we've just never noticed them," Jimmy said, placing his phone back in his pocket.

I snorted. "We're gonna get our Visa bills and they're *just* going to be from scooters," I laughed.

"Hey, I'd totally be okay with that. It's not very expensive in the end. What was that? Like . . . six dollars?" he asked, and I nodded.

"Okay, let's find where we wanna sit on the beach. The sun is starting to go down," Nils said, leaning her scooter up against a bike rack.

Getting to the sand, Nils took off her heels and carried them since it was too hard for her to walk. I thought about doing the same since sand was getting inside my shoes and it was uncomfortable, but I honestly couldn't be bothered. Sitting in the sand, both Nils and Jimmy were quick to open the bag and dig into our gourmet meal.

"I can't remember the last time I wore a dress . . ." Nils mumbled, stuffing her face.

Jimmy started laughing. "Oh, c'mon! Don't you remember when you went on that date with . . . oh God, what was his doughebag name again?"

"Oh *God*. Tyler? That guy was an asshole."

"Why did you wear a dress, then?" I asked.

Nils stuffed her face again and frowned while chewing obnoxiously.

"Nilly felt like being girly. She curled her hair and wore pretty makeup and a little summer dress—"

Nils swallowed her food and kicked out, pushing Jimmy over with her foot. "I was going on a date with a guy I liked at the time!" she yelled, frowning at him laughing on the ground.

I smiled at the two of them, then went back to staring at the Ferris wheel. Jimmy sat up and nudged me.

"What's your deal with the pier?" he asked, sipping his Coke and chewing on the straw. "You keep zoning out at it," he laughed and I shrugged.

"I've lived here my whole life and I've never been down here. It's pretty; the lights 'n' stuff," I mumbled.

The sun was lower now, and the sky was starting to turn bright orange and pink. The Ferris wheel lights had just turned on and were bright neon green.

"You've never been to Pacific Park?!" Nils choked, staring at me with wide eyes.

I shrugged again. "Need friends to do this sort of stuff with, I suppose," I laughed.

The two exchanged looks and Nils stood, patting the sand off her dress.

"Alright. Let's go," she said.

Jimmy stood up beside her, also shaking the sand off his pants. I stared up at the two of them, taco still in my hand.

"What?" I blinked.

"We're taking you to the pier. You can't live in LA and *not* come here. It's awesome," Jimmy smiled, offering me a hand to stand up.

I frowned, taking it and pulling myself up. "But—"

"Grab your food. Let's go!" Nils said, having already picked up her heels and her bag of tacos.

Jimmy grabbed his stuff and ran off to catch up with her while I stared at the back of their heads, confused. It all just happened so quickly. Laughing, I quickly picked up my food and drink and ran after them. Nils eventually made her way into the water and was splashing around getting the bottom of her dress all wet.

"Why wear it and not enjoy it?" she asked, a huge smile on her face.

I laughed, shaking my head. *These two are nuts,* I thought. Jimmy walked beside me and nudged my arm a little, smirking at me. I stared at him and frowned, knowing exactly what he wanted to do.

"No."

"Don't be so gay! Go in the water!" he yelled.

I laughed and nudged him back. "No!"

He nudged me once more a little harder, but before I could trip into the water, I grabbed his jacket and pulled him along with me. Nils jumped out of the way just as soon as Jimmy and I went crashing into the ocean, both completely submerged for a few seconds. I sat up laughing, now completely drenched.

"That's a whole other level of enjoying your outfits," Nils laughed, looking down at us.

It was dark now and the only lights we had were coming from the glowing colourful pier right beside us.

Sitting up, I looked over at Jimmy, who was still laying down in the water, laughing.

"God, salt water is *disgusting*!" he spat, sitting up.

Both eventually standing, I walked back toward the sand and scooped up our ruined bags of food and ran to the garbage to throw them out. I only had one taco out of the five that were given to me in my family pack. Hearing Nils scream behind me, I turned around and saw Jimmy carrying her into deeper water. She was screaming and laughing at the same time and trying her best to squirm out of his grip.

"JAMES ANTHONY ECHO, DON'T YOU FUCKING DARE!" she yelled, kicking her legs.

I stood at the shoreline ringing out my clothes and laughing harder when Jimmy reached hip level water.

"Bye, Nilly!" he yelled, and tossed her in.

One last final scream from her until she splashed into the ocean. He ran out to come join me and killed himself laughing when Nils came to the surface.

"*James!*" she screamed, running back out.

Her dress stuck tight to her body and her makeup was smeared all down her face.

"You fucking twat!" she laughed, trying her best to wipe her eyeliner off with her hands.

The black smeared onto her palms and she sighed. "Whatever. Let's get some rides," she mumbled, grabbing her heels that had floated to shore and walking ahead of us.

We finally got to the pier and rode some rides, laughing when we got strange looks from people. We were dressed like we were ready for a wedding, but we were all dripping wet and Nils had makeup all over her face.

"I'm uncomfortable. This dress couldn't possibly get any tighter. I'm gonna buy some clothes to change into. And I need the bathroom to fix this makeup," she said, looking around.

"Aww, you look hot though," Jimmy laughed.

She stuck her tongue out at him before leaving.

"We're gonna go on the Pacific Wheel!" he yelled out to her, holding my hand.

I stared at him with wide eyes. "We are?"

"Yep! C'mon!" he grinned, squeezing my hand and leading the way.

Nils walked off laughing.

This ride had a short line, so we were next to get on and I was instantly uncomfortable. I liked rides, for the most part, but I was actually terrified of heights. And there was something about Ferris wheels that didn't sit right with me. It wasn't *too* windy tonight, but windy enough that while we stood in line and I looked up at the ride, I saw each individual cage rock back and forth. It made me feel sick. Sitting down, Jimmy got in after me and sat directly across from me, smiling. One of the ride attendants came by and closed the tiny gate, locking us in, and I stared at him with pure horror.

"That's all we get?" I squeaked, looking at Jimmy.

He started laughing. "What did you expect?"

"I dunno, like . . . a seat belt or something?!"

"How fast do you think this thing goes?" he laughed.

"I dunno! It's windy out!"

"Relaaaaax," he smiled, leaning back in the seat and stretching out his legs.

Looking all around, I felt myself start panicking even more once the ride started to move. Jimmy was still laughing at me. We didn't get very far before stopping again, and it was such an abrupt stop that our cage swung back and forth.

Closing my eyes, I swallowed the lump in my throat and sighed. "I remember why I never came to the pier now . . ." I mumbled and Jimmy chuckled.

"Dal, it's a *Ferris* wheel. *Children* go on this," he explained.

Opening my eyes to glare at him, I sighed once more. "Yeah, well . . . whatever. Children don't understand consequences," I said, slightly leaning to my right to look down below.

We weren't very high, but I still wasn't enjoying myself.

Jimmy was laughing even harder now. "Consequences? Consequences like what?"

"Falling! From high places!" I explained, sitting up right and placing my palms in my lap.

He smirked and rolled his eyes, scooting over to the side to get a better view of down below.

"*Don't!* Do that. Please," I panted, starting at him with wide eyes when our cage moved some more.

"Okay. We gotta get your mind somewhere else. You're being ridiculous," he mumbled, no longer smiling.

I swallowed the lump in my throat once more and stared at him. "What did you have in mind?" I asked.

He stood and walked over to my side of the cage and I stared at him with wide eyes.

"*What are you doing?!*" I hissed. "The sign says no standing!"

And there was in fact a sign on the inside of the cage that said **No Standing At Any Time While The Ride Is In Motion.** He sat beside me and wrapped his arm over my shoulders, pulling me in closer to him and sighing.

"Let's take a picture," he said, and it threw me off.

"What?"

"Let's take a picture together. I want a birthday picture," he smiled.

I ducked my head and laughed a little, feeling embarrassed. "I'm not good at pictures," I explained.

"I don't care. Get out your phone," he said.

Frowning at him, I awkwardly—and cautiously—sat up and grabbed my phone from my back pocket, holding it out and opening the camera app. He was quick to take the phone from me and extended his arm out in front of us.

I side-glanced at him and smiled a little. "I can't just smile on command, J. I told you. I'm not good at pictures. You gotta make me laugh or something," I said.

Turning to look at me, he stuck his tongue out and made a farting noise. It was childish, but it wasn't what I was expecting, and sure enough, I laughed pretty freaking hard. He was quick to face the camera again and took a few pictures.

"Wow," I laughed, shaking my head.

"Hey, it worked, didn't it?" he asked, bringing the phone back so he could examine the pictures with a closer look.

"Again," he smiled, extending his arm again.

Now I couldn't *stop* smiling and rolled my eyes. Staring straight ahead at the camera, I kept my genuine smile and Jimmy was quick to lean in and kiss me on the cheek, blowing a few raspberries.

"Shit yeah, that one's gonna be cute as fuck," he mumbled, bringing the phone back to stare at it.

Placing the phone on my lap, he stared at me. "Now. Go on to your Instagram page, delete your embarrassing drunk pictures from Jack's party, since I told you to do that back in October and you still haven't done it, and upload these ones instead. And change your username," he explained with a smirk on his face.

I frowned, staring down at my phone and opening the Instagram app. Staring at my drunken pictures, I snorted and started laughing, holding my phone up to show Jimmy, then saw that we had already gone around twice and were stopped at the very top.

"Jeeeesus Christ!" I hissed, staring out at the beach front and putting my phone down.

Instagram would have to wait for another day. This was fucking terrifying.

"Well, I distracted you a *little* bit," he shrugged.

I turned to look back at him and sighed, forcing a smile. "You did. Thanks, J," I mumbled.

I thought about leaning forwards and kissing him, but just when I built up the courage to do so, the ride started moving again and I closed my eyes.

"Here. Gimme this," he mumbled, taking my phone from my lap and opening my Instagram app again.

I watched with interest as he changed my username to just my normal name and deleted all my embarrassing drunk pictures.

"You're good at this," I mumbled, still watching as he uploaded one of the pictures he just took of the two of us.

"I use it *mainly* for tattooing. The odd time I'll post a personal life thing here or there . . ." he mumbled, focusing on writing a caption.

He changed my picture to the one where he was kissing my cheek, then handed the phone back and smiled at me.

"There! Now people won't think you're some sort of drunk," he laughed.

I stared at the picture on my account and smiled, looking back at him and smiling wider. This time, I didn't care that we were however high in the sky, spinning in circles. I leaned forwards and pressed my lips against his.

"Happy birthday, J," I mumbled, my lips still pressed against his.

I felt him smile. "Thanks, babe," he mumbled in return.

Finally, the Ferris wheel came to a stop and it was our turn to get off. I climbed out first and walked straight for Nils who was standing in the crowd waiting for us. Resting my forehead on her shoulder, she laughed and reached back to pat my head.

"Awww, didn't like the ride I take it?" she asked.

"No," I mumbled.

"Shut up, you were fine!" Jimmy snapped, laughing at me.

"Don't like heights?" she asked, turning to look at me.

I shook my head. "Hate them."

"*Hates* them," Jimmy repeated. "But hey! I fixed his Instagram. Oh, and I made him follow you and myself," he smiled.

Standing up straight, I giggled. "I didn't know how to use it," I said, looking at Nils and shrugging.

She nodded. "I assumed, since your username was atrocious and your only pictures were drunk ones from Jack's party," she explained.

I scrunched up my nose.

Chapter 18

December 2016

Normally in December, we ranged anywhere between low sixties to mid eighties, but for the first week, we had a random heat wave roll through and it was almost ninety-five degrees out. I loved it. The sidewalk outside the parlour was currently under construction and everyone from No Regrets had to stay home for a week until the construction was done. Jimmy wasn't impressed.

Today, Nils was hanging out at our apartment, and when I got home from work, she was hanging upside down off our couch, talking about the beach.

"And since the shop is closed for a while, why don't we try and get *everyone* to come? Like, I mean the *whole* gang," she smiled, swinging her head back and forth and watching Poppy play with the ends of her hair.

"If you wanna go ahead and text everyone, be my guest," Jimmy laughed.

Quickly sitting up, Nils blew her hair out of her face and scrambled to grab her phone. "It's already late! I gotta start texting now!" she panted, hunching down in the couch and frantically texting her friends.

"We should wake up earlier and go to the H sign for the sunrise," Jimmy added.

Walking over to the bed where Jimmy was laying, I crawled up and laid beside him, leaning on his chest and smiling at Nils who continued to chaotically text.

"Ha! There. I just wrote a massive text and *spam* texted everyone," she grinned, turning and smiling at us.

We both started laughing.

"Nilly?"

"Hmm?" she smiled,

"H Sign?" Jimmy asked.

"Oh. Yeah, yeah. I'm down," she said, laying back on the couch and going back on her phone.

Grabbing my own phone, I went on my Instagram account for any updates. After Jimmy fixed my page and showed me how to actually use the app, I had recently been having fun with uploading pictures of drinks from work. Apparently, the people of Instagram *loved* the hipster pictures of various coffees.

"Sure? Because last time I asked you to come with me for the sunrise hike, you whined the entire time about how early it was and how you hadn't had a coffee yet," he explained.

I remained staring at my phone and snorted.

Nils sighed. "I mean . . . it *is* stupid early. But I love the view, so it's worth it," she mumbled.

"Okay. Your words. I'm holding you to them," Jimmy said.

❧

Flinching at the shrieking sound of our phone alarms going off, I quickly reached out and slid my fingers across my screen until the noise stopped. Jimmy did the same to his own phone. Sighing and stretching my arms above my head, I smiled when Jimmy rolled over and curled his body around me. Grabbing his arm that was hugged around me, I squeezed myself into him. He rested his forehead against my back and sighed happily into my ear.

"Good morning," he croaked, and I smiled wider at his raspy morning voice.

Kissing his wrist, I leaned back and tried to push my body in even closer to him. He forced a laugh and squeezed me, kissing my collarbone down to my shoulder.

"Mmm. You're so warm," I mumbled, tangling our legs together under the sheets.

Suddenly, his phone started ringing and it made me jump. He laughed but sighed, kissing my shoulder one more time before turning over to answer whoever was calling.

"Yeeessss?" he answered, putting it on speaker.

"I hope your cute asses have gotten out of bed and are almost ready. I'm already on my way," Nils said.

She had gone home the night before; ever since we decided we were waking up early and going on a hike, she claimed she had to be home to prepare the right outfit. She left shortly after we agreed on the task.

Jimmy closed his eyes and started laughing. "We're up," he said.

"Good," she said, then she hung up.

I smiled and nudged him. "C'mon. Let's get ready . . ." I mumbled.

❧

"I've never been to the Hollywood sign . . ." I admitted, looking at Jimmy and laughing at the face he was making.

He didn't seem impressed.

"What *is* it with you people?!" he snapped, opening the door for me and closing it behind us once we walked out.

I turned to watch him lock it and laughed again. "You people?" I asked.

He shoved his key back in his pocket and sighed, taking my hand and leading the way toward the elevator.

"I swear I'm the only local that's been to the H sign. Nils has never been. My ex had never been—"

"So . . . two people," I teased, looking at him and sticking my tongue out.

"All I'm saying is . . . it was right up the hill from you. That'd be like, what . . . an hour walk, one way?" he asked, reaching the elevator and letting go of my hand.

I shoved my hands in my pockets and shrugged. "Dunno. But who would I have gone with?" I asked.

He had taken out his phone and was texting Nils. "Angela? She has a kid, doesn't she? That hike would be great for him to burn off some energy!"

"Nah. Ang doesn't do the outdoors," I laughed.

Putting his phone back in his pocket and taking my hand once more, he frowned and stepped onto the elevator once the door opened.

"She's a strange lady . . ." he mumbled and I laughed and nodded.

"She is."

We stood in silence as the elevator lowered and once we stepped out into the front lobby, he grabbed his phone again with his free hand.

"Mkay, Nilly said she's almost here," he said, glancing at his phone before putting it back in his pocket.

I nodded. "Cool."

Standing outside and waiting for Nils, Jimmy lit himself a cigarette and I leaned against the wall, staring out and people watching. It was early and the morning rush hour was just starting.

"You're still down for the beach later, right?" he asked, smoke flowing through his lips as he spoke.

I smiled and nodded. "Yep," I said before glancing at a woman walking her little dog past us on the sidewalk.

"This is all new stuff to you, isn't it?" Jimmy asked and I arched a brow.

"What?"

"Just like . . . doing things and hanging out with people," he stated.

I shrugged. "Pretty much, yeah. But it's fun cause I know everyone now. This would have been an anxiety attack if everyone was a stranger," I smiled.

"That's true. Well, I'm glad I came as a package deal and brought friends along," he laughed.

Moments later, Nils could be seen making her way up Highland toward us. Cigarette sticking out of her mouth, her hood was up and she was frowning. Her hair popped out on either side of her face, messy and knotted. I snorted.

"Why are we doing this so early again?" she asked, her cigarette staying between her lips as she spoke.

"Because sunrises are cool and you love it. So, shut up," Jimmy said. "Plus, turns out Dal has never been, so this will be a great first impression," he added.

I turned to Nils and smiled.

She snorted and poked my nose. "Cute," she said, then finally took her smoke into her hand and sighed. "Well, let's get going, then."

"Why the hoodie?" Jimmy asked, taking my hand again once we started to walk.

"Because it's fucking cold as balls, James!" she snapped and I snorted. "Also, are we still going to the beach after this? Cause I don't want to freeze my ass off. Like, what happened to that heat wave we were promised?" she vented.

I looked down at my hand linked with Jimmy's and smiled at our tattoos. It was kind of my new favourite thing to stare at.

"It's going to warm up soon, and then you're gonna regret that sweater," Jimmy explained.

She rolled her eyes. "That's a future me problem," she smiled, taking another drag of her cigarette and adjusting her hood.

Reaching the beginning of our hike up the Hollywood hills, Jimmy stared ahead at the darkness and sighed, raising his phone and pointing his flashlight app in front of us.

"What's wrong?" I asked and Nils giggled, tossing her hundredth cigarette off to the side and opening Spotify on her phone.

"James is scared of snakes," she explained.

I looked at him and smiled, shrugged and squeezed his hand. He looked at me.

"I get it. I'm petrified of spiders, so . . . I kinda get it," I said and Nils giggled again.

"Yeah, but that makes sense. Spiders can get you in your house and like . . . can hide in small places and have a shit ton of legs. Snakes . . . when are you *ever*—"

"What about that?" Jimmy asked, stopping and pointing ahead and shining his light.

Nils chose a song on her phone and we both looked up, and sure enough, there was a generously sized rattlesnake, coiled up in a ball, not more than a few feet in front of us.

"Oh," Nils snorted, then bent over laughing.

Jimmy stayed where he was and I turned to look at him.

"We'll just slowly go around," I said.

"I wanna take a picture of it!" Nils gasped, taking her phone out once more and opening her camera app.

I sighed and Jimmy whined.

"Can you nooooottt? I really don't want anyone going to the hospital for—"

But by the time Nils got close enough to even *attempt* to take a picture, the snake turned and disappeared in the long grass. Jimmy loosened up and sighed.

"Ha! That's karma for trying to get us all killed!" he yelled, smiling and proceeding to walk on.

I wasn't sure how long we were walking for, but eventually we could turn off our flashlight apps and give our phones a rest. The sun was slowly rising and providing natural light. Thankfully, we didn't see anymore snakes after the first incident. After a sharp left curve in the path, we were facing out toward the city and the glowing skyline could be seen clear as day.

"Eurgh! *This* is when it becomes worth it!" Nils enthused, finally taking off her hoodie after having previously rolled up the sleeves.

Continuing our climb, the mood did a sudden shift when "I Will Follow You into the Dark" by Death Cab for Cutie came on Nils' Spotify playlist. She didn't change it and I frowned at the ground as we walked.

Breaking the silence, Nils sighed. "When I die, I want this song to be played at my funeral," she said, and I glanced up at her, slightly mortified.

Jimmy snorted. "That's dark. This song is *incredibly* sad, Nilly," he said, staring at the ground as he spoke.

She shrugged. "Yeah, that's the point. I'm fucking dead. People *better* be sad! No smiling or laughing," she teased, winking at me and sticking her tongue out.

I laughed and Jimmy huffed, not as amused.

"Well, I'll make sure it's played at your funeral, Nilly. Make sure everyone is nice 'n' sad," he said, looking at her and smiling.

She frowned. "Oi. What makes you think I'm dying before you?" she asked and I snorted, looking down at the tiny rocks I started kicking.

"Oh, *please!* Between the cigarettes and the Red Bull addiction, I'm surprised you haven't croaked *yet*," he teased in return.

Nils started laughing. "Whatever. I *hope* I go before you. That way I can *haunt* your ass until you come join me," she smirked and I started laughing all over again.

"What if I go to heaven and you go to hell?" he asked and she gasped, reaching out and punching him.

"Sod off! You're going to hell just as bad as I am!" she yelled, punching him once more.

He turned his back to her and burst out laughing.

The hike was exhausting, but I think more so because we got up at 5:00 a.m. and I had never done this kind of cardio. The path slowly got brighter and brighter as the sun slowly began its climb into the sky and I could start to actually make out the trail. The hills were twisting, winding, climbing, and slowly inclining. We finally did one full clockwise turn before reaching the top. I was somewhat out of breath, but the view did not disappoint. The sky was a dark shade of blue with the stars and the moon still in sight, but down over above the ocean was a tiny, bright orange ball. It slowly started glowing a bright pink before turning the above clouds into a dark purple. Along with the city lights, it made a Kodak moment.

"Wow," I panted, leaning forwards with my hands on my knees.

Jimmy smiled, standing behind me and stretching his arms above his head. "Yep," he mumbled.

"*Oh!* I just love it. Absolutely love it," Nils smiled, taking out her phone and taking a bunch of pictures.

I sat down on the edge and stared down at the sign. "Wow," I said again.

Jimmy sat beside me, occasionally kicking my feet with his own. "Pretty cool, huh?" he asked, resting his head on my shoulder and sighing.

Suddenly forcing herself between us, Nils was ecstatic as she sat down and held out her arm, angling her phone to the side and smiling wide.

"Say Dallas' H Sign Virginityyyyyy!" she grinned, taking the picture regardless of what we looked like.

Jimmy had said the phrase with a wide grin, but I burst out laughing. Bringing her phone closer to look at the pictures she had just taken, she smiled wider and sighed.

"Adorable," she said, grabbing onto my shoulder and helping herself back to her feet.

I watched her walk off and started laughing, looking at Jimmy confused.

He shrugged. "She's a simple creature, really. Not a fan of cold mornings or cardio, but *loves* herself a good sunrise. She's taken her pictures, now she's ready to go home," he smiled.

"I'm ready to go when you are!" Nils yelled out, face deep in her phone as other hikers showed face and stepped around her.

I ducked my head laughing.

"We'll come another time just the two of us," Jimmy said, patting my thigh before standing and stretching as he headed toward Nils.

I stared out at my city once more and sighed, smiling a little as I took in the view once more.

I had already changed into my bathing suit and was sitting on the couch, petting Poppy and watching TV while Jimmy got ready. Smiling at Poppy and scratching under her chin, I jumped when Jimmy abruptly opened the bathroom door and stood with his hands on his hips.

"I'm ready," he said, already wearing his sunglasses and a backwards snapback.

His swimming shorts were black with white stripes along the side, and he wore a black sleeveless shirt that read *Young And Reckless* across the front in a bright yellow font. I turned off the TV and smiled at him, getting up from the couch and walking up toward him.

"Hot," I laughed, staring at his somewhat childish shirt.

He grinned, holding his arms out straight on either side. "I know, aren't I?" he grinned, wrapping his arms around me and kissing me on my forehead.

Throwing our towels in a bag, we set out for the nearest bus stop to make our way down to Santa Monica. Walking down the ramp toward the pier, I smiled at the view in the daylight, seeing as I had only been here at night.

"I wonder if anyone is here yet," Jimmy thought out loud, swinging our linked hands back and forth.

I glanced around at either sides of the beach, mainly scanning for Nils' beacon-like hair.

"Ah-ha!" he smiled, pointing to the faint light blue dot in the distance to our left. "She's like a fucking highlighter . . ."

"*Used* to be. She's not so vibrant anymore . . ." I pointed out.

When I first met Nils back in the summer, her hair was an electric ice-like blue. If Windex and bleach had a baby.

"Hmm, yeah. Good call. I'll point it out to her and watch her freak and get all self-conscious," Jimmy laughed, leading the way down the left side of the boardwalk.

I adjusted the bags straps on my shoulders and did my best to walk at Jimmy's pace, while also looking all around my surroundings. He started laughing and I looked at him and frowned.

"What?" I asked.

"Nothing. You're just cute. Lookin' around and stuff," he smiled.

I scrunched up my nose and stuck out my tongue. "It's nice here," I said, looking up at the palm trees.

Getting closer to the crew, I started laughing when I realized that all hair things considered, Nils was still wearing a neon yellow bikini and resembled a highlighter. I snorted and shook my head. She was playing volleyball with Lilly, Megan and Jillian, but got distracted when she saw us and got a volleyball to the side of her head.

"Oi! Lil!" she snapped and Lilly started laughing.

"Sorry! Pay attention!" she snorted.

Nils kicked the ball back before running toward us. "Hi boys!" she greeted, grabbing us at the same time and hugging us.

"Ehhh! Wet titties!" Jimmy whined and I started laughing, staring down at the wet spot on my shirt.

"Yeah, I went swimming already," she grinned, stepping back, pressing her palms against her boobs, and pressing the water out of her top.

I snorted. "Nice."

"Jack also filled a bunch of Gatorade bottles with booze!" she enthused, grabbing a bottle once we reached everyone and taking a sip. "This is vodka and cranberry juice," she grinned.

Jimmy started laughing and I dropped our bag at our feet.

"Of course," Jimmy mumbled, opening the bag, grabbing his towel, and flattening it out on the sand.

I did the same and instantly sat down with my legs out in front of me, staring around at everyone.

"Eyyyy! Jimbo!" Jack yelled, coming over with a joint sticking out of his mouth.

Jimmy started laughing and patted him on the back. "Weed too?" he asked and Jack shrugged and nodded.

"It's legal, bro. Why not. Plus, when's the last time we all hung out like this, hmm?" he asked.

"Your party," I stated, remembering the first night I met everyone.

Jimmy smiled and nodded. "He's right."

"Well, whatever. I'm just happy, is all. It's nice to finally have a break from work, y'know?" Jack asked, handing Jimmy a Gatorade and walking off. Jimmy laughed again and sat beside me, sighing and leaning back on his elbows.

"I'm not drinking this," he said, staring at the bottle in his hand.

I turned to look at him. "Why not?" I asked.

"I bet it's tequila. It's clear and Jack handed it to me *way* too confidently," he explained and I started laughing.

"Smell it," I said.

Twisting the lid open, he brought it closer to his nose and gave a tiny sniff.

"DON'T BE LIKE THAT!" Jack yelled in the distance and everyone started laughing when Jimmy shook his head in disgust.

"YOU DICK!" he yelled, closing the lid and whipping the bottle in Jack's direction.

"Tequila?" I asked.

"Tequila," he confirmed, shaking his head and laughing. "Wanna go swimming?" he asked, looking at me and smiling.

Grabbing the hem of his shirt, he lifted it up and over his head. I watched with a smile on my face and sighed.

"Sure," I mumbled, staring at his tattoos.

The whole gang was here: Lilly, Caleb, Liam, Jeremy, Megan, and Jillian who also brought her boyfriend Carlos, then there was also Matt and Evan, obviously Jack and Nils and then Jimmy and myself. We had pitched some sun tents and umbrellas, plus we rented a volleyball net and we were even set up near one of the firepit barrels. We had coolers and coolers of alcoholic and non-alcoholic, plus the odd water bottle. There were skateboards present and rollerblades, plus the one surfboard. Apparently, Jeremy could surf, but I had yet to witness it. We spent the day drinking and smoking—for some—and swimming and playing games of volleyball. It was the most fun I'd had in a while. Anything I did with Jimmy and his friends was fun; it was never a dull moment.

"Why didn't we do this *every* time the shop was closed?" I asked, watching the volleyball get tossed around.

Jimmy and I ran at the same time toward the ball, both laughing, until I psyched out and allowed him to spike it. He threw himself forwards, hit the ball, then fell in the sand on his knees. I started laughing and helped him up.

"Nice."

"Because . . ." he panted, dusting the sand off his knees and getting back into position. ". . . the shop's schedule is all over the place. Our days off are kind of hectic. It's very rare that we have a full *closed* day," he explained, staring back up at the ball. "Head's up!" he yelled, and I quickly looked up and punched the ball with my fist before it hit me in the face.

Everyone dove for it at different times until they all missed and the ball landed right beside Megan's leg.

"*Fuck!*" she screamed, punching her hand into the sand, and I burst out laughing.

Jimmy was already bent over laughing before coming over and slapping me on the back. "Dude!" he laughed, bending over to continue laughing.

Everyone was basically laughing at this point and I wasn't really sure what was so funny.

"What?" I laughed, awkwardly looking around at everybody.

"Just . . . your *face* and you just kinda . . . *punted* it and got us the winning point!" he spat, laughing all over again.

"Oh," I smiled, feeling my face get hot.

⚬∞⚬

I watched Jimmy and Jack skate around the Venice skate park for a bit and found it thoroughly entertaining. The park was filled with skaters and rollerbladers of all ages and all skill levels. There was even a boy who had to be only seven years old and he was kicking ass. Eventually having enough of falling and eating shit, Jack made his way back to the group, whereas Jimmy and I opted for walking along the boardwalk. He gave his skateboard to Jack so he didn't have to carry it around.

Walking hand in hand, we struggled to carry our bags of freshly purchased clothes as well as ice cream cones in our other hands. Jimmy kept his shirt off, whereas I felt more comfortable with mine back on. Plus, watching people gawk over his body was hilarious.

"Are you having fun?" he asked, turning and looking at me.

For some reason, the sunglasses and the backwards hat made him *that much* more attractive and I almost couldn't stop staring at him.

"The most fun," I smiled, leaning in closer and kissing him as we walked.

He smiled and stared straight ahead. "Good."

"Really? Do you *have* to do that in public?!" someone yelled from behind us.

Both frowning and stopping to turn around, I felt my body tense when a taller, larger man was staring at us with disgust. He was on the heavier side and appeared red in the face; his hands were already curled into fists. I stared him up and down and sighed quietly.

"J, leave it," I whispered, staring at him and squeezing his hand.

"I'm sorry? What was that?" he asked, ignoring me completely.

Sighing once more and closing my eyes, my shoulders dropped.

"I mean, the hand holding is already gross enough. You don't have to go around French-kissing!" the man snapped.

I opened my eyes and arched my brow. It was hardly French-kissing, but okay. Letting go of my hand and leaving his bags with me, Jimmy walked forwards and continued to casually lick his ice cream.

"It's a free country, my man. I didn't know it was illegal for two dudes to be in love," he said.   And while I tried my best not to make eye contact with the scary homophobic man, I couldn't help but smile at Jimmy's comment.

"It's fucking disgusting, is what it is!" the man barked and I instantly went back to feeling shitty.

"And how does our relationship affect your life, hmm?" Jimmy asked, standing in front of him and continuing to lick his ice cream.

The man stared at Jimmy's cone and curled his upper lip.

"Oh. I'm sorry. Is my *gay* tongue making you uncomfortable?" Jimmy asked, licking the vanilla ice cream once more.

"Fucking quit it!" the man yelled, taking an aggressive step forwards, but Jimmy didn't even flinch. "Take your ice cream and your redhead *twink* with you!" he added.

I saw Jimmy's shoulder tense, but he didn't budge.

"Are you *hitting* on me?" he asked, licking his ice cream once more.

I frowned and looked around, realizing that a crowd was starting to form. Staring back at Jimmy, I could feel myself starting to overheat. The man's face was redder than before and he clenched his hands into tighter fists.

"Shut the fuck up!" he snapped, stepping in closer.

"Awww, am I hurting your ego—"

But before he could really finish his sentence, the man brought his fist up and straight into Jimmy's face. Dropping his cone and falling back, he stared up and had a smirk on his face as he licked the blood off his bottom lip.

"James!" I yelled, running toward him.

He quickly held up an arm and motioned for me to stay back. "It's fine. I wanted him to make the first move," he said, then got to his feet and threw a fist right back.

Connecting with the man's jaw, he was quick to punch again, but this time, he got him in the gut. He didn't stand a chance with Jimmy's agility and didn't have a window to fight back. Swinging his leg under the man's ankles, Jimmy slammed him onto the ground and pressed his knee into his neck. The man started coughing; his face bleeding.

"I'm sorry, I'm sorry!" he panted, coughing at the end.

Spitting blood off to the side, Jimmy stared down at him, slightly out of breath. "Now, we're going to think twice before harassing people about their sexual orientation, right?" he asked and the man nodded ever so slightly; the movement being difficult with Jimmy's knee still being pressed on his neck.

"Good," Jimmy smiled, patting him on the head before getting back to his feet.

Brushing off his shorts, he walked over to retrieve his glasses and hat from the ground before making his way back to me.

"Are you okay?" he asked and I frowned.

"Am *I* okay? Are *you* okay?!" I asked instead.

He smiled and sighed. "I'm fine," he said, pressing his thumb against his cut lip and staring at the blood. "Nothing I couldn't handle," he added, licking his lip.

I sighed, staring back as the man quickly got to his feet and ran away.

"Bit ticked off about my ice cream, though . . ." he mumbled, staring at his fallen cone.

I pouted as well, then stared at my ice cream in my hand, still perfectly intact.

"Here," I said, handing it over.

"No, no. That's okay. You have it," he smiled, shaking his head and taking my hand back into his.

Unannounced, we both decided to make our way back to the group.

"No, seriously. Here," I said, holding the ice cream up to his mouth, close enough for him to lick it. "We'll share," I smiled.

Licking my ice cream, then side-glancing at me and smiling, he licked the ice cream once more before sighing ever so slightly.

"You're adorable," he said.

His bottom lip had stopped bleeding but had started to swell and bruise ever so slightly. It was visible enough for Nils to lose her shit when we got back to everyone.

"Like *just now*?!" she yelled, grabbing Jimmy's chin and tilting his head in every direction.

He stared up at the sky and rolled his eyes. "Like five minutes ago, I dunno. It happened and we made our way back here," he explained.

"Why didn't you come get us?" Jack asked, staring at me.

I frowned. "It's not like we were all very close to each other. Plus, James had it under control," I smiled, looking back at Jimmy who was smiling at me and winked.

"Yeah, I mean, he was a big guy and he got the first hit, but I got him in the end," he explained, walking over and helping himself to a mysterious alcoholic Gatorade.

"Why'd you let him get the first hit?" Matt asked and Jimmy shrugged, sitting on one of the lawn chairs and sipping his drink.

"In case authorities got involved. That way I could say he started it. Literally," he grinned, taking another sip.

I snorted. It was crazy but it was smart.

"Uggghhhh, I'm just so sick of you getting beat up all the time," Nils whined, standing with her arms crossed.

She was still in her bikini bottoms but was now wearing a t-shirt over her top.

"All the time? I'm not getting beat up all the time," Jimmy frowned.

"You definitely get beat up the *most*," Megan added, laughing a little.

I frowned, feeling a sense of concern. Was this a normal occurrence? Were we not allowed to show public displays of affection? Were the consequences of being gay punches to the face?

"Dal?" Jimmy asked, getting my attention.

I jumped out of my train of thought and stared at him. "Hmm?" I asked.

"You okay?" he asked and I nodded and forced a smile.

"Mmhmm! Yep," I smiled, then tried thinking about something else.

Chapter 19

By the time the sun started to set, almost everyone had made their way back home other than me, Jimmy, Nils and Jack. Most of the beach had cleared out, actually. I guess it was a weekday and people had to work tomorrow, but the shop was closed all week, and it was extremely rare that Jimmy, Jack and Nils had time off together. It never happened, actually, so today had to have been a nice break. Not to mention our humid heat wave.

After going for one final swim, the four of us sat on our towels and watched the sun go down. Jack was passing a joint around, to which I politely declined, and for the most part, we sat in silence. Receiving the joint from Jack, Jimmy pinched the end, took a tiny drag, held the smoke, then blew out his infamous smoke rings. I watched with interest.

"Oh, yeah. Nilly?" he asked, leaning back and staring at Nils who sat on Jack's other side.

"Hmm?" she asked, wrapping herself up in her towel and bringing her knees up to her chest.

"You're not vibrant anymore," Jimmy added.

Staring out at the ocean, Nils frowned before blinking slowly and turning her head to stare at Jimmy with heavy eyes.

"Pardon me?" she asked and Jack gasped with wide eyes.

"Rude! Nilly is *always* vibrant!" he yelled, reaching out and placing both hands on her ears. "Don't listen to him. You're still a highlighter," he slurred and she bit her lip to refrain from laughing.

"She's not! Dal and I were looking for your bright head when we got here earlier and we almost didn't see you! You're faded," Jimmy smirked.

"Well, you know what that means, don't you?" she asked.

Face falling, Jimmy frowned. "No? What?" he asked.

"You're going to have to redye it for me," she grinned, grabbing the tiny joint from Jack and finishing it off.

Laying back on his towel, Jimmy whined loudly and I started laughing, glancing at him over my shoulder and smiling.

"I don't *wanna! You* do it! You do it to yourself all the *time!*" he whined.

I laughed again and Nils stuck out her tongue.

"Tough shit. You're mean to me, so you have to do me this favour to make it up," she explained.

He turned to stare at her and frowned. "I wasn't being mean; I was just being honest. You're dull! Look how non-vibrant it is!" he repeated and Nils went back to frowning.

"You don't have to use such harsh adjectives!" she yelled and this time Jack started laughing.

An hour after the sun set, Nils was curled up on her towel and was using Jack's towel as a blanket. Jimmy and Jack were talking amongst themselves, whereas I was daydreaming about the glowing rides on the pier. It was the most peaceful thing I had ever experienced. The sky was pitch black, the moon was bright, and other than the odd scream coming from the rides, the waves crashing in front of me and the low mumbles of Jack and Jimmy's voices were all I heard. There was a quiet hum as tourists continued to walk the boardwalks and my face flashed vibrant colours as the Ferris wheel lit up.

"Well, boys . . ." Jack mumbled, and it was enough to spike my attention away from the rides. "I think we'll be heading home," he said, turning and placing his hand on Nils' shoulder.

"Hmm?" she mumbled quietly.

"C'mon, crumpet. Let's go home and to our designated beds," he said.

"Mmhmmm . . ." she whispered.

Looking at us and smiling, Jack got to his feet and gently picked Nils up.

"C'mon, Sawyer," he said, placing her on her feet and squatting in front of her. "Jump on."

Drunkenly grabbing onto his shoulders, Nils gave a tiny, pathetic hop and jumped up on Jack's back. We laughed. Adjusting her on his back, Jack turned and smiled at us.

"Text me later," he said, bending down and picking up their bags.

"Night, Jacky," Jimmy laughed, taking my hand and waving at Jack with the other.

Swinging our hands back and forth while carrying our flip-flops in the other, Jimmy and I walked in the shallow water in silence. The pier was staring to empty out and the low mumble of tourists got quieter. The waves continued to splash—occasionally riding up my leg—and the moon was our main source of light.

"Are you okay with what happened today?" Jimmy suddenly asked and it almost made me jump.

"With that big dude on the boardwalk?" I asked, looking at him.

He nodded, staring at our feet splashing through the water. I nervously played with my lip ring.

"I mean . . . I'm not really sure *how* I feel, to be honest," I mumbled, also staring down at our feet.

He sighed quietly, then remained silent. Continuing to play with my lip ring, I sighed as well and squeezed his hand.

"This . . ." I gestured to our hands. "I like this. I like being able to be myself, with you, in public. But I have to be honest . . . it's terrifying every single time we touch, or hold hands, or kiss. For the exact reason of what went down at the boardwalk," I explained quietly.

He looked at me and looked sad. I sighed once more because I wasn't sure if I was explaining myself properly, or if I was just talking myself in circles.

"I really like you, Jimmy. And I really like what we have going on." I stared down at our hands again and smiled ever so slightly. "But today was low-key terrifying and it makes me hesitant to . . . touch you," I explained, looking up and meeting his eyes.

He was nervously chewing on the inside of his cheek and in the moonlight, I could see his swollen lip.

"I know. I'm sorry you had to see what you saw. I didn't mean to take it so far, but . . ." he sighed. "I get it. If you don't wanna—"

"That's not what I'm saying," I cut him off. "I guess what I mean is . . . I'm scared. But it's a risk I'm willing to take—getting punched in the face," I said, smiling at him.

We had reached the pier and stopped underneath it. Squeezing my hand and turning me to face him, he stared at me with sad eyes but smiled. Staring back and forth between my eyes and my lips, he gently reached out and cupped my chin, bringing our faces closer together and softly pressing our lips together.

With the shop being closed, Jimmy remained home for the week and enjoyed some well-deserved time off. Mainly lounging around in sweatpants, he lived on the couch playing video games, but I'd always wake up to breakfast being made and I'd come home to dinner. It was something different every day.

Thursday, I walked in and jumped when I saw him topless, in his boxers, with gloves on and dyeing Nils' hair in the middle of the room.

"Hey!" he grinned, glancing at me over his shoulder before focusing back on adding dye to Nils' head.

I started laughing, closing the door behind me and kicking off my shoes.

"Hey," I mumbled, tossing my keys on the counter and walking around Nils who sat on a stool and was wearing a dye covered tank top and dye covered short shorts.

"This was his doing," she said, smiling at me as I walked a circle around her.

There was a towel placed on the floor and the stool in which Nils sat on was placed on top of said towel. I guess dyeing hair was a messy activity. I giggled at the dye on Jimmy's arms and stared at the minor splatter on his chest.

"I thought you were supposed to be an artist?" I asked, taking off my socks and heading to the bathroom to toss them in the laundry hamper.

He frowned. "This is *not* the same thing as tattooing!" he yelled in defense, and I snorted, walking back out to grab a change of clothes.

"I'm teasing," I said, walking past him and kissing him on the cheek.

Closing the bathroom door, I took a quick shower, then walked back out in a t-shirt and sweatpants. The heat wave was getting a bit ridiculous and Jimmy and I decided to leave the AC cranked. Sitting on the couch, I turned around and hung over the back so I could watch the hair dyeing process. Nils smiled at me.

"So, how was work?" she asked, and I shrugged.

"Same shit, different day," I mumbled, crossing my arms on the back of the couch.

"Well *that's* no fun," she said.

I shrugged once more. "It is what it is, I guess," I mumbled, laughing a little.

Averting my gaze to Poppy who had just jumped off the bed, she appeared uncomfortable and I frowned. Continuing to watch her, I suddenly realized what she was about to do and I jumped up to grab some paper towel.

"Uhhh . . . what's Pops doing?" Jimmy asked, staring down at her with wide eyes.

He looked mortified as she convulsed back and forth making an ungodly sound. Bending forwards, she threw up a hair ball right by Jimmy's feet before making a dash for the bathroom.

"*EW! POPPY, THAT'S DISGUSTING!*" he yelled, taking a step back.

Nils burst out laughing and I sighed, grabbing a handful of paper towel and quickly cleaning it up.

"It's just a hairball. That's normal," I explained, throwing it in the garbage and grabbing a damp sponge.

"That's revolting," Jimmy mumbled with his upper lip curled.

"You're a child," I teased, glancing at him over my shoulder and smirking.

He stuck his tongue out, turning and focusing once again on finishing Nils' hair.

Nils ended up staying for dinner and we ordered pizza. Jimmy and I sat on the couch, whereas she sat on the floor, her hair rolled up in a bun on the top of her hair. She had yet to wash the dye out, and instead stuffed her face with pizza while we watched a movie.

"When do you wash that stuff out?" I asked, staring at the blue mop.

She shrugged and I laughed.

"Are there not instructions?" I asked and she shrugged once more.

"I mean, there *are*. Do I follow them? No."

"Should you?"

"I look at it more as suggestions. It says to leave the dye in for half an hour," she explained and Jimmy choked on his pizza.

"Nilly! That was over an *hour* ago!" he yelled and she started laughing, looking at me over her shoulder.

"I usually like to keep the dye in for almost two hours? Makes it nice and vibrant," she grinned, facing forwards and eating more pizza.

Jimmy looked horrified at her hair and I started laughing.

∞

The next morning, I woke up and Jimmy had made us eggs, bacon and toast. I was smiling before I even opened my eyes. Turning on my side, I opened one eye and saw him cooking the bacon, topless. Sometimes I wish he *stayed* topless. It was always a nice sight to see. Glancing at me, he saw that I was awake and smiled widely.

"Good morning!" he grinned, distributing the bacon onto our plates along with the eggs and the toast. "Good timing. Breakfast is served," he smiled, carrying both plates over to the coffee table.

Slowly sitting up, I yawned and stretched my arms above my head, yawning so hard that my eyes started to water. Throwing my legs off the side of the bed, I stretched my back and groaned before hopping to my feet and shuffling toward the couch.

"I didn't make any coffee 'cause I figured I'd come to Starbs and get something," he smiled, turning on the TV and shoving bacon in his mouth.

I yawned and nodded. "Sounds good," I mumbled.

After feeding Poppy, we made our way to Starbucks hand in hand. Jimmy talked about how he missed work and he was ready to get back to tattooing. We walked on the other side of the road, since the sidewalk was still drying, and once we got to Vine, I stared across the street at Starbucks and frowned. Jimmy snorted. Outside the front door was a man holding a giant cardboard sign that read *They Are Coming* in a bright crimson paint. It was eerie. Sighing, the crosswalk changed and we walked toward the building.

"THEY'RE COMING! THEY'RE GOING TO BE HERE BEFORE YOU KNOW IT AND WE'LL ALL BE FUCKED!" he yelled, shaking the sign above his head.

I sighed, letting go of Jimmy's hand and crossing my arms. "Hi there . . ." I mumbled.

The man turned to stare at me and his eyes were bloodshot. It made me tense.

"They are coming," he whispered and I arched my brow.

"Uh huh. I'm gonna have to ask you to do . . . this, somewhere else," I said, gesturing to his sign.

His eyes got wider and he shook his head. "No! No, no, no! I need to *warn* people!" he snapped and Jimmy frowned, shoving his hands in his pockets.

"Warn people about what?" he asked.

"*Them!*"

"*Who?*" I asked, sighing.

"The Six! The Six is coming! We're their target and they're going to kill us all!" he yelled and I sighed again, rolling my eyes.

Closing my eyes and pinching the bridge of my nose, I took a deep breath. "Dude, this is terrible for business and I'm about to open up. Go find another curbside to scream your nonsense," I said, shooing him away.

"But—"

"Off y'go!" I added, giving him a light push in the other direction.

Glaring at me, he lowered his sign. "You'll be first," he whispered, then crossed the street and continued to yell.

I frowned and Jimmy started laughing. "What a fucking nutjob," he mumbled.

I continued to watch the man walk away and chewed on the inside of my cheek. "Yeah . . ." I said quietly, feeling slightly uneasy about the whole thing.

Chapter 20

Unlocking the front door and stepping inside to lock it again behind me, I sighed loudly and walked behind the counter to start getting the coffee machines ready. Jimmy sat on the counter and dangled his legs back and forth.

"Think Ang would mind if I hung out here all day?" he asked with a grin.

I snorted, grabbing my apron and tying it around my waist. "Ang isn't working today. It's me and Tiff," I added, flicking on the final coffee machine.

Jimmy scrunched up his nose. "Oh, ew," he mumbled and I started laughing.

"I know. My thoughts exactly."

"Well, in *that* case, I'm for *sure* going to stay. It's Friday and you're off tomorrow, so let's make today fun!" he grinned, continuing to kick his legs back and forth.

I continued to laugh and walked into the kitchen with Jimmy not too far behind.

"Sounds like a plan," I said, starting to bake.

Baked goods and pastries placed in the front display, Jimmy and I sat at our table and drank our coffees in silence. Jumping at the phone ringing, I sighed loudly and slowly got up to go answer it.

"Starbucks, six fifty-five Vine Street," I mumbled.

"Hey, Dallas."

It was Tiffany and I instantly rolled my eyes. She was bailing and it was going to be some lame excuse. As always.

"Hey, Tiff. What's up?" I asked, closing my eyes and leaning against the counter.

"Would it be okay if I took a sick day? I'm not feeling very well. I think I have food poisoning," she explained and I rolled my eyes once more.

"Oh?" I asked, pretending to care.

"Yeah. I woke up this morning and I feel nauseous."

"You sure you're not just hungover?" I asked and she was silent for a moment.

"I . . . wasn't out drinking last night," she stuttered and I shook my head.

The lying was *pouring* out of her mouth.

"It's fine, Tiff. Take the day," I sighed.

I didn't have the energy to deal with her bullshit, whether she had food poisoning or not.

"Cool, thanks," she said quickly, then hung up.

Frowning at the dead end, I hung up as well and headed back out to the front to sit with Jimmy again.

"Who was that?" he asked, slightly distracted by Instagram on his phone.

"Tiffany isn't coming," I mumbled, taking a sip from my coffee and staring outside.

He looked up at me from his phone and frowned. "What? So, you're working alone?" he asked and I shrugged, looking at him.

"I guess so, yeah. It's okay. Wouldn't be the first time," I smiled.

He frowned harder. "Not okay. I've seen how swamped you guys can get."

"J, it's fine," I smiled, resting my elbows on the table and sipping my coffee once more.

"I'll work with you," he grinned, suddenly pushing his phone to the side and staring at me.

I ducked my head to laugh, then looked back up at him and smiled, tilting my head to the side.

"Oh yeah? You're gonna take people's orders and make their coffee?" I asked, arching my brow.

He shrugged, pursing his lips. "How hard can it be?" he asked and I leaned back to laugh.

⌒∞⌒

Shockingly, he was doing surprisingly well. He failed his first attempt at making a single coffee order, so I left him in charge of *taking* orders and I made everything. When the drinks were made, he also called people's names out so they could grab their order. He was tickled pink about the fact that he got to wear an apron, even though I told him it wasn't necessary, but he insisted. Standing in the kitchen, I leaned against the doorframe and crossed my arms, staring at him and smiling. He closed the register with his hip after cashing out the final customer—they just ordered a muffin and an orange juice, which Jimmy could handle—then turned and saw me staring.

"What?" he asked, smiling.

I shrugged and shook my head. "Nothing. You're a natural," I laughed, walking toward him and wrapping my arms around him.

He slid his hands into my back pockets and brought me closer, gently kissing my lips. "That's because your job is easy," he whispered before kissing me again.

I leaned my head back to laugh out loud, trying to be insulted, but he started pressing kisses against my neck and it tickled. Quickly pushing him off, I laughed harder and turned my back to him.

"No! Bad!" I laughed, walking back to the kitchen to get back to cleaning dishes.

The heat wave finally came to an end and we dropped down to our regular December temperatures. Los Angeles didn't get snow, but it was still cold as hell. Cold for Californians anyways. But I loved the winter. Winter meant a whole new menu at work and every day was beyond crazy busy. It was stressful, but paycheques were usually amazing. The only downtime was usually *right* after lunchtime and that was when Jimmy would come for his daily visit. Angela knew about us, obviously, and she was totally cool with me taking my break whenever he showed up, so we'd sit at our usual table and talk.

"So, what do you want for Christmas?" he asked Sunday afternoon.

I shrugged. I honestly hadn't given it a single thought. I was so preoccupied on saving for his present that I hadn't even thought about myself. Plus, I had been alone for all these years, so gifts never really came to mind.

"I don't know. I haven't thought about it really . . ." I mumbled.

He forced a laugh. "Dallas. Christmas is in two weeks. What do you mean, you haven't thought about it?"

I shrugged again. "You have to remember that until I met you, I did everything by myself. I never had Christmas. I bought myself a tree once, but it ended up just being more work than I wanted it to be and it was more depressing than anything . . ." I laughed.

He was frowning. "Not okay. You're going to get a real Christmas this year."

I rolled my eyes. "Oh God. This is going to be like one of those super dumb motivational Christmas movies, isn't it?" I asked and he grinned.

"Yep! We'll buy the tree today after work."

"Do you even have any Christmas decorations?" I asked, arching a brow and smirking.

"Nope! I usually go to Nils' for Christmas, so we'll get those too! In the meantime, I gotta get back to work. I want a Christmas list from you by the time we get home, you understand?" he asked, standing and shoving a finger in my face.

I started laughing. "A *list*?!" I squeaked, and he nodded.

"Yes. A list. Then that gives me a variety to choose from," he smiled.

"Okay, *dad*!" I mocked.

He tossed out both our cups and walked back to me laughing.

"Smart ass," he said, then cupped my face and bent down to kiss me. "I'll see you at home," he smiled, and then left.

I sighed, smiling as I watched him leave.

Going back to work, Angie was smiling at me in the kitchen. She did this every day.

"You guys are so—"

"*Cuuuuuuuute!*" I laughed, mimicking her at the exact same time.

"Speaking of which . . . I can totally work Christmas morning this time. You have someone to spend it with now, so—"

"Angela, no. You have a kid! You need to be there for him on Christmas morning. It's only until noon. I don't mind. I'll bring Jimmy with me," I smiled.

Her shoulders sank and she smiled at me. "Thanks so much, Dallas," she said and pulled me into a hug.

Nils helped me a bit with Jimmy's present, and thankfully, it got delivered on a day I had off and Jimmy was at work. Our tree was up and decorated and was beautiful, so I spent the afternoon wrapping his present and smiled when I placed it underneath the tree. Sitting back and staring at it, I tilted my head to the side and sighed. Jimmy's present for me was already under the tree and even though it looked kind of sad with only two presents, it was still perfect in my mind. We didn't need to buy each other a lot, let alone *anything*, but it was fun. Maybe next year, we'd invest in stockings and I could spoil him with his favourite candies.

The night of the twenty-fourth, Jimmy had surprised me with a big huge fancy dinner that I could smell from the hall. Walking in, I started laughing when I saw that he was cooking and dancing in an apron that said *Kiss The Cook*. I didn't know this apron even existed, but it wouldn't surprise me if he had bought it *just* for this occasion.

"Hi!" he grinned, swaying his hips to the beat of the music and starting to sing along.

I closed the door and took my shoes off, laughing when I saw Poppy sitting on the couch with her ears pinned.

"Having fun?" I snorted.

He was still dancing and singing, blasting the music from the TV. "You bet! Dinner's almost ready!"

"Okay," I laughed, walking over to Poppy and picking her up to snuggle.

It must've been weird for her to go from living just the two of us and then moving in with Jimmy. I know I hadn't been giving her my full attention like I normally did, but she also wasn't a kitten anymore and didn't need as much. Putting her back down, I walked outside onto the balcony and stared out at the view. I turned around and watched Jimmy dance around the kitchen and laughed to myself. Life was good.

I saw him set our little coffee table with our plates that were stacked with food, then poured glasses of red wine. He did that a lot. Whenever he felt the night had an occasion, which most of the time it didn't, he'd pour us both a glass of wine, regardless if we drank it or not. Tonight, I would. He finally turned the music off and looked up at me and grinned, motioning for me to come back inside. Throwing his apron on the bed, he walked over with our glasses of wine and sat down on the couch, still grinning up at me as I walked in and sat beside him.

"Ta da!" he grinned, arms out wide.

I looked at the plethora of food and was actually shocked.

"Holy shit, J! How long did all of this take?! Did you cook a full turkey?!" I laughed.

He grinned. "I'm off for a few days and it's Christmas Eve, so I wanted to do something nice," he said.

Our plates were filled with turkey, vegetables, mashed potatoes, and he even had a little basket filled with a few buns. Holding up his wine glass, he waited for me to do the same, then clinked the glasses together.

Laughing, I shook my head. "You didn't have to go through all this trouble for lil' ol' me," I said.

He took a sip of his wine, then scrunched up his nose and stuck his tongue out. "Fuck, I hate this shit," he mumbled.

I started laughing. "Then why do you buy it?!"

"Cause it's fancy! Gimme this . . ." he said, taking the glass from my hand and running to the kitchen.

He drained both glasses, rinsed them, then came back with apple juice, placing mine back in my hand.

"Now it looks like white wine. It's not though. It's apple juice," he grinned.

I threw my head back laughing. "Oh my God, James."

He was smiling at me. "Plus. I want you to have the best Christmas ever because it'll be your first time being all traditional 'n' shit."

He took a sip of his apple juice, holding out his pinky, then started eating. I couldn't help but watch him and smile. His eyes glanced at me and he frowned.

With a mouthful of food, he said, "Eat!" and I jumped, laughed, and then started eating.

I ate until I physically couldn't eat anymore, and I had the biggest food baby I had ever experienced. But it felt good.

"J, that was delicious. Thank you," I said, then slouched in the couch and groaned, placing both hands on my stomach. "I don't even want to think about food."

"Oh. So, I guess I shouldn't tell you that I bought dessert?" he asked, pouting.

I stared at him, eyes wide. "What?!"

"Ha, I'm kidding. Fuck food. I'm stuffed too."

"Now all I want to do is sleep," I groaned.

"Yep," he laughed.

"Sooooo we get to go to sleep now?" I asked, smiling.

He stared at me and pouted, instantly making my face drop.

"What?"

"Well . . . I was hoping we could have festive Christmas sex . . ." he mumbled.

My shoulders sank and he started laughing.

"I'm just joking, Dal! If I move, I'll fucking throw up. C'mon, let's go to bed!" he laughed, standing and starting to clean up. "I'll do dishes in the morning," he mumbled.

I quickly stood and gently pressed on his chest, forcing him to sit back down on the couch.

"No, no, no! I do this. You sit," I smiled, taking the plates from his hands and bringing them to the kitchen where I started to stack things in the sink.

I got into bed first and by this point, I was completely comfortable sleeping in whatever, whether it was boxers or nothing. I slid down under the covers and brought the blanket up to my chin, letting out a huge yawn. Jimmy disappeared into the bathroom and came back out in nothing but his Christmas themed boxers and a Santa Claus hat.

I threw my head back laughing. "James, what the fuck?" I giggled, staring at him.

He jumped on the bed and stared at me, trying his best not to break character and laugh.

"Have you been naughty, Dallas Penske?" he asked, biting his bottom lip to refrain from laughing.

I was laughing so hard, I was crying. "Shut the fuck up," I laughed, reaching out and taking the hat off. Placing it on my own head, I smiled at him. "And I'm *always* good," I explained, getting comfy under the covers again.

He started laughing and got off the bed, walking around the apartment and turning lights off. He walked up to the Christmas tree, and I sat up and yelled at him.

"Wait!" I squeaked.

He froze and stared at me, confused.

"Can we sleep with the tree lights on?" I asked, smiling. "I like how it looks."

"Of course," he smiled, then came back and joined me in bed.

I turned on my side and stared into his eyes, smiling. "Thank you for everything tonight," I said, and he giggled.

"I can't take you seriously in my Santa sex hat, but you're welcome," he laughed, leaning forwards and kissing me.

"Santa sex hat?" I repeated, looking horrified and he nodded, sitting back and tucking himself in.

"Yeah. We were gonna fuck and I was gonna wear that," he smiled, yawning.

"Oh my God," I laughed, taking the hat off and tossing it away.

"Next year," he mumbled, then turned on his side and closed his eyes. "Night," he smiled.

Chapter 21

December 25, 2016
Hollywood
Los Angeles, California

9:00 a.m.

The morning came and my alarm went off to go to work which was normal for me on Christmas morning, so I didn't moan and groan too much. Jimmy was a different story.

"What the fuck . . ." he whined, turning onto his other side and pulling the blankets over his head.

Suddenly remembering what day it was, he threw the blankets off and sat up just as I was getting out of bed.

"What the fuck?! Where are you going?" he asked.

I gave him a funny look. "Work?"

"Why?!"

"J, I work every Christmas morning."

"Who the fuck goes to Starbucks on Christmas morning?!" he yelled; eyes still half closed from being asleep seconds before.

I pulled my pants up and grabbed my belt. "You'd be surprised," I mumbled, searching around for my shirt.

He fell back down and rubbed his face with both hands. "What the fuuuuccckkkk," he continued to whine, and I frowned.

"What's the big deal?"

"The big deal, Dallas, is that it's fucking Christmas morning and we're supposed to spend it together with breakfast and presents and . . . together! Why didn't you tell me you had to work?" he snapped, sitting back up and moving to the edge of the bed.

I bit my bottom lip. "I dunno. I've never had to tell anyone that I worked today before . . . I'm sorry. I just forgot. It's not a long shift, though. I finish at noon," I forced a smile.

He sighed, rubbing his face again. "Alright. Whatever . . ." he mumbled.

I walked over and sat beside him on the bed. "J, I'm sorry . . . do you wanna come with me? Or do presents right now before I go?" I asked.

He shook his head. "No. We can wait until we get home. I'll come with you," he said, stretching his arms above his head and standing to get dressed. "I'm gonna lecture every single customer you have today about how it's not normal to need Starbucks coffee *so badly* on Christmas," he mumbled, grabbing his ripped jeans and pulling them up.

I leaned against the couch and laughed, crossing my arms and watching him get dressed. The room was quiet but there was a subtle rumbling in the distance outside. Arching my brow and turning my head, I frowned a bit when another rumble happened a bit closer. This time, Jimmy looked up after throwing on a shirt and frowned.

"Did you hear that?" I asked and he nodded.

"Yeah . . ." he said.

Instantly after, our lights flickered a few times before remaining off. I stared at him and frowned.

"Uhm . . . what?" I asked with an awkward laugh.

The rumbling continued to get louder and closer until it sounded like it was right next door. Jimmy sat on the edge of the bed and was putting on his socks when I decided to go out onto the balcony to see what was going on. Leaning over the banister, I looked left and right and frowned as I saw that people were slowly filling the streets, screaming and crying. Staring at the city skyline in the distance, one by one, the buildings were exploding and falling to the ground. Everywhere I looked, buildings were crumbling to the ground.

"Uhhhh, J?!" I squeaked, still looking down.

Suddenly, there was a giant explosion and the apartment building next door crumbled into a giant pile of debris, the aftershock making our entire building shake. Every picture frame hanging on the wall fell, glass going everywhere and the dishes from the countertop fell and smashed.

"*JESUS!*" I yelled, falling backwards.

Jimmy came running out and grabbed me by my armpits, pulling me back up to my feet.

"Are you okay?! What the fuck just happened?!" he yelled.

He looked down below and I quickly grabbed him by the back of his shirt and pulled him back just as soon as a giant missile went flying past our faces. It hit a building down the road and made our building shake again, the lights flickering back on.

"What the fuck was that?!" I yelled, dusting myself off and glancing back outside.

The city was loud with screams, and sirens could be heard from all over as explosions were going off all throughout the city. Each one felt like a mini earthquake. Running back outside, I leaned against the banister and looked to my left where the newest building was just hit, and Jimmy joined me.

"Holy shit . . ." I whispered.

The entire building was gone. Just like that. Only a pile of ash remained with giant clouds of black smoke and flames. I ran back inside and fell on the couch, scrambling for the TV remote and quickly turned on the news. Every channel was talking about the same thing, the scene of the city being filmed from several different helicopter angles and anchors looked panicked as they talked about what was going on.

> "—to be the work of The Six. Late last night, we had been informed that a few locals had seen them around town and this horrible incident is proof enough. Police are advising to stay calm and for everyone to reach lower ground. Basements if possible or if you live in an apartment building or condo complex, please gather your children and your pets and make your way to the lowest possible floor of your building—"

There were more quakes when surrounding buildings fell to the ground and the power flickered off once again. I stared at my reflection in the TV screen, forgetting how to blink and feeling my eyes fill up with tears.

"What do we do?" I whispered.

Jimmy opened and closed his mouth like a fish out of water—speechless.

"I don't know . . ." he finally said.

"Does this building have a basement?" I asked.

"Underground parking . . ." he mumbled.

"Okay, so let's pack up our shit and let's go!" I said, quickly standing to my feet.

I grabbed a bag and shoved as many articles of clothing inside as I could.

"What do we pack?" he asked, running and grabbing a bag of his own.

"I have no idea. Whatever you can think of, I guess. I'm grabbing clothes!" I called out once he ran into the bathroom. I grabbed a bit of everything. My bag was already overflowing, but I ran to the kitchen and packed canned foods and Poppy's cat food.

"Canned food. Smart. I got first aid shit," Jimmy said, standing beside me and grabbing a few water bottles from the fridge.

"What else?" I asked, quickly putting on my shoes and scanning the room, looking for anything that would be necessary for survival. I didn't know what was going on out there, but I had a funny feeling we wouldn't be coming back here. I thought about not tying my shoes, because currently, that was the least of my concerns, but the thought of my clumsy ass tripping and falling was highly likely. Quickly kneeling, I started tying the laces to my Vans and stared at Jimmy who was running around and packing things.

"Flashlight!" he yelled, opening the cupboards in the island and grabbing two flashlights and a handful of batteries.

"Matches?" I asked, my panicked expression feeling permanent on my face.

I switched knees and quickly tied my other shoe.

"Wouldn't hurt," he said.

"Phone chargers!" I gasped, jumping to my feet and running to the bedside, grabbing both our phones and their designated chargers.

"Heh, yeah. If the power ever comes back on . . ." he mumbled.

There was another crash close by and our building shook once more, making me lose my balance and fall to my knees.

"Kay, Dal, we gotta go!" Jimmy yelled.

"Where's Poppy?!" I yelled back, grabbing onto the bed to get back to my feet.

"I got her, I got her! Let's go!" he yelled from the front door, carefully placing Poppy in his bag. Holding the door open, he stepped to the side and motioned for me to go first.

"Wait!" I yelled, turning on my heel and quickly running back inside.

Another explosion and we both fell.

"Dallas! We have to go!" he yelled.

I slid on my knees in front of the Christmas tree and quickly grabbed my present for him and his present for me, shoving them in my bag, then running back out into the hall. He didn't bother closing the door behind him.

We ran down the hall and took the stairs all the way to the lobby which was overflowing with the rest of the residents. The stairwell to the underground parking was packed and there was a lineup that filled the lobby. Everyone was panicking. There was another distant roar that got louder and louder until it crashed into the building behind us, again, shaking ours. People started screaming and crying, then a group of them had to jump out of the way as the front lobby chandelier crashed to the floor. Opening my bag, I grabbed a hoodie and threw it on, quickly tossing the bag back on my back. Jimmy looked at me and almost laughed.

"Aren't you hot?" he asked.

I shook my head. "I'm freaking out and actually really cold," I huffed.

Both my hands were in my pockets and I looked around, trying my best to remain calm, but the harder I tried, the harder it was.

"We can't stay here . . ." Jimmy thought out loud, looking around the room.

I stared at him, eyes wide. "Where else are we going to go?" I asked.

"I don't know but it can't be here," he mumbled. "Okay. Let's switch bags. You take Poppy," he said, carefully taking his bag off his shoulders and handing it to me.

Gently tossing the bag on my back, I stared at him. "Any ideas?" I asked.

"C'mon," he said, taking my hand and leading us out of the building.

He led the way and I did my best to keep up as we ran down the chaotic streets. People were running all over the place screaming, crying and even starting to attack each other. There was panic as everyone was trying to get out of the city whether it was by foot or by car, whereas the rest were starting riots, breaking windows, stealing things and setting things on fire. Pure chaos broke out within seconds.

"Get in the car!" Jimmy ordered, sliding across the hood of a parked car and opening the driver side door.

"J!" I screamed, ducking behind my side of the car just as someone ran up to him and threw a knife.

Ducking just in time, the knife flew past his head and went right into the guy inconveniently standing behind him. The knife thrower was gone before we could do anything and the guy who got stabbed had fallen over and was dead before we could help.

"Jesus Christ . . ." I panted, slowly standing.

"Dallas, get in the car," Jimmy ordered again, his voice getting darker.

He ran over to the guy with the knife in his head and took it out, running back to the car and getting in, locking the doors.

"What the fuck?! What the fuck are you going to do with that?!" I yelled, placing my bag in the back seat and instantly putting my seat belt on.

Tossing his bag in the back as well, he wiped the blood off the knife on his pants, then jabbed it into the ignition and forced it to turn. To my surprise, the car roared to life. I opened my mouth to say something but figured there was no point.

"Where are we going?" I asked, reaching over and grabbing his seat belt, buckling him in.

"We're getting the fuck outta here," he said, jamming the car into gear and burning rubber.

He did his best to avoid people, but some were literally throwing themselves in front of us. Someone was on fire and I watched them intentionally jump in front of us. I winced and cringed every time we hit someone, and it was happening more than I'd like to admit.

9:40 a.m.

Buildings and trees were on fire and people were killing each other out in the middle of the streets like it was nothing. It was honestly the scariest fucking thing I'd ever seen.

"J, what the fuck's going on . . ." I whispered, crossing my arms and sinking lower in my seat.

"I don't know. Try not to watch . . ." he mumbled, grabbing the e-brake and drifting around the corner onto Santa Monica Boulevard.

Quickly slamming on the brakes, both of our seat belts locked when he came to a sudden halt. The road was jammed with stopped cars.

"Of course," I sighed.

The air was echoing with honks and yelling, people reaching out of their windows and shaking their fists and exchanging middle fingers. I turned around and opened my bag a bit more so Poppy could crawl out if she wanted, then faced forwards and tucked my knees up to my chest, trying my best to get comfortable.

"What do we do, wait it out?" I asked, looking at Jimmy for all the answers.

He said nothing and chewed on the inside of his cheek in thought. His attention was distracted by three army fighter jets shooting by in the sky, and I closed my eyes to try and remain calm.

"We can't stay here . . ." he finally said.

I opened my eyes and stared at him, feeling my breathing pick up. "Where are we supposed to go?" I asked.

Leaning forwards on the steering wheel, he looked all around, then nudged his head to my right.

"There," he said.

I turned to look and frowned. "Walgreens?" I asked. "You want us to take cover in a Walgreens?"

"We need supplies. What we grabbed won't be enough," he added, putting the car in park and unlocking his seat belt.

"Fuck . . ." I hissed nervously, unlocking my seat belt as well and quickly placing Poppy back in the bag.

Handing Jimmy's bag to him, I cautiously got out of the car and stared down the car-packed road.

"Let's go," Jimmy said, adjusting his bag on his back and walking up to the Walgreens.

I turned to join him but continued to stare down the road. *Why isn't anyone getting out of their car?* The road was at a complete standstill; no vehicle was going anywhere, and all anybody was doing was sitting and honking.

"Dallas!" Jimmy called and I jumped, turning and running inside.

Joining his side, I stared with wide eyes and almost wanted to go back outside. With the power being out, the only lights on were a few emergency lights, and they weren't looking too good—flickering every now and then. People were using their phones for flashlights and the streaks of lights were flashing all over the place. Visible panic.

"Don't use your phone. We have to conserve the battery power," Jimmy whispered to me.

The overflowing building was filled with people running in every direction, down every aisle, filling their arms or their carts with as much as possible.

"What are we looking for?" I asked, looking all around and not sure where to start.

"I don't know. Anything, really. But we gotta be quick. Shit's going quick. Just grab it, shove it in your bag and let's get the fuck outta here. Got it?" Jimmy asked, looking at me.

I nodded.

"Okay. Split up. Meet back here in five."

"'Kay," I mumbled, and he took off.

The shelves were almost empty, but the floor was covered in stuff. People were moving so fast that they weren't even grabbing anything at all. Finding an abandoned basket, I quickly picked it up and started to shove as much as I could inside: food, drinks, whatever the store had to offer. Working up a sweat, I noticed a shelf with a few batteries and was quick to snatch that up and throw it in my basket. Turning on my heel, I was making myself dizzy with all the fast thinking and fast moving I was doing, but I knew now was not the time to slow down. Taking off my bag, I placed it in the basket and started placing some items inside with Poppy. I knew she was uncomfortable, but there was nothing I could do. Seeing the pharmacy sign flicker a few aisles down, I turned a corner and made a run for it. I mean, I had a headache *now*, and a little Advil never hurt anyone. Getting to the counter, one of the employees quickly stood up from behind the counter and was pointing a shot gun straight in my face; their hands were shaking. Jumping a few feet back, I froze and threw my hands up.

"Whoa, whoa!" I could feel myself shaking as well.

"What do you want, man? Just tell me what you want, and I'll give it to ya . . ." he mumbled, his hands barely able to keep the gun still.

"Advil. I just want some Advil . . ." I said, my voice shaking.

I never once moved my eyes from the double barrel aiming directly at my face.

"We only have Tylenol," the kid said and I nodded quickly.

"Yeah, fuck, whatever. Tylenol is fine," I stuttered.

Keeping the gun aimed with one hand, he awkwardly reached under the counter and grabbed two boxes of Tylenol Extra Strength, then threw them at me. I caught them and threw them in my basket.

"Tha-thank you," I said, taking a few steps back.

He lowered his gun and walked backwards as well, staring at the chaos behind me and starting to cry.

"Thank you," I said again, then turned and went to run.

Suddenly getting an arm slammed into my throat, I fell straight onto my back and got the wind knocked out of me.

"Take the redhead's basket!" someone yelled.

Struggling to open my eyes, I coughed for oxygen, then sat up. "No!" I croaked. "Stop! Please!"

"Shut the fuck up!" another one yelled and kicked me in my spine.

Instinctively curling into a ball, I did my best to protect my ribs as the two men kicked the shit out of me. My hand still holding onto the basket, I refused to let go.

"JAMES!" I screamed, now curling up to protect my face. "*JAMES!*" I screamed again, whimpering when I got a jab in the ribs.

"HEY!" he screamed, sliding around the corner with a gardening shovel in his hands.

Swinging it back like he was playing a game of baseball, he swung and hit both men one at a time in the head, knocking them clean unconscious, if not dead. Dropping to his knees, he curled himself around me and tucked his face into mine.

"Are you okay?" he asked, panting.

I blinked away my tears and winced at my ribs screaming in pain, but nodded anyways.

"Yeah . . ." I muttered.

"Let's go," he said, standing and helping me to my feet.

Wrapping an arm around my core, I closed my eyes and bit my lip.

"Dallas, are you sure you're okay? Your ribs . . ." he mumbled, taking the basket from me.

I opened my eyes and stared down at the two men who now had bleeding heads, then looked at the bloody shovel.

"I'm fine. Let's get going," I whispered.

Reaching out and placing a hand on the back of my neck, Jimmy leaned forwards and kissed me on my forehead.

"Okay. C'mon," he said, taking my hand and leading the way.

Getting back onto the streets, a lot more of the cars had finally been abandoned, but a lot still remained. Squinting up at the sky, I frowned at the police helicopters hovering above.

"C'mon," Jimmy mumbled, keeping my hand linked in his and walking us further down the street and away from the chaotic Walgreens.

Dropping his bag, he knelt down and opened my bag as well, smiling at the supplies and Poppy.

"Hey, kitten . . ." he said quietly, scratching the top of her head. Placing our supplies in both bags, he nodded with approval. "Good find," he added.

With my arm still wrapped around my stomach, I continued to stare up at the helicopters. Next thing I knew, they were exploding into a million pieces and the debris was falling on the tops of the cars below.

"JESUS CHRIST!" I yelled, wincing when I ducked.

Jimmy jumped and glanced at the explosion over his shoulder, then stared up at me with wide eyes. Closing our bags, he stood and handed mine to me.

"Jesus Christ . . ." he hissed, tightening his straps over his shoulders.

I stared back down the road and narrowed my eyes, waiting to see through the smoke. Whoever it was had a rocket launcher and they knew what they were doing. The honking suddenly stopped, and the yelling and cussing turned into panicked screams.

"Dallas . . ." Jimmy said.

I stared at him, eyes wide.

"We gotta go! Now!" he yelled, quickly walking past me.

Turning to join him, I glanced over my shoulder and saw a huge mob of people running in our direction, screaming and crying with gun fire in the distance behind them.

"DALLAS!" Jimmy screamed.

I stared at him, then quickly stared back at the hoard of people running in our direction, only now they were all doing face plants as they got shot in the back.

"*DALLAS!*" Jimmy screamed again and I turned on my heel to run away, practically tripping on my own feet.

Looking ahead, Jimmy had jumped up onto the hood of cars and was jumping to and from their roofs.

"You good?!" he called back, and I nodded, jumping from my car onto the one he was currently standing on.

"Yep!" I panted.

More gun fire shot behind us and we were quickly on our way again. The firing was the perfect motivation to focus really hard on your feet, making sure you didn't fuck up and fall on your face.

"Now where?!" I yelled up to him, jumping from one car to another.

"Parlour!" he yelled back, and I frowned.

"*Seriously?!*"

"Seriously!"

10:50 a.m.

We eventually ran out of cars and turned back down Highland, running down the street. Only this time, we were dodging people instead of vehicles.

"How are we going to be safe at the parlour?" I asked, catching up to his side when he finally stopped running.

"These guys . . . *The Six* they seem to call themselves . . . they're obviously out to kill. They're targeting tall buildings, like skyscrapers and apartments . . . the parlour is a bungalow—low to the ground. Why would terrorists target a tattoo shop?" he kept his voice low.

I was playing with my lip ring and sighed. "I feel like it doesn't matter what they blow up, J. They just like doing it," I said and he frowned.

"Well do *you* have an idea?" he asked, and I sighed again.

"Lead the way," I said quietly.

He took my hand and linked his fingers with mine, squeezing.

So many things were on fire that the sky was black with smoke. What looked like falling snow was actually falling ash. Jimmy quickly turned and stood in front of me, placing both his hands on my shoulders again and stared straight into my eyes.

"Okay. Now we're going to run again and I need you to only focus on me. Don't pay attention to anything else but me, okay?" he asked.

I nodded, not saying anything. I winced when an explosion went off down the street from us, followed by horrendous screams and he snapped his fingers in front of my face.

"We're going to get through this. Just focus on me and focus on that little feline of yours, okay?" he said.

I secured the bag over my shoulders and sighed, nodding.

"Okay . . ." He turned and looked all around: left, right and then up into the sky. "Let's go . . ." he said, then suddenly took off into a sprint.

I followed as close behind as I could.

Chapter 22

This can't actually be real, right? It feels like a really bad dream. There were dead bodies scattered throughout the streets from the explosions and collapsing buildings, helicopters flying all over the place and police cruisers screaming by in every direction. Firefighters were at every building, trying to control the flames, but they couldn't keep up. Suddenly, air raid sirens were blasting through speakers I never noticed attached to light posts and it only seemed to send everyone into a bigger panic. People were bumping into me from every direction and it was making it harder to follow Jimmy, and the thick smoke was starting to make my eyes burn and water. We finally got to the intersection across the street from the tattoo parlour and I looked down toward Starbucks, although couldn't see further than a few feet from all the smoke. Jimmy grabbed my hand and squeezed it, bringing my attention back to him.

"C'mon," he said and stepped out onto the street.

Looking to my right, I saw a car coming in our direction and they were out of control.

"WATCH OUT!" I screamed, forcing my hand out of Jimmy's and pushing him ahead of me.

I jumped backwards as soon as the car came swerving in our direction and I spun around at the last second, so I landed on my chest and not my back. My ribs took the impact, but it was better than Poppy inside my bag. The brick wall I fell into collided with my face and I knew my cheek would be bleeding. The people inside the car died on impact, blood splattering across the windshield. Jimmy landed on his hands and knees and looked at me over his shoulder, tears in his eyes.

"Are you okay?!" he screamed.

I was swatting smoke and ash out of my face and coughing. "I'm fine!" I called back, pushing off the wall and pressing my bleeding cheek into my shoulder to dab the blood with my shirt.

"Kay, c'mon!" he yelled, back on his feet.

"Right . . ." I mumbled to myself, running across the street to grab Jimmy's hand again.

The tattoo parlour had its *closed* sign lit up and Jimmy was quick to smash his foot through the front window, elbowing all around to remove any glass shards that could hurt us, then stepped back, motioning me to go first.

"Okay. Go on," he said.

I crawled through, careful not to touch any glass, then Jimmy followed close behind. We walked to the furthest room in the back and closed the door when Jimmy jumped, making me jump.

"Nils?!" he screamed, running over to the far corner where she was curled up in a ball, shaking.

Her left shoulder had a huge slice going from one end to the other and was pouring blood all down her arm.

"Jesus Christ . . ." he mumbled, crouching down in front of her. "Are you okay?" he whispered.

She looked up and nodded, her cheeks stained with eyeliner and tears. "It's stupid, really. I was leaving a Christmas party from the night before and was on my way home when a fucking missile or some shit went by and blew up the building behind me," she mumbled. "Debris went everywhere."

"And that's what this is?" Jimmy asked, motioning to her exposed arm.

She nodded.

"Nilly, that's gonna need so many stitches . . ."

She forced a laugh. "Dude, the hospital is probably *overflowing* right now. Have you seen the streets? Hey, Dal," she added in at the end, giving me a little head nod.

I forced a smile and nodded back. "Of course. We were just in them," I said.

Jimmy sighed and pinched the bridge of his nose. "Nils, I'd feel a whole lot better if we got you to the hospital," he said and she frowned.

"James . . ."

"No, I'm serious. That for *sure* needs to be looked at and bandaged up properly or it's going to get infected. Not to mention all the blood you're losing . . ." he explained and she sighed.

"Fine. But I'm telling you now the hospital is gonna be fucked," she said, reaching up with her good arm for Jimmy to give her a hand up. Wiping away her tears, she stretched her neck from side to side, then shrugged. "Lead the way," she said, motioning to the door.

Jimmy walked out first, followed by myself and then Nils, and once we got to the hole in the window, she sighed loudly.

"You couldn't have just used the door?" she asked, opening it instead of crawling through the hole.

Jimmy frowned. "I didn't think it would be unlocked. Common sense isn't really a thing right now, Nilly."

"John's gonna be *pissed* when he sees that," she said, joining our side and I laughed.

"I think he's going to be pissed about a lot more than just that window," I said and Nils rolled her eyes.

"Whatever," she mumbled, then the three of us were silent.

Looking out at the streets of chaos, I sighed. "Shall we get going?" I asked and Jimmy nodded, his shoulders falling limp.

"Yeeeeep. Ready?" he asked, looking at me and Nils over his shoulders and we both nodded.

The three of us broke out into a run and ran down the street, dodging people and cars. I was noticing less police cruisers and even saw a fire truck on fire; the firemen were all laying dead around the vehicle with bullet wounds in their bodies. Quickly focusing back on my footing, I tried my best not to think about it.

"What the fuck is going on?!" Nils yelled as we ran, but neither Jimmy nor I had an answer.

Quickly dodging out of the way as a mob made their way into an electronic store with Molotovs, I huffed loudly and tapped Jimmy's shoulder.

"We need a car. It's going to take us forever to get to the hospital on foot."

"He's right," Nils added, then we stopped running and kept our backs to a building.

"Fuck, kay. Let's find a car then," Jimmy said, glancing around at the craziness.

The cars that weren't on fire were upside down or in the process of being broken into, and if they weren't being broken into, it was because they were already being driven all over the place by crazy people.

"There," Nils said, pointing across the road to a nervous looking man who was attempting to break into a red Honda Civic.

"What?" I asked, tilting my head and frowning.

Quickly glancing to her left and right, she ran across the street and snuck up behind the man, elbowing him in the back of his neck with her good arm. He instantly fell to the ground and was out cold. Jimmy and I ran across to join her and I was staring at her with wide eyes.

"Nils, what the fuck?!"

"He's only unconscious, don't get your knickers in a knot," she mumbled, smashing the driver side window with her elbow and reaching in to unlock the doors.

Jimmy opened the driver door and started giggling. "I love when you say that. It makes you sound *extra* British— Dal? You gonna get in?" he asked, now sitting in the car with his door closed.

I was still staring at the unconscious man in complete horror.

"Dallas, it's a dog-eat-dog world right now. And right now, we're fucking starving . . . so if you could just get in the car so we could get a move on?" Nils said bitterly, sitting in the passenger seat.

I frowned at her and got in the back, putting my seat belt on. Just like the guys back at Walgreens trying to take my stuff, we had just become the bad guy by taking this guy's car. It really was a dog-eat-dog world and we were all just trying to survive.

12:00 p.m.

The drive was just as ridiculous as before. Jimmy tried his best to dodge all the obstacles, but people were still throwing themselves in front of us and we'd run them over like speed bumps. I continued to cringe every time. When the hospital was finally in view, there was suddenly someone standing in the middle of the road, holding a flat screen TV.

"What the—" Jimmy mumbled, then abruptly made a hard left and crashed us into a wall when the man threw the TV at our windshield, missing us by a foot.

My face ached being pressed into the back of Jimmy's seat while he and Nils were face planted into the airbags.

"Awesome. A nosebleed," Nils mumbled, licking her top lip.

Jimmy groaned and rubbed the back of his neck, undoing his seat belt. "Are you guys okay?" he asked, and I nodded.

"C'mon. The hospital is right there. Maybe it won't be filled with assholes," Nils said, opening her door and getting out.

My door was bent out of shape, so I had to climb over to the other side to get out, but once I did, I regretted it almost instantly. Staring at the hospital down the road, a giant missile flew by on our right and exploded into the building, sending us flying backwards from the shock and the building burst into explosive flames. Landing on my side and sliding all down my arm, I quickly grabbed my bag off my back and checked Poppy to make sure she was okay.

"Fuck," I panted, laying back down on my chest and closing my eyes.

My head was *pounding,* and my ears were ringing. When I slowly came to, my eyesight was blurry for a bit and I could vaguely make out Jimmy and Nils beside me in the exact same state.

"J . . . Nils . . ." I mumbled, slowly sitting up.

Horrendous screams echoed down the streets coming from the hospital, then suddenly the bottom caved out and the entire building came crashing to the ground, forcing a thick wave of black smoke in our direction. Ducking for cover, chunks of debris flew by and I felt a sharp sting in my right arm. Once the dust finally settled, I looked down and almost laughed when I saw a shard of glass sticking out of it.

"Kinda wish that the hospital was still kicking . . ." I mumbled.

Jimmy crawled over to me and swore loudly, smacking the ground with his hand.

"Just leave it. It's probably better in your arm than out. At least you won't bleed out," Nils added.

She reached down into her boot and pulled out her pack of cigarettes, as well as a lighter.

I glared at her. "How can you *possibly* be smoking right now?" I asked and she shrugged.

"I smoke when I'm stressed, and right now, I'm fucking stressed. Got a problem?" she snapped, and I continued to frown.

"Both of you just *shut the fuck up right now*!" Jimmy yelled.

Covering his face with both hands, he sighed loudly, sat back on his heels, then stared at me. "You know I have to take it out," he said, and I nodded.

"Yeah. Just do it," I mumbled, turning and looking the other way.

He was quick to grab hold of the glass and pull it out, the pain amplifying even more, and I couldn't hold back my scream. Covering my mouth and biting my hand, I watched as the wound filled with blood and poured all down my arm. Jimmy was quick to grab the first aid kit from my bag, take out gauze and wrap it around my arm. Nils giggled when it instantly soaked with blood.

"Gross," she snorted, and I frowned back up at her.

Packing the kit back up, Jimmy stretched his neck from side to side and sighed.

"Okay. So, the fucking hospital is a fucking write-off . . ." he mumbled, standing and beginning to pace back and forth with his hands on his hips. "Now what?" he asked, staring at me and Nils.

I shrugged and she pursed her lips in thought.

"We could head back to No Regrets. There are at least cleaning supplies there. We'll just have to make do with what we have and do what we can to my arm," she said, blowing smoke out between her lips as she spoke. Her nose was still bleeding. "And I guess now your arm too," she added, gesturing to my new wound.

Jimmy sighed loudly and clenched his jaw. "Fine. But I don't want to hear *once* from either one of you how this was a waste of time. If we had just left a little sooner . . ."

"Yeah, if we had just left a little sooner, we could be fucking dead like the rest of them, James," Nils snapped, gesturing to the flames.

I forced myself to my feet and checked up on Poppy once more.

"There's no sense in fighting with one another. We're all we have. Let's just get another car and head back to the parlour and figure out our next move from there," I mumbled, dusting down my clothes.

12:30 p.m.

The streets were overflowing with bodies at this point, dead and alive, and it was almost impossible to find a working car. Making our way along Fountain Avenue, I slowed down when I looked down an alleyway and saw a group of people sitting in a circle, holding hands and praying.

"They're wasting their time," Nils mumbled, and I frowned at her.

We searched until we found a minivan missing all its windows with the driver dead at the wheel.

"Better than nothing. Get in," Jimmy said, quickly opening the door and dragging the body out and onto the ground.

I winced when their limp body fell and quickly got into the passenger seat. Thankfully, the keys were in this one and we roared the van to life, fighting our way back to the parlour. Jimmy was basically leaning on the horn the entire drive to tell people to get out of the way since the crowd was so thick; the dead ones we could do nothing about. A few times, I had to peel people's hands off the van because they were grabbing at my windowless door, crying and begging me to bring them with us. It was scarring and heartbreaking all at the same time.

Finally getting back to the parlour, there thankfully nobody inside. I thought for sure with the door being unlocked this whole time and the hole in the window, it would have been an open invitation for people to seek shelter, but that was not the case. Ditching the van, but keeping the keys, we carefully made our way back inside and went to the furthest room in the building, closing the door and locking it. The power was still out on this grid of the city and with the sky filling with smoke, there was barely any sunlight. We were practically sitting in the dark with an uncomfortable red glow from all the flames.

"Dal. If you go to my room, I have a collection of candles on my shelves. Could you go and grab them all so we could have a little light in here? I don't wanna use our phones . . ." Nils mumbled, sitting on the floor so Jimmy could assess her arm.

I nodded, leaving Poppy with them, and running to do the task given to me. Just as described, Nils' room was filled with used candles. It was kind of cool, to be honest. Gave the room a very gothic vibe, which I'm sure was exactly the vibe she was going for. She had them in every size, colour and scent, and the flow of wax was dripping down the sides, drying them in place. Breaking them off her shelves, I filled my arms and ran back.

"So . . . why'd you decide to come here?" Nils asked Jimmy, glancing at me and smiling when I walked back in.

"Safer," he mumbled, and she nodded, wincing at the alcohol wet naps pressed to her skin.

"My thoughts exactly," she mumbled back.

There were some more distant shakes as buildings continued to fall to the ground and the screaming felt like it was never going to end. Placing the candles around the room, I searched for the matches Jimmy and I packed and lit each and every one.

"Better?" I asked with a smile, and Jimmy nodded.

"Thanks, babe," he mumbled, still focused on cleaning Nils' arm.

Suddenly, all of our attention was averted to outside, where the air raid sirens had stopped, and someone was talking over a megaphone. Jimmy went to stand, but I placed my hand on his shoulder to stop him.

"I'll go," I said, cautiously opening the door and running outside.

Looking around, it was almost quiet, apart from all the screaming coming from further within the city. Shit was obviously going down everywhere. Down the street, there was a giant swarm of people staring up at a rooftop where six men stood, all holding different variations of guns. I slowly walked toward the crowd and stared up at the men as well, curious about what they were saying.

"Nobody thought we'd be able to do it, but here we are! We've caused chaos and havoc down the state and now it's time for Los Angeles to pay for what it's done to us! It is the city of angels, after all! We'll kill every one of you little ants!" one yelled.

I was squinting through all the smoke and ash until the speaker's face came into view and I felt my body turn cold. It was Connor Evans, the leader of The Six, yelling through the megaphone. I looked around and saw people talking amongst each other, panicked and confused. Realizing this wasn't going to get any better, I stopped and started walking backwards. I was the only one with this idea.

All six of them stood on top of the roof, all carrying guns. Connor stood in the middle with Ryan and Dylan on his left, then Jason, Luke and Benji on his right. The megaphone was handed off to Ryan Burke—sentenced to ten years for raping several women—and he was smirking, staring down at the crowd below.

"Merry Christmas, Hollywood!" he screamed, throwing the megaphone behind him and they all aimed down at the crowd, firing at random.

At this point, I had already turned around and was sprinting back to the parlour, ducking and wincing at the gun shots behind me. The screaming started up all over again as people started running for their lives, hiding where they could. Typical me, I wasn't paying attention to my feet and tripped and fell.

"Fuck!" I hissed, quickly getting back up.

Looking to my right, I saw a little boy, about five years old, on his hands and knees, bawling his eyes out. I did a quick scan around to see if I could find anyone who he belonged to and there was a woman across the street, frantically looking around. Running over to the boy, I picked him up, tossed him over my shoulder, and ran toward the searching woman.

"Miss!" I screamed.

She turned and saw me and instantly looked furious. I stopped and started walking backwards, holding up my hand in defense.

"No, no, no! I'm helping! He fell!" I quickly yelled.

She grabbed her son from my shoulder and placed him on his feet, holding his hand. With her other, she made a fist and swung at me, hitting me square in the jaw, then turned and ran off with her son. I fell again, using my hands to catch myself.

"*FUCK!*" I screamed, looking at the fresh cuts on my palms and stretching my now aching jaw.

I blinked a few times to regain focus, then jumped when I heard the familiar hissing sound of a missile.

"RPG MOTHER FUCKERS!" Jason Wright—Connor's right-hand man—yelled, resting the large weapon on his shoulder.

My eyes grew wide and I quickly got to my feet.

"*WAIT!*" I screamed after the mother, running in her direction.

I was immediately blown backwards from the impact and slid on my back across the debris covered pavement. Slowly sitting up, my ears were ringing and I had a splitting headache. Ignoring my screaming body, I sat up, eyes bulging out of my skull. The explosion happened directly in front of them, killing them both instantly. They basically ran into it. Realizing that all the wind had been knocked out of my lungs, I started having a coughing fit. My focus was quickly averted from my aching lungs to another explosion beside me and I ducked and rolled just as a car exploded and flew over my head. My tears and sweat stung my bleeding face and my ears were ringing so loud that my surroundings were drowned out completely. I felt light-headed and found it difficult to stand.

Slowly getting to my feet, I blinked back to reality and looked around. The men on the rooftop were gone and people were back to causing their own chaos, throwing things into windows and stealing as much as they could. More firearms had come out and people were shooting each other. Everything was moving in slow motion. Jumping to another explosion nearby, I looked down at the Melrose and Highland intersection and saw that the gas station that once stood there, stood no more. The police were useless at this point and were starting to fall back. Even the SWAT teams had shown up and were useless against the explosives The Six had with them. Blinking in slow motion, I looked up at the sky and saw a few military helicopters flying around. Blinking slowly once more, I looked down the street and saw the tattoo parlour in the distance. Shaking my head, I took in a deep breath and stumbled in its direction.

Quickly getting back, I practically dove back through the hole in the window and ran to the back room, slamming the door shut behind me. Panting out of breath, I slid down the door and closed my eyes.

"What? What's wrong?! What the fuck happened to you?!" Jimmy yelled, handing Poppy to Nils and kneeling in front of me.

I caught my breath and opened my eyes, staring at him with fear. "It's fucking chaotic out there. I don't even know ... I ... it's them though. It's definitely those six guys from the news ... they were on a rooftop with guns. They started shooting everyone and things were exploding—cars and buildings ... " I couldn't catch my breath fast enough. "I tried to come back here, but then there was this kid ... and this woman ... and I tried to save them ... but then there was an explosion and just ... I couldn't," I said, staring at the floor. I couldn't even feel the tears; my whole body was numbing with pain.

"Jesus Christ ..."

"We won't be safe in here forever, y'know," Nils stated. "They'll eventually kill everyone out there and they'll start searching buildings."

I buried my face in my arms and sighed. "That's comforting," I panted.

"Thanks, Nils," Jimmy said.

She shrugged. "Just being honest."

"Well, do you have a better plan?" he snapped.

She was silent and shook her head.

Sighing loudly, he looked back at me and frowned. "You're bleeding ... like a lot," he pointed out, and I shrugged.

"I can't really feel it, to be honest. I have my adrenaline to thank for that . . ." I panted, falling back on my butt and leaning against the wall. I closed my eyes and continued to catch my breath; my ears still ringing.

"Your palms though . . ." he said, taking both my hands into his and examining them.

I opened my eyes and stared at my hands as well, sighing at their state. "They're okay. If anything, it's my . . . everything else," I said and he forced a smile for my sake. I sighed once more.

"Well, now what?" I mumbled.

Nils slowly stood and walked over, handing over Poppy, then stretching everything but her bad arm which was now bandaged up, thanks to Jimmy.

"I don't know about you two, but I'm fucking starving . . ." she said.

Jimmy started laughing and shook his head. "Nilly, not now. This is serious . . ." he said and she frowned.

"I *am* being serious . . ."

1:25 p.m.

There was a sudden loud bang at the front of the building, and we all jumped, Nils eyes growing wide. Jimmy brought his finger to his lips, mouthing to stay quiet.

"They're here . . ." she whispered, her eyes filling with tears.

I felt my heartbeat quicken and I could feel more tears forming in the corners of my eyes.

"The candles," I whispered.

Glancing around at the glowing lights, Jimmy quickly licked his fingers and crawled around to put each one out, slowly bringing us back to darkness. Nils made eye contact with him and nudged her head to the right, motioning to the closet.

"Closet," she mouthed, no longer whispering.

I was quickly looking back and forth between the two as they were now only communicating with hand gestures. Jimmy shook his head, but Nils was nodding.

"James, yes. Now," she hissed, so quietly it was almost impossible to hear.

Jimmy sighed and grabbed the front of my hoodie, forcing me to stand up. I tucked Poppy back in my bag and brought her with me, grabbed Jimmy's hand and stood to my aching feet. We all tiptoed to the closet and got inside, closing the doors slowly behind us. Nils stopped the second door with her foot and looked at Jimmy, forcing a pained smile. She opened the door and stepped out, resisting Jimmy's death grip on her wrist.

"Don't—" he started, staring at her with pleading eyes.

She closed her eyes and shook her head. "Shhhh. Just stay here. Both of you," she said.

"No," Jimmy whispered, his voice cracking.

She reached behind my head and grabbed a shotgun that was on the top shelf. My eyes grew wide and she grinned, cocking it.

"God bless America," she said, winking, then closing the closet door and walking out.

Jimmy reached out at the last second, but she had already closed the door on us. Covering his mouth with his own hand, he ducked his head and held back his sobbing, whereas I stared at the closed door with wide eyes and mouth ajar. I couldn't believe she just did that. Whatever her plan was . . . she probably just saved our lives.

Jimmy's head suddenly shot up when we could hear the faint mumbles of voices in the front room. We couldn't make out what anyone was saying, but it was clear Nils wasn't alone. At one point, it almost sounded like she was laughing, but she was always sort of cocky. Could be a defense mechanism. Releasing Jimmy's hand, I gently pressed on the closet door, allowing it to quietly open. He shot me a look and grabbed my hand, blocking me from walking out.

"What are you doing?" he whispered.

"Just . . . trust me," I replied, equally as quietly.

Tiptoeing over to the closed door, I very cautiously turned the handle and very quietly opened it just a sliver, just enough that I could get a better look.

"What do you see?" he hissed, slowly walking toward me. Wincing, I closed my eyes just as Nils punched Ryan Burke in the face, forcing him to swallow and choke on a cigarette he had between his lips. Opening my eyes and glancing at Jimmy over my shoulder, I smirked.

"You should see this," I whispered.

He walked toward me and leaned on my shoulder, glancing through the crack of the door and watching Nils. Ryan was bent over, coughing profusely, until a soggy cigarette popped out on the floor in front of him. His face was almost purple.

"You fucking—"

"I don't want to fucking hear it!" she snapped, kneeing him in the face and knocking him out cold.

Jimmy covered his mouth with both hands and held back a laugh. "She's kicking ass!" he hissed.

I watched with a smile on my face. That she was. Kicking Luke Kelly—sentenced to twelve years for multiple counts of sexual assault—in the chest, he dropped his gun and she caught it midair. Shoving it into the waistband of her shorts, she picked up her shotgun that was on the floor and aimed back and forth between the two men.

"Let's just give Nils a gun and she can protect us," I laughed in a whisper.

Jimmy still had his hands over his mouth and nodded.

"Well? Who's it gonna be?" she asked.

"Shoot her!" Luke yelled, looking at Dylan Toner who stood by the front door, stunned by Nils' actions.

He had been put away for first degree armed robbery. Got ten years.

Turning and aiming her shotgun at Luke, she smirked.

"Sorry, babe. That's not how the game works," she said, and then pulled the trigger.

At first, I winced. I winced because she was aiming point-blank at a man with a shotgun and that was going to be messy. But then her gun didn't do anything and just like that, she lost.

"Not so tough anymore, eh?" Luke asked.

Retrieving his gun from her shorts, he twirled it around his finger and watched as Dylan grabbed her by her wrists and forced her arms behind her back. I wasn't smiling anymore and now Jimmy watched in horror. Reaching out and placing his hand on the doorknob, I was quick to stop him before he opened the door any further. He shot a glare at me.

"Don't," I mouthed, shaking my head.

Looking back through the crack in the door, Nils was nowhere to be found, but instead, Dylan Toner was walking in and searching every room. Staring without blinking, I reached out until my hands found Jimmy and I turned to stare at him with watery eyes.

"Go. Go, go, go!" I hissed, pushing him back toward the closet.

Both quickly shuffling back behind the closed doors, I could feel and hear my breathing getting faster and louder. Jimmy looked at me and I bit my bottom lip.

"You're breathing like a fucking dragon!" he hissed.

I stared at him and felt a tear run down my cheek. "Someone's coming," I mouthed, closing my eyes and wincing once one of the doors in the front room was kicked in.

Jimmy tensed. Hearing the door to the back room open fully, I clenched my eyes shut tight and Jimmy reached out, covering my mouth with his hand. My tears were falling down my cheeks and over his hand. I could feel my whole body shaking. I was petrified.

"Yo! Dyl, we gotta get going!" someone yelled from outside.

Hearing Dylan inside the room sigh, he turned and walked out.

"Looks like she's been hiding out here for a while! Candles everywhere!" he called out; his voice thankfully getting quieter in the distance.

I held my breath and opened my eyes, waiting to hear him leave the store. And sure enough, we heard the doors of a car slam shut, an engine roar to life, and just like that, they were gone. Pushing open the closet doors, Jimmy fell to his knees and stared up at me with tears rolling down his cheeks.

"They took Nils," he choked.

CPSIA information can be obtained
at www.ICGtesting.com
Printed in the USA
LVHW010836190821
695649LV00002B/271